# Raised In Air

SARAH HEGGER

Copyright © 2022 Sarah Hegger
All rights reserved.
No part of this book may be reproduced in any form or by any electronic or mechanical means, including information storage and retrieval systems, without written permission from the author, except for the use of brief quotations in a book review.
Cover: Deranged Doctor Design
First Electronic Edition: October 2019
ISBN: 978-1-7771903-8-5
ISBN: 978-1-7771903-9-2

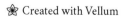

*To Caitlin*
*Because you're my magic.*

# CHAPTER ONE

D*rip!* The cave folded open before Mags. She knew the cave well in the landscape of her mind, had visited often, and lately, nearly every night. In the musty and damp air, a strange, almost sweet aroma hovered at the stiletto edge of her ability to identify it. Earth, wood, and musk she recognized, but what their combination meant eluded her. What the cave meant eluded her. As familiar as it was, she had never visited it in the physical realm.

*Drip!*

Darkness flattened the rock to variegated shades of gray. To the left, the sharper outcropping rose nearly twenty feet to midway up the wall. On her right, lay a haphazard scattering of fallen boulders like crumbs at a giant picnic. They meant something, those boulders.

*Drip! Drip!*

The something escaped her, and the more she peered at the strewn rocks, the more they remained merely lead-hued riddles. The cave, the smell, the very air, were all sensory messages like clues to a riddle.

*Drip! Drip! Plonk!*

The sound she knew, and Mags braced for what came next, what always came next. Not water dripping, but blood. Spreading like charcoal stains over the dusty floor. Sweating from the rocks in bubbles that swelled full, quivered a moment, and then seeped down the rock.

Blood became obscenely, brilliantly red against all the monochrome around her. It snaked in rivulets down the rock, on to the sand, and crawled toward her bare feet.

Every instinct in her willed her feet to step back from the encroaching scarlet, but she couldn't move. The blood would not be denied, inescapable in its forward creep until it oozed tepid and tacky between her toes.

The earth-wood-musk-scented breeze ruffled her hair, pressing her linen skirt and blouse to her body. Blood licked at her ankles. Claggy wind chafed her skin, the smell now so strong it etched into her sense memory.

Then. Absolute stillness. Not even the beat of her heart.

Springing from all around her, strands of gray and red silk wove through the cave. Like crazed worms, the silk threads wound over and through the rock, the blood, even the darkness itself. They worked faster, speeding to a frenzy of squirming, wriggling strands. Propelled by an unseen hand, the threads were woven into a static image, forcing her outside of the weave. Now she stood beside a giant tapestry and watched it.

In the sharper ledge to her left, a figure coalesced in the weave. Handsome, aquiline features. Dark hair. Darker eyes. Alexander.

He blinked at her, and then as fast as the threads had created him, they unraveled him, and the rockface reformed.

In a sickening twist, the cave imploded and vanished in a pop that left Mags blinking as reality reasserted itself in front of her.

She was standing beside her window in her bedroom. The

land surrounding Baile spread beneath her in a gentle, verdant blanket, blurring into a powder-blue sky littered with puffy clouds.

From within Baile came the sounds of her coven, Niamh calling to one of her many animal companions, Sinead and Roderick bickering about something, the clatter of feet on the stairs.

Probably Warren's daughter, Taylor. The youngest witch at Baile, Taylor never walked when she could run.

More than merely seeing or hearing, Mags sensed and felt the coven occupants.

And she could sense him. Jack Langham. The largest, scariest man Mags had ever clapped eyes on, which was saying a lot, as she lived with Roderick, Warren, and Alexander. None of them slouches in the big and bad category.

But Jack Langham was different. For one, he wasn't here to be bonded to a witch as her coimhdeacht. Mags didn't know exactly why Jack was at Baile, other than that he was hers. That and the little matter of the four children they were fated to have together.

For a woman not that comfortable with strange men in the first place, that knowledge certainly dialed her awkward up to excruciating.

# CHAPTER TWO

Life had a funny way of turning the tables. Fiona stood over Edana's bed and tried to summon her customary dislike of the woman. She'd even settle for indifference, but no, Fiona ached for the prone woman on the bed.

Hundreds of years they'd been bound together by a series of momentous decisions neither of them had truly understood the extent of. Sometimes Fiona wondered if she'd known way back when what she had been signing on for, whether she'd still have made the same decision. Probably. Baile had never been big enough to contain her ambition. It was way too late for doubts, and the hint of regret could get her killed.

"Fiona?" Edana's fever-bright brown eyes found her face. "Is there any water?"

Fiona slid her hand beneath Edana's neck and raised her mouth to a glass of water. "Here."

Edana licked her dry, chapped lips. Her teeth rattled against the glass as she drank. The effort exhausted her, and she limply allowed Fiona to lower her head back to the pillow. "Thank you," she whispered.

"You're welcome." Fiona meant it too. She wished she could

do more than her pitiful attempts to make Edana more comfortable.

Rosy light from the setting sun fell softy on Edana's face. Her poor, ruined face. None of Edana's staggering beauty remained on the pitiful collaboration of skin and bones.

Edana's dark lashes fluttered shut. Her breath wheezed past her cracked and bleeding lips. She flinched in her uneasy sleep, pain chasing her even into unconsciousness.

And all Fiona had for her was water and over-the-counter paracetamol.

Mistress had refused Fiona's requests for a doctor.

And Edana's fever raged unabated. Not even her longevity and accelerated healing ability could help Edana's body fight the result of the two jagged slashes across her face. The deeper and longer of the two ran from two inches into Edana's hairline, through her left eye, over her nose, and down over her cheek. About an inch below the first gash, the second dissected her cheekbone and chin.

Puffy, red, swollen, and seeping, those wounds would leave horrible scars. Even if Edana did survive, she had lost what made her quintessentially her. Edana had been walking temptation with her gleaming blond hair and melting brown eyes. Her curves had silenced rooms and dropped jaws wherever she went.

For as long as she could remember, Fiona had envied Edana her beauty. Envied that beauty until it had nearly become an obsession. She'd lain awake countless nights and fantasized about a time when Edana didn't have her sultry, golden looks. Now Fiona mourned their loss, almost as if they were her own.

"It's bad, isn't it?" Edana's pecan-colored gaze locked on her. She'd been so appallingly, impossibly vain about her looks. Now, Fiona took no satisfaction in the reason for Edana's conceit being gone.

"I've seen worse." Fiona took the chair beside the bed and

schooled her features into something less grim. Her back ached, and a numbing shroud covered her brain. If Edana had drawn her arrogance from her looks, Fiona had based hers on her reasoning. Logic, intelligence, astuteness, those had been Fiona's boasts. Thinking hurt. Feeling hurt worse.

Edana attempted to smile. It ended in a crooked grimace. "You're such a fucking liar."

"And you're a dumb slut." Fiona's response was rote and lacked any malice.

Dammit, but Fiona was tired. Tired of pretending, tired of lying, tired of the senseless loss, and tired of hanging on to the fraying thread of her life.

"Hey." She went for distraction. "Do you remember when we were first tossed out of that coven?"

Edana had hated the rules of being part of the Baile coven, railed against having her natural inclinations tempered by relentless self-righteousness. Edana had been born in the wrong century. If she'd been a child of this time, her wildness and her willfulness would have gone unremarked.

Edana's hoarse chuckle grated against Fiona's ears. "We got drunk."

"You got drunk." Fiona nudged them back into their familiar pattern. "I got a little tipsy."

"If you say so." Edana took a shuddering breath. "That was fun."

"Yes, it was." They'd been giddy with success, riding the soaring high of power and freedom. "We should do that again."

Edana nodded and turned her face to the beautiful sunset painting pinks and oranges across the horizon. "How long?"

"Three weeks." Fiona didn't pretend not to understand what Edana asked. Three weeks since a wild leopard had attacked Edana as it defended the guardian witch, Niamh. Edana would wear the results of that attack for the remainder of her days. If they had still been part of Baile, Goddess would have healed the damage to Edana. Healers would gather around her bed and transmute her pain and raging infection.

Three weeks ago, Fiona would never have thought Edana's days numbered. But now? Now Fiona faced an uncertain future without Edana. How had she never realized they were a team?

Hindsight had a brutal clarity to it. When Rhiannon vented the worst of her rages and her desperation, they had stood side by side. Together, they had overcome any lingering traces of doubt over the things Rhiannon demanded they do. It had been the two of them staring down the constant fear of their deaths, fused by time and decisions they'd both made.

Fiona didn't know if she had the strength to face all that alone. Lying to herself didn't help. She knew, down to her marrow, she didn't have the strength to face the future alone. Taking her own life, however, would not just kill her but cut her from the cycle of death and rebirth forever. The end of life in its ultimate form, and she'd done that to herself when she'd made the choice of Rhiannon over Goddess, blood magic over crémagic.

Desperation clawed at her. Endless years stretched ahead. "Stay with me," she whispered. "Please. Stay with me."

Edana was asleep again, sweat beading her fever-flushed face. Raised, angry red skin surrounded the oozing wounds.

Fiona stood. She had to do something, had to try.

Fear twisted her belly into a tight knot. Always unpredictable, Rhiannon had been frenzied since their return from South Africa. Two of the four cardinal points were now active: fire and water. They'd been activated by cré-witches and their power now fed Goddess. A strong Goddess could reincarnate and destroy all Rhiannon's plans. Unless Rhiannon could gain control of the power points, hundreds of years working toward her goal would disappear if Goddess grew strong enough to defeat her. So much death and blood saturated Rhiannon's plans. Funny, the killing had never bothered her before, but now Fiona felt like they were all drowning in it.

There was only going forward. Her and Edana's part in Rhiannon's plans had put them irrevocably on the anti-Goddess team.

Alexander had walked away. A traitorous voice whispered deep, deep inside of her. Mistress's own son had found a way to escape his doomed coil, and now lived safely behind Baile's wards. Those wards were forever closed to her and Edana. That water witch, Bronwyn, the healer, she could help Edana, but that way was mired in pitfalls. Even if Fiona could get to Bronwyn and get her to consider helping, Rhiannon would kill them for sure.

Fiona walked down the narrow, dark hallway to the main part of the cottage. With all her power, wealth and influence, Rhiannon could have lived anywhere. Even taken over the beautiful estate Alexander had lived on before he'd defected.

Mistress's fury hung over the cottage like the gathering power of a hurricane.

Fiona entered the living room with her head lowered. "Mistress."

"What?" Rhiannon kept her attention on the view outside the window. Deepening twilight caught in her pitch-black hair.

"Edana grows worse." Fiona kept all hint of rebuke from her tone.

Rhiannon snapped her head around. Her eyes, darker even than her crow-black hair, glimmered with banked fury. "She failed me."

The plan had been beautifully simple. Let Niamh find the fire point, follow her there, and get her to activate it. Then, enact the loophole Rhiannon had discovered. A cré-witch's blood spilled into the point she'd activated would corrupt it to blood magic, and all that power would have been theirs. No more of the searing agony of twisting cré-magic to respond to them. It would have been theirs for the asking, a powerful source now of blood magic, and lost to cré-magic forever.

"Yes." It made her a coward that she allowed all the blame to fall on Edana's shoulders. They'd all failed to gain control over fire. "But she might die. The infection could kill her."

Rhiannon shook her head. "And why should that concern me?"

"Edana has her uses." Any inference that she cared for Edana would only work against both of them. "She is a powerful witch. The new ones don't have her skills or her natural ability."

She and Edana were the last of Rhiannon's followers to have been trained in their magic. Rhiannon recruited anyone with latent power and turned them, but in this new world, magic had suffered from the steady dilution of years of non-practicing. "If we lose her, we lose her magic."

Rhiannon turned back to gazing out the window. "Tell me, Fiona, have you discovered some tendril of fondness for that slut?"

"She is familiar to me." Fiona forced a shrug. She wouldn't have thought it possible either. "Edana is the devil I know."

Silence lengthened alongside the growing shadows in the room. Furniture, art, and bric-a-brac crowded every available space, a veritable antique treasure trove by this time's standards. Rhiannon refused to get rid of anything. Like a grumpy dragon, she hoarded the reminders of the eons she had lived.

Finally, Rhiannon stood. "Take me to her."

Fiona bowed her head, not allowing hope to bloom.

At her back, Rhiannon's seething presence made her force down panic.

In the room, Rhiannon stalked over to the bed and stared down at Edana. She leaned over and studied Edana's sleeping face. "She is ruined." Face tight with anger, she said, "You brought me here for this? She is useless." She jabbed a finger into Edana's wound.

Edana screamed herself awake. She blinked at Rhiannon's face as if trying to bring her into focus.

The pain must have been unbearable, but Fiona kept any expression from her face. "Her looks are gone, true." Fiona fought down her gorge as Rhiannon dug a forefinger into Edana's wound. "But her magic remains."

Rhiannon studied the smeared blood and pus on her finger. She licked her finger and closed her eyes. A beatific delight lit her exquisite face. "Ah yes! She has her power yet."

"More even than me," Fiona said.

Rhiannon's gaze sharpened. "Do you know what the inherent problem with using blood to drive our magic is?"

"Tell me, Mistress." Nobody told Rhiannon anything.

"It's over too fast." Rhiannon clicked her fingers. "The blood carries the life force, but the life drains as fast as the blood does. We expend so much of the life force in gaining control of the magic."

Fiona kept her head bowed. She didn't know where Rhiannon was going. Blood magic drew on the life force contained within a person's blood.

"I have been thinking of that South African witch," Rhiannon said.

Mistress spoke of the old sangoma she had killed trying to overpower Niamh. It would have worked as well, had the animals not responded to the guardian witch's life being in danger.

Rhiannon picked up Edana's arm and stroked the inside of her wrist.

Against the creamy pallor of her skin, the pale blue lines of Edana's veins pulsed.

Edana's gaze flit to Fiona and then fastened on Rhiannon. Even through her illness, the terror won out. Edana wanted to live.

"So much power." Rhiannon shook her head, her thumb stroking Edana's veins. "And lost so soon."

The slower the person bled to death, the more power they could tap, but they didn't always have the luxury of time. "You had to take the old witch's power fast. You had no choice but to kill her."

"Hmm." Rhiannon placed Edana's arm tenderly beside her on the bed. She nodded as if she'd made a decision and turned back to Fiona. "Look at me."

The brightness of Rhiannon's smile almost blinded her. "Mistress?"

"You have done well." Rhiannon very rarely praised anyone.

Fiona bowed her head again. Her life might depend on working out what she'd done well.

"You have pleased me by bringing this possibility to my attention." Rhiannon swept from the room. "I think a doctor is a perfect idea."

# CHAPTER THREE

Mags stared around her room. Not surprisingly, her lost journal didn't throw itself in front of her. She'd lose her own head if it wasn't attached. The perishing journal had been lost since yesterday, and she needed it. She wrote all her visions in her journal, a habit she'd had since childhood. It appalled her how much her conscious mind forgot about her visions, and she'd made a habit of recording the details.

Dropping to her knees, she tried under the bed for the third time. The last time she'd had her journal was after another dream about him. Although she strongly suspected that last dream about Jack had been part fantasy. Heat bloomed in her cheeks. She didn't need her journal to remember the details of that dream.

She crawled over to her dresser against the far wall and peered under. The journal was way too fat to have wedged under there, but you never knew. There were days when she even forgot what she was looking for while she was looking for it. She'd blame menopause or dementia, but at twenty-six neither seemed probable.

"Aha." A beaded bracelet she hadn't seen in over a month

gleamed in the dullness under her dresser. She slipped the amethyst beads over her hand and reunited it with the other bracelets on her wrist. She liked the way they clinked and clattered together.

She took a second to appreciate how the weak light from her huge window gleamed in the profusion of crystals and beads. She did like pretty things, and bright things, and things that sparkled.

Her feet tangled in the multicolored layers of her floor length organza skirt as she stood. Plenty of practice stopped her from face-planting into the floor. "Now where?"

She'd been through all the drawers of her dresser, the old chest at the foot of her bed, her bathroom, her bedside tables, her wardrobe, even the countless tiny drawers of the large apothecary cabinet she used to keep the treasures life offered her. When an object crossed her path that called to her, it ended up in that cabinet—feathers, rocks, crystals, beads, shells, interesting bits and pieces that spoke to her. Sometimes she used her collection for jewelry, other times they got sewn into clothing, or glued anywhere the fancy took her.

Which reminded her, she wanted to make new curtains for around her bed. She imagined feathers all over them, maybe with dried flowers. Or maybe she could use ribbons with the feathers. Or ribbons, feathers, and dried flowers. It would be like waking up in summer every morning.

"Journal." She yanked her mind back to the business at hand. Her mind had been showing a stubborn insistence on going for a walk with the fairies lately. The vision with Alexander was important. It had happened many times before. You didn't ignore visions that repeated. Each time, she detailed the vision in her journal for comparison purposes. With visions and seeings, the details could make a vital difference, provide the clue that unlocked the mystery.

Somehow her journal must have wandered out of her room.

The last time she'd seen it had been after her Jack fantasy, but she couldn't remember where she'd been when she'd had the vision. It had been yesterday. Or maybe the day before. No, it must have been yesterday, because she remembered not seeing the journal since yesterday, and she'd been looking since yesterday.

Or had that been earlier today?

Or even the day before yesterday.

She tugged on her hair as if she could get her mind to reset its date and time, which reminded her she could do with a trim. Without her paying much attention, her hair had reached her waist and kept growing. There was too much hair in her life.

Haircuts, however, and the timing of her lost journal weren't as important as finding the blasted thing. Anyone could pick it up and read her entries. That spelled disaster. She didn't want Alexander reading about his image being soaked in blood and unraveling. Or Jack reading what she'd written about him. Her cheeks heated and she got moving.

Mags loved living at Baile, loved the gentle, reassuring presence of the old structure, but searching an entire castle for a lost journal was a daunting task.

She took the back stairs and stopped at a flash of red on one of the stairs. Bending, she picked up a sparkly red apple hair slide. The sort of hair slide a young girl would wear. There hadn't been any children at Baile in years. The coven were all grown up now, and none of them had children yet.

"Taylor." She tucked the hair slide in her pocket. They did have a young witch at Baile. Their newest coimhdeacht had a young daughter, who'd been staying here for the last few weeks.

Something had happened to Taylor recently. Mags couldn't remember what. Goddess, if she had her journal, she could consult that.

Goddess! That was it. Taylor had wandered into the caverns

and discovered she was a witch. Mags had definitely not seen that coming. Or had she? No, she hadn't. She was sure of it because she saw nothing about Taylor. It was so rare for her to get nothing from someone that it stuck in her mind. She hadn't even seen Taylor's arrival at Baile, only sensed it moments before her mother had driven her here, and that knowing had been connected to the mother and not Taylor. The mother would be back. What was her name?

Never mind. It didn't matter because Mags wouldn't be here. She didn't know why she wouldn't be here, but she did know she wouldn't. Goddess, but visions could be frustrating. When she saw something, it would be super if it could get specific. Like on the 16th of whatever, so-and-so would show up there, wearing that, and do the other. But no. What she got instead were feelings, sensings, notions, and vague details. Other than Jack. She'd seen Jack in brilliant detail, down to the shirt he'd worn. And in her latest vision, the shirt he hadn't been wearing.

Oh my! That man had muscle in places other people didn't have places.

Back stairs opened into the pantries behind the kitchen. When Roderick had built the castle, he'd probably had these stairs built for servants to use. Mags giggled as she imagined Roderick finding instead an entire coven of witches living in the caverns beneath his newly built castle. A coven of witches who had then moved in, and for all intents and purposes, taken over his precious castle.

One leading into another, the pantries were Alannah's domain. Neatly labeled jars lined the shelves. Storage bins sat obediently in rows against the walls. Drying herbs hung from the ceiling, and the air was redolent with scents of all the spices Alannah used in her cooking.

Bright green apples made a vivid, lovely picture in their woven basket. Her stomach grumbled, and she snagged an apple. It was crisp and tart and delicious. She might have missed breakfast.

Alannah didn't hear her come in. She stood with her back to Mags rolling out pastry on the large kitchen table. A brightly patterned summer dress hugged her lithe body and displayed miles of long, gorgeous leg.

Mags suspected it was Thomas perched on the edge of the table and not her pastry holding Alannah's attention. Lounging there in jeans with a T-shirt hugging the dips and swells of his gorgeous torso, he could be an advert for some trendy menswear line. He also looked as corporeal as she and Alannah. Thomas was one hundred percent ghost, however, and Mags was one of a growing chorus who wasn't happy about his attachment to Alannah.

"Heya," she said to them.

Alannah looked over her shoulder with one of her stunning big smiles. Her hair didn't need a cut and cascaded down her back in a gleaming auburn mass of loveliness. "Magsie! Where have you been all day? I haven't seen you once."

She must have missed breakfast. "This and that," she said, instead of trying to tackle the overwhelming task of remembering what she had been doing all day. "I was looking for my journal. Have you seen it?"

"Mags, you keep a journal?" Thomas's eyes glinted. The man—sort of man—would flirt with anyone.

She cursed the heat in her cheeks. It would only encourage him if she blushed. The curse of the redhead, that propensity to blush.

Alannah laughed and brandished a rolling pin at Thomas. "Don't you start."

He gave her a slow, lazy smile that smoldered with private conversations and joint secrets.

Alannah blushed and giggled but turned to Mags. "I haven't seen it, and I cleaned the kitchen before I started on these pies."

"Pies?" Mags's appetite poked at her. "Chicken?"

"Chicken for you and Sinead." Alannah dusted her rolling pin with flour. "Steak and kidney for the boys, veggie for Niamh." She smiled and got to work on the big glob of pastry. "A few Cornish pasties to keep everyone happy, and a fresh green salad."

"You make me wish I could eat." Thomas stared mournfully at the pastry.

Alannah smiled at him. "Roderick eats enough for both of you."

Thomas laughed and said to Mags, "If you tell me what your journal looks like, I'll keep an eye out."

"It's about so big." Mags showed him with her hands. "And it's got a bright pink cover. With some beads sewn on to it."

"I'll let you know if I see it." He winked at her. "And I promise not to read it."

Blushing again. Mags tripped on her skirt going up the stairs and out of the kitchen.

"I'm fine," she yelled over her shoulder. Not that her clumsiness took anyone by surprise anymore. Stopping at the top of the stairs, she cast her senses out to find the remainder of the coven. Yelling from the great hall saved her the effort.

A game of French cricket was underway with Taylor on bat.

"All right, kiddo." Sinead gave an elaborate wind up. "Don't think I'm going to take it easy on you just because you're a kid."

Giggling and flushed, Taylor set her chin. "Bring it."

"I warned you." Sinead nodded to her fielders.

"Eyes on the ball." Warren played wicket keeper behind his daughter. "She's all talk."

"Hey!" Niamh called from the other side of the hall. "Whose side are you on?"

Wolf pups gamboled and yipped at her feet. Their mother spent more and more time outside with the rest of the pack as the pups grew older.

Taylor hit the ball with a solid *whack* and sent it bouncing and bumping across the hall.

Pups surged after it, two of them losing interest immediately and stopping to wrestle.

"Get it." Sinead lunged after the ball.

"Mags!" Taylor waved the bat at her. "Are you coming to play?"

Was she? It looked like fun. Nope, she was looking for her journal. "No, I was actually looking for my book."

"Don't you know where it is?" Taylor scrunched up her face.

The kid had a point. "My blessing doesn't always work like that."

"What kind of book?" Sinead jammed her hands on her hips. Alannah's identical twin, but in looks only. Sinead wore combat pants with a black Arcane Activist T-shirt.

Mags didn't want to get into a full explanation, so she waved her hand. "Just my journal."

"Can you describe it?" Niamh approached, a pup tugging on the hem of her jeans. Niamh had a kind of animal grace and moved like her own rhythm played through her muscles. She'd have made a great burlesque dancer. Mags liked that movie about the burlesque dancers with what's-her-name, the popstar.

"About yea big." Mags showed them with her hands. "Pink."

"Sparkly?" Sinead grinned at her.

"Sparkly." She grinned back. Sinead knew her well.

Niamh's gaze went unfocussed as she reached out to her animal companions. They made useful eyes, ears, and noses about the place.

"Why do you have a journal?" Taylor cocked her head. "Do you write your secrets in there?"

"It wouldn't be a secret if she told you." Warren tugged one of her ponytails.

Seeing Warren as a dad required a reset. A big, rough man

with a face too hard for conventional good looks, but with his daughter he was a big softie.

"The library," Niamh said. "Look in the library."

"Of course." Mags slapped her palm on her forehead. As if that would somehow dam the holes in her brain. Of course, she'd left it in the library because the Jack dream had come to her while she was taking a nap on one of the massive leather sofas. The fire had been warm, her belly full of Alannah's home baked bread and cheese. A glass of wine had gotten her nice and relaxed and sleepy. "I don't know why I didn't think of the library."

"You sure you don't want to play?" Taylor held the bat out to her. "It's still my turn but you can have it."

"That's very kind." She liked Warren's youngster. Taylor fit right in at Baile. More than Warren was happy about, to be sure, and she didn't need her blessing to see trouble brewing on that front. "But I'm a danger to myself and everyone else when I play games."

Warren made a face. "Surely not—"

"No, really." She appreciated Warren's attempt at kindness, but a lifetime of trips, falls, bruises, and swollen body parts couldn't be denied. "I'll probably take one of you down with me."

Niamh and Sinead were too sweet to outright say anything, but their silence spoke for them.

"Come on then." Niamh threw the ball to Sinead. "Let's get her out."

Mags watched Taylor crack another ball across the hall before she went to the library.

As she opened the door, a glorious view of the sea confronted her. Sunlight glimmered off the water like a thousand crystal beads bobbing beneath the surface. Books lined the towering walls and made the air smell of ink and paper. The space above the gaping fireplace was still empty, since

Alexander and Bronwyn had taken down the map to all the power points that had hung over it.

Her journal lay open and facedown on the arm of the sofa she'd taken a nap on yesterday. "There you are."

A massive dark form unfolded from the sofa with a smirk. "Here I am."

# CHAPTER FOUR

Sodding hell but Mags was gorgeous. Jack cranked to his feet to face her.

He couldn't say exactly what made her such a knee to the bollocks, but he suspected the truth lay more in a combination of factors.

Her big green eyes always looked slightly startled, like she'd only that moment brought the world around her into focus. Her long, willowy shape was always in motion, most of that clumsy as hell, and so adorable she was like pure candyfloss for the soul. He constantly wanted to rescue her from all the things she tripped over, bumped into, and slipped on. Girl could go arse over tit on free air.

She had the true ivory skin of a redhead, and it looked cool and silky to the touch.

Blinking those huge greens at him, she went brick-red. She flushed a lot around him, and he chose to take it as a good sign that his attraction was reciprocated. "Jack!"

"Margaret." He wanted to kiss each and every freckle spackling her tilted nose. She wasn't a sexy pin-up like Niamh or super model gorgeous like Sinead and Alannah or even soft and curvy like Bronwyn or channeling a Disney fairy like Maeve, but she had something he wanted.

"Magdalene." She wrinkled her nose at him. "Not Margaret."

"Magdalene." He drew the syllables of her name out and liked them. "How are you today?"

She giggled, and her blush deepened. "F…fine. Good actually." Her voice rose. "I'm fine. Good."

"Good and fine." He got such a kick out of teasing her. "Sounds like a great day."

"No…I mean I am…but it's not." She huffed a lock of hair out of her face and drew a deep breath. "My journal." She pointed to the pink sparkly book on the arm of the leather sofa. "I just came to find it."

"Here we go then." He made to pick it up.

"No." She leaped forward, tripping over the hem of her skirt.

He lunged to intercept the trajectory of her forehead with the table, but she managed to rescue herself.

"I mean." She straightened her skirt. "I can get it myself."

"No worries." He leaned down and snatched up the book. "I'm closer."

Her eyes went huge as she stared at the book. She wrinkled her nose at him. "Can I…"

"Sure." He handed it over.

"Good. Thank you." She hugged it to her chest. The question she wanted to ask gathered in her eyes. The woman had no poker face.

He couldn't stop his grin, even though he was about to catch hell. And deserved it. "Yes."

"What?" She blinked at him.

"Yes. I read it." To be fair, he hadn't meant to. He'd seen the pink sparkly book, assumed it belonged to Taylor and glanced at the open page. After he'd caught his name, he'd read a bit more. When he caught the gist of the entry, you couldn't have stopped him from reading it with a bulldozer.

Her eyes snapped at him. Thunder gathered in them as her outrage grew. "You read my journal?"

"I didn't mean to." Lame, but the truth. "I thought it belonged to Taylor, and I glanced at it to confirm it was hers."

"You read my journal." Her voice rose and her face went from flame-red to ice-white. "You had no right to read my journal."

"True." He held up a hand, hoping she'd give him two minutes to explain. "But once I saw my name, I got curious and couldn't resist."

She opened and shut her mouth, struggling to find words. Woman had no trouble expressing herself on paper, by the way. "That's outrageous."

"You're right." Truth was truth, after all. "But if you saw your name, wouldn't you read on?"

"No." She was the crappiest liar on the planet.

He couldn't let that go unchallenged and raised his brow. "Really?"

"Yes, really." Her knuckles went white around her book. "I would never read someone else's journal. Never." Her tirade gathered steam. "It's the grossest, most awful invasion of privacy."

"You're right. Of course, you're right." Wanting to reach her, he stepped closer. She smelled like spring, fresh and floral with notes of jasmine and almond. God, that journal entry. He got hot remembering it. She might blush and stammer every time someone said anything even slightly racy, but her mind was a darker, twistier, and far more interesting place. "But there's nothing you wrote that I haven't thought about."

"Really?" He'd shocked her out of her outrage. Momentarily. Two seconds later she went right back to being pissed off at him. "That is so not the issue."

"I know." He wanted to get closer still, but she might hit him. "But I'd rather talk about what I read."

She choked and coughed. "No. Not the point. And stop looming."

"I'm not looming. I'm tall." And so was she. Five-eight, five-nine to his six-five, and that was perfect as well. "And I'm trying to get closer to you."

"Then don't invade my privacy." Tears flooded her eyes.

That shook him out of being a smart ass. "I really didn't mean to, Mags." He'd only meant to tease her, flirt with her, try and smooth the way toward some of those things she'd written about him. "And I'm sorry." He reached for her hand, but she stepped back and gripped her book. "I really am sorry."

"You had no right."

"That's true." Need to make this better clamored in him. He'd made her cry, and that made him the biggest wanker of all. "It was inexcusable."

Her shoulders sagged. "Anyway, it's not a journal."

He was fairly certain she'd called it that, and it did have Mags's Journal on the first page. "I thought you called it—"

"Well, yes. But that's only what I call it. It's not a journal-journal." She flapped a hand and frowned. "What I mean is it's not one of those journals that I write my hopes and what happened in my day."

"Right." Bollocks, and here he was really hoping she'd wanted what she'd written to happen.

"It's more of a logbook," she said.

"Logbook?" As this was probably the longest conversation they'd had since he'd gotten here, he wanted to keep her talking to him for as long as she'd let him. "What sort of things do you log?"

"Well, you know that." She scowled at him. "Because you read it."

"Not the whole thing." He kept the wince under wraps, because so not the point. Then his prat of a mouth kept going. "Only the parts with my name."

Her scowl deepened, and he couldn't blame her. Also, he kind of loved that she gave him what-for. Most women looked at him and got intimidated. He'd learned to stand back, give them physical space, keep his voice even and low, and never mention the nicknames he'd gotten slapped on him through the less than stellar parts of his history. "I only read that last entry."

"Right." She nodded and shook her head, as if trying to clear her thoughts. "I log my...visions. My precognitions."

His nape prickled. So much went on in this castle that made him twitch. The longer he stayed, the less guarded they were speaking around him. There'd been a lot of chatter about magic, elemental power points, healing people, and Doctor Doolittling it with animals. And he'd heard all about Mags and her nifty ability to see the future. "Tell me about that."

She looked taken aback. "What's to tell? I see possible futures."

He made an encouraging noise. Silence often made people talk more than questions. Another handy trick he'd misused in his past.

"I can also see people." She raised her chin for a knock back. "I can scry them."

"Scry?"

"See them." She flapped a hand. "Like from a distance." Her pretty face fell. "At least, I should be able to do that according to Maeve, but my abilities are still a bit iffy."

"Because of your element not being active?" He'd picked up a thing or two.

She nodded. "I'm the next witch who needs to activate my point."

"And Niamh went to South Africa with Warren for hers?" He'd come here looking for his friend, and he had refused to leave before he saw for himself Warren was hale and hearty. Turns out Warren was more than hale and hearty. In fact,

Warren was loving life and a fair way down the road to loving that Niamh of his.

Mags nodded. Her silky, hip-length coppery hair dropped over one shoulder. It made him think of fairies and elven princesses. Also dark, sweaty nights and hot skin.

"She activated fire, because she draws her blessing from the fire element," Mags said, yanking him out of his fantasy. "Maeve is also fire. Bronwyn is water, and she activated that here at Baile. In the caverns."

The infamous caverns he'd heard so much about but never seen. "They're under the castle, right?"

"In the cliffs." She tilted her head. "I'm sure if Baile let you inside the wards, she'd let you visit them."

They all talked about the castle like it had its own personality. He'd tried a few subtle questions at Warren, but the bloke went mum. As for Roderick, he'd had better conversations with the rock walls of the castle. "Would you take me?" He didn't rate his chances, given how their encounter today had started out, but if you don't ask…

"No." She had no hesitation in shutting him down. "That's between you and Baile."

"Right." He went for a quick direction change. "When I first came here, you acted like you knew me. Was that because of your…um…" The word got away from him.

"Precognitions." She nodded. "Yes, I saw you, and I also saw that you're important."

He didn't know how he felt about that. Being seen before he arrived gave him the itch, but curiosity got him asking, "In what way?"

She fired up again and cleared her throat. "To me."

"You?" He could get behind being here for her. Except some clarification would be a good idea. "Like Warren?"

"Eh?" She blinked at him as if she'd spaced out for a moment.

"Like Warren," he said. "You mean be there like Warren is for

Niamh." He couldn't remember that tongue-wrenching word they used to describe what Warren did at Baile.

She took a fixed interest in her skirt. "No-o-o, you're not coimhdeacht."

Whatever the hell that was when it was at home. "Then what?"

"Um…" She pleated her skirt between her fingers, then looked up. Her gaze direct and unflinching. "Are you sure you want to know?"

"Yes." Not really that sure after all. She could have seen him impaled on a castle turret. In which case, wouldn't he like to know beforehand. Maybe. Then again…

*Christ, Jack, get a grip.* He didn't believe people were chained to fate. "Yes."

"Before I tell you, you need to understand nothing is definite." She sounded like she'd made her speech before. "Just because I see something, it doesn't mean it's going to happen. It means if things continue on their current path, what I see will come to pass."

And wasn't that bloody convenient. Here, this is your fate, but just in case it doesn't work out like that, here's my escape clause. "Hit me with it."

"You're connected to me." She cleared her throat and stared over his left shoulder, her cheeks red again. "We're…going to… be together."

"Be together?" He could have told her his plans lined right up with her visions, and he didn't need a crystal ball. Taking her hand, he tugged her closer. "That sounds about right."

She stared at her hand against his chest and frowned. "But it's not set in stone. It's only a high likelihood."

"A very high likelihood." He covered her entire hand with his. "If you stop ducking away every time you see me."

"I don't—" She wouldn't make eye contact and huffed. "I do, but only because this is so terribly awkward."

He'd been warned she was shy, and he sort of liked it. "It doesn't have to be awkward. I'm a man, you're a woman, and we share a mutual attraction." A nasty thought put the mental brakes on. "Unless you aren't feeling the same kind of way."

"Oh, no." And she managed that without a blush. "I do feel the same way. But..."

As far as he was concerned, they could crack on right here and now. "But?"

"I know too much."

Did she see some future scenario where he didn't get it up or something? "Like what?"

"Like the fact that we're going to have four children together." She frowned. "Also, I might die."

# CHAPTER FIVE

"Hey, little witch."

*My man.* Alexander leaned against the doorjamb to the healer's hall, breeze playing in his dark hair, sun backlighting him and slamming the all-round gorgeousness point home. Bronwyn didn't think there'd ever be a day she wouldn't melt every time she saw him. Of course, sometimes the melting was more about annoyance than romance, but he could handle whatever she threw at him.

"Hey, yourself." She straightened from her worktable and eased the pinch in her lumbar. "You got nothing better to do than hang around looking hot?"

"Nope." He grinned at her. "And the hot thing comes naturally."

"Asshole." She grinned back and eased off her stool. "What brings you this way?"

"It's dinnertime." He met her halfway and slid his arms around her. "And I'm here to remind you to eat."

Bronwyn had to laugh at the futility of reminding her. The twins in her belly had been tugging the "feed me" bell rope for about forty minutes. "Your kids beat you to it."

"Hello, tiny people." Alexander leaned down and put his mouth near the gentle curve only beginning to make itself known. "Tell your mother that Dad says it's time to eat."

Part of her was still getting used to the idea of being pregnant. Prophecy, as it turned out, laughed in the face of planning, and got right on with making pregnancies happen. "Does it freak you out?"

"Becoming a dad?" He tucked her against his side and walked them toward the door. "I always thought it would, what with it being the raison d'être for yours truly here, but no. I'm good with it." He kissed her temple. "More than good with it."

They had been thrown together by an ancient prophecy. *The son of death shall bear the torch that lights the path. And the daughter of life shall bring forth water nascent and call it onto the path of light. Then they will bear fruit. And this fruit will be the magick. The greatest of magick and the final magick.*

"Hmm." He had a way of rolling with the punches that soothed her concerns and fears. Probably a side effect of him having rattled around the earth for hundreds of years. "I never saw myself as a mother."

Not seeing herself as a mother had become a lot more academic since the last part of that prophecy had sidestepped condoms and the pill, and she was now pregnant with twins.

She and Alexander walked across the bailey with a setting sun doing a bang-up job of adding pink, red, and orange mood lighting.

"I was never one of those women who wanted to hold the baby or got all broody over pictures of babies."

"I'm fairly certain those are not prerequisites for the job," he said.

His accent killed her. Tom Hiddleston and Colin Firth rolled into one, and all hers.

"I hope not." Her mother had died young, and she'd been raised by her maternal grandmother. Deidre had been lovely, but not the conventional model for motherhood. Then again, Alexander had been raised by Satan's handmaiden, and he was doing okay.

Proving he could read her thoughts, he said, "You've got this, little witch." He pressed her closer to him. "We've got this." He indicated the kitchen with a head tilt. "And a raft load of backup if we need it."

Her babies would be raised by the coven. A small bubble of happiness pulsed from her womb. The twins liked that idea.

---

WARREN TRIED to release the tension knotting his shoulders as Taylor accepted a Cornish pasty from Alannah. The homey, everyone gathered around the table, atmosphere of the kitchen did nothing to soothe his nagging worry. If anything, it made it worse. How could they all be sitting down to dinner, business as normal, when shit was heading for the fan at warp speed?

"I could be any kind of witch. Right, Niamh?" Taylor turned sparkling eyes, the same hazel as her mother's, on Niamh.

His bonded witch, sensitive to what he felt and thought, Niamh glanced at him before replying, "It seems that way."

"Cool." Taylor responded to Sinead's nudge with the salad bowl and ladled greenery on her plate. "Maybe I could be some kind of witch that nobody's ever heard of."

Roderick looked struck by that idea and studied Taylor from across the table with his pale-blue predator's gaze.

Sodding great! Not only had his daughter uncovered her latent magical potential, but her discovery might be a lot more wait-and-see than he had bargained for. Already, there were enough complicating factors to the equation.

Not the least of which was Debra. She was going to love this new development. Not.

Touching his hand, Niamh murmured, "It will be all right. Goddess assured you of that."

"Right." He didn't bother to hide his doubt from her. Goddess had assured him Taylor would be all right and they'd be together again. All true as it turned out, but Warren didn't know if her promise had extended to Taylor being a witch, and her mother having no idea.

Debra was still in Australia nesting with her new man, Adam. She was in for a bugger of a surprise when she got back.

"Hey, Bronwyn," Taylor called, and waved hello with her fork.

Warren's irritation got away from him. "Don't wave your cutlery around."

"What?" Taylor blinked at him, both of them surprised by his sharp tone.

"I beg your pardon," Warren corrected, uncomfortably aware of the sinking atmosphere in the kitchen. "And don't wave your cutlery around. It's bad manners."

"More like life-preserving." Roderick winked at Taylor. "In my time, when you waved your eating knife around, you lopped the ear off the person next to you."

"Hello, sweet girl." Bronwyn dropped a kiss on Taylor's head. "What's got your dad all grouchy?"

"Magic." Taylor pulled a face. "He doesn't like that I'm magic."

*Ah, fuck!* All heads snapped his way. All expressions wearing varying degrees of WTF.

Niamh broadcast her WTF loud and clear through their bond.

Picking up his fork, he tried to power his way through. "It's not the magic that worries me, it's what's going to happen now."

"I think that's fairly self-evident." Roderick snorted.

The man didn't have a kid; he had no idea what Warren was going through. Also, the bugger was how many hundreds of years old. He didn't even understand the concept of divorce, let alone how this would play out in modern times.

"I can't believe I'm saying this." Alexander looked ill. "But I agree with Roderick."

Maeve dropped her fork and gaped at him.

Alexander winced. "Yeah, I know. Surprised the crap out of me too."

Warren knew what they thought he should do, keep Taylor at Baile so she could be safe and learn her blessing, but as neither Roderick nor Alexander were a sod's worth of help with the how he was going to pull that off, he didn't want to hear it.

"Taylor needs to stay here." Bronwyn broke the silence as she took a seat at the table. "She needs to train in her element, and then we need to discover what her blessing is."

"Yes!" Taylor fist pumped, then subsided with a guilty side look at Warren. "I mean, I think Bronwyn is right."

Warren grasped for his waning patience. "And what about your friends? Your school?"

"But, Dad." Taylor turned an imploring face to him. "I can learn everything I need to know here. Mags and Alannah and Sinead, and Niamh were all homeschooled. And I can make new friends." Her eyes gleamed as she pressed her point home. "And Bronwyn went to school. She didn't like it there, so she was also homeschooled."

Warren hated to be this guy, but he needed to keep her grounded. "And your mother?"

"She's in Australia." Taylor's voice grew small. She clenched her lips together like she was trying not to cry.

It killed him, it really did, but he owed it to his daughter to keep a level head here. "She's coming back, Taylor. In two weeks. And she's going to want to see you." His gut clenched around the words. He wasn't going to let Taylor go without a fight, but that was between him and Debra, and he refused to involve Taylor in their battles. "How are we going to explain any of this to her?"

Taylor put her fork down on her plate and dropped her chin to her chest. "I dunno." She shrugged. "But we just will."

Yeah, because Debra was known for being reasonable and understanding.

"Eat your dinner, loveliness." Alannah pushed Taylor's plate closer to her. "You love pasties."

Taylor picked up her fork and poked the salad. "You don't know she won't understand."

Umm yes, he most certainly did. Debra would blame him for all of this, and she would not be wrong. He'd wanted Taylor here, and he'd gotten her here. Then, she had wandered off one day and into the caverns. Next thing they all had known, Taylor had burst out of the caverns with the super thrilling news that Goddess had been waiting for her and had accepted her in water.

The potential stumbling blocks were miles high. Taylor could never tell anyone about what had happened to her, but she was twelve. Twelve-year-old girls were not exactly known for their discretion, and neither should they be. She shouldn't have to keep secrets, and for damn sure not one this huge.

Fuck! He could see it now. Debra getting called in to school because her daughter said she was a witch. Taylor being teased and ostracized by other kids. Debra dragging Taylor off to counseling for her delusions.

"Hey." Niamh put her arm around Taylor. "You're not in trouble. You didn't do anything wrong."

Warren hated that he now felt like a bully. "I know she didn't do anything wrong. I'm not saying she did."

Niamh kept right on talking to Taylor. "I honestly don't know how, but we can trust Goddess to find a way." She leaned closer to Taylor. "After all, she brought you here to us, didn't she?"

Niamh's naiveté staggered him, and worst of all, she was making promises to Taylor nobody could keep. He opened the bond wide and let her feel his anger. "Until we have the answers, I think we should keep this realistic."

Not one particle bothered by his mood, Niamh shot right back, "Which part of any of what happens around Baile is grounded in your so-called reality?" She waved a hand to encompass all of them and the castle. Her dark eyes flashed at him. "We're living through something extraordinary. We're beings who practice magic on behalf of a goddess who lives underneath our sentient castle."

Alexander chuckled. "She's got you there, brother."

"Twelfth-century knight. I'd be more specific about the date, but we weren't big on record keeping back then." Roderick raised a meaty hand. "Sitting right here, as flesh and bone alive as you."

Maeve giggled and raised her hand. "I was born in sixteen twenty-three, which makes me three hundred and ninety-eight years young."

"As a gentleman, I could never disclose my age." Alexander smirked.

They didn't bloody get it. None of them did. Niamh's lack of understanding irked him the most. The woman was inside his mind, body, and soul. She should know what Taylor's discovery was doing to him.

"I talk to animals." Niamh nudged Taylor and got a smile out of her.

Her betrayal smarted, and he let her feel it.

Raising her chin, she met his gaze and stared him down.

Bronwyn joined in. "I heal people." She snapped her fingers. "Just like that."

"I talk to the dead." Maeve made her voice creepy.

Thomas popped into view beside Alannah. "I am dead."

"Enough!" Warren pounded the table.

Everyone jumped, except Roderick who kept right on eating.

Taylor stared at him with huge eyes, and he hated that most of all. He'd allowed her to see his fucking rotten temper. He hauled back on his anger and tried for a reasonable tone. "None of you get it, okay." His attempt at reasonable came out more bark than words. "Making jokes and pretending like it's all going to work out is making the situation worse. Wake up, the lot of you."

Silence reigned. Even Roderick stopped mid-chew and stared at him.

He couldn't believe he had to explain this to them. "This is not some magical make-believe where everything works out. We might be magic." He scowled at Niamh. "But so far, that's caused as many problems as it's solved. Taylor is part of this century." He slammed the table to make his point clear. "This time. She's not some isolated weirdo, living in some messed up alternate reality, pretending like everything is going to come right. This is her life, and she deserves a normal life. I'm going to make sure she gets it." He was breathing heavily when he ran out of words.

A wolf pup whined. The fire in the kitchen range popped.

"Come on, Taylor." Sinead picked up both their plates. "Let's go finish our dinner outside. There's a beautiful sunset this evening."

Gentle Alannah shook her head at him, her beautiful face sad, as she also stood. "I could go for a sunset too."

"Me three." Bronwyn pushed to her feet and snatched up her plate.

Alexander stood with her. "Whither she goest and all that."

"Oh, Warren." Maeve sighed and shook her head. "You shouldn't have said that."

"Any of it." Standing, Roderick grabbed the huge dish of pies in the middle of the table and followed the other witches.

Maeve took their plates and went with him.

Niamh took the salad bowl and a bunch of cutlery. The look she tossed him was underscored by the scathing scorn and fury screaming through the bond at him. The door shut behind her.

Even the she-wolf was giving him the stink eye from her place by the stove.

"Wow!" Jack glared across the table at him. "Well done. You managed to call everyone in the room a delusional weirdo and upset your daughter. Bang-up job. I can't wait to see what you do next." Jack's chair scraped against the floor. "Got a bit of bullying, maybe some mild torture planned for the rest of the evening?"

# CHAPTER SIX

Sinead liked getting up with the sun, loved the way it warmed and woke Mother Earth for the day. Closing the keep door behind her, she breathed deep of the fresh, new day. Her blessing connected with the abundant growing things around her and tingled beneath her skin. A crisp morning, a pure day, and after last night's shit show courtesy of Warren, she felt doubly blessed.

She let herself into the walled kitchen garden and shut the door behind her. It seemed they'd picked up an extra inhabitant.

Taylor sat in the kitchen garden, covered in mud and wolf puppies. She must have gotten up at first sparrow's fart.

Sinead wasn't good with children. Mostly, she scared the crap out of the poor little buggers, but Taylor didn't seem to mind her, and she really liked the girl. Whatever Warren said about his ex, she'd done a good job raising their daughter.

Sinead should be having a shit fit about Taylor and the pups destroying her tomato plants, but the plants would recover, and the girl looked like she could do with a bit of tending.

Well, she'd give it her best.

"Hey." She parked it next to Taylor.

A dark brown pup immediately attacked the laces on her Converses, determined to remind them who was the apex predator.

Taylor gave her a wan smile. "Heya."

"What are you doing out here?"

Taylor tumbled a pup and rubbed her belly. "Playing."

Ask a stupid question. Sinead hunted for another lead, but tact really wasn't her thing. "You upset?"

"No." Taylor shrugged.

"You look upset." Sinead elbowed her. "And you're covered in mud."

Taylor gave her another shrug and went back to the pups.

Two males got into a tussling showdown and Taylor giggled.

"Your dad is worried." Sinead got straight to the point. As much as she wanted to thump Warren for how he'd handled that interaction in the kitchen last night, she did get what had his knickers in a twist.

Taylor sighed and scrubbed her palms against her knees. "I know."

Kids were hard work apparently. "Want to talk about it?"

"No."

Stupid question number two, and she was sinking fast. "Want to garden?"

"Maybe." Taylor gave her a squinty-eyed look, like she didn't trust the offer at all.

But it wasn't an outright rejection, so Sinead got to her feet. "Looks like those green beans are ripe. We should pick them."

"These too." Taylor jerked her head at the tomato plants.

"Yup." Sinead fetched two baskets from the supplies stacked against the wall. "And I think we've got some carrots ready to come up, and some parsnips."

Taylor took a basket and screwed up her nose. "I don't like parsnips."

"Don't like parsnips?" The heresy of it, and Sinead gave her a look that said just that. "Maybe that's because you haven't tasted what Alannah can do with a parsnip."

"Maybe." But this time Taylor said it like she was giving the option due consideration. She followed Sinead to the green beans. "Alannah's a really good cook."

"That she is." Sinead crouched and took a bean pod in her hand. "We want to pick ones where the beans inside the pod are not bulging yet. Like this one."

Taylor nodded. "Did you grow all these?"

"Alannah and I did." Sinead relished the snap of the pods as she took them off the stalk.

Taylor snapped a pod and studied it. "But you don't cook."

"Nope." Sinead moved down the neatly staked row. "Never had the patience for it."

"How come?" Taylor squinted at her.

"I dunno." Sinead dusted soil off a pod. "I guess my twin got my share of patience."

Taylor giggled.

"Here." Sinead handed her the bean pod. "Taste that. Young and fresh, they're always the sweetest when they're newly picked."

Wrinkling up her nose, Taylor eyed the pod. "It's dirty."

"A little dirt is good for you." Sinead spread her fingers in the warm, fragrant earth. An answering pulse went through her as her element connected. As earth witches sharing a warden blessing, she and Alannah were doubly connected to all the growing things and the planet itself.

"It glows." Taylor pointed to her hand in the earth. "Are you using your magic?"

"Just saying hello-how-are-you." Sinead never felt more peaceful than when she could connect to her element. Unlike fire or water, or even air, earth had a peace and a steadiness to it that kept her stable.

She moved on and snapped pods as she went.

Taylor took a tentative bite and chewed. Her face lit up. "It's sweet."

"Told you." Sharing the earth's bounty satisfied her at a soul level. Earth gave its gifts with such a free and gracious hand.

Sun was warm on her back and head, but summer was waning. She could feel the plants readying themselves for their long dormancy, and the annuals coming to the end of their cycle. The earth herself prepared her offspring for winter. Through the earth, she absorbed the ponderous constancy of the great trees surrounding the castle. Their lifecycle was slowing down. "Autumn will be early this year," she said.

"How do you know?" Taylor whispered.

"I can feel it." Sinead loved how she responded to earth, aware as only a cré-witch could be of the presence of magic in everything. It connected her to all things growing in and of the earth, and reminded her of the constant cycle of life, death, and rebirth. It anchored her, made her feel intrinsically part of a greater whole.

Her expression reverent, Taylor crouched beside Sinead. "Can Alannah?"

"Oh, yes. We share a blessing." She brushed dirt off Taylor's cheek and smiled. "Come on. Let's get these veggies harvested."

They worked in silence for a while, finished the beans and moved to the carrots.

Sinead sunk her fingers into the soil. Earth rose up to greet her, smelling of roses and cloves. She pushed a little deeper, feeling the health of the land all around them. She let her magic spread like a root though the earth. The wards touched her awareness and her magic recoiled.

That was new.

She pushed her magic into the wards again. There. Nothing you'd pick up at a cursory glance, but a smudge on the pure, crystalline energy of the wards. She and Alannah had sensed the anomaly before, but it had grown. That couldn't mean anything good.

Taylor crunched on a bean. "How does that work, the whole sharing a blessing thing?"

"We're twins." Sinead released earth and sat back on her heels. She needed to talk to Alannah about what she'd found, but she didn't want to alarm Taylor. "We're identical twins. I guess we share our blessing like we share our DNA."

"Hmm?" Taylor snagged another bean from her basket. "I'm not sure that's how twins work."

Sinead had to laugh at her earnest tone and straightened to look at her. "Then how does it work, smarty-pants?"

"I'm not sure." Taylor wrinkled her nose. "But does that mean you can only do half the magic?"

"Nope." Sinead moved on to the parsnips. Alannah roasted them in butter and honey with a handful of thyme. Her mouth watered. "It means we need to be together to work our blessing."

"What if one of you dies?"

And she thought she had a lack of tact. The idea alone of losing Alannah terrified her. People who knew them always thought she was the tough one, and Alannah the sweet and gentler twin. She and Alannah knew the truth. Alannah had a backbone of pure steel beneath all that sweet, and Sinead would be nothing without her. She answered with honesty. "I can't even think of that. Alannah is the other half of me."

"Sorry." Taylor looked contrite. "That wasn't a good question to ask."

"It wasn't a comfortable question," Sinead said, but she liked the way Taylor kept it real. "But because it's not comfortable, doesn't make it bad."

"Like my dad," Taylor said.

The insight stopped Sinead mid parsnip inspection.

"Indeed." Not all kids could possibly be this bright and switched on. "Exactly like that."

"He's not comfortable with me being a witch."

"Right." Sinead tugged a parsnip free of the rich, beautiful soil and inspected it. "He's not comfortable with the idea because he's your dad, and he wants to protect you." Not that she knew much about dads. Men didn't stick around Baile much longer than it took to plant a kid in someone. But she'd seen dads on TV. "You having magic is going to make things more difficult, and he wants to shield you from that."

Taylor nodded and chomped another green bean. She pointed the chewed end at Sinead's parsnip. "What's that?"

"Parsnip." Sinead smelled a lie. "How come you don't like them, and you don't even know what they look like?"

Taylor gave her a duh face. "Because I've never seen them like that." She stepped closer and studied the parsnip. "They look like a pale carrot."

"Maybe it is a carrot." Sinead leaned closer and winked. "A carrot that's had a fright."

Giving her an adult look, Taylor said, "Lame."

So true, and part of why she was no good with kids.

"I'm not cross with him about that part." Taylor scuffed the dirt.

The switch took Sinead by surprise, and she suspected they'd drifted into more complicated territory. "Then which part are you angry about?"

"The way he spoke to everyone." Her face hardened. "He had no reason to be so rude. Even if he was upset."

Sinead knew many adults who could learn that lesson along with Warren. "No, he didn't."

"I'm going to tell him so." Taylor raised her chin.

"If you don't, you can bet Roderick will."

Taylor gaped at her and then giggled.

Sinead selected a few more parsnips and then motioned the tomatoes. "We can leave those for today. Let's go and see Alannah." Maybe Alannah had already noticed that smudge on the wards and had an explanation. She leaned closer to Taylor and pretended to check for spies. "I know she's baking something to cheer you up."

Grinning, Taylor turned with her, and they walked out of the kitchen garden. They entered the keep through a small door nearly hidden by rampaging ivy. The hallway beyond was dark and cramped. Hooks lined the wall. In days of yore, they would have been used for hundreds of boots, coats, riding whips, and hunting paraphernalia. Alannah's cheery yellow raincoat contrasted with the gray walls. A broadbrimmed sunhat occupied the hook beside the raincoat. Sinead toed off her Converses.

Doing the same, Taylor said, "I like Roderick. He's big and scary when you first meet him, but he's harmless."

Yeah, the kid totally had the big lout dead to rights. She motioned Taylor closer and whispered, "Don't tell him, but I like him too."

"I knew it." Taylor jabbed the basket toward her. "I knew you just pretended not to like him."

Sinead slung her arm over Taylor's shoulders. "Well, someone has to keep him humble."

"So true." Taylor sighed.

The passage led into a large laundry. A modern washer and a dryer looked out of place amongst the huge copper, wood, and cast-iron tubs. Alannah had taken over one end of the vast space for her fuel of the future experiments. The stench got Sinead and Taylor walking faster.

Sinead shut the door on the far side of the laundry with a sigh of relief. Shelves of cutlery, glasses, jugs, platters, bowls, and crockery lined the walls of the small storeroom, which opened to the kitchen.

Vanilla, cocoa, and sugar scents escaped the kitchen from

Alannah's baking. Sinead took an appreciative sniff, and Taylor copied her.

Thomas was there. Of course, he bloody was. That damned ghost had glued himself to Alannah, and Sinead didn't like it.

As she and Taylor walked in, Thomas straightened from where he had been leaning way too close to Alannah.

Alannah flushed and looked guilty.

True, part of Sinead was jealous. It had always been the two of them first. Part of her, for sure, resented another being—if you could even call a bloody ghost a being—between her and her twin, but with Thomas, it was more than that.

Alannah liked him. As in really, really liked him. She played it cool and kept her affection close, but she wasn't fooling her twin for a second. Another man would have meant sharing her twin, but Sinead couldn't stand back and watch Alannah's heart get broken. A ghost and a human woman had heartbreak scrawled in sky writing all over it.

"Hi." She tried to keep her dislike hidden from Alannah.

Alannah tensed and gave her a tight smile. "Hi."

Yup, the not being able to get one over your twin went both ways, and Alannah could sense her dislike of Thomas. It wasn't Thomas, really. The ghost was amusing, clever and insightful, and had he not been sniffing around her sister, Sinead would have enjoyed him a shit ton more.

Taylor bounded up to Alannah and showed her the basket. "We picked green beans."

"How lovely." Alannah tugged Taylor's ponytail and motioned the sink. "Put them over there, and I'll wash them."

Trying to lighten the mood, Sinead said, "There were more, but someone kept eating them."

"You told me to." Taylor shrugged and did an excellent job of looking innocent.

"That's a shame." Alannah made a face. "I guess that means you won't want any cupcakes."

"Cupcakes?" Taylor spun away from the sink. "Chocolate ones?"

Alannah laughed and kept her gaze clear of Sinead. "Are there any other kind?"

"Well, there's vanilla and strawberry…"

Sinead let Taylor prattle on, glad the kid was looking more cheerful, but she and Alannah needed to talk, and her twin couldn't hide in the kitchen forever.

# CHAPTER SEVEN

Warren hadn't needed the lecture that had followed from Jack last night to get how much he'd screwed up. Instead, what he needed was to get his head together, and he took a long walk. His life had been one episode of *Supernatural* after another since he'd first started getting weird dreams several months back. With no specific destination, he let instinct guide him. A warm, breezy day seemed to mock his dark mood, but the fresh sea air helped clear the funk in his brain.

The forest around Baile teemed with life. As Niamh's coimhdeacht, he was aware of living things in a way he never had been before. He couldn't connect with them in the same way Niamh did, unless she were with him, but he could sense creatures going on with the business of life all around him.

He cleared the forest and kept going, climbing the rise to the meadows beyond. A stiff breeze tugged at his clothes and hair as he walked. Overhead, gulls wheeled and shrieked. A hare startled out of the undergrowth, sat up and stared at him, and then shot away.

Warren stopped on a bluff scattered with jagged gray rocks. Here he'd come face to face with probably the only remaining wild wolf pack in England. The first time had been a shock to the system, but now pack were intrinsic to him, part of his bond with Niamh.

Alpha tapped at his awareness a few seconds before he slunk around a large boulder. A large gray and white wolf, with piercing amber eyes, Alpha ambled toward him and sat about six feet away.

"I fucked up," he said, dropping into a noncombative crouch.

Alpha lay down with a sigh and rested his chin on his front paws. Those intelligent eyes locked on Warren. He seemed to share the Baile consensus on Warren's fucking up.

"I can't see how the situation with Taylor is going to sort itself out." Too wound up to sit still, Warren plucked out a long strand of grass and shredded it.

Niamh nudged at Warren's mind, concerned about his turmoil.

Raising his head, Alpha flared his nostrils as he tested the air.

"You haven't met my ex." The weirdest part of their conversation was that it didn't feel at all strange to be talking to a wolf. "She's just looking for an excuse to take Taylor away from me for good. If she gets wind of this whole witch thing—" Warren attacked another blade of grass "—that'll be all she needs to lock me out for good."

*Pack.*

Alpha didn't speak words as a human would but conveyed a series of sense impressions.

"Yeah, yeah, pack is best." He didn't know why he'd thought a wolf could help. "But I'm trying like hell to keep my little pack together."

Alpha belly-crawled closer and nudged Warren's hand.

This was new, but Warren laid his hand on the wolf's ruff.

Springy, coarse hair threaded through his fingers. The bond snapped into place.

Warren experienced the lurching of his awareness into the wolf's. His eyesight went monochromatic, his ears sharpened, and his sense of smell increased exponentially. The wind blowing across their nostrils was alive with scent and it brought a bounty of information.

And then he felt the earth beneath their paws and belly, warm from the sun and alive. The essential state of being that flowed through everything of and on the earth. He stilled inside as the awe-inspiring completeness of existence itself drifted through him and carried him with the current. There was balance to be had here, harmony, a knowledge that he formed part of a greater whole, which sank marrow-deep into him.

His mind quieted as instinct took over. Life and death swirled through him and over him in an endless cycle. The individual parts formed the whole and were simultaneously dependent on it.

They breathed deeply and let the surety of the rightness of each moment sink into them.

And Warren got it.

He had to trust. His familiar horned demon of doubt had raised its head and destroyed his belief that a greater good worked with and for him. Life ebbed and flowed and completed one cycle only to start another immediately. Events came and went, and the greater good remained. Everything had a time and a place, and everything was as it should be.

Alpha chuffed and dropped his connection to Warren, but the peace he'd shared with Warren stayed.

Their gazes met and held. *Pack.*

"Thank you." Warren stood and dusted grass off his jeans. "I get it, but first I'm going to have to make nice with a number of people."

Alpha grinned at him, stood and loped away.

Niamh clicked off the television and pressed her palm heels into her eyes. She managed to stop her tears, but not the growing desperation inside her. Animals everywhere, suffering and in distress, and she was stuck here crying into her coffee. It wasn't good enough. She had only recently gained full access to her powers, and she was failing already. She was animals' guardian, their voice, and their advocate, and they were crying out to her to help them. Humans went through life in ignorance and cruelty, convinced that they were somehow more valuable, and their lives mattered more. Her job was to reeducate and redress the balance.

Balance. Harmony. These were the essence of Goddess, and these were the things so desperately missing from the world.

A hedgehog trundled across the rug and stopped at her feet. It blinked bright, black eyes at her and continued on under the sofa. One of the Baile dog pack jumped onto the sofa beside her and rested his chin on her thigh. Their trust stabbed her through the heart. They were counting on her.

Ever since Roderick had requested Baile allow satellite television, she'd been watching Discovery, National Geographic, Animal Planet—anything animal related. Goddess, but part of her missed the days when she was ignorant of her responsibility.

The dog looked toward the door.

"Heya." Warren stood in the library doorway, hands in his jean's pockets, a sheepish look on his face.

Niamh had half been expecting him since his meltdown in the kitchen. She had felt his turmoil through the bond. Now she got a sense of peace from him, and also the apology he was getting ready to make. She didn't need to hear him say the words to know how crappy he felt. "It's okay." She stroked the big ginger and white tabby snuggled on her left. "I know you're worried about Debra and Taylor."

"Yeah." He strode closer. "But that doesn't excuse me being a total prick."

"No." And his bluntness made her laugh. Life had made him a hard man, and he was hardest on himself. "You should probably save your groveling for Roderick."

Warren grunted, then focused his pale blue eyes on her. "What's wrong?"

"I've been watching wildlife shows again." The cat purred and butted her hand. All about the castle, animals pressed into her awareness, questioning her emotional state, and trying to give comfort.

Warren crouched at her feet and took her hands. "China again?"

"India." His warmth spread from where they touched. "They have this organization that is trying to help. But the things I see—"

"Hey!" He squeezed her hands. "You're torturing yourself."

"I'm here to do something about this shit." She jerked her head at the television.

"And you will." Standing, he drew her to her feet. "Just like we'll find a way for Bronwyn to do her healing, we'll find a way to get you out there being a guardian."

Niamh leaned into his physical strength. His heart beat against her ear, steady, solid, comforting. Their bond glowed warm and constant through her. "When?"

"I don't know." He wrapped his arms around her waist and drew her closer. "Alexander says Rhiannon is back in the village. He went outside the wards a couple of days ago and could sense her."

"I wish she'd burned to a crisp." In her activation of fire, Niamh had incinerated the inside of a cave in South Africa. Rhiannon and her minions had been gone by the time she,

Warren, and the two surviving South African witches had awoken.

Warren stroked her spine, leaving tingles in his palm's wake. "That would have been useful."

"I've never felt anything like her." Niamh shivered at the memory of Rhiannon trying to take control of her power. "Her magic is strong. Stronger than I could have imagined."

"Yep." Warren's voice grew gruff. "She certainly got around me fast enough."

With a finger click, Rhiannon had immobilized all of them in that cave, Warren included. Then her people had attacked him and knocked him out.

Niamh hugged him. "It's not your fault."

"Right." He didn't believe her. His guilt nagged at him, and registered prickly and sour through their bond. "My first job as your coimhdeacht, and I'm as useful as tits on a tortoise."

That got another chuckle from her. "She's always one step ahead."

"The lads and I were talking about that in the barracks." He stayed where he was, and Niamh was happy to let him. He touched her more and more, like he sought the physical connection as well as their bond. Warren's trust was a hard-won battle, and all the more treasured for its scarcity. "There are two points left to activate, and she knows we have to get them up and running."

"Who's next?" She shifted and stared up at him. "Mags or the twins?"

"That is the question." He looked down at her, his eyes warm in a way that made her breathless. His desire for her sparked and crackled between them. "Mags would be good because she's a seer, but the twins are earth, and they could strengthen the wards."

"Let me guess." His face had already become as familiar to

her as the one she saw in the mirror. "Roderick is pushing for the twins."

The side of his mouth quirked. "Which means Alexander is all about Mags." Warren shifted infinitesimally closer until their thighs brushed. "And none of them have a coimhdeacht."

"The twins would have to go together." Niamh found it harder to concentrate on the talking part of their interaction.

He cleared his throat. "And that would also put two witches in danger."

"You or Roderick could go with Mags." Even as she made the suggestion, everything in her rejected Warren going anywhere without her.

He tangled his fingers in her hair. "It doesn't work like that, Niamh."

"No." She breathed deep. He smelled of the summer wind with the barest trace of the strawberry-basil scent combo of her magic. Her magic had fused with his DNA and become part of him. "Maeve wouldn't want Roderick to go."

"No." He could read her every thought and emotion and he knew what his proximity did to her. His voice had deepened and grown huskier as he asked what he already knew the answer to, "And you?"

"I wouldn't want Roderick to go either." Just because he had an unfair advantage didn't mean she wasn't going to put him through the wringer a bit.

Warren laughed and it delighted her. "You're a wicked woman, Niamh."

"Uh-huh." She nodded and grinned at him. "You're only working that out now?"

"I had a sneaking suspicion." He lowered his head until their mouths almost brushed. "Now I'm certain."

Niamh's pulse hammered, and the tiny space between them shimmered with possibilities. She had worked her way beneath his tough exterior. "Are you planning on doing anything about it?"

"Oh, yes." He touched his mouth to hers. "I plan on doing a lot about it."

Oh, Goddess! Her knees melted. She suspected the heat from her core had burned the cartilage to goo.

"Dad!" Taylor clattered into the library. She saw them and stopped. "Are you kissing?"

"Trying to," Warren grumbled before stepping away from Niamh.

Niamh swayed toward his retreating form before righting herself and turning to Taylor. "What's doing, loveliness?"

The she-wolf and her pups had followed Taylor into the library.

"We need to talk." Taylor looked all grown up as she faced off with Warren.

With a grimace, Warren nodded. "We do, but first I owe you an apology."

"Oh." Taylor deflated.

"I shouldn't have spoken to you like I did in the kitchen." Warren put his hand on Taylor's shoulder. "I let my fears get the better of me and took that out on you. I'm sorry."

Taylor gaped at him and then Niamh. "Well, that was easy."

"He still has to talk to Roderick." Niamh laughed. She didn't want to witness that conversation.

"Right." Taylor had her mother's hazel eyes, but in all other ways she was Warren's child. "And the rest of the coven."

"And the rest of the coven," Warren said.

Taylor nodded, and then her expression grew mischievous. "And now, let's get back to the kissing business."

"I would." Warren tugged on her blond ponytail. "But you're here and killing the mood."

Giggling, Taylor tugged her hair away. "You're so gross."

"Want to come with me and protect me from Roderick?"

The way Warren looked at Taylor was so beautiful it made Niamh want to tear up. His love for his daughter thrummed down their bond like a warm, glowing coal. All fathers should feel that way about their children.

The she-wolf looked at Niamh with her sharp, yellow eyes, as if she'd heard the thought and approved.

"Go on, you two." Niamh shooed them. "I have some more reading to do."

Warren looked at her, his expression firm. "No more watching wildlife shows."

"No more watching wildlife shows." At least for now, but the need lurked beyond Baile, and as a guardian witch she couldn't, and wouldn't, ignore it for long.

He got her thought and raised a brow.

Niamh shrugged. It was not like she could stop herself. Her blessing demanded she act. "I'll get back to reading about dead guardian witches."

"Sounds boring." Taylor screwed her face up.

"Not really." Niamh had to smile at her expression. Then again, Taylor hadn't read any of the memoirs and diaries she had. When guardian witches had sat down and written about their lives, they'd been honest to the point it even had Niamh blushing. Guardians were linked to animals. They shared animal's more pragmatic and instinctive attitude toward sex. Through some of their scribblings she already knew so much more about Roderick and Thomas than she ever wanted to know.

Warren grinned as he read her mind. "I'll see you later."

The promise behind those words made her belly tighten in anticipation. "Not if I see you first."

On a laugh, he and Taylor left the library.

Resolutely, Niamh pushed the television remote away and gently nudged a pair of squirrels off the pile of books she hadn't gotten to before their trip to South Africa. She pulled them toward her and stopped.

Something was off. She trailed her fingers over the cover, and then started at the evidence on them.

Dust. *Dust?*

Baile never got dusty.

# CHAPTER EIGHT

Jack was annoying himself. He spent his days wandering around Baile like a lost fart in a thunderstorm. He'd come here to find Warren. Well, he'd found him. Warren was good, great even, and Jack was still here.

He was officially out of excuses to stay.

And yet...

He crossed the great hall—big enough for a couple of rugby games at least—to the staircase leading up, a massive wood and stone creation that must have broken several backs to erect in the first place.

Yesterday, Warren had manned up, like the solid bloke he was, and apologized for being a prat the other night. Now, Warren, Thomas, Roderick, and Alexander were all in the practice yard, whacking at each other with wooden staves and arguing about which witch went next to activate her point.

To be clear, only Alexander and Roderick were seriously trying to hit each other. Warren was trying to learn how to sword fight and Thomas was trying to teach him. Warren showed a typical soldierly aptitude and an unapologetic boyish delight at learning how to sword fight.

Everyone at Baile had a higher purpose, a calling. Everyone except for him.

He had a life up north he needed to get back to. Not much of a life. Warren had been one of the few he called friend. For the most part, people got on his nerves. His family had refused to have anything to do with him after his conviction, and Jack couldn't really blame them. And the people he met on his security job were generally too shit scared of him to get close. Probably a wise choice, given his notoriously short fuse.

He reached the upper hall. Jack didn't know bollocks about art, but he had a suspicion Baile was loaded with all kinds of rare and valuable. The witches lived in a relatively small part of the castle. Most of the doors stayed shut. Roderick had told him the castle used to be filled with witches. The place must have been alive with noise and action. Jack got the sense Baile missed those days. She had a waiting quality about her, like she wanted her people back. The idea of a castle having feelings was insane, which went to show he needed to get back to his normal.

When he got to the door of the room he was using, he kept on walking. If he went in, he'd only have to stare at the bag he should be packing. He hadn't been called here to take care of a witch like Warren had. He wasn't hiding out from his homicidal mother with his baby mama like Alexander. And he for damn sure hadn't animated out of a statue like Roderick.

At the end of the hallway, he reached a turret with a stone spiral staircase. He knew where the stairs went, and if he were honest with himself, that had been his destination all along.

Mags had a room at the top of those stairs. He hadn't seen her alone since that scene in the library.

He climbed.

Roughly halfway up, a small semicircular landing interrupted the ascent. Jack knocked on the arched wooden door. It would take a battle axe like Roderick enjoyed swinging to get through the metal studded door.

"Come in, Jack," Mags called from the other side.

Jack stepped into the chaos that Mags surrounded herself with. Billowy pink and green curtains danced in the breeze coming from the open casement.

Mags sat in the middle of a bright, floral rug with an honest-to-god crystal ball on the floor in front of her. A garish sea of bits of fabric and shiny stuff made an island of her.

The restless itch inside Jack settled down.

She frowned into the crystal ball.

Toeing aside a pile of lurid red, yellow, and blue feathers, he crouched close enough to catch the enticing jasmine and almond smell of her.

Maeve had told him each witch had a unique scent combination to her blessing, and that's what he smelled.

Jack liked it. It sank inside him and made him want to be around her.

"See anything?" He gestured the crystal ball. It was as good a conversation starter as any other.

He couldn't say how much of what he'd heard around Baile he truly believed. Witches, goddesses, ancient curses, and magic all seemed a bit farfetched to him. But he had seen things he wouldn't have believed possible. He'd stood right next to Bronwyn as she healed a gash Alexander had given Roderick. Animals followed Niamh everywhere, and she always knew what they wanted or what was wrong with them.

And Mags did have an uncanny way of knowing stuff.

Mags shook her head. "I'm not sure."

"You're not sure of what?" Either she saw something or not.

"It's my head." Mags scrubbed her fingers across her forehead, leaving a red mark on her lily-white skin. She turned her huge green eyes to him imploringly. "It's all getting jumbled up."

Her look snuck past his guard and yanked at his heart. "What's getting jumbled up, sweetheart?"

"Time." She sighed and chewed her lip. She banged her hand against her head. "Time is all mixed up."

Jack took her hand and held it before she could do any damage. He wasn't sure what she was getting at, but he did know he couldn't be here and let her hurt herself.

"Jack." She stared at him, her gaze keen and penetrating. "What if I'm going mad?"

A chill chased up his spine. "You're not going mad, sweetheart."

"But what if I am?" she whispered. Dropping her head, she tightened her hold on his hand. "I can't sort out the when anymore. It all goes around and around my head and it won't stop."

"Breathe." He dropped to the floor beside her and used his other hand to stroke the long, knobby ridge of her spine. She didn't eat enough. Some days she even forgot to eat at all. "First you need to breathe."

Obediently she inhaled and exhaled.

"Again."

She complied, and her shoulders relaxed.

"Now." Jack kept his voice low and soothing. "Tell me what's getting confused."

"I did." She blinked at him. "Time is getting confused. I don't know when things happen. If they've already happened or if they're going to happen."

Jack was way out of his depth, but he'd be buggered if he left her like this. "You know I'm here with you now, right?"

"Yes." She frowned. "But I see so many things about us." She shrugged. "So many possible futures and they get tangled up with the past."

"Tell me one." He needed to talk to one of her coven sisters about this.

She blushed and it was fucking adorable. "We have four children."

"Well." He choked that one down with a great gulp of not-in-this-lifetime. He wasn't the fatherly type. His own old man had screwed it up enough for both their lifetimes. "I can tell you we don't have four children."

"No?" She cocked her head.

"No," he said, decisively. And nor would they if he had anything to say about it. According to Mags, the future was fluid anyway, and talking kids at this stage was getting way, way ahead of the curve. Honesty, though, compelled him to say, "Although I'm not sure that's me you saw with the four kids." He smiled to gentle the impact. "I'm not the fatherhood type."

"Hmm." She gave him an enigmatic smirk and a soul stripping with those wise eyes. "That remains to be seen."

She seemed oddly confident on the kids thing, and it made him twitchy. "Maybe you should talk to one of your…er…coven sisters about the time thing." Never had he thought a day would come when the phrase coven sisters would come out of his cakehole.

"No." The confusion vanished, and she grabbed a handful of feathers. "I'm making bed curtains."

The subject change left him catching flies, and he snapped his mouth shut. "Don't you have those?"

"Yes." She arranged the feathers in a spray, cocked her head and studied her creation.

He wanted to stay, but he'd run out of any real reason to do so.

Shaking her head, Mags removed a yellow feather and replaced it with another yellow feather. She grinned at him. "Much better."

"Right." He didn't see the difference.

"What now?" She tapped her pouty bottom lip and studied the crap ringing her. She nodded. "Yup. Sparkle."

The woman must have a conference going on in her head.

"Oh!" She snapped her fingers and looked at him. "I almost

forgot to tell you." She sifted through a little heap of sparkly shit. "No."

Now Jack knew he wasn't brainy. He'd barely made it through school, but up until right now he'd been fairly confident in his ability to follow most conversations. "No what?"

Frowning, she flicked away a couple of shiny pebbly things. They skittered across the floor, one disappearing beneath the bed.

"You shouldn't go," she said. With a huge grin she held up a purple bead. "Perfect."

He rather liked the purple sparkly. "Nice."

"I'm bored of them."

And there went his grasp on their chat. Silence seemed the best policy.

"The bed curtains." She flapped one long elegant hand at the bed. Her wrist looked too fragile for the weight of jewelry she had on it. "I'm bored of them."

"Aha!" For clarity, he waded in. "You can't talk to your coven sisters about your time thing because you're too busy making new bed curtains?"

She nodded and went back to sifting like a busy magpie.

"And you're making new bed curtains because those—" he jabbed his thumb at the bed "—are boring."

"Me." She held up her forefinger at him. "They're boring me."

"Got it." And he felt stupidly relieved that he did. "Also, I shouldn't go."

"No." She picked up a glue gun and touched her forefinger to the tip. Hissing, she sucked her finger. "Bums!"

"Hot?"

Sucking that finger, she nodded.

"Isn't that the point?" And no, he would not get cranking on that mouth and that finger and the possibilities.

Mags giggled and applied hot glue to the underside of her feather arrangement.

"You haven't said why I shouldn't go." He rather liked the colorful nest she'd made.

"Oh." She rolled her eyes. "I warned you about the jumble."

He barely stopped her in time from tapping the glue gun to her temple.

Her gaze sharpened as she looked at him. "I'm going to need you."

"Yeah?" That really shouldn't make him want to puff his chest.

"Absolutely." She went back to her gluing. "I'm sure about that."

Clearing his throat, he tried to keep the question neutral. "How? I mean, what are you going to need me for?"

"I'll die if you don't come with me." She leaned back and studied the knot of feathers and beads she'd just made. Then she threw him a naughty grin. "And for the four children, of course."

# CHAPTER NINE

Maeve did like Jack. She propped her chin on her palm, her head already spinning a little. The tapestries on the wall looked fuzzy, but the warm buzz in her middle made her not care. She'd found him alone in the library pouring himself a drink and looking troubled.

Well, he'd offered her a drink. She'd said yes. Then they'd chatted about Mags for a bit. Even in her lovely, happy state, what Jack had told her worried Maeve, but she'd deal with that later.

They had chatted a bit more. Maeve forgot what about. Somehow the subject had come up about how things were so different in this time.

While Jack listened to her about that, she'd had another glass of wine. He'd been such a good listener and an even better teacher, and she'd had more wine. Now she felt wonderful.

She liked the feeling almost as much as she liked Jack. Jack was handsome in a craggy, rough kind of way. He also really liked Mags.

"Hmm." She'd ended up in a pool of sunlight on the floor beside the huge windows. Flopping to her back, she closed her eyes and let the warmth seep into her bones. "The sun is lovely."

"Yes." Jack chuckled. "Would you like a glass of water?"

"No!" Why'd he have to suggest water? Who wanted water when there was more of the yummy wine? She held her glass in the air. "But I will have more wine."

"Let's talk for a bit." He crouched beside her. "How we doing, Miss Maeve?"

Maeve giggled and opened her eyes. Nobody in this time frowned at a woman for lying on the floor. She stretched her arms above her head, and it felt lovely. Jack had been teaching her all kinds of modern ways of speaking, and she tried one out now, "We're killing it over here."

"Yeah, you are." Jack winked at her.

Jack was funny too. "More wine?"

"Tell me first why you don't drink alcopops." Jack stood and went over to where the drinks were. On a cart. By the other wall. Glass clinked and Jack poured something as he said, "Alcopops and fruity drinks with umbrellas in them are for..."

"Basic bitches," Maeve said.

"That's my girl." Jack grinned and brought a tall glass filled with clear liquid. "And do we want to be a basic bitch?"

"Ah, hell no." Proud of herself, Maeve smiled and took the glass. "What's this?"

"Water." Jack sat beside her.

Maeve glared all three of him into focus. "I said I didn't want water."

"I heard you, but you'll thank me later."

She took a cautious sip and pulled a face. Thrusting the glass at him, she gave him her most winning smile. "More wine."

"Take another sip." Jack nudged the glass back toward her.

Maeve shook her head. "Absolutely not."

"Do it for…Mags."

Well, all right, if he was going to bring Mags into it. She took another sip. Actually, her mouth did feel dry and sticky, and she took another sip.

"Good job." Jack motioned her to take another.

He really had the loveliest smile, and she should tell him so. "I like your smile."

"Thank you."

"You should smile more."

"More water?"

"Maybe later." She dropped to her back and closed her eyes. Patting the floor next to her, she said, "Lie down here. It's so warm and comfy."

"I don't think I—"

"Lie down." He should smile more and argue less.

Jack settled next to her. "Just a stab in the dark here, but you're not much of a drinker, are you?"

"No." She sighed. There were so many things she hadn't done and wanted to do. "I'm not much of an anythinger."

"No?"

Jack was such a good listener. He might be her new best friend. "Did you know I'm a virgin?"

Jack made a choking noise. "Umm…no."

A shadow blocked her sun and she frowned.

"Maeve?" A voice that sounded a lot like Roderick's came from above her.

Maeve cracked open her lids. It was Roderick. She liked Jack, but she loved Roderick. "Hello, darling."

Face impassive, Roderick looked at her, then Jack, then the glasses on the floor beside them. He didn't appear angry, but she got the feeling he was.

She probed their bond and came away blank.

Roderick picked up her glass and sniffed it. "What are you doing?"

She really hated it when he made her feel like a naughty little girl. "Learning not to be a basic bitch." Raising her brow, she dared him to challenge her. Roderick was her coimhdeacht, not her father.

"I see." Roderick stared hard at Jack. "If you would excuse us, I need to speak with Maeve."

"Mate." Jack took his time getting to his feet. "There's no problem here."

"Really?" Roderick's expression hardened into a glare. "And yet I find I have a problem with everything going on here." He glanced at her. "Get up, Maeve."

"Then talk to me about your problem." Jack got between her and Roderick.

*Uh-oh.* He shouldn't do that. Roderick wouldn't like that. At all.

Maeve scrambled to her feet. The world went black and squiffy, and she reached out to catch her balance.

Jack caught her hand and steadied her. "Slowly, buttercup."

A blaze of Roderick's emotion shot through the bond. He wasn't angry. He was livid. And just like that, her fun afternoon was over, because Roderick said so and came here and glowered and loomed. Well, she wasn't going to stand for that, and it was about time Roderick learned he could not push her around. "You got no chill. Dude."

Jack made that choking noise again.

"Maeve." Roderick used his infinitely patient, long-suffering tone. The one he reserved for lecturing her about what a foolish little girl she really was. "Would you please come with me?"

"No." She wanted to shock him out of his stodgy self-righteousness. "Because I'm an independent woman, and I have rights."

Jack winked at her. "Give him hell, buttercup."

"Stay out of this." Roderick got close enough to Jack to kiss him.

Jack didn't budge. "Make me."

But there wasn't going to be any kissing between those two.

*Oh no.* There would be punching and blood and lots of other stuff that burst her happy little bubble.

"Come on then." She shoved herself between the two huge slabs of man. "Let's go, Roderick."

Jack put a hand on her shoulder. "You don't have to go with him."

"Yes, she does." Roderick's gaze locked on Jack like he wanted to rip his throat out.

Maeve didn't want Jack getting hurt because of her.

"It's fine." She touched Jack's arm to make him look at her. "I probably should go with him."

"No." After a glance her way, Jack went back to glaring at Roderick. "You should do what you want to do."

Jack trying to protect her went beyond sweet, but he really didn't need to.

"What she wants to do is come with me. Now." What was not so sweet was Roderick being all silly and demanding.

"No, I don't. Not really," she said to Roderick. "But I will because you're going to be all butt…sore" She forgot the term Jack had taught her.

Jack's lips quirked. "Butt hurt."

"Right." She tugged on Roderick's arm. "Come on then. Let's get the lecture over and done." She had the satisfaction of seeing that little muscle in the side of Roderick's jaw tick. The more she got under his skin, the more the muscle would tick.

Silky smooth, the careful evenness to Roderick's voice conveyed how angry he really was as he said to Jack, "Keep your distance from Maeve."

The staggering assumption that he could decide who she did and didn't spend time with made her want to smack that arrogant expression right off his face. However, there was enough aggression stinking up the library already. "Oh, be quiet, Roderick. And stop glaring at Jack in that ridiculous manner."

Some of the tension seeped out of Jack. He looked at her. "You sure?"

"Yes, she's—"

"You." She poked Roderick in the broad chest and ended up hurting her finger. "Come with me."

Roderick was at her heels as she left the library and stalked across the great hall. His breath fanned her nape as she climbed the stairs to her chamber. And he shut the door behind them with a decisive click when they reached her chamber.

Leaning his back against the door, he crossed his arms. "You're drunk."

"I was drunk." And it had been a glorious feeling. "Now I have a headache and a pain in my arse."

He blinked at her. Then he got it, and the glowering started up all over again. "I don't want that whoreson near you."

"Why?" She threw her hands up for lack of any better way to express her frustration. "He's really nice and he was teaching me—"

Roderick growled. "I don't want to hear what he was teaching you."

The oddest notion popped into her head. "Are you jealous?"

"No." Roderick looked past her shoulder and glared out the window.

Part of her wanted to laugh, another part experienced a distinct thrill of satisfaction, and still another wanted to box his ears. "You are." She stepped close enough to stare right into his face. "You're jealous."

"Maeve," he grumbled. "This has nothing to do with me being jealous. I am not jealous." His expression took on an insufferable, self-righteousness cast. "I am tasked by Goddess to protect you against everything and everyone who would do you harm, including yourself."

Roderick's face got all hard and stony when he was angry. It was kind of thrilling. Hot! She liked that word. *Hot, hot, hot.*

He wasn't being truthful with her. He was hiding, and she wanted to ferret the truth out of him. "No."

"I most certainly am." He fired right back, raising his chin, and squaring his shoulders.

Oh, he needn't think he was going to get away with his line of crap. "Bullshit!"

"Maeve." He frowned at her.

"Bull. Shit." She took particular delight in enunciating the words. "You saw Jack and me in the library and got all jealous." She remembered something else Jack had taught her. "Peanut butter jelly time."

"I do not get jealous, Maeve." He sniffed. "But you are little better than an innocent, and I—"

"You. Are." She stood on her toes and whispered in his ear. "Jealous."

He smelled delicious, and a girl could collapse into his broad chest and stay there. She'd seen him without his shirt, and she'd like a closer view of all that skin and muscle.

"This is so tiresome." Roderick sighed.

"But it's okay to be jealous." She pressed her advantage home. "Because I get jealous too."

His mood shifted. A hot surge of satisfaction coursed down the bond from him. "I don't do anything to make you jealous."

"But you did." Although their bond was hundreds of years old, the time they'd spent out of stasis and conscious only amounted to a few months. "When we were first bonded, I was jealous all the time."

His hard face softened, and his arctic blue eyes blazed down at her. "There was no need, my Maeve. It has long been only you for me."

Her breath caught in her throat, and she gave in to the urge to touch him. She pressed her fingertips to his lips. "And you for me."

"Maeve." His voice deepened. "You should not say such things."

"Why?" Her breath came faster, and her heart raced. "It's the truth."

For a long moment they looked at each other. She could feel his answering desire though the bond, and the battle he waged within.

"Autumn solstice," he said.

And Maeve wanted to kick him. The stupid bargain she'd agreed to with him was the last thing on her mind right now. He wanted her to be sure she was ready to take the next step in their relationship, and she'd agreed to take time and think it over. But thinking was not high on her priorities when he stood so close to her, and smelled of leather and soap, and his mouth hovered so tantalizingly close. "I don't need any more time."

His jaw tightened, even as his eyes smoldered. "Tell me that when you're sober."

"Just so you can come up with another reason to run away from this?" Frustration washing away desire, she motioned between them.

"Maeve," he growled.

She growled back, "Roderick."

"You tell me that when you're sober and thinking straight, and there won't be any running away." He pressed a hot, possessive kiss on her mouth. "For either of us."

---

GODDESS, but she would be the fucking death of him. Resisting the urge to slam her chamber door, Roderick shut it and strode away. He'd closed his side of their bond down tight to prevent her from sensing how much he had wanted to toss her on that bed and have done with all this waiting and wanting.

He'd nearly killed Jack Langham when he'd walked into the

library to find them both lolling around on the floor together. Maeve had pinned him to rights; he had been jealous. Searingly, stunningly, uncontrollably sodding jealous.

His rational mind knew Jack's defense of her had been born of the intention to protect Maeve. If he'd been listening to his right mind, Roderick would have applauded the bastard. It had been an honorable action and one Roderick would have taken if he'd seen a man being domineering with a woman.

Striding through the barracks, he followed the sound of swordplay outside into a small portion of the bailey reserved for coimhdeacht. From here they could practice weapons and see the gatehouse.

Jack was there, and Roderick's heightened senses closed in on the man.

Standing as Roderick approached, he squared his shoulders. "You got a problem with me, mate?"

"Aye." His blood still ran hot, and he now had the perfect outlet for his sexual frustration.

"Lads." Warren popped up in front of him, getting between Roderick and his target. "What's going on? Let's use our words here."

Alexander appeared beside Jack, and bonus! Roderick now had two targets for the violence simmering in his blood.

Aye, he had asked Maeve to take time and think on whether she wanted him in her bed, as well as being her bonded warrior, but that did not mean he would stand by while another dog pissed in his garden. He tried to shove past Warren, but the newest coimhdeacht had grown stronger since he'd bonded Niamh.

Roderick jabbed a finger at Jack over Warren's beefy shoulder. "Stay away from Maeve."

"Oh dear." Alexander smirked. "Did someone take your toy?"

"Fucking hell!" Jack glared at Alexander. "That's a woman you're talking about. Show some fucking respect."

Alexander grinned back at him. "Quite right. I adore Maeve, respect the hell out of her. But I do like winding the big guy up just as much."

Jack gaped at Alexander. "How old are you?"

"Don't answer that." Warren glanced at Alexander before turning his attention back to Roderick. "I'm sure Jack meant no harm."

"It's probably more a case of Roderick suffering chronic blood loss to the brain," Alexander drawled.

Warren swore and glared over his shoulder. "Want to shut the fuck up?"

"Must I?" Alexander grimaced.

"Yes!" Roderick shouted along with Warren and Jack.

Sinead called it getting his medieval up. Roderick didn't care what anyone called it. In his mind, it meant making his point well understood. "Maeve is mine."

"Were you born in the fucking dark ages?" Jack bared his teeth at Roderick.

"Don't answer that." Warren glared at Roderick before he turned to Jack. "What did you do?"

"Me?" Jack shook his head. "I gave her a glass of wine or two."

"You got her drunk." Roderick's hold on his temper slipped. He well understood why men of Jack's ilk fed women alcohol.

Alexander stiffened, and his voice went quiet and deadly. "You got Maeve drunk?"

Even Warren wasn't looking at Jack with quite so much indulgence now.

"No!" Jack looked horrified. "I mean, not on purpose." He spread his arms wide. "I was having a drink in the library because...it doesn't matter. I was having a drink. Maeve came in. I offered her one, and she said yes. Nothing more sinister than that."

"I'm waiting for the part where Maeve got drunk." Having

been on the receiving end of that murderous look from Alexander, Roderick almost pitied Jack.

"She had three glasses." Jack held out three fingers. "Small ones at that, and of wine. I had no idea she'd get pie-eyed."

Roderick trusted Jack about as far as he could toss the big sod.

"On the level," Jack said to Warren. "We got chatting. I filled her glass a couple of times. I didn't realize until it was too late, and then I tried to get her to switch to water."

Alexander studied Jack's face. Shrugging he turned to Roderick. "Maeve doesn't normally drink."

"She doesn't like it." Roderick didn't want to believe the sod, but his Maeve was a—what was Sinead's expression?—ah, lightweight.

Jack snorted. "She does now."

And his ire rose again. "Stay away—"

"Yes, we've covered that part." Alexander waved him to silence. "What we haven't established yet is Jack's intent."

"Fucking hell!" Jack's voice bounced off Baile's stone walls. "I like Maeve just fine, she's sweet and pretty, but if I was going to get anyone drunk it would be Mags."

"Stay away from Mags," Warren and Alexander snapped.

"Fine!" Jack folded his arms. "But I never got Maeve drunk. She did that all by herself. And if you don't believe me." Jack stared at Roderick. "You try telling her not to do something."

Roderick couldn't, in all conscience, deny that point. Maeve had a will of steel when she chose to exert it.

"Ah, Mr. Cray!" A man's voice broke the tense silence. "I'm so glad to catch you at home."

Roderick swung around as a tall, slim man with brown hair and glasses strode across the bailey toward him. What had Warren said about this man? Something about taxes.

Either oblivious or studiously ignoring all the large, tense men glaring at him, the newcomer walked right up to Roderick.

He held out a large brownish envelope. "As you have not responded to my last estimated assessment of your property, I have brought my request in person."

Roderick didn't want to take the envelope. "How did you get in here?"

"I drove." The man blinked at him. "And I must say, I cannot fathom how I didn't manage to find the castle entrance before. It was right at the end of the road."

Stepping forward, Alexander took the envelope. "Hello. We met before. At the Hag's Head. I'm Mr. Cray's…er…cousin."

"Lord Donn." The man nodded. "I remember." He held out his hand. "Andy Braithwaite. Valuation Office Agency."

"Taxes, property taxes," Alexander said to Roderick.

"Indeed." Andy pushed his glasses up his nose with his forefinger. "And according to our records, there is no indication that council tax, community charge, or domestic rates have been paid on Baile Castle and its surrounds. Ever." He tapped the envelope in Alexander's hands. "Using Windsor Castle as a comparative point, I estimate the amount owing to be somewhere in the region of three million, seventy-eight thousand, four hundred and five pounds."

Roderick's head swam. He could not have heard that number right.

Andy kept speaking. "Of course, I will require access to the castle and its surrounds to make a more accurate assessment."

Jack whistled. "Motherfucker!"

This time, Roderick was entirely in agreement with him.

# CHAPTER TEN

Dr. Hannah Maxwell pushed her laptop down her thighs and rubbed her eyes. It didn't matter how many times she looked at the test results and scans, they still didn't make sense to her. She'd been over Gemma's results so many times, they were imprinted on her eyelids. The same test results that had kept her tossing and turning for the last four weeks. She was a doctor, a scientist, and mysteries bothered her.

Her patient, Gemma Andover, aged 12, didn't have brainstem glioma anymore.

Beside her on her king-size bed, Charlie had fallen asleep on his favorite purple stuffed whale. She should have sent him to his bed earlier, but she had so little time with him that she didn't like to spend what she did have arguing with her five-year-old. Hannah smoothed his white-blond hair off his forehead. He was all she had now. Just her and Charlie against the world.

Her laptop screensaver came on, and she stared at the image of red rocks and blue sky without really registering it.

She'd been treating Gemma since her DIPG had first been diagnosed, and Hannah had known from the start it wasn't good. Years of working with Gemmas had given her a kind of sixth sense around outcomes. DIPG prognoses were poor at the best of times, and Gemma's had been well advanced, spreading in a hateful series of masses through her brain cells and stem.

Now Gemma was cured. Completely.

Charlie snuffled next to her, his little body hot against her thigh.

Hannah would love to take credit for Gemma's recovery, even obliquely, but she couldn't. However Gemma had been cured, it had nothing to do with her, and that same sixth sense about outcomes bellowed at her now. Something had happened to cure Gemma.

Gemma lived with her mother, Hermione, in Greater Littleton.

"Fancy a trip to the seaside?" she whispered to a still-sleeping Charlie.

She had plenty of leave time saved up, nowhere else to go, and nothing to do with it. After all, she was doing some old-time doctoring and making a house call on her patient.

---

ALEXANDER SAT at the kitchen table studying the reams of printouts from Andy Braithwaite and trying not to throw up. Baile had more land than Windsor and wasn't listed with either the National Trust or the National Heritage. His brain ache was not being helped, in any manner, by Roderick fuming and pacing at the kitchen window.

He'd had hundreds of years of hiding in plain sight amongst the mundane. In the earlier days it had been so much easier to hide assets and investments, transfer property deeds, that sort of thing. Mundanes tended to suffer irreparable sense of humor failure when they discovered ancient beings amongst them.

Andy Braithwaite's paper bomb was out of his league, however. If he'd still been part of Rhiannon's unholy tribe, he could have called on one of her many minions who had experience with this, and they would have solved it.

Roderick rapped his knuckles against the window ledge and huffed.

"Do you mind?" Alexander glared at him. If the stupid shit thought this was so easy, he could wade in here and sort this.

Stopping suddenly, Roderick peered out the window. "She's back."

"Could you be a tad more specific?" They lived in a fucking castle with seven shes.

"That woman from the village. The one with the daughter." Roderick strode for the door.

Alexander scrambled after him. "Hermione?"

He hated the sinking feeling in his gut.

Hermione stood beside her compact SUV looking like she was facing a firing squad. She started when she saw him. "Lord Donn."

He smiled to put her at ease. "Alexander."

"Right. Alexander." She glanced at Roderick. "Mr. Cray."

Roderick smiled at her. "Roderick."

"Right. Roderick."

One of Niamh's dogs barked inside the castle. The SUV engine pinged as it cooled.

"Would you like to come in?" Look at Roderick suddenly being warm and approachable.

Alexander couldn't quite believe his eyes as Roderick motioned Hermione inside.

Hermione cleared her throat and stayed beside her car. "I'm not sure I should."

Once, just once, Alexander would love it if the sinking feeling turned out to be a false alarm, or indigestion. "Then you had definitely better come in."

Dragging her feet, Hermione stopped inside the kitchen door, her handbag clutched to her chest. "There's a problem."

"With Gemma?" Alexander hoped like hell Hermione's daughter hadn't gotten sick again. Bronwyn had healed Gemma of her tumor, but fucking cancer had a way of coming back.

"Yes and no." Hermione took a deep breath.

"Hermione?" Bronwyn came in from the bailey. She must have been in the healer's hall and seen Hermione arrive. She frowned and glanced at Roderick and Alexander. "What's wrong?" She paled. "Is Gemma sick again?"

"No." Hermione shook her head. "And I know you're going to think I have no right to ask, but please don't make her get sick again."

*Bugger it!* Secrets always found a way to come out, and in Alexander's long, long life he'd had more than enough experience to know this definitively. And now it looked like another of his evasions was about to get an airing. "We've got this," he said to Bronwyn. "No need to stop what you're working on."

"You're being weird." Bronwyn tilted her head and studied him.

Roderick pulled out a chair for Hermione. "Why don't you have a seat and tell us what's happening?"

Bloody, sodding Roderick! Most days he was all for lifting the drawbridge and filling the moat with piranha.

"We would never make anyone sick." Bronwyn frowned at Hermione. "Why would you even think that?"

Hermione glanced at him. "Well, Alexander—"

"Tea," Alexander yelled. "Let's have tea. Or maybe something stronger."

Bronwyn narrowed her eyes at him.

"Definitely something stronger. Sun's over the yard arm and all that," he said. He'd never told Bronwyn about the oblique threat he'd leveled at Hermione to assure her silence around Bronwyn healing her daughter. He may have implied—definitely had—that if word about Bronwyn got out, Gemma would get sick again. "Whisky?"

His little witch would have his balls roasted and toasted when she found out. In his defense, the world would go crazy if they knew about Bronwyn's abilities. First would come the dying and the desperate, and after them the skeptics, and the coven was in no way ready to handle all that. It's not that they wanted to keep Bronwyn's blessing to themselves—she wouldn't have allowed it even if they did—it was more a matter of controlling the script in a way they could manage.

Bronwyn took a seat beside Hermione. "Why would Gemma get sick again, and what would that have to do with us?"

"Vodka!" Alexander threw a desperate look at Roderick. "Wine, port, brandy?"

Smirking, Roderick crossed his arms.

"Lord Donn." Hermione blinked at Bronwyn. "I mean, Alexander. He told me—"

"It was more an intimation." Alexander went for damage control.

Bronwyn's green eyes locked on his. "What did Alexander say?"

"That the healing would go away." Hermione scrubbed her palms against her denim-clad thighs. She wasn't wearing her tour guide outfit today, but jeans and a large sweatshirt. "That if we didn't keep silent, it could disappear."

Bronwyn's stillness made Alexander flinch. And thus endeth the life of Alexander. "Not go away, per se, but that maybe—"

"I didn't do it." Hermione's breath hitched on a sob. "I didn't say anything."

Roderick threw him a look loaded with *you did what now?*

It's not like that brainless lout didn't ever open his mouth and insert both size thirteen combats.

"First off, the healing doesn't work like that." Bronwyn kept her voice gentle and reassuring for Hermione. She wouldn't even look at him, and that spelled trouble with a capital T. For him. "When I heal someone, it's not reversible."

"Really?" Hermione burst into tears. Losing the death grip on her handbag, she opened it up and rummaged inside. Pulling out a pack of tissues, she tried to mop up tears that were falling faster than she could manage. "I...I...was so afraid." Her shoulders heaved. "I've only just got her back. She's my daughter and I..." The rest got lost behind a tissue.

Bronwyn nailed him with a look that made his balls retract. "I'm sure you were terrified."

He made an apologetic face, but she wasn't even a tad impressed.

"Hermione." Sitting on her other side, Roderick took the tissues from Hermione's fist and drew a new one from the pack. "Here. You've seen what Bronwyn can do."

Eyes huge, Hermione nodded and stared up at him.

Another tissue. "And we're afraid what will happen if word gets out."

Another nod.

"And that's the only reason Alexander told you that." Roderick applied the tissue this time. Who knew the big guy could be that gentle? "Bronwyn is pregnant and there are people out there who would be a danger to her."

"Danger?" Hermione hiccupped and went even paler.

"It's a lot to explain." Roderick held the tissue over her nose. "Blow."

Hermione obediently blew her nose, but never took her eyes off Roderick's face.

"And there's a lot that I can't tell you." He pried her handbag from her and put it beside the wad of soggy tissues on the table. "But before you tell us what happened, you need to know your daughter is fine, and will stay that way, Goddess willing."

Nodding, Hermione peered at Bronwyn. "The cancer won't come back?"

"I can't promise that." Bronwyn took her hand. "But it won't come back because of anything you say or don't say. If it comes back, and I pray to Goddess it doesn't, it will be because it's cancer and it sucks."

"Okay." Hermione took a shuddering breath. "Okay."

"Now." Roderick's tone firmed. "Tell us what happened."

"She's denying it, but Gemma must have said something at school." Hermione shook her head. "I don't know why, but she's only twelve and—"

"So, people know?" Roderick kept it gentle.

"Gemma's best friend's mother called me." Hermione picked at the table wood grain. "She wanted me to know that Gemma was making up stories." Hermione looked wounded as she glanced at him. "I lied. I told her I would speak to Gemma. I pretended Gemma was telling lies."

Relief swept through Alexander. Perhaps the situation could be controlled.

"But she's not lying," Hermione said. "And I feel like the worst kind of mother for even saying that about her."

"You were doing what you thought you had to in order to save her." Bronwyn squeezed Hermione's hand. "You should never have had to do that. You shouldn't have been put in that position."

Yup, he was going to lose several working parts as soon as Hermione left. And he deserved it. Sure, his motives had been to protect Bronwyn and their babies, but he'd not thought the repercussions through.

"I thought that would be the end of it." Hermione took a deep breath. "But I was out shopping, and another mother approached me. She'd heard it from the first one." She glanced at Roderick and then Bronwyn. "You know what people are like. This could be everywhere."

Bronwyn grimaced. "Yeah. People love this sort of thing."

"There's more," Hermione said.

Fucking hell! Of course, there was.

"Gemma's oncologist is in Greater Littleton." Hermione dug

her fingers into her thighs. "She came to see us, and she had questions. She's confused and amazed by Gemma being cured, and she wants to know how it happened."

"What did you say?" Tension radiated from Roderick.

Hermione shrugged. "I didn't know what to say. I said I didn't know but was too grateful to care."

"Well done." Bronwyn looked concerned. "I think the less you say, the better."

Alexander couldn't not chime in at this point. "Do you think she's heard the rumors?"

"I can't say." Hermione shook her head. "But you know what this village is like. Nothing stays secret for long."

"Okay." Bronwyn's cheeriness fell flat in the grave atmosphere of the kitchen. "Well, it's not great, but it's not the end of the world. The most important thing is that now you know Gemma is not going to get sick again because of this."

"Umm…" Hermione bit her lip.

For fuck's sake. Alexander couldn't hold back a groan. "What else?"

"Jasmine—the mother from the shops. She came to see me, and she wants me to arrange for her son to have an appointment with Bronwyn."

"That won't happen," Roderick said and stood. He paced over to the window.

Bronwyn glared at his back. "But—"

"Blessed." Roderick squared his shoulders. "You must see—"

"She's not the only one." The words burst out of Hermione. "I've had four strangers stop me on the street and ask the same thing. And that's today."

That ended Bronwyn's planned tirade at Roderick. "Oh my."

"I keep saying I don't know what they're talking about." Hermione grabbed the wad of tissues and balled them up. "I had to come and tell you."

"You did the right thing." Roderick nodded to Hermione. "And we need to ask you to keep denying it."

Hermione nodded vehemently. "Of course, but what are we going to do?"

"We'll think of something," Roderick said it with such quiet confidence Alexander almost believed him. "The best thing you can do is go about your life as if you have no idea about any of this."

"Okay." Hermione looked doubtful. "But it's true, isn't it? The women of Baile Castle really are witches."

Alexander let Roderick field this one.

Looking grim, Roderick said, "Yes."

---

VOICES AND OPINIONS raged around Mags, but she couldn't follow them. A coven meeting had been called after Hermione had left, and because of their growing numbers, it was being held in a sunny sea-facing parlor. The parlor had been closed until recently. Then Baile had popped open the door and given them all access to the large room. Double groupings of two sofas and two armchairs each ensured everyone had a seat.

The large Aubusson rug beneath Alexander kept capturing her attention. Like in her vision, the carpet threads kept writhing out of the carpet and covering Alexander. Then they would dissipate, and Alexander would disappear. Only for her vision to reset, and he'd be sitting there again, arguing with Bronwyn and Niamh.

She pinched her thigh to ground herself in the present. Her repeating vision was not happening in the now, and as far she could remember it hadn't happened before. She was seeing the future, but in a way that made no sense.

The deep sense of foreboding, however, she got with gut-clawing clarity.

"Mags?" Niamh was looking at her with an impatient expression like she'd been trying to get her attention. "You've not said what you think."

What were they talking about? She forced her gaze off the carpet and to the bracelets on her wrist. Hermione had come here with the news that the secret was out about Bronwyn. Niamh was pushing to be allowed to work her magic as well. Bronwyn wanted to take advantage of the situation and do more healing.

Sinead and Alannah wanted the coven to wait until all four cardinal points were active.

Alexander wanted to take the fight to Rhiannon instead of always waiting for her to find and attack them.

Roderick?

With one arm on the mantel, he stood glaring into the empty hearth.

Mags couldn't remember what he wanted, but she would guess it would involve nobody leaving Baile.

Warren sat opposite Niamh in a large wingback chair. Frustration carved grooves in his forehead. "We need a strategy that works for everyone."

"We do not." Roderick pounded the mantel. "We need to lie low until we can find a safe way forward. I have seen what happens when we act impulsively."

A woman screamed. A sword flashed. Blood welled at the gash across her neck. Another woman was dragged by the hair, her long skirts tangling in her flailing legs. Roderick was there, blood-splattered and sweaty, his sword rising and falling. More blood. All that screaming. Men grunting and bellowing. Steel clashing. Broken bodies littering the ground. Big boots careless and cruel as they stamped through blood and limbs. Smoke everywhere.

"Mags!" An urgent voice penetrated the melee. "Magdalene, sweetheart, look at me."

Jack's voice.

Mags blinked, and the horror vanished. She was sitting beside Bronwyn, on a sofa, in the parlor.

Jack crouched at her feet, worry in his caramel eyes.

"Magdalene." Jack chafed her freezing hands. "Where the hell did you go?"

Mags tried to piece back the lost moments. She'd been looking at Roderick as he spoke. And then…

She shuddered. She couldn't go back there and see it again. Smell the sweat and blood and smoke.

Goddess, how had Roderick survived that night? How did he not wake screaming every night thereafter? "I saw you," she said to Roderick.

Roderick stilled. "A vision?"

"Not of the future." The clothing in her vision provided the clue. "It was the night Rhiannon attacked the coven."

"What?" Roderick paled. "How could you see that?"

"You were fighting." Mags didn't want to close her eyes in case she went back to that awful night, but her eyes burned. "You were so tired, and you knew you would lose, but you kept fighting."

Maeve went to stand beside Roderick and put her arm around his waist.

He pulled her close to him as if Maeve could keep the nightmare at bay.

"So many dead." Mags's cheek itched and she touched it. Her fingers came away wet. "So many dead and dying and you kept fighting. You watched them die. Your brothers, all those witches, you watched them die."

"Stop it." Roderick's voice grew hoarse. "Stop."

Maeve was so pale, she looked like she would faint. "You're torturing him. Please, Mags."

What was she doing? Nausea churned in her stomach, and she pressed a hand to her mouth. "I'm sorry. So sorry. I didn't…"

She couldn't find the words, couldn't make sense of any of what she'd seen and why she'd seen it. "I'm so sorry."

Sorry for making him and Maeve remember. Sorry they had been forced to live through that night. Sorry it would happen again, and there would be more death.

# CHAPTER ELEVEN

In his thirty-six years, Andy Braithwaite had never broken a law, no speeding tickets, not even a parking ticket. Then again, in his thirty-six years, Andy had also never had the sort of feeling currently thrumming through him.

Fifty-three minutes earlier, he'd arrived at Baile Castle for his second visit in as many days. Like the polite and civilized being he was, he tapped on the kitchen door and waited. Then waited some more and tapped a bit louder.

An extremely large dog, which looked disturbingly like a wolf, answered his second knock.

"Good dog." He nodded at the beast.

The dog stared at him with piercing, yellow eyes, and Andy reconsidered his notion of putting his hand out for it to sniff. Cesar Milan maintained that was a waste of time in any case. Dogs, with their vastly superior sense of smell, didn't need you shoving your hand beneath their noses in order for them to smell you.

It still baffled him that after weeks of driving around in circles trying to find the castle, he'd driven in yesterday and today like it was child's play. Reaching Baile should have been child's play. The castle sat on a hill above the village of Greater Littleton. According to his GPS and his maps, and a google maps search, there was only one road from the village to Baile Castle. Yet, up until yesterday, he'd driven around and around with the castle always up ahead of him and him never reaching it.

The dog trailed him as he stepped into the kitchen. It sighed and then lay down beside a large kitchen range. The kitchen stopped Andy short. He'd been inside enough ancestral homes to know this was the real thing. Modern appliances aside, the kitchen could have been a leap back in time. A large wooden table dominated the space. Drying herbs hung from the rafters and filled the air with aromatic scents. The range had been built into what would have started its life as a cooking hearth. Blackened stones bore testament to centuries of fires lit beneath them.

After waiting in the kitchen for a while, he took the stairs upward.

"Hello?" he called out to warn the inhabitants he was on the premises. He would hate to be accused of trespassing, which technically he was doing.

Nobody came, and Andy climbed the stairs and found himself in a great hall.

"Oh, my Lord." He stopped to take it all in.

It was the sort of great hall that explained how it had earned the descriptor great. Stone vaulted ceilings soared above the flagstone floor. Banners hung over the supporting pillars, and Andy walked over to examine them. Typical heraldic stuff, but fascinating, nonetheless. Fascinating to one such as he, particularly.

He didn't strictly recognize the heraldic symbols, but he'd studied enough heraldry to recognize certain elements.

Andy lived for history. Deep within, he had the feeling he'd been born in the wrong century. Two minutes after entering the great hall of Baile Castle, and Andy knew, with an inexplicable certainty, his tidy, two-bedroom home in a desirable up and coming neighborhood would never feel as much like home as Baile did. Neither had he experienced this odd sort of completeness in his respectable, middle-class family home.

Andy was where he was meant to be.

At the far end of the great hall, a stained-glass window held him transfixed. Three women were depicted beneath a large tree at the edge of a pool. The space beside the three women in the window set his teeth on edge, like a knife slipping on a plate.

The dog joined him and sat beside him staring at the window with him.

"Good dog," he said, and considered patting its head.

The dog gave him a stare that made him abandon the notion and settle for a nod.

He voted against taking the large staircase upwards and chose instead a heavily fortified arched door to the right of the window. He knocked, of course, before opening the door and entering a long passageway. Light poured through windows on one side. On the other, Andy had to stop again and again to study the tapestries adorning the long, stone wall.

They even had a dragon depicted in one of them.

The battles, though, that's what kept him moving from one to the other. Glorious scenes of knights at war, beautifully stitched in vibrant silks. Andy could almost smell the sweat, blood, and horses, hear the clash of steel and the clank of armor.

The corridor opened onto an armory. And Andy stumbled into heaven.

The swords alone took his breath away—falchions, falxes, gladii, kopis, spatha, long swords, broad swords, curtanas, claymores. He'd never dreamed such a collection existed, let alone seen one. They even had a harpe, and several scholars believed that to be entirely mythical.

"Mr. Braithwaite?" Frowning, Lord Donn approached him from across the armory. The man frowned at him.

As well, he might, considering Andy was trespassing and had, legally speaking, broken into the premises. His cheeks flushed, and he was acutely and mortifyingly aware he had no business there. "Good morning. I'm…er…" He ran out of adequate words to explain his actions, so he shrugged. "Admiring your collection."

"Right." Lord Donn glanced at the swords and then back at him. "How did you get in here?"

"The door was open." The words came out too fast. "I knocked first."

Still frowning, Lord Donn nodded. "You walked right in?"

"After I knocked. Twice." He was bold, not a criminal. "And I called out. Twice. Three times if you count the time in the great hall, and I rather think we must. Don't you?"

Lord Donn's lips quirked. "Must we?"

"Indubitably."

"What the hell?" Mr. Cray entered, and Andy wanted to curl up and hide. Cray had two other men with him, all three of them looking grim and upset.

"I must apologize." Andy hadn't a leg to stand on here. "I did knock."

"Twice," Lord Donn said.

Andy nodded his thanks. "And called out."

"Thrice," Lord Donn said.

Andy suspected the man might be teasing him, but he needed to reassure them on the breaking and entering first. "I am fully aware that I should not have walked in without first obtaining permission, but I saw your collection and I needed to study them."

Mr. Cray raised an eyebrow at him. "Needed?"

"Indeed." Of this there could be no doubt. "Do you have any idea what you have in your possession?" Stupid thing to say, and his cheeks warmed again. "Of course you do. They're your collection."

"How did you get in here?" The fair-haired man beside Mr. Cray stepped forward.

They seemed to be rather fixated on the details of his ingress.

Lord Donn spoke before Andy could. "The door was open, and he walked right in."

"Bullshit!" Mr. Cray glowered, but at Lord Donn and not at Andy.

Before the ferocious expression turned his way, Andy needed to clarify. "I can assure you, that's exactly what happened. I parked in the bailey and knocked on the kitchen door. Nobody answered."

"So, you took that as an invitation to walk right in?" The blond man folded his arms. Muscle bulged beneath his T-shirt.

Andy opened his mouth, but he had nothing to say. He had, in fact, walked right in and kept on walking unti—*Was that a makhaira?*

The second man with Mr. Cray snapped his fingers. "Eyes this way, mate."

"But…" Words failed him again. A makhaira. An actual makhaira. "Ancient Greeks carried those." He pointed. "Ancient Greeks."

"The saber thingy?" The blond man frowned.

Andy opened his mouth, but nothing came out. He took a deep breath to steady himself. "That is not just any saber—"

"Ancient Greeks." Lord Donn winked at him. "I was paying attention."

"Alexander," Mr. Cray thundered. "A moment, please?"

It wasn't a request, and Lord Donn made a face. "Don't go anywhere."

Like he would. *Dear Lord, was that a nagamaki?* Andy's gaze drifted over the swords and stuck.

From Roderick's bellicose expression, Alexander guessed he was in for stormy weather. He couldn't deal with it right now. He was still trying to get his own brain to accept that not only had Baile allowed Andy Brathwaite inside the wards, but she'd had no objection to that man wandering around.

"How the fuck did he get in here?" Roderick looked about ready to lop Andy's head off with one of the swords the man was still transfixed by.

Really, though, glaring and hissing at him would accomplish nothing. "I have no idea." He met Roderick's gaze. "You're the one with the bloody connection to the castle; ask her."

"He has to go," Roderick said, typically ignoring any inconvenient truth Alexander presented him with.

Warren joined their twosome. "What's the plan?"

"Ask Roderick the Brute." Alexander had managed to make that moniker stick a couple of hundred years ago. He still rather liked it.

"I thought you told me Baile doesn't allow just anyone to get in here." Warren was becoming a master at walking the tiny strip of neutral space between Alexander and Roderick.

Roderick carried on scowling at Andy, so Alexander stepped in. "In theory, she doesn't. She didn't let me in until recently."

"Her first lapse in judgment." Roderick never missed an opportunity to drive home how little he wanted Alexander there.

Warren shook his head at Roderick. "Can we stay on topic here?"

"Baile letting in human detritus is the issue."

Goddess, there were days—this being one of them—when Alexander would love to forget they were all trying to work together and belt the bastard. He was here. Roderick knew why he was here, and he was staying. "Baile must have her reasons."

"Jesus." Warren scrubbed his face with his palms. "The whole sentient castle thing does my fucking head in."

It took some getting used to. "Given that she does nothing without a reason, I think the more pertinent question is why he's here."

"For the sword porn." Warren watched as Andy went nose to nose with six feet of gleaming steel. "Is he some kind of history nutter or something?"

"Or something," Roderick grumbled. "What if Baile got it wrong?"

That must have cost him to say. Roderick adored this old pile of stones. Given that Roderick had built her, Alexander got his attachment. Of course, Roderick hadn't known he was building a place to house a coven at the time he'd done so. Roderick of that time had been constructing a monument to his own battle prowess, celebrating his elevation in life. "You're thinking about that ward anomaly Sinead spoke of?"

"Yup." Roderick set his jaw in a grim line. "Your mother created those wards. She could have infiltrated them."

"She could have." Alexander controlled his wince at Roderick calling Rhiannon his mother. She'd birthed him and raised him, but they'd parted agendas the night she'd tried to destroy the entire coven and kill everyone in it.

"Then why wait until now to do it?" Warren crossed his arms. "If she had the ability to penetrate the wards and attack, wouldn't she have done so years ago?"

"To steal a word from our smitten friend over there, indubitably." Alexander had suffered through enough of Rhiannon's tantrums to be sure if she could have gotten inside Baile, she would have. "No, I think if he's here, he's here for a reason."

"We can't take that chance." Roderick's frown reappeared. "Not with everything we have to protect."

Alexander knew all about what was at stake. His Bronwyn was pregnant with their twins. The same twins Rhiannon would love to get her hands on. If Rhiannon ever managed to pull that off, the consequences didn't bear thinking about.

"We could always roll with it," Warren said.

Roderick looked confused. "What are we rolling?"

Warren chuckled. Roderick had made great strides in adapting to this century, but the language still tripped him up. "I mean, we could always let things play out and keep an eye on him."

"No." Roderick shook his head.

"Strange how you sound exactly like Fiona when you say that." Alexander got a shot in at Roderick. "She made a unilateral decision to close Baile off too. And look what happened then?"

Fiona had been working with Rhiannon, weakening Baile from the inside, until Rhiannon's forces could attempt to infiltrate and overthrow the coven.

Roderick's eyes blazed at him. "Don't you fucking dare!"

"Enough." Warren made a chopping motion between them. "Let's deal with the real problem here."

He made an excellent point, so Alexander tucked his growing frustration away.

"Um…guys?" Jack called from beside Andy.

Alexander didn't have time to deal with Jack and Roderick. "Ignoring Andy didn't work out so well for you last time, did it?" Roderick had been so sure Andy could never get past the wards. "And if we toss him out, there's every chance he'll come right back."

"Guys?" Jack called, more urgency in his tone.

"He can't be here." Roderick growled.

Way to state the sodding obvious. "But he is here."

"He has to go."

"He'll only come right back again. The world is finding us, and we have to deal with it." Alexander wanted to pound Roderick's stubborn head until some daylight made its way in there.

"We stay behind the wards." Roderick stuck his chin out.

"The problem with your strategy is standing right there."

"Guys!" Jack yelled.

They all turned.

Andy had a shield and a helmet on, and he was brandishing a broadsword at them. "Avast there, you scurrilous rogues! Show me the temper of your steel."

# CHAPTER TWELVE

Jack had run out of reasons to stay, which meant it was time to go. He'd heard Mags and how she needed him with her. Frankly, her assertion that she'd die if he didn't stay did worry him. But he wasn't the sort to forward chain letters, he rolled his eyes at conspiracy theorists, and he didn't even have a lucky number.

Jack folded his spare jeans and shoved them in his duffel. Only planning to stay a day or two, he'd only brought the two pair with him. The spare pair was clean and sat atop a stack of his folded T-shirts in a tidy pile on one of a pair of large armchairs beside the window. His laundry being handled for him and ready to pack he was taking as a sign. That and the near knock-down drag-out he'd had with Roderick after they'd managed to disarm Andy. Not ten minutes ago, Roderick had made it clear outsiders were not welcome at Baile, and that's exactly what Jack was. His friendship with Warren didn't give him a place here.

Roderick was a sexist throwback, and Jack would like nothing more than to toss him back. Way, way back and on his arse. But Roderick lived here, Jack didn't, and he might not win any Miss Manners quiz, but he knew better than to beat the crap out of his host.

Picking up his T-shirts, he stopped to admire the view outside his window. He caught a slither of seascape where it kissed up to the beach. People strolled along the pier like a diorama of a seaside holiday. A small boy threw food to the swooping gulls, as his parents stood behind him and watched. It was beautiful, like the holidays other kids had gotten when he was growing up. But he wasn't one of those kids. He was Jack Langham. His dad was a drunk doing life, his mother and sisters liked to pretend he was dead, and he had his own special file with the boys in blue.

With summer ending, the tourists would be packing up their happy lives, with another memory added to the perfect picture, and head home in a couple of weeks. Jack wouldn't be here to see it, but he bet the sea view got dramatic in winter, all crashing waves and brooding skies.

He couldn't blame his departure all on Roderick though. That scene in the library with Maeve was about him being a loose end. A childhood of being barely raised by a drunk who'd left, and a mum working two jobs had taught him he could get into all kinds of shit when he had too much time on his hands.

He'd miss Mags though. Not that anything had ever gotten off the ground with her, but she'd burrowed beneath his skin, and he cared what happened to her. More than a shit like him had a right to. Again, though, he needed to be straight with himself. He didn't even believe in half the crap they bandied about Baile, so what possible help could he be to her? Gary, who ran his anger management support group, wouldn't be a big fan of the pull-yourself-together style of support, which was all Jack could offer.

Magdalene needed a different kind of bloke, a gentle one, somebody who could comfort and encourage her. A good man.

She didn't need an ex-con with his list of deal-breaker character traits.

His door flew open and banged into the wall.

Jack reached for the knife he kept in his duffel.

"Jack!" Mags ran for him, tripping over her long dress. "Jack! We have to run."

He caught her before she fell. His heart pounded in his chest as adrenaline kicked it. "What is it?"

"They're coming, Jack." Tears spilled from her panicked eyes and ran down her paper-pale cheeks. "They're going to kill us all."

"Mags?" He tucked her against his side and swung to face the threat.

A seagull shrieked from outside. A man laughed from down below.

"We have to go." Mags tugged on his shirt. "We need to save the others and go."

There was no faking the terror on her face. "Who's coming, Mags?"

"Rhiannon." She sobbed and tugged on him. "She wants all of us dead. I can feel her." She grabbed the front of her dress and dug her nails in. "She's inside me. Her hatred. It's in me."

"Mags." He stared at the empty passage outside his bedroom. Nothing. He strained his ears for any sign of violence. "Can you tell me, calmly, what's happening?"

Her nails raked the exposed skin above her dress. "She's in me. I can't get away from her."

"No." He took her hands in one of his, wincing at the raw scratches she'd made. "There's nobody here."

"You don't understand." She sobbed, struggling to break free. "She's coming, and we are all going to die."

"Mags." He gave her a tiny shake. "Magdalene."

Her full name calmed her slightly, and she stopped fighting him. "They're here, Jack. They're everywhere. They're killing everyone." On a soft moan, she collapsed. "The blood is everywhere. So much blood."

Jack braced his weight and caught her. "Magdalene, I'm going to need you to take a breath."

"But, Jack—"

"Breathe, sweetheart, breathe." He drew her against him.

She took a shallow breath. "I—"

"Breathe."

Mags nodded and managed a longer, shuddering breath.

Leading her over to the bed, Jack took another look outside his window. He couldn't see the front of the castle. He angled his body to catch the road up to the castle. Nothing there.

He sat down and tugged Mags down beside him. "Rhiannon is attacking?"

Mags nodded. Her eyes grew unfocussed, her breathing shallow, and she lurched up again.

"No." He took a firmer tone and kept her beside him. "There's nobody here, sweetheart. Just you and me."

"No." She shook her head. "I saw it, Jack." Fresh tears tracked down her face. "I saw them killing everyone. There's so much blood."

"Look at me." He waited until those tormented green eyes locked on him. "Remember what you told me about time? How it gets mixed up for you."

She nodded slowly and bewilderment replaced the terror.

He could work with confusion. "You told me how you can't always tell when you were."

"Ye…e…es."

"Now take another breath." He waited until she complied. Years of listening to Gary's counseling in group came to his rescue. "Now tell me five things you can see."

She blinked at him. "I see you."

"What else?"

Her gaze flickered to the side. "The curtains, the chairs, the hearth, the carpet."

"Right. Four things you can touch."

She frowned and splayed her fingers over his arms. "You, the bedspread, the pillow, your duffel bag."

"That's good, Magdalene. Give me three things you can hear."

"I can touch your duffel bag." She stared at the bag. "Why are you packing?"

He'd get to that, but the edge of her panic had receded. "Three things you can hear."

"Sea, gulls, dog barking." She flapped her hand and gaped at him. "You can't leave."

"Two things—"

"Enough, Jack!" And just like that, lucidity returned. Her gaze cleared, and she stared right at him. "I told you, you can't leave. You're needed here."

"We need to calm you down before we get to that. Tell me two things you can smell."

"I'm calm," she said, as astonishment covered her face. "Why would you leave if you know you're needed here?"

She looked and sounded every bit as calm as she claimed to be. "I only came here to find Warren. I found him, and now it's time for me to go."

"No." She shook her head at him. "You're coming to Russia with me. I know it."

Nope. Going to Russia with her didn't sound like anything he'd do. He kept it reasonable. "I can't go to Russia with you, Mags. I have a job waiting for me. I have people up north expecting me."

"Phone them. Tell them you need to stay here."

Jesus, she wasn't going to be logical about him leaving. He gave it one last try. "I don't even have a passport."

"Alexander will get you one." She tossed out a hand as if

getting passports was the simplest thing imaginable. "We go to Russia together. I've seen it."

"Mags." He really didn't want to hurt her feelings, but she had to be rational. "You're not even sure what you see is happening or has happened. You told me that."

She glared at him. "That's not fair, Jack. I'm not mixed up about everything."

It felt like kicking a starving dog. "Not five minutes ago, you burst in here convinced the castle was under attacked.

She opened her mouth to argue.

Jack got there first. "Is it possible that maybe the Russia thing is the same? Maybe it's not what you think you saw."

"No." She shrugged. "That's not at all possible."

"Why?"

"Because…" She cocked her head and studied him. A sad smile creased her full mouth. "Ah, I see now."

"See what?" Honestly, nothing that came out her mouth in response to his question would surprise him.

She leaned forward and tapped his chest. "You don't believe me."

"I believe you believe what you see." Gary would be so proud of his tact.

Mags laughed. "You think I'm off my rocker."

Their conversation had him tied in knots. Her rabbit-hopping emotional state left him far behind. "I don't think you're off your rocker." Not at this moment, at least, but the way she'd burst into his room had left him seriously considering the idea. "But I think your confusion is playing tricks on your mind."

"Tell me, Jack."

He braced.

"Do you believe I can see things?"

"Sure, you can." She had eyes, didn't she?

Mags tapped where her finger had rested. "Stop being cute. You know what I'm really asking."

"Right." Underestimating how sharp she could be landed him in even deeper crap. Time to take the gloves off. "No, I don't."

She smiled, as if pleased with him. "I can understand that."

"You can?" He was sprinting to keep up with her again.

"Oh, yes." She nodded and gestured outside the window. "Most of them don't believe it either."

"The village?"

"The world." She wrinkled her nose. "People are frightened by what they don't understand."

"That's called being human."

"Yup." She stood and stared at his bag for a long time. "You know what?"

*Not a fucking clue.* He stood with her. "No, what?"

"You should go." She stood on her toes and kissed his cheek.

Her warm lips tingled where they pressed, and the waft of almonds and jasmine weaved around him.

"I should?" He reached for her, but she evaded his arm and slipped away.

Stopping at the door, she turned to him. "I'm a seer, Jack. I catch glimpses into times that are not this one. My being able to do that is not dependent on you or anyone else believing it." Her sad smile yanked at his heart. "And I'm never wrong."

# CHAPTER THIRTEEN

Bronwyn laughed as Alexander reached the end of the story. Stretched out on the leather sofa she'd had installed for him in the healer's hall, he looked like a big, lazy cat. "And you just left him with Roderick?"

Alexander crossed his ankles and tucked an arm beneath his head. Biceps bulged against his shirt in a deliciously distracting way. "Andy didn't challenge me to a sword fight."

Although her man appeared relaxed, she could sense his worry. "What do you think him being here means?"

"No idea." He turned his head and looked at her. "But maybe you should come over here and help me think."

Goddess, he was beautiful with that sinful body and those wicked, smoldering eyes. "If I come over there, we won't be thinking."

"I love how clever you are." He grinned and managed to look even more irresistible.

So, why was she still standing all the way across the room?

"I didn't put that sofa there so you could distract me from working." She walked toward him, putting a little sass in her step as she went.

His gaze drifted over her breasts, and then her hips. "Yes, you did."

"You're right." No sane woman would resist, or should resist. "You planning to make it worth my while?"

His grin was pure sex, as he said, "I always do."

Her belly fluttered, and she stopped, putting her hand against the swell.

"Is it them?" Alexander uncoiled and put his hand beside hers.

Bronwyn nodded.

The babies' movement strengthened, and then an awareness brushed her mind. Once, twice. No, not twice. Two separate beings tapped at her consciousness.

Alexander cocked his head. "Did they..."

"I think so." Bronwyn couldn't believe the conclusion blossoming inside her. "It's the twins."

Eyes intent, he spoke to her belly. "Say hello back."

"What? How?" She'd never heard of such a thing. The babies were still so small, barely bigger than a raspberry.

He glanced at her, wonder in his expression. "I don't know."

Bronwyn gently nudged at the awarenesses.

She got happy back, and two distinct beings—one male and one female.

"A boy and a girl," she said.

"Do they even have brains at this stage?" Alexander stroked her belly.

"Not really. Not according to what I've read." Then again, she hadn't been paying much attention to pregnancy books. Nobody had written one about magical babies in any case. Their twins were making their presence known. "We should name them."

Alexander looked taken aback, and then he smiled. "We absolutely should."

"Any ideas?" She might end up regretting making the suggestion.

Alexander cocked his head and then said, "Actually, yes."

"Hit me." Bronwyn waggled her fingers for more.

"Well." He pursed his lips. "They're supposed to be the final magic, so maybe something regal."

She liked that idea. "I'm listening."

"Regan and Rian." Alexander shot her a nervous glance. "They mean sovereign or ruler."

Both babies pressed into her mind, a warm glow of rightness that felt like a perfect fit. "I like it." She cupped his handsome face. "And they like it too."

"That's it then." Alexander whispered to her belly, "Hello Regan and Rian."

And they both felt the twin's happy reaction.

"Now." Bronwyn bent and pressed her mouth to his. "About that other idea of yours?"

Alexander looked torn. "They'll know."

"Nah." No way she was spending the next thirty weeks not touching her gorgeous man. "They're not that aware."

"Are you sure?" He side-eyed her belly. "Because—"

"You talk too much." She sucked his bottom lip. "And that's never a good quality in a man."

His dark eyes lit from within as he bracketed her hips with his hands and pulled her astride him. "You should respect your elders."

"I'm trying." Bronwyn rocked against him. "But he's putting up a helluva fight."

"Bronwyn." Warren strode into the healer's hall with Jack on his heels.

They both stopped and eyed her and Alexander.

Jack looked like he might retreat.

Chuckling, Warren said, "I was going to ask if you knew where Alexander was, but clearly you do."

"You can go now," Alexander grumbled.

Jack looked adorable wearing a blush. "We really should leave."

"No." Warren smirked. "We've found them now."

"Yes, but..." Jack made an awkward gesture. "They're...you know."

"I can see that." Warren folded his arms. "But if we wait for a time when they're not at each other, we'll be waiting for years."

Moment gone, Bronwyn climbed off Alexander. She shot Warren a glare for good measure. Maybe if he got himself laid, he wouldn't be so happy about cock-blocking them. "What is it?"

"Can't it wait?" Alexander whined.

She knew exactly how he felt.

"Unfortunately, not." Warren lost the grin. "Jack is concerned about Mags."

"Mags?" Bronwyn had been meaning to talk to Mags about that scene in the parlor with Roderick.

"She's...uh." Jack frowned and looked uncomfortable. "I don't think she's doing well." He squared his shoulders. "In fact, I'm bloody sure she's not doing well."

They had her undivided attention now, and Bronwyn motioned Jack to continue.

"She's getting her time snarled up." Warren took up the explanation. "From what Jack tells me, she's not entirely sure whether what she's seeing is past, present or future."

Mags had tripped into Roderick's past the other day, and that dovetailed too neatly with what Jack had said. She looked to Alexander. "Is that something you know about?"

"No." He shook his head. "We can ask Roderick if seers in the past have struggled, but I've never heard of it."

Bronwyn battled with phrasing her words delicately. Jack had only been here for a short time. "Mags can be different."

And her gift could be straight-up creepy at times. "You know, it's easy to get freaked out by her."

"Especially when she busts in on you and is crying about death and blood." Jack's jaw firmed, and he folded his arms. "And she's not pretending to be scared either. The woman was terrified out of her fucking mind."

Protectiveness radiated from him, and Bronwyn had to ask, "You're sure you've experienced no calling?"

"I'm dead sodding certain," Jack said. "From what Warren's told me, I've had none of that. No dreams, no woman nattering in my head, no itchy arm. Nothing."

"Was it like the other day, in the library?" Alexander stood and approached Jack. "When she saw Roderick and the coven massacre."

Bronwyn's heart went out to Alexander. His pain and regret about the events of that day scarred deep. Roderick and Maeve had not been the only ones affected by Mags with that seeing.

"Worse." Jack shook his head. "She was trying to get me to run, and she didn't seem like she was seeing something that happened in the past." Then he sighed. "But I can't be sure, and she can't either."

Bronwyn hated the direction her thoughts were heading but she voiced them anyway, "Could this be similar to what happened to Roz?"

Roz had been caught in the awareness of an owl. They'd only recently lost her when she'd chosen to pass with the owl rather than live separately from it.

"Who is Roz?" Jack looked from one to the other of them.

"She was Niamh's aunt." Warren grimaced. "Her blessing was untethered from her cardinal point, and without Goddess to ground her power, it overcame her. She thought she was part of an owl."

"I really don't like the sound of that." Now Jack looked ready to go to war. "I'm not going to like how this story ends, am I?"

"No." Warren's expression carried the weight of Niamh's grief. As her coimhdeacht, he would have experienced Roz's loss along with Niamh. "She died."

"That's not happening to Magdalene." Jack scowled.

"We don't know that it's the same thing." Bronwyn didn't want them all going off half-cocked. "I'm only suggesting it as a possibility."

"But it's too fucking close for comfort." Alexander drew her against his side, his warm body anchoring and comforting her. "It makes a horrible amount of sense."

Even though she'd made the suggestion, Bronwyn wanted more than anything to be wrong. "Let me examine her and see what I can find."

"And then you fix her." Jack glared at her. "You make sure she comes right."

"Steady on." Warren put a hand on Jack's shoulder. "Bronwyn will do what she can, but she's—"

"Mags is not going to die." Jack ground out. "She's not going to go fucking mad either."

"You need to ease off." Alexander met Jack's stare with a scowl of his own. "There are factors at play here you know nothing about, and I'll be fucked if I let you put this on Bronwyn."

Warren spread his hands in a conciliatory gesture. "Look, we're getting off track here. Jack is not putting this on Bronwyn, but he is worried about Mags."

That made four of them. That scene in the library with Roderick had not been Mags's usual brand of weird, and Bronwyn had not followed up with Mags like she should have done. She was so fired up to get out there and save the world that she had missed something right under her nose. "I'll go and see her now."

Jack stepped into her path. "And you'll tell me what you find?"

"I will." They might not know why Jack was here, but Mags had said he had to be, and he seemed to care for her. Bronwyn squeezed his arm. "We're not going to let anything bad happen to our Mags."

Warren glanced at Jack and then Alexander. "What about activating her cardinal point?"

"What does that mean?" Jack answered him. "Is it dangerous?"

"It wouldn't hurt," Alexander said. "Goddess provides an anchor to cré-magic, and the more magic she anchors, the stronger she gets."

Bronwyn spoke aloud for Jack's benefit. "And Roz got lost in the owl because fire wasn't activated, and her magic couldn't be grounded in Goddess."

"Activating air would certainly ground Mags." Warren nodded.

Jack folded his arms. "Then we'll do that."

"We have every intention of doing that." Alexander's accent grew crisper as he got annoyed. "But a trip to Russia takes careful planning and preparation. You can be damn sure that Rhiannon knows we're going after another point next and she's waiting for us to leave Baile's wards."

"He's right," Warren looked at Jack. "Niamh and I had the advantage of surprise. Mags or Sinead and Alannah won't have that. Two points are active already. Rhiannon is not going to stand back and let us wake up another one and do nothing."

After a terse nod, Jack said, "I'll need a passport."

"You?" Warren looked shocked. "You're not her coimhdeacht."

"Don't have to be to go with her." Jack planted his feet and squared his shoulder, looking like it would take an act of nature to stop him. "Magdalene told me I'm the one going with her to Russia, and that's good enough for me." He shrugged one meaty shoulder. "I'm good in a fight, and I can take care of both of us, with or without those sodding arm squiggles."

Warren looked down at the coimhdeacht markings on his right arm and smiled. "Markings," he said. "They're not squiggles, they're badges of honor."

"Right." Jack threw him an apologetic glance. "Didn't mean nothing by it, mate."

Warren nodded.

"But he hasn't got them either." Jack motioned Alexander. "And he takes care of Bronwyn."

Neither Alexander nor Warren looked eager to explain why Alexander was different. Jack had picked up a lot since he'd been at Baile, and nobody guarded their words around him, but there was knowing a thing and *knowing* a thing. Coming right out and letting Jack know Alexander was several centuries old might push the big man over the edge, and he was teetering already.

Bronwyn went with a partial truth. "Alexander has a very specific set of kills."

"What is he, fucking Liam Neeson?" Jack scowled.

"Only much better looking." Alexander smirked. "But besides that, if Mags says you're the one who needs to go with her, that's good enough for me. I'll get working on that passport."

"How do you do this shit?" Warren frowned at Alexander. "Do you have some kind of super-secret network going?"

"Of a sort." Alexander winked at her and then got serious. "I've gotten to know people over the years. Not everyone who starts out working for Rhiannon wants to stay that way."

# CHAPTER FOURTEEN

Fiona forced her hand way from her mouth before Rhiannon noticed her horror. If she had known this was where her insistence on a doctor would end, Fiona would have slit Edana's throat herself.

Only a mind as truly twisted as Rhiannon's could have formulated this travesty. She had Dr. Maxwell milking Edana for blood, pushing Edana to the verge of death time and time again. Fiona didn't know what had driven Dr. Maxwell to comply, but it had to be vital enough to make a good woman override her principles and her oaths as a physician.

"I'm losing them." Rhiannon looked every inch the deranged witch of grisly tales as she leaned over her scrying bowl. Her dark hair clung to her pale, sweating face, and her dark eyes burned with a terrifying fervor.

The doctor looked ready to vomit. "I can't."

"Do you need a reminder of what's at stake for you?" Spit flecked Rhiannon's bottom lip.

"No." Palpable hate filled Dr. Hannah Maxwell's blue eyes as she ran a blood-encrusted hand though her shoulder-length brown hair. She looked nothing like the calm professional who had appeared in Edana's sick room several days ago.

How long ago had that been? Time blurred for Fiona in a ghastly haze.

Rhiannon threw her head back and screamed, the tendons on her neck standing out.

Forcing her hands to stay by her sides, Fiona wanted to clap them over her ears and block out the awful noise.

On the bed, Edana stirred, her eyelids fluttering. Please let her not be conscious through what was happening to her.

"I need more blood." Rhiannon thrust her finger at Edana. "Give me more of her blood."

"I can't," Dr. Maxwell yelled back. "I'll kill her if I do. I've already taken as much as I can."

"Her blood pressure is dropping." From some deep inner core, Dr. Maxwell found the strength to master her response. "Her heart rate is increasing. Her body is going into traumatic shock. If I don't stop, she dies."

For a long moment, Fiona waited to hear Rhiannon tell the doctor to do it anyway.

Rhiannon's shoulders slumped and her face fell like a grotesque parody of a thwarted child. "But I saw them."

A fine tremor shook Dr. Maxwell's hands as she drew the needle from Edana's arm and applied pressure to the puncture wound. From the needle, the blood went into a bag and through a second tube into Rhiannon's scrying bowl.

"Who did you see, my lady?" On rubber legs, Fiona moved to shield Dr. Maxwell with her body. "Did you see inside Baile?"

"I saw them." Rhiannon sobbed. "My babies, my beautiful babies."

"That is wondrous, my lady." Fiona was amazed her voice sounded so steady. Her pulse pounded in her throat, and she felt sick to her center. Sweaty runnels slid down her sides.

"They have named them." Rhiannon scowled at the scrying

bowl. "I should be the one to name them." She looked up again and sniffed. "Rian and Regan. But the names are fitting."

Behind Fiona, Dr. Maxwell worked on Edana, but she dared not look. She bowed her head. "Venerable names, my lady. Names worthy of you."

"Right." Rhiannon stood, her chair screeching on the wooden floor. "They spoke of the seer."

Fiona waited.

"There is something not right with her." Rhiannon paced away from the scrying bowl. "But I did not see it."

"We can try another day," Fiona said.

"Don't be a fool." Rhiannon rounded on her. "Do you think they have not found the chink I'm whittling through those wards?"

Fiona hadn't known about any chink. Rhiannon kept more and more from her. Disappearances for days to meet with people Fiona knew nothing of. Magic worked without her being a part of it. "I beg your pardon, Mistress."

"And they will find him too." Rhiannon scowled at her scrying bottle. "The weak point in the wards allows me to reach him. That one." She pointed to Edana. "Gives me more power, longer reach."

Dr. Maxwell made a noise of desperate protest, but Fiona kept her attention on Rhiannon.

"I heard much, but I didn't hear it all." Rhiannon lunged forward and grabbed the scrying bowl. With a scream she hurled it against the wall. Copper clanged against the white wall and bounced to the floor. "I cannot rely on her living much longer, and I must use what I have learned."

Rhiannon charged from the room and slammed the door behind her.

Spots and rivulets of blood rorschached the wall. Edana's blood. Edana's life.

Dr. Maxwell let out a sob in the sudden vacuum of Rhiannon's departure. "This is not me. This can't be me," she whispered. "Dear God, please don't let this be real."

Fiona had never prayed a day in her life to the Christian version of God, but she echoed Dr. Maxwell in her mind. Turning, she motioned Edana. "Tell me how to help."

## CHAPTER FIFTEEN

Alexander picked up the bow and handed it to Warren. "Right. Stand straight. Feet shoulder width apart and at ninety degrees to the target."

"Why do I have to learn this again?" Warren glared at the bow in his hand.

"Because there is nothing like archery for aim, and Roderick really wants you to." Alexander grabbed an arrow. He couldn't quite believe he wasn't the one putting up a fight about teaching a modern soldier to fire a bow and arrow. Besides, it went against the grain to tamely agree with anything Roderick said. It also kept them all busy and away from each other's throats as they got organized around sending out the next witch.

"Who doesn't want to know how to fire a bow and arrow?" Jack leaned against the castle wall in a patch of sunlight.

Alexander had to grin at Jack's enthusiasm. "I have another bow. Right here."

"Yes." Jack peeled away from the wall and strode to them. He took the bow and copied Warren's position.

"Shoulders back." Alexander corrected Warren's stance. "And relax."

"I feel like fucking Robin Hood." Warren scowled.

Alexander kicked his right foot slightly forward. "No, you're nothing like him. He was a bit of a prat."

Jack and Warren blinked at him.

It was too easy to mess with them, and Alexander handed them both an arrow.

"Actually—" Andy appeared from the barracks "—most scholars agree that there is no one person associated with the actual Robin Hood."

Where the hell had he come from? The barracks, obviously, but how the man kept getting into Baile and what he was doing here were the more pertinent questions. "Back again, are you?"

Andy nodded and studied Jack and Warren with narrow eyes. "Historian and archivist Joseph Hunter found several references with variances in spelling referring to Robin Hood. The oldest of which dates back to 1226."

Roderick followed Andy outside. "Is there a reason you're here again?"

"Good morning." Andy went ramrod straight and then bowed. Really badly. He'd topple over if he bent any lower.

Fucking Roderick would be impossible—even more impossible—if all the genuflecting carried on. How Andy had managed to get Roderick to show him the rudiments of sword fighting would go down as another mystery in the cré-witch annals.

"The reason you're here?" Roderick crossed his arms.

Andy flushed. "I thought I might do some more sword fighting."

"That presupposes that what you were doing the other day was sword fighting," Roderick said.

Going an even deeper shade of red, Andy huffed. "I'll have you know I am a founding member of the Mashbury Marauders."

"Eh?" Roderick glanced at Alexander for an explanation.

He had nothing and Alexander shrugged. "Mashbury in Essex?"

"You've heard of us?" Andy's eyes sparkled.

Alexander hated to break it to him. "I've heard of Mashbury."

"I saw a sign for it on the way down here." Jack tossed Andy another bone.

Warren went to the heart of the matter. "What are the Mashbury Marauders?"

"We are historical renderers." Andy puffed his chest out. "We're well known for our version of the battle of Maldon."

"Now that was even before my time," Roderick said.

Jack cocked his head at Andy. "Are you one of those blokes who dress up and run around playing war?"

"I beg your pardon." Andy smoothed the front of his immaculately pressed shirt. "But we do not dress up like children at a birthday party. We meticulously research every detail of dress and—"

"They're re-enactors," Warren murmured to Roderick. "They re-enact historical times."

Roderick gaped. "Why the fuck would they do that?"

"Our main goal is the preservation of history." Andy straightened his shoulders. "After all, if you don't know where you come from, then you don't know where you are, and if you don't know where you are, then you don't know where you're going."

"Huh?' Roderick eyed Andy askance.

"Terry Pratchett said it." Alexander clued Roderick in. "He was an author, wrote books."

"I know what an author is." Roderick glared at him.

That's what happened when you tried to do something nice. Enough of that crap. "Really?" Alexander drew the word out. "Because they didn't have those in your day."

"We had books." Roderick's glare deepened into a glower.

Too easy. "Yes, but you probably couldn't read any of them."

"That's what we had monks for." Roderick stepped into him. "Want me to make a monk out of you?"

"Technically, only the church can make a monk out of him," Andy said.

"Aye." Roderick growled. "But I can still rip his balls off and feed them to him."

"How would that make him a monk?" Andy frowned. "A monk is—"

"Leave it." Warren motioned Andy to silence. "Can we get back to this arrow crap?"

Andy made an excited chuffing noise. "I adore archery."

"Like you knew how to sword fight?" Brow raised, Roderick stared at him.

Andy sniffed. "I was not in possession of my usual weapon."

"Right," Roderick drawled.

"I will have you know—" Andy raised his chin "—I am the best archer in the Mashbury Marauders."

Alexander toed a third bow behind him and out of Andy's eyeline. "Really?"

"Yes, indeed." Andy nodded. "It's not in my nature to puff myself up with conceit, but I am known for it. At least in Mashbury, I am."

Roderick motioned the bow behind Alexander. "Let's see it then."

"Couldn't we take his word for it?" Alexander had seen enough of the sword fighting to know he really didn't want to put a sharp projectile in Andy's hand.

"Oh, aye." Roderick's grin was borderline evil. "Let's see what he can do."

"Bow!" Andy shot his hand out imperiously.

Grinning, Jack handed his over.

"Arrow!"

Alexander needed to be the voice of reason. "I really don't need to see what he can do."

"My abilities have been maligned," Andy declared. "Allow me the opportunity to prove my prowess."

It sounded a bit dirty when he put it like that. "I'm sure you have all kinds of prowess, but I don't need to see those."

"I do." Jack chuckled. "I'd give my right nut to see Andy's prowess."

"I'll toss in my left nut." Warren smirked. "Let's see this prowess, Andy."

Andy took the bow and nocked the arrow. He turned to face the straw bale they'd set up at the far end of the bailey.

He drew back.

"Stop!" Roderick strode forward. "Goddess alone knows what you'll shoot if you start like that."

Alexander had a nasty feeling about this.

"Square to the target." Roderick jerked Andy into a better position. "Narrow your stance."

"I beg your pardon." Andy lowered the bow. "But I am well versed in the correct stance for archery."

Roderick kicked his left foot closer to his right. "No, you're not. Now narrow your stance."

"I'd listen to him." Alexander had spent enough time ducking Roderick's arrows to know how good he was. "He's the best archer who's ever tried to kill me."

Jack gaped at him.

Warren shook his head.

"Not that good." Roderick glanced at him. "Or you wouldn't be standing there."

"Oh, you're good," Alexander said. "I just duck better."

Roderick threw back his head and laughed. "I swore I had you that time outside Bath."

"You did." Alexander's left bicep gave a phantom throb. "You got me in the arm."

Roderick snorted. "I was aiming for the eye." He turned back to Andy and shoved the small of his back. "Straighten up."

Andy sighed. "I know how to—"

Roderick glared at him.

Andy snapped his mouth shut and straightened.

"Draw." Roderick stepped to the side.

Drawing the bow string back, Andy sighted down the shaft.

"Not like that." Roderick shook his head. "One finger above the arrow and two below."

"I know how to fire an arrow." Andy turned, bow still raised. He demonstrated his hold on the string and drew back.

The bow string pinged, and the arrow flew straight for where Alexander stood with Warren and Jack.

Alexander shot his hand up.

Light shimmered. His hand tingled. The arrow pinged against the shield his hand had become and dropped to the ground.

"What the fuck?" Jack stared at the shield that had been Alexander's hand.

Roderick's mouth dropped open.

Light shimmered again, and the shield dissolved back into his hand.

"What the fuck indeed?" Alexander stared at his hand. Had that just happened?

"What did you do?" Roderick strode over, grabbed Alexander's hand, and scowled at it.

"I don't know." Being too struck to speak was new for Alexander and the truth came out. "I saw the arrow, had this thought that I needed a shield, and stuck my hand out."

Jack cleared his throat. "Did he turn his hand into a shield?"

"Looks that way." Warren shook his head.

Andy hurried forward. "I beg your most humble pardon. I assure you I know—"

"Not now." Roderick focused his pale blue eyes on Alexander. "You've been experimenting."

"No, I haven't." Alexander yanked his hand back and stared at it. "Not since that day with Maeve."

The day Maeve had stepped into the middle of sword sparring session between him and Roderick and he'd somehow deflected his sword from taking her head off her shoulders.

"You lie." Roderick growled. "You have been wielding magic in secret."

Alexander's temper ignited. "Watch your fucking mouth."

"Or what?" Roderick stepped right into him. Their chests an inch apart. "Are you going to make me. I told you if you practiced magic, I would end you."

"Lads." Warren tried to push them apart. "This isn't helping."

"This whoreson is using magic." Roderick went nose to nose with Alexander, fury leaking from him. "I should never have allowed him into Baile."

"You didn't." Alexander had reached the limit of his tolerance with Roderick and his bullshit. "Baile let me in, and I'm here for Bronwyn. You need to get the fuck over yourself. I'm here, and I'm here to stay."

Roderick bared his teeth. "You traitorous cur."

"Traitorous?" Alexander wanted to wipe the floor. With Roderick's face. His fist burned to plow straight into that arrogant mug. "I've proved my loyalty to this coven and my mate. I don't owe you a fucking thing."

"Oi!" Warren got serious with the shoving and separated them. "You both need to cool off."

Jack stared at the arrow. "That is too weird."

"There's no such thing as magic." Pale, eyes wide, Andy shook his head. "Science. Science exists. There must be a logical explanation."

Alexander took a breath and stepped away from Roderick. Getting into a brawl would benefit nobody. He was shaken to his core by what he'd done. There had never been a male witch. Men couldn't wield cré-magic. Goddess only ever called women to channel her magic. Even the magic he'd used to awaken Roderick and Maeve from the statue had been borrowed from Rhiannon.

Thoughts churning, he went to find Bronwyn.

She smiled when he entered the healer's hall and then got serious. "What is it?"

"It happened again." He held his hand out to her like she could see what had happened.

Bronwyn took his hand. "What happened again?"

"The magic." Saying it aloud made it even more real, and he had to sit down. He pulled out one of the stools tucked beneath the large refractory table Bronwyn used to mix herbs. He told her what had happened.

"Wow." Bronwyn popped onto the stool beside him. "And you're sure no man has ever been able to do this before?"

"I'm sure." Alexander tried to sort his careening thoughts. "Did Goddess give me magic?"

"That is the third time something's happened." Bronwyn pressed against him. Her body provided a stable point in his tilting reality.

The first time he'd experienced something out of the ordinary had been after Bronwyn had activated the water point. The second had been to protect Maeve, and today he'd reacted on instinct.

"You know what I think?" Bronwyn took his hand and threaded her fingers through his.

The soft silk of her hand penetrated his confusion and he held on. "What?"

"I think you should find out more about this."

Alexander missed her meaning. "I could always do some research. The library is full of information."

"No." Bronwyn put her head on his shoulder. "If this had happened before, you can bet Roderick would know. He was here long before the library even."

"He was here before dinosaurs."

Bronwyn giggled. "I think you should start using this." She raised their joined hands. "Whatever this is. I think you should try to use it deliberately."

And wouldn't Roderick be thrilled to hear that. "You mean practice magic."

"Yes." She snuggled closer. "And I think you should do it with Roderick so he can see you're not doing anything suspicious."

"Roderick can hang." The urge to punch the prick returned. "I don't owe him any explanations, and I don't have to prove myself to him."

"But you do to the coven." Warren stood in the doorway. "If everything you've told me is true, we have a massive fight ahead of us. We're going to need every asset we have to win, and part of that is working together."

---

BRONWYN FOUND Mags sitting at the kitchen table eating a thick slab of Alannah's homemade bread covered in giant wedges of cheese. She looked up at Bronwyn and grimaced. "I know."

"Know what?" Bronwyn took a seat at the table opposite her.

Mags rolled her eyes and put her bread and cheese down. "Jack is worried about me and came to see you."

"He cares about you." Bronwyn's belly grumbled at the yeasty smell of bread and reminded her twins they were hungry. Again.

Nodding, Mags picked up her bread and took a huge bite.

Alannah entered the kitchen from the pantries. Her beautiful smile felt like being trapped in a ray of sunshine. "I thought I sensed a hungry soul."

"I could eat." Her twins were always ready to eat. Goddess alone knew what they'd be like as they got bigger.

Thomas appeared beside Alannah and smiled a greeting to Bronwyn.

Those two were getting closer by the day, but that was tomorrow's problem.

She waited until Thomas had followed Alannah back into the pantries. "It's not just Jack," she said to Mags.

"I know." Mags sighed and swallowed. "It's also what happened with Roderick." She made a face. "I really am sorry about upsetting him like that."

"Roderick's tough," Bronwyn said, but Roderick's visible upset had shaken even her. He was always so steady and sure that it was easy to forget he experienced the same human emotions as the rest of them.

Mags finished her snack and took her plate to the sink. "The truth is, I'm not sure what's happening to me."

Bronwyn waited for more.

"And it frightens me." Mags stared out the window.

She looked so fragile in the pale light that Bronwyn got up and slipped an arm around Mags's waist. "Let me help you."

"I will." Mags smiled down at her. "But not today."

"Fair enough." Bronwyn gave her a squeeze.

From the pantry, Alannah giggled, followed by Thomas's husky chuckle.

Mags stared toward them. "There's big trouble coming there."

"Did you see something?" Bronwyn's gut tightened around an anxious ball.

"He's a ghost, and she's a woman." Mags's mouth turned down at the corners. "I don't need my gift for that." She breathed deep. "But there is something big coming around Alannah and Sinead." Her eyes went jade and opaque. "A wolf howls in the darkness, and it howls for Sinead."

# CHAPTER SIXTEEN

Hannah's back ached, and her head throbbed as exhaustion burrowed into her bones, but she dared not sleep. She didn't know anything about the woman on the bed with the unsightly wounds on her face, but she did know that—however reluctantly on her part—the woman was her patient, and she was all that stood between her and death.

Actually, they were both keeping each other alive in a weird way. She had no doubt if her patient died, Hannah's usefulness would be over, and the psychotic bitch would get rid of her.

The other one, Fiona, had drifted off to sleep a couple of hours ago. Despite the clear, bright day outside, she slept deeply, and Hannah suspected it was only because she was here that Fiona felt she could sleep at all. Fiona had an oddly detached way of caring for the bedridden patient, but care for her she did.

Hannah didn't understand any of what had happened in the past week or so. Time blurred in the room she was locked in with her patient. She didn't understand anything beyond psycho bitch had Charlie.

God, her beautiful little boy in the hands of that woman made her want to vomit. The things she had done to this poor unconscious woman to save him made her sick to her soul. A lifetime spent prolonging life and fighting to save the chronically ill, and here she was, actively participating in an act that went against everything she believed and had sworn to preserve.

Fiona snuffled, her lank brown hair falling over her pale face.

The one on the bed must have been beautiful before whatever had happened had left her with those suppurating wounds. Fiona had mentioned something about a leopard, but Hannah was beyond asking questions.

Quick footsteps clattered down the hall.

Hannah braced herself and Fiona jerked awake.

Psycho bitch threw open the door and stood in the doorway like something from a Steven King novel. "I need more blood." Dressed in a long, silk gown of scarlet, she was stunning, but the maniacal gleam in those sin-dark eyes marred her beauty. "I need to get inside the wards. The answer lies with the seer."

"My lady." Fiona got to her feet, a neutral mask sliding over her unremarkable features. "You have a plan?"

"I always have a plan." Rhiannon turned on Fiona, hands raised like claws. "And this one will answer all our difficulties."

Fiona stilled and took a careful breath. "What difficulties, Mistress?"

"We are blind." Rhiannon tapped her head. "We are stumbling around in the dark while they cower behind those wards."

Hannah shook off her fatigue and adopted the same non-expression as Fiona. Psycho bitch fed on emotion, it was her drug of choice, and Hannah would be fucked before she gave her that as well.

"You have a way to spy?" Fiona tilted her head.

Rhiannon strode for the bed. "More than that." A smug smile lit her expression. "I have a tool that could even supersede my son's usefulness to us."

Jesus Christ, this hell-bitch had actually spawned something. Rhiannon turned to her and snapped her fingers. "I need more blood."

"I can't take any more of her blood." Hannah's belly knotted. Charlie's life depended on her not pissing the woman off. The poor soul on the bed's life depended on her too. "If I take blood now, she'll die."

Rhiannon made a strangled scream in her throat and bunched her hands. "I must have it. I care not if you have to kill her to get it." Her eyes burned into Hannah. "I cannot let this opportunity pass me by. Do you not understand?"

"I understand that you want more blood." Hannah didn't know how she kept her tone even. "But I also know if I take another drop, it'll kill her."

"Then kill her." Rhiannon snapped her fingers. "Kill her and give me what I need."

So many lives depended on the woman in the bed staying alive. Hannah's head whirled, and she couldn't form thoughts into sentences.

"Mistress." Hands spread in a placating gesture, Fiona slid between them. "I beg you to reconsider."

Rhiannon turned on her. "What are you talking about? I could not have planned this better. I must act now."

"Indeed, you must." Fiona showed as much emotion as the wall. "But once Edana is dead, then you can no longer use her for blood."

Tossing her hair, Rhiannon said, "This means more than the life of one useless witch. When she is used up, I will find another source."

"But none are as strong." Fiona spread her hand over her chest. "Not even I possess the magic Edana does."

That seemed to give Rhiannon pause.

Hannah held her breath and prayed to whatever or whoever might be listening.

"Mistress," Fiona said, "you have discovered a way behind those wards. The access we now possess is unprecedented. We will know the moment they decide which point they activate next, and we can plan ahead."

"That is only temporary." Rhiannon bared her teeth. "They will find him, and they will find the gap, and then I will be completely blind again."

"But they have yet to find either of those things. Let us think of this together and find another way." Fiona held up one hand. "We are so close and acting in haste now could undo much. Besides, she might not have enough blood to give you for what you require, and that would be a great pity."

Not even her years of medical training could give Hannah the kind of calm Fiona tapped into. Hannah didn't want to think what had gone behind forming that mask.

Rhiannon turned her back to her. "Are you certain you can draw no more blood?"

"You know what's at stake for me." Hannah tried to channel some of Fiona's calm. "I would do anything for my son, but I can't change the limits of the human body."

"She can heal fast." Rhiannon loomed over an unconscious Edana. "She is more than merely human."

Hannah had noticed the former and been too freaked out by the entire situation she found herself in to contemplate the latter. "But she's not there yet."

"How long?" Rhiannon watched Edana like a hawk eyeing a mouse.

"I can't say for sure." Hannah glanced at Fiona. "If you say she has accelerated healing powers, that's out of my area of expertise."

"Two days," Fiona said. "Three at the most, and then you will have what you need."

More like weeks or even months, but Hannah kept her mouth shut.

"Watch yourself, Fiona." Rhiannon slapped the other woman. "Don't make the mistake of thinking you are cleverer than I. I concede to this because it makes sense, not because of anything you have said."

Fiona bowed low. "I understand, Mistress."

In a rustle of her long silk gown, Rhiannon was gone, shutting the door softly behind her. A key turned in the lock.

Footsteps moved away from the door.

Hannah took a breath. "She locked us in."

"Yes." Fiona moved to the bed and adjusted the covers around Edana. "I have bought her a day, two at most, but Rhiannon won't be stopped next time."

"Do you know what she's planning?"

Fiona stared at her with an inscrutable expression and then shook her head. "She doesn't share everything with me, but I would guess it has something to do with what she saw the other day."

Dark lines of fatigue were carved into Fiona's face, and in that moment, she looked more human than she had since Hannah had first seen her,

"Have you been with her long?" Hannah needed information, and Fiona was her only source.

Fiona gave a bitter laugh. "Longer than you can imagine."

"So, I take it the accelerated healing comes with a longer lifespan." Hannah couldn't believe she was even considering the idea, but when you had eliminated all options, the impossible started to look plausible.

Fiona nodded and moved to one of the straight-back chairs at a wooden oval table and sat. She propped her chin on her hand. "She has your son?"

Pain and panic lanced through her, and Hannah nodded. "Charlie."

"Makes sense. I guessed it would have to be something like that to get you to cooperate." Fiona nodded.

"He's five." He would be terrified without her. God alone knew what that hideous creature had done to him. Hannah couldn't dwell on the possibilities, or she'd lose it.

Fiona sighed. "She'll kill him, you know. Once she's done with you, she'll kill both of you."

"Yes." Hannah clawed her sanity back from the edge of panic. Bile burned her throat. "But we're still alive now, and I'll do what I must to keep us both that way."

Staring at Edana, Fiona nodded. "We've been together a long time, she and I."

Hannah didn't care, but the conversation kept her sane.

"Tell me, Dr. Maxwell." Fiona's brown eyes met hers. "Do you believe in magic?"

What the hell? "No. I'm a scientist."

"Of course." Fiona put her hands on the table and studied them. "I'm a witch."

A week ago, Hannah would have laughed if someone had said that to her. "Is she?"

"Rhiannon?" Fiona breathed deep. "Yes, at least she was. Now..." She shrugged. "She is becoming something so much more than a witch. I don't even know what that is."

Hannah went to the table and took the other chair. "Why the blood?"

"Is it story time?" Fiona sneered.

Hannah waited. She sensed Fiona needed to talk.

"A long, long, long time ago." Fiona sat back in her chair and stared out the window. "In that castle."

The big, beautiful gray castle overlooking Greater Littleton dominated the view. The place didn't look evil. It looked like it guarded and sheltered the village at its feet.

"Actually, I need to go further back." Fiona took a breath. "Long before Christianity, long before any religion you would recognize, there was Goddess."

Paganism?

"She ruled over all living things and loved her creation. But her creation was flawed." Fiona met her gaze. "You know the story of Cain and Abel?"

"In the bible?"

"The bible." Fiona snorted. "Nothing but a bunch of men stealing stories from wherever they could." She sighed. "Anyway, the gist of that story is right. Goddess's creation got a bit unruly and started killing and stealing." She waved her hand in a dismissive gesture. "All your major sins basically. Goddess withdrew in horror."

Hannah had never been particularly religious, but this was a new take on everything she'd ever known or heard.

"A woman came to Goddess and begged for her to come back." Fiona went back to staring at the castle. "She prayed so long and hard that Goddess regretted her decision to leave her creation to their own devices and returned to earth."

The story Fiona told was unlike any version of paganism Hannah had picked up. But she'd seen things in the last week that forced a mind open.

"Goddess gave her creation one last chance and called four women to serve her."

Sometime during the telling, Hannah must have sat forward because her elbows now rested on the table. "Serve her to do what?"

"To keep the divine harmony." Fiona raised her hands. "In science, I believe you refer to any action having an opposite and equal reaction?"

Hannah nodded.

"Well, it's a bit like that. There must always be balance for life to prosper and harmony for it to grow."

Fiona was silent for so long, Hannah was on the verge of prompting her, when she spoke again.

"So, Goddess called four witches to teach the rest of creation how to live in balance." She raised four fingers. "One for each element; fire, earth, air, and water. And she gave them each a gift, a blessing." Fiona dropped her hand. "What you would call a magical ability."

"Magic." Hannah would never have believed it possible.

"Deidre, the one who did the praying in the first place, drew fire and was a healer. Tahra, drew water, and her blessing was guardian. Brenna, the air witch, had the gift of sight." Fiona gave her a wry smile. "And Rhiannon. Element, earth. Gift, Warden."

Fiona couldn't mean—"Rhiannon?"

"Oh, yes." Fiona chuckled. "One and the same."

Hannah had to digest that for a long moment, and then another even longer one. "You're telling me Rhiannon—" She jerked her head toward the door. "The same Rhiannon, is thousands of years old."

"Mind blown yet?" Fiona studied her.

Hannah could only nod. Fiona had to be making this up. Exaggerating at the very least.

"Everything was great. Hundreds of years passed. The four witches collected followers. Women with latent power, whom Goddess activated. Followers practicing magic meant a stronger Goddess, and they all settled there." She pointed at the castle.

"In the castle?"

Fiona laughed. "Oh, there wasn't a castle back then. The witches lived in the caverns beneath Baile. In the center of the caverns is a pool, Goddess pool, and it's the source of waterpower. It's also a kind of portal for Goddess to move between her realm and this." She sniffed. "There are other portals, but they've been forgotten over time. Anyway, for the purposes of this story, let's stay with the witches living under Baile."

Fiona waved her hand. "More time passed. Christianity came. Men didn't like women with so much power, and the witches got more circumspect."

"If they had all this power, why didn't they defend themselves?"

"It's not Goddess's way. There are only two big rules to being a cré-witch. One—" Fiona held up her index finger "—you can never use your magic to take life, or cause harm. Two, you can never touch blood magic."

Hannah glanced at Edana, sensing this was the crux of what she was doing here. "What's blood magic?"

"That's what you're helping her do," Fiona said. "It's using blood to work magic. It's not the blood so much as it is the essence of life contained within. So, essentially by breaking rule two, you're breaking rule one as well."

"Right." Hannah nodded like she wasn't getting the biggest head fuck of her life.

"Goddess lives on magic and worship. Essentially, they're the same thing. The practice of magic is what feeds her. As magic disappeared more and more from the world, so did she."

"And she did nothing about that?"

Fiona shrugged. "Apparently not. That's the part of this whole thing that has always confused me, but…" She shrugged. "I can't tell you what Goddess was thinking, or what deeper games are at play here."

Hannah's gaze was drawn to the castle. "Then what happened?"

"I won't get into Roderick." Fiona grimaced. "But eventually the castle was built, and the witches moved in. Now, Rhiannon." She pointed at the door. "That Rhiannon was starting to get pissed off. All that power, and they were living like criminals and keeping their magic under wraps."

Guessing, Hannah said, "She rebelled?"

"She did." Fiona nodded. "And they threw her out for it and cut her off from the magic." She jabbed a thumb at Edana. "Rhiannon can no longer access her magic through the elements, so she's forced to use blood magic." Fiona pulled a face. "We all are. It hurts like a bugger, but the magic…" Her expression grew dreamy. "It's worth it to use the magic."

"Were you around then?" Hannah had to shake her head that she'd even asked that question.

"No." Fiona chuckled. "I came along later. Just a girl with a gift who was drawn to Baile to practice it."

"You lived in the castle?"

"I led the coven." Her face glowed with pride. "I led that coven and ruled over it. That's where I met Edana." She shook her head. "I hated her, at first. In fact, if you'd asked me a couple of weeks ago, I would have told you I still hated her." She winced. "Maybe I still do, but it's only her and me left now. From the old days."

"How did you end up with Rhiannon?"

"Not a very interesting story." She sniffed. "I was a woman with ambition beyond what I could satisfy at Baile. Rhiannon is good at finding those of us like me. She persuaded me to join her." She held out her hands and shrugged. "And here I am."

Hannah sensed more to Fiona's part of the story, but she let it lie and said, "Was it worth it?"

Fiona stiffened. "It hardly matters now. My decision was made hundreds of years ago, and there is no going back."

# CHAPTER SEVENTEEN

Maeve drew fire, and the beloved orange and lily scent of her magic filled the air. She took a moment to revel in the newly restored fullness of her blessing. Too long, she'd been using only vestiges of magic, but since Niamh had awoken fire, she was complete again.

Time to get to work.

Around her, spirits of witches past hovered, waiting for her to open their portal into the sacred grove and to release them from the physical plane.

So many witches, it pressed down on her and made her want to weep. All the souls that had passed that dreadful night she and Roderick had gone into stasis, plus all the witches who had passed in the three hundred odd years she had been a statue. Mags's trip into the past the other night had shaken both her and Roderick. Neither of them liked to think of that terrible night. Like war survivors, they tucked it into a chest of things never to be thought of and moved on. Every now and again, however, some memory crept out of storage and rose to haunt them.

As there could only ever be one spirit walker per coven, and with her frozen with Roderick into a statue, no other spirit walker had served the coven since that night. The dead witch's souls had remained at Baile, caught in a nether region—unable to move forward or reincarnate. She'd been working long hours to give them peace and their deserved rest. Still, for every soul she granted rest, another ten came forward.

Focusing, Maeve drew a soul forward. The witch's journey passed through her as the soul did. Images of her life immersed Maeve. Her magic chose the crystals, rocks, and shells and guided Maeve's hands to form them into the pattern. When she was done, the soul slid free and through the portal the sigils had created.

Another done. Deliberately, she didn't turn and see the many gathered hopefully about her. Too many, and her heart ached for every one of them. Then there were still the lost souls on the village green. Thirteen witches and one acolyte had taken their own lives the night of the coven massacre, using the forbidden blood magic to forge her and Roderick into stasis. Since she was the only witch who could walk the sacred grove with dead witches, they had made the sacrifice to preserve her and cré-magic, but what a huge sacrifice it had been. Having used blood magic, the fourteen souls had severed their bond with goddess and been removed from the cycle of death and rebirth forever.

Maeve's bond warmed like a gentle ember in her chest as Roderick approached the cavern. She quested through their tether to read his emotions. Resonances of frustration and anger spiked back at her.

Physically, he stepped into the central cavern, a large basket flung over his arm. "Maeve."

"Hello." She leaned into the strength his presence always provided.

Roderick put the basket beside her. "Alannah thought you might be hungry." He frowned, his dark brows a slash over his pale, blue eyes. "She says you've been in here for hours and skipped lunch."

"I wasn't hungry." But the smell of roast chicken coming from the basket had her stomach begging her to reconsider.

Putting the basket between them, he lowered himself to the ground beside her and propped his back against the wall. "I thought I'd join you for a late lunch."

"You didn't have lunch?" That didn't sound like Roderick.

He gave her his half smile, the one that reached his eyes, that he kept for her. What she felt for him was so much more than love. He was the other half of her.

"I had lunch." He shrugged and dug in the basket.

He handed her a chicken sandwich on hearty wedges of Alannah's home-baked bread.

Maeve's mouth watered as she took a huge bite. The bread was fresh and soft, the chicken tender and flavor-packed, and the mayonnaise Alannah's own. She moaned as she chewed.

Roderick raised a brow at her. "Good?"

"Mmm-hmm." She ate another bite. "What's bothering you?"

"Maybe I just wanted in on your sandwiches."

She looked at him over her sandwich. He should know better than to try to put one over her. Goddess, she was part of him, mind and soul. Not body though. They hadn't ventured there. Yet. She bit into her sandwich.

"It's Alexander." He took a sandwich for himself.

It often was Alexander with Roderick, so she kept on eating.

Roderick's sandwich disappeared in three bites. He handed her another before taking one for himself. "He's got magic."

"You told me." She went at the second sandwich with as much enthusiasm as the first.

"No." Roderick shook his head. "It happened again."

That stopped her mid-chew. "Again?"

"This morning." Roderick finished a second sandwich and

went basket hunting again. He chuffed his approval and showed her a palm-size flaky, buttery pastry. "Jam tarts."

"Don't you eat them all." You had to stake your claim on food with Roderick around. "What happened with Alexander?"

"He created a shield from his hand." He popped a tart into his mouth.

Maeve let that sink in. "How?"

"I don't know." Roderick's frustration leaked astringent through their bond. "I haven't got a sodding clue how he did it. One moment there was an arrow heading for him, Warren, and Jack, and the next, Alexander's hand turned into a shield."

She'd been raised in a coven, and seen things most people hadn't, but hands becoming shields was a new one on her. Motioning the wall, she said, "I could ask them if they've ever heard of it."

"Yes." He nodded and frowned at the wall. "But I've never seen anything like it."

Roderick had been here for longer than most witches past, and if he hadn't seen a thing, chances were, it had never happened before. Still, she could ask.

Maeve accepted a jam tart from him and bit into it. Never mind hands and shields, what Alannah could do in the kitchen was magic in its purest form. She closed her eyes and groaned.

When she opened her eyes, Roderick was staring at her. He brushed a crumb from her lip with his thumb and licked it off. "Where do you put all the food? You're such a tiny thing."

"Everyone is tiny compared to you." The man set her insides to the slow boil when he did things like the thumb thing. It was intimate, and sensual and—how did Sinead put it? Sexy as fuck. Her voice came out deeper than normal, as she asked, "Did you fight with Alexander?"

He grimaced. "Don't we always fight?"

"Yup." She accepted another tart.

"Warren is pissed off with the pair of us." He shrugged. "He says we need to learn to work together. For the good of the coven."

Maeve made sure to meet his gaze, so he knew she was serious. "He's right."

Roderick growled.

Also sexy as fuck.

"I know that," he said. "But you were here that night when Alexander killed so many of our brothers and sisters."

She knew he might say she was splitting hairs, but she said, "I didn't see him killing anyone."

"Maeve." He gaped at her. "The fucking man tried to drown you."

Alexander had led a village mob intent on subjecting her to trial by water. A flawed little test where if you sank and drowned, you were innocent of being Satan's minion, but if you floated, they killed you—often by drowning you in the handy body of water they were testing you in. Roderick had come to her rescue. The memory of Roderick cleaving through people, sword raised and bellowing for Alexander to fight him swept through her. She had never been so grateful to see anyone in her life. He'd been gravely injured in the rescue. "Thank you," she whispered, emotion squeezing her throat. He'd been prepared to die for her that day. He almost had died for her that day.

"Maeve." His harsh face softened. "I will never not come for you. There is no need for gratitude." He touched her cheek. "Or guilt."

She didn't see it that way. Her impulsivity had cast the die for what had happened, and he had paid the price. She pressed her cheek into the warmth of his palm.

"Come here." His voice rasped as he settled her against his side and put an arm about her shoulders. "You are my witch, sweet Maeve. I will allow nobody to take you from me."

"You never even shouted at me." She snaked her arm around the firm flesh of his stomach and snuggled closer.

He chuckled, the deep bass vibrating through her. "Would it have changed anything?"

"No." Her face discovered the hot skin of his neck, and she drew the scent of him into her. "But then I could have shouted back and convinced myself what a tyrant you are."

Resting his cheek against her head, he said, "I'm a man of my time, Maeve. I can learn new ways—and Goddess knows, Sinead is determined to make me—but I will still be a warring brute at my core."

"You're not a warring brute." He gave off so much heat, it melted her insides. She wanted to be closer to all his glorious warmth.

He tilted her chin up, and his blue eyes laughed down at her. "Maeve. Even you do not believe that."

His feelings flooded their bond. Something so akin to adoration it took her breath away. "All right, you have warring brute tendencies."

"Hmm." His gaze caressed her face and settled on her mouth. "I most certainly do."

Tingles. Everywhere. Heat through her limbs, settling between her thighs. "Roderick." She could wait not one minute longer. "I'm not drunk now."

He froze. His eyes blazed. "Maeve?"

"You said the other night—"

He surged to his feet, taking her with him. One huge hand engulfed hers and he tugged her after him. Almost running, he pulled her through one cavern after another.

"Alannah's basket." She didn't care about the basket, but she felt breathless and giddy.

"Don't care." He took the stairs to the bailey two at a time.

"Roderick." She panted after him. "Slow down."

"Nay." He scooped her into his arms and kept to his pace.

His jaw was set like granite and his eyes fixed before him like a man on a holy quest.

What all his intensity meant made her laugh. "Roderick!"

"Maeve," he growled. "Every day since I first saw you as a woman, I have waited for this. Every. Single. Day."

He barged through the door to the bailey and strode for the kitchen.

"I don't think you can count the ones we were in stasis."

He shook his head. "I'm counting them."

Alannah whirled from where she was standing by the stove as Roderick bore them across the kitchen. "Roderick, Maeve did you—"

"No." Roderick cleared the kitchen.

Over his shoulder, Alannah giggled and winked at her. "Oh my."

The stairs to the great hall presented no challenge to Roderick, and he wasn't even breathing hard as they cleared them.

Warren strode toward them, frowning. "Roderick we need to talk—"

"No." Roderick shook his head and started the stairs to the upper level.

"About you and Alexander." Warren shouted after them. "It's important."

Roderick shook his head.

"Oh, hi." Thomas appeared in the living-quarters passage, and barely managed to dematerialize before Roderick went right through where he would have been.

He didn't put her down until they'd reached her chamber and the door banged shut behind them. He lowered her to the ground slowly, her interesting parts brushing his on the way to her feet.

"Maeve." He lowered his head and stopped an inch from her mouth. "After today, there will be no going back. You will be mine."

"I know." His words thrilled her, and she wrapped her arms around his neck. "Last chance for you to back out."

He took her mouth in a kiss so possessive it stole her breath.

No hesitation, he breached her lips with his tongue. His hand tangled in her hair and kept her where he wanted her. He was strong and hard against her, imprinting himself upon her.

He grabbed the hem of her blouse and tugged, breaking their lip seal only long enough to pull it over her head. Then his big hands were on her breasts, cupping, kneading.

Lust shimmered through Maeve. Her breasts ripened beneath his caress. She craved his skin on hers.

"Sweet." He lowered his head to her breast and sucked her nipple through her bra.

Wet and hot, the sensation seared her, and her knees weakened. She grabbed his silky hair and held him to her. More, she wanted so much more.

On a low grumbling purr, he circled her hips and hoisted her off her feet. He worshipped her breasts with his mouth.

The ache at her core intensified, and she parted her legs around his waist.

The bed was beneath her, and his big frame pinned her from the top.

Between her thighs, she throbbed for him.

As if sensing her need, he pressed into her.

Sensation shot through her from the point of contact, and she moaned.

Straightening his arms, he rose above her. A flush colored his cheeks and he breathed hard. He fisted the back of his shirt and tugged it over his head.

Maeve needed to touch all the hard flesh bared to her. She spread her hands over the molded slabs on his chest, followed the fascinating dips and ridges of his stomach, and reached his waistband. "Off."

"Maeve." He kissed her, demanding and thrilling, before rising again. Long, strong fingers snapped the button, and lowered his zipper.

She couldn't look away.

He shucked his trousers, and she saw what she had only ever imagined. Larger, and harder than how he existed in her mind, and she wanted to touch.

"Do it," he rasped. "Touch me."

His cock was hot, the skin delicate as silk as she caressed him.

Roderick hissed, his eyes glued to what she was doing to him.

Before she'd even halfway finished her exploration of him, he caught her hand and moved it from him.

He removed her bra, and then peeled her trousers and panties off.

Gloriously naked, she lay before his hot, hungry gaze. The way he looked at her was like a touch and she moved restlessly.

There was so much more, and she needed it now.

Roderick pressed her legs apart.

Bared to him, she had a moment's hesitation, and then his emotions and thoughts roared down the bond and engulfed her.

She was beautiful. His want was akin to agony. He wanted to sink deep inside her and never leave.

He touched her then, where she was hottest and slickest for him.

Maeve whimpered and pressed her needy flesh into his caress.

She caught his intention moments before he lowered his mouth to her core. The barrage of sensation was almost too much. His lips and tongue working her where she ached most.

Her climax blazed through her, and she bucked against his mouth.

His satisfaction magnified the sensation and sent her over the edge.

Their bond was wide open. She both felt his hands and

mouth on her and felt her beneath his caress. Both their feelings swelled and bloomed inside her, all over her.

When he entered her, it was almost too much, and she clung to him.

"It will always be thus between us, my Maeve." He rasped against her ear. "We are joined now in every way we can be."

He moved inside her, and she felt him within her and her clasping him in a wet, tight fist. Their impending completions fed on each other until there was nothing but the sensation of him and her. He drove them both higher and Maeve dug her nails into him. She climaxed with him, their twined sensations feeding into and from each other. Her world tilted, and she surrendered with him.

In the still of the aftermath, it was impossible to separate her awareness from his, and she didn't want to. His body, slick with sweat, covered hers and she wanted to keep him there forever.

"Maeve." He kissed her neck where his face pressed against her. "You are everything."

She nodded. She had no words, and somehow, I love you didn't seem enough.

# CHAPTER EIGHTEEN

Alannah added a dash of lemon juice to her pot of simmering sugar and brambles. With autumn coming upon them fast, the hedgerows were bursting with fruits. In her and Sinead's garden, thanks to their earth element and their warden blessing, things always grew more abundantly and ripened faster.

In her search through the journals of dead cré-witches, Niamh had found the old recipe Alannah was using. Of course, Niamh had been looking for the location of the fire point at the time and had no use for the old recipes and household tips, but Alannah liked the connection making the jam gave her with witches from long ago.

Although the author of this recipe had suffered from a ridiculous sweet tooth and Alannah was balancing the flavor. Roderick would like bramble jam, and with his rapacious appetite, he was always a joy to cook for.

"What do you fancy for dinner?" She asked the litter of sleepy wolf pups napping to the side of the range. Their mother came by to feed them a few times a day, but they were mostly left with Niamh and the coven to raise.

Niamh said it was part of man's original pact with the wolf; the wolf would help man to hunt, using its superior instincts, man would help with the kill and raise the pups.

The largest pup yawned wide, its pink mouth and tiny, spikey teeth on full display. Alannah couldn't resist a quick belly rub. "I know what you'd like for dinner." She evaded the needle-teeth and scratched behind an ear. "Meat, meat and more meat. With maybe a side of chicken."

The pup emitted a squeaky little yawn and his eyes drifted closed.

"But what to feed my humans." Alannah stood and washed her hands. The bailey outside her kitchen window was bathed in the crisp, champagne light of early autumn. She loved this time of year and the coming celebration of Samhain. It was a time of the death of the old year and the birth of the new. A time to take stock of your life.

Her sigh shivered up from the deepest part of her. Her life was a sloppy mess with no solution in sight.

She felt him before he became corporeal beside her, a soft brush against her nape. "Lurking again?"

"It's what ghosts do." Thomas appeared to her right, his hips braced on the sink behind him.

He looked so real, it was hard to remember he was nothing but smoke and ether. His beautiful hazel eyes studied her, their gaze roaming her face like a caress. "You're sad," he said.

They never spoke of the thing between them. By tacit agreement they glossed over the sticky details. She forced a smile for him. "I'm just feeling a bit mopey today." She gestured outside the window. "It's that time of year."

"Hmm." His look said he wasn't buying it but asking further might take them into the perilous territory of *we don't talk about it*. "What's for dinner?"

He also could read her disconcertingly well. "I was just discussing that with the gang."

"I'm guessing they went with meat." He glanced at the pups and smiled. "It's hard to believe they'll be huge and scary by this time next year."

"Not our pups." Alannah adored each one of them. Niamh refused to let her name them, but that didn't stop Alannah from recognizing their different personalities. The biggest one was always first into trouble. The smaller black female didn't take any of his crap. The one with the white tip to his tail was a bit shyer than the rest but loved cuddles. Who didn't love cuddles?

You know who didn't get cuddles, though? A woman in love with a ghost. At least, she didn't get cuddles from the one she wanted them from most. A fist tightened around her heart and squeezed.

"Don't." His smile dropped, and his eyes filled with sadness.

He was right, and she tried to shake her melancholy. "I have some fish left over from yesterday, I thought I might make kedgeree."

"With cream?"

His enthusiasm made her laugh. Especially coming, as it did, from a being who would never sample her cooking. And why did even that have to hurt? "Is anything without cream in it worth eating?"

"Not that I can think of," he said. "I would like to eat kedgeree, just once."

Thomas had been dead by the time kedgeree had found its way to England. Alannah nudged the thought aside and moved to the huge fridge and took out butter, the leftover fish and, of course, the cream. Thomas had told her kedgeree had been one of those dishes he would love to have eaten. Maybe that had played into her decision to make it tonight. She did that a lot, as if she could feed him by providing his favorites.

Goddess, she was maudlin today. Leaving Thomas playing with the pups, she went to the dry pantry for the rest of her ingredients—olive oil, basmati rice, sultanas. Returning to the kitchen, she watched a moment as Thomas stroked a gray and white female. For some inexplicable reason Thomas was able to physically touch animals. Not human animals, however. He said it had something to do with his bond with a guardian witch still being partially active. Thomas's witch was one of the fourteen souls trapped on the village green.

Thomas's big hand caressed the female from ear to flank.

*Lucky little wolf.*

Argh! She needed to stop this. Spices! She went back into the pantry to her spice cupboard and gathered cumin seeds, fresh ginger, turmeric, and curry powder. After snagging a jar of her homemade tomato puree, she went back to the kitchen.

Thomas sat by the range with a wolf pup on his lap. It was the mostly white male, who loved chewing on fingers. "I wanted to talk to you about the wards."

"And here I thought it was for the pleasure of my company." She'd meant to toss the comment out lightly, but it came out loaded with all sorts of *if only*.

"Always that."

His gaze met hers. Pleasure heated her cheeks, and she bent over her jam and gave it a pointless stir. "What about the wards?"

"You remember that anomaly you and Sinead found?"

"Yes." He had her full attention now, and for entirely different reasons. As wardens, she and Sinead had a direct connection to the wards, rooted as they were in the earth of Baile. Some weeks back, they'd stumbled across something. It was hard to put into words, but it was a minute hiccup in the constant power flow to the wards. So tiny, they might have missed it, but then they'd picked it up a second time. Roderick hadn't sensed it, however, and his connection to Baile was like he was plugged into the mainframe.

Thomas let the pup chew on his forefinger. "I can sense it now. It's like a distortion."

"Yes." That was as good a description as any. Sinead called it a disturbance in the force, but then she would. After turning the heat down beneath the jam, she grabbed a small onion and chopped it. "Did you speak to Roderick?"

"Not yet." Thomas winced as the pup got enthusiastic with chewing, and he gave it another finger to work on. "I wanted to chat with you first about it."

"I'll ask my sister." Alannah had not seen much of her twin lately. Sinead really didn't like Thomas hovering around her, and it had driven a small wedge between them. "She's more sensitive than I am to those kinds of things."

"Let me know." Rising, Thomas carefully deposited the pup with his siblings. "I'll talk to Roderick in the meantime."

Alannah stared at the neatly chopped onion in front of her. The other day, when Sinead had come into the kitchen with Taylor, she'd looked like she wanted to talk, but then they'd gotten sidetracked. Or rather, Sinead had chosen not to speak to her.

She put down her knife and washed her hands again. She didn't need to start dinner for another half an hour, and the wards couldn't wait.

Maybe it was because they were twins, or maybe because they shared a blessing, but she always had a sense of where Sinead was, and she walked to their shared suite. Roderick had told them that these two rooms with their sitting room between had once belonged to Fiona.

That had gotten Sinead out with the sage sticks, doing her damnedest to eliminate any trace of Fiona's energy from the space.

Sinead was sitting on the floor in the sitting room, sunlight gleaming on her auburn braid. She looked up when Alannah entered. "Hey. I thought you were making jam."

"I was." Alannah joined her sister on the floor. "I am, but I needed to ask you something."

Sinead nodded and resumed her basket weaving.

Basket weaving? "What are you doing?"

"Making a basket." Sinead frowned down at her creation. "Very badly I might add."

Alannah didn't have the heart to agree with her. "Are those to sell?"

"That was the idea." Sinead pulled her face at the wonky half-woven basket. "But I'd actually have to learn how to do this properly first."

Sinead had been on a tear for ways to generate income since the news about that property tax bill had come in.

"Thomas came to see me," Alannah said.

Sinead stiffened. It was so minute, another person might have missed it, but Alannah knew her twin inside and out. She stayed on topic. For now. "That anomaly we sensed in the wards. Apparently, he can feel it now."

Sinead put her basket on the floor and frowned at her. "Can Roderick?"

"Thomas is going to ask him." Alannah stared at Sinead until their gazes met. She got the feeling Sinead was hiding something from her. "Have you felt it strengthen?"

"Yes." Sinead nodded. "The other day I was working with earth in the garden. When I was with Taylor. The anomaly is stronger now."

Keeping stuff from her was not like Sinead. They were a team. "Why didn't you tell me? Why did I have to hear this from Thomas?"

"I forgot." Sinead picked up her basket again.

As explanations went, that one fell way short of ideal. "You forgot to tell me something this important?"

"I got distracted." Sinead's jaw firmed into a stubborn line. "And I haven't really felt it since."

"Haven't really or haven't at all." Alannah pushed. She hated the distance between them, but she couldn't bridge it. Sinead wanted her to push Thomas away, and that was something she couldn't do. Wouldn't do.

Sinead poked at her weaving. "Haven't really. It comes and goes."

Not sharing the information was crazy, and dangerous. The wards were their last line of defense. It took Alannah a moment to formulate her thoughts into polite words. "And you didn't tell me?"

"No, Alannah, I didn't tell you." Sinead looked up, anger blazing in her eyes. "I didn't tell you because every time I come near you to talk to you, that bloody ghost is hanging around."

And there it was. The truth laid bare between them. Alannah knew Sinead had an issue with Thomas, but the vehemence knocked her back. "Thomas is my friend."

"Your friend?" Sinead's expression hardened. "Don't lie to me, or yourself. There is nothing platonic about what you feel for that bloody ghost, and we both know it."

"Stop calling him a bloody ghost." Alannah's temper sparked.

Of the two of them, Sinead was the fiery one. What few people realized was that Alannah's temper, although a slow burn, was by far the higher flame when it did ignite. And it was simmering and spitting now like fat in a frying pan. "Just what is your problem with him anyway?"

"With him?" Sinead raised her eyebrow.

She knew Alannah hated that, and that's why she did it.

"I have no problem with him," Sinead said through gritted teeth. "What I have a problem with is you and him."

"There is no me and Thomas." And her statement was loaded with all the regret and pain and longing inside her.

"You say that." Sinead stood and tossed her basket to the ground. "But I don't think you really get that. In fact, I know you don't get that."

Alannah stood with her. Angry tears prickled, but she blinked them away. She didn't need Sinead rubbing her nose in the truth. "What's not to get. He's a ghost. There will never be a him and me. There will never be more than there is." She took a deep breath to catch her flyaway emotions. "And you should have told me about the wards. You should never have let your personal issues jeopardize the safety of this coven."

"Me?" Sinead's eyes widened. "You're saying that to me?" She rushed right on before Alannah could speak. "You're the one mooning around over something you can't have. You're the one who doesn't even work earth anymore but locks herself in that kitchen cooking meals for a man who will never fucking eat them!"

"Fuck you, Sinead. You're just scared he'll come between us." That her sister was right made the truth harder to swallow.

Sinead's eyes blazed. "You're right, I am. You and I are a team. We need to work as a team." She gesticulated the castle. "This coven needs us to work as a team."

"Funny how you bring that up now." Alannah stepped in and went toe to toe with her twin. "When you're the one who's withholding information."

"I can't talk to you." Sinead shook her head. "You've locked yourself away with a dead person."

That she knew her sister was bang on smarted. "That was just ugly, Sinead. I don't deserve your ugly."

And with that, she left before the threatening tears could escape. If they escaped, Alannah knew she'd be crying her river before she could stop herself, and she would be the one getting swept away in the deluge. There were no tears, or anger, or avoidance that could change her situation. She was in love with a ghost, and there would never be a happy ending for her.

---

SINEAD WATCHED Alannah stalk out of the room, waited about two seconds and followed. "Could we talk about this?"

"No." Alannah left a rage contrail in her wake.

"Ala—"

"No."

"We need to talk about this."

"No, we don't." Alannah whirled to face her. "What I need is for you to get out of my face and stay that way. You don't understand. You're not even trying to. Now, leave me alone before we both say things we can't take back."

Sinead let her go. Alannah didn't lose her temper often, but when she did, a wise woman took cover. A wise woman also went to the heart of the problem.

When they reached the great hall, Sinead turned right to the barracks as Alannah stormed off left to the kitchen.

Sinead almost flattened Warren in the passageway with the tapestries.

He leapt aside. "Blessed?"

"Coimhdeacht." Not an easy word to snap but a great one to growl.

"May I help you with something?" Warren called after her.

Sinead made like Alannah. "No." Then because she hated bad manners: "Thank you. No, thank you."

Alexander and Jack were playing cards at one of the four tables in the communal area of the barracks. They glanced up and froze.

"Good day, Sinead." Alexander put his cards on the table and stood. "Are you looking for someone?"

Her irritation and upset from her argument with Alannah ripped free. "A fucking ghost. I'm looking for a fucking ghost."

"She means that literally, doesn't she?" Jack glanced at Alexander.

Alexander grimaced. "I'm thinking that's a definite yes."

"Thomas." Sinead bellowed so loudly it echoed through the vaulted ceilings and ricocheted off the stone walls. "You get your arse out here and talk to me."

Jack flinched. "That's a good set of pipes she's got there."

They'd heard nothing yet. "THOOOMAAAS."

Thomas popped into being and bowed. "Blessed."

"You." Sinead jabbed a finger at him, in case her bellowing hadn't clued him in. "I need to talk to you."

"Certainly." He bowed again and motioned her to precede him down the hall toward the sleeping chambers. "Unless you require an audience for this conversation."

Sucking in deep breaths for calm, Sinead only shook her head and marched down the passage. She went past the sleeping chamber Roderick didn't use, and the one Alexander never slept in. On the opposite side, two doors opened into Warren and Jack's rooms, respectively. Next was what she needed. An empty room.

Except there were a pair of pressed khakis lying on the bed and a pale blue button down draped over the wooden chair at the desk. A pair of glasses sat on the desk.

"Perhaps next door." Thomas motioned to the room.

She had bigger things on her mind than the room's occupant, however, and she brushed past Thomas to the next door on. Slamming the door behind them, she took childish pleasure in doing so through Thomas.

Bloody ghost didn't even wince but reformed his scattered molecules and perched with his hips against the desk. "I'm all ears."

"Leave my sister alone." Sinead didn't believe in dragging a thing out, so got right to the point.

Thomas raised his brows but didn't look surprised, so he must have been expecting something of this nature. "Isn't that for Alannah to tell me?"

Damn it! He had a point there, and Alannah was going to spit in her dinner for the next five years if she found out. Sinead did a mental ten count, and then went for another calming breath. When she spoke again, she had her voice more under control. "This thing—" she didn't have the right word and didn't want to give it the weight of calling it a relationship "—you have with Alannah has to end."

"Our friendship?" His handsome face was inscrutable, but those hazel eyes held a warning.

She chose to ignore the warning. He didn't scare her. "You know it's more than a friendship, so let's not piss around."

"As always, Blessed, your form of expression is refreshing." He lounged against the deck looking poised, sophisticated, and urbane.

She didn't give a shit what he thought of her language. "Alannah and I just had a fight."

He frowned.

"About you."

He looked genuinely apologetic as he said, "I'm sorry to hear that. I know how close you two are."

"Then stop doing what you're doing."

His frown deepened, and he sighed. "Look." He spread his palms in front of him. "I like you, Sinead, and I really don't want to add to your crappy day by getting into an argument with you. Can we not discuss this reasonably?"

If he'd come at her any other way, she'd have taken his head off. And she liked him too. When he wasn't flitting after Alannah.

"I love my sister." Her heart spasmed. "She's the most important person in the world to me."

Thomas's tone was gentle as he said, "I know that, and she feels the same about you."

"We hardly ever fight." As the anger drained, her hurt and upset flooded into the void left behind.

Thomas's face softened. "I am truly sorry to have been the cause."

"Yeah." He meant it as well, but what she had to say was too important to back off now. "I just want her to be happy."

"We want the same thing." He shrugged, but he looked sad now.

"And do you really think that's you?" She didn't believe in hanging a person on their reputation, but Alannah meant too much to her. "You didn't have the best reputation when you were flesh and bone."

Thomas winced. "I'm not that man anymore."

"Aren't you?"

"I'm not dallying with Alannah." His hazel eyes met hers.

She saw the truth reflected in them, which made what she had to say even worse. "It doesn't matter, in the end, though, does it?" She believed in plain speaking, but that didn't mean hurtful words, and she hated that hers had to be. "You can't be what she needs."

Thomas looked down at his feet. His form flickered, going transparent and then strengthened. "I love her."

"Then I'm as sad for you as I am for her." Sinead wanted to cry for the two of them. "Because I'm fairly sure she loves you too."

He shoved his hands in his pockets and nodded. "There have been no words. I mean, we've never said…"

"Does it change anything?" Goddess, she would give anything not to have her sister cursed by a love she could never have.

Thomas shook his head.

"And if you really do love her, you'll let her go," she said, her voice barely above a whisper. She was an absolute shit to kick him when he was down, but someone had to call their relationship for what it was, and what it wasn't. "Because there's nothing between you two but a whole fucking raft of heartache."

# CHAPTER NINETEEN

Andy entered the library, laptop tucked under his arm, and retreated. Niamh was sitting there with Taylor, and they were chatting in a way that suggested they didn't want to be disturbed. Alexander and Warren were playing cards in the barracks, and Alannah was banging pots in the kitchen. Now, he couldn't claim to be a man sensitive to women's feelings, but the way Alannah was rattling the cookware gave him pause to reconsider bothering her.

He needed a quiet place to gather his thoughts and put some ideas together. The great hall was devoid of furniture, and he had not yet dared go up the stairs to the sleeping quarters. He had a fair notion Roderick, Alexander, or Warren would object.

A door on the other side of the stained-glass window from the barracks entrance stopped him. It was a fairly unremarkable door, large and wooden like all of Baile's doors, but he'd not noticed it before. In the handful of days he'd been in the castle, he'd done a lot of exploring and an exhaustive study of the great hall. The door had not been there before. A feeling of rightness tingled through him, and he made for the door.

Light and warmth greeted him as he opened the door, and

he stood a moment to appreciate the room. It was a roughly octagonal shape, like it formed the base of one of the towers. Sparkling windows on four sides of the octagon revealed a breathtaking view of the sea. Another wall held a fireplace, and the others, neat rows of shelves. A section of the shelving was separated into compartments jammed with scrolls.

A massive dark wood desk faced the view. Andy suspected walnut. Behind the desk, a high-back, dark-green leather chair perched like a throne.

"Oh my." Andy put his laptop on the edge of the desk. "This is rather lovely."

The quiet, warm satisfaction coming from Baile radiated through him. He didn't find it odd in the least. In fact, he rather enjoyed the sensation. "Is this for me?"

Fire crackled to life in the hearth. A large landscape that looked familiar hung over the dark wood mantel. It bore a strong similarity to the Constable landscapes he'd seen in the National Gallery. Two wingback chairs, the same leather as the desk chair, sat cozily side by side in front of the cheerful blaze.

Moving slowly, because one really wouldn't want to anger a castle, Andy approached the desk chair and sat. The desk patina gleamed like it had recently been polished and smelled deliciously of beeswax.

Andy did appreciate a desk with heft to it. The chair cradled him as if it had been made for him. Leather cushions provided the perfect amount of support and padding.

"This is a glorious place to work." He admired the delicate work of the oriental rug in front of his desk. "And the colors are marvelous."

Pulling his laptop closer, he opened it up.

No networks to connect to.

"Hmm." He stared at his laptop before looking up. "My lady, if I might trouble you further." He pointed to his screen. "An internet connection is rather imperative to my work."

In his teens, he'd been a bit of an internet maverick. He despised the term hacker. It implied a deplorable lack of skill and finesse.

The network bar loaded to full signal and Andy bowed again. "Thank you, my lady. You have been most generous." He bent to his work and stopped. "I am assuming this is a secure connection?"

He jumped as scrolls tumbled out of their cubbies to the floor.

Andy stood and bowed deep. "I most humbly beg your forgiveness, my lady. To have questioned your wherewithal was unconscionably rude and maladroit."

To demonstrate the depth of his contrition, he stood and picked up the fallen scrolls. The spidery writing on the outside of the first one caught his attention.

"Assets?" He placed that on the desk. The next one read household expenses.

Andy blew a kiss to Baile. "And even in this, you have given me what I needed."

---

Mags peeked around the doorjamb. She'd never been in this room before, never even noticed it. But Baile did that. She opened and closed literal doors as the castle inhabitants needed them.

Andy was tap-tap-tapping at a laptop. Scrolls lined the left of his desk like good little soldiers. Three piles of precisely stacked ledgers perched to his right.

"Hello." She spoke softly, not wanting to startle him.

Andy looked up. "Ah, Mags, isn't it?"

"Yes." She walked further into the room and stopped to admire the view. "This is lovely."

Andy beamed. "Isn't it?"

"I need to read your cards." She got down to the reason for her visit.

Raising his brows, Andy smiled politely. "I beg your pardon?"

"Your cards." Mags raised the tarot deck in her hand for him to see. "I need to read them."

She could have done it without the cards, but the man seemed a bit skittish.

"That is a most generous offer." Andy's smile stayed plastered to his face, but his gaze slid away from hers. "But I am a trifle engaged right now."

"I'm sorry." And she really didn't want to interrupt him, but he had to do what he had to do, and she had to do what she had to do. "But this can't wait."

"Really?" He tilted his head.

She shrugged. "Really."

"Right." Andy stood and snapped his khaki trousers back into their crisp creases. He motioned the two chairs by the hearth. "Perhaps you would care for a seat whilst you do?"

"Lovely." Mags took the chair facing the view.

And wow! Baile had rolled it out for Andy. The room and the view were a wall-to-wall welcome carpet. The setting sun had turned the sea to molten gold and limned the puffball clouds in silver.

She placed the cards on the table between the chairs and said, "You have to shuffle them."

That much, she'd seen on telly.

"I see." Andy took the deck like it might grow fangs and shuffled them, inverted the deck, and cascaded them like a card sharp. Clearly, he had hidden talents.

Mags held her hand out and retrieved the deck. She flipped the top one over. A male figure sat on a kind of throne with a short staff in one hand and the other hand raised. He looked vaguely religious.

"Ah." She peered at the card. "The meaning is clear."

Andy leaned closer and stared at the card.

"This is the…er…bishop!" Inspiration struck, and she grinned at Andy. "And it means you have the blessing of higher powers."

Andy frowned. "Forgive my presumption." He tapped the card. "But is that not, in fact, the hierophant?"

Bugger! Mags didn't know tarot from tapioca. She slapped a superior look on her face. "Are you doing this reading?"

"I beg your pardon." Andy sat back again.

She flipped the next card. It looked like a joker juggling two pentacles.

"So…hmm…interesting." She leaned over the card.

Andy whispered, "Two of pentacles."

"You know tarot?" Her stomach sank.

Andy made an apologetic face. "I'm a geek. I spend a lot of time watching fantasy movies and going down internet rabbit holes."

"Right." She gathered up the cards and handed them to him. "Then these will do better with you."

Andy took the deck and frowned. "No reading then?"

"Well, no." Her cheeks heated, and she locked her gaze on the view. "I don't read tarot. But I do need to tell you something."

"What?" Andy sat up straighter.

"You belong here." Mags didn't see the point in any more pretend. "Your soul is connected to Baile, and this is not the first time you've been here."

Andy gaped at her. He sat back and then leaned forward. "Eh?"

"Your connection to Baile." Mags indicated the walls around them. "It runs deeper than this lifetime. You have been here before. In other forms, of course."

"Of course." Andy paled. "Are you sure?"

"Oh yes." The ground firmed beneath Mags. "I brought the tarot because I was trying not to freak you out, but I see things."

"Things?"

"The present, the past." She took a pause before hitting him with the big banana. "The future, too."

"Ah." It came out like he'd been strangled. "Are you quite certain?"

"Yes."

He sat back and stared at the tarot deck in his hand. "Oh my."

"You have a place here. Your soul has searched for its place here before and been turned away, but in this lifetime, you are exactly where and who you should be, to do what you need to do."

"Right." Andy nodded and swallowed. "I'd best get on with it then."

## CHAPTER TWENTY

**D***rip!* It was the dream again. Mags breathed deep. Only a dream, and it couldn't hurt her; it could only frighten her. She knew this dream. Except, it was different in some way. She scanned the familiar stone walls surrounding her. Were they darker, more shadowy?

*Drip! Drip!*

The blood part had come too soon, and the walls were different. They were glistening. Her horror pierced the dream. The walls ran thick with blood. The red overtook the gray in a flood and gushed across the floor toward her.

*No! No! No!*

The blood clung to her like it had tiny tentacles. It climbed to her knees.

The part of her that knew she was dreaming separated from her physical body. She saw herself lying on her bed, moonlight glowing on the white of her nightie. Her physical body writhed, her legs tangling in the sheets. Her spirit was still trapped in the dream.

Blood lapped at her thighs.

It was just a dream, just a dream. She screamed at her physical self to wake up and end the dream.

A face coalesced in the blood. His features at first indistinct and then becoming clear.

Alexander. Except his eyes were dull and flat. A tiny air bubble escaped one nostril and burst on the blood's surface.

Dear Goddess. The blood had reached her waist. She tried to run through it and escape, but it weighed her down.

Her body on the bed refused to wake up. Her legs scissored, her back arched as she contorted herself to escape.

Alexander's face sank beneath the blood.

She lurched for him, plunging her hands in the tepid, clinging blood to get to him. The silky strands of his hair snagged on her fingers, and she grabbed for him. His hair unraveled and disintegrated in her hold. And then his face.

The blood reached her breasts, and still she could not wake.

She screamed the first name that came to her mind. *Jack!*

On the bed, her mouth opened and formed his name, but no sound came out.

Blood lapped at her collar bones.

*Jack*, she screamed in her mind. *Jack!*

---

JACK WOKE with a start and jerked up in bed. His mass moved before he'd formed the thought to do so. He bolted down the passageway.

A door opened, and Taylor stood in the doorway. "Hurry." She hugged her body and sobbed. "Please hurry, Jack."

Taking the stairs three at a time, he sprinted to Mags's room.

He didn't understand the why, only the imperative drumming through him to get to her.

Bursting through the door he leaped on the bed beside her.

Her spine was arched, her fingers clawing at the sheets. Her eyes were open but vacant, and her mouth opened and closed as if she were trying to say something.

"Mags." He shook her. "Magdalene."

Her legs flailed, and she made choking noises.

"Magdalene. Sweetheart, you have to wake up." He grabbed her shoulders and raised them off the bed. "Wake up for me. Wake up, dammit."

"Keep talking to her." Taylor stood in the doorway, a small wraith in shortie pjs, the female wolf by her side. "Your voice will pull her out."

"Mags." Jack folded her against his chest, trying to warm her cold, clammy skin. "Sweetheart, you've got to listen to me. Hear me now and wake up."

"She's lost." Taylor dropped to her knees and wrapped her arms around the wolf's neck. "Keep talking, Jack. She wants to come back."

Dear Jesus, he'd deal with what was happening to Warren's girl later.

"Sweetheart." His mind emptied, and he couldn't think of words. "Jesus, Magdalene, you're scaring the shit out of me right now. You need to come back to me. Anything you want, Mags. Anything damn fu—blasted thing you want, my sweet girl, but you've got to come back."

His mouth moved, words came out, but he had no idea what he was saying.

He pried her hands off the sheets and wrapped them into his embrace.

"Taylor?" Warren spoke from the doorway. "What are you doing here?"

Jack kept on talking, holding, rocking, fucking praying to whoever and whatever could hear him.

Taylor responded to Warren as if from a distance. "It's Mags, Daddy. She's trapped and she can't get out."

"I don't understand," Warren's voice was rough with concern.

"Get Bronwyn," Jack snapped over his shoulder. And then he went right back to word spewing. He fought against his own desperation. He wasn't getting through to her. He had to get through to her. It didn't end like this, before it had even begun. It didn't end before he got the chance to discover what the thing between them was. It for sodding sure didn't end with him losing Mags.

"Please, Magdalene, sweetheart." He pressed his lips to her head and pulled her into his lap. "I need you here. With me."

Mags stiffened in his arms and gasped. She blinked and focused on his face. "Jack." She scrambled to put her arms around his neck and wept. "Jack."

"Jack." Someone touched his arm. "It's Bronwyn."

He couldn't let Mags go. Managing to raise his head he said, "I couldn't reach her."

"But you did reach her." Bronwyn's big green eyes radiated quiet assurance. "Can I check her?"

His arms tightened reflexively around Mags. Her tears trickled down his neck to his bare chest. Only then did he realize he was only wearing boxers.

"Mate." Warren's hard, warm hand hit his shoulder. "We've got her now. Let Bronwyn take a look and see if she can help."

He tucked his head close to Mags. "Mags?"

Nodding, she squeezed him tight and then uncoiled her arms.

"Bronwyn is here." He didn't know how much she was tracking. "She wants to see if she can help you."

Mags drew a shuddering breath. She felt fragile as a snowflake in his arms. He wanted to bare his teeth and snarl at the world to get back. He needed to keep her safe.

Roderick perched on the bed on the other side of Mags. "I

know." His gaze met Jack's. "Last thing you want to do right now is take your arms away from her."

Jack read a world of understanding in that steady gaze.

"She's yours to shelter, yours to shield."

"I couldn't get to her," he rasped, his throat asphalt-dry.

Roderick nodded. "I understand." He put one hand out and touched Jack's where it was tucked around Mags's torso. "But nobody is going to hurt her here. We're going to make sure she's okay. Try to stop this from happening again."

It took everything in him to let Roderick unfold his hand, and then his arm from Mags, but he kept her in his lap.

All the time Roderick kept their gazes locked, and Jack knew that he knew the torture of letting go that which he'd almost lost.

"It's okay." Mags raised her head.

She looked like hell. Snarled hair stuck to the sweat and tears on her cheeks, and her face was translucently pale in the dim light.

"Here." Roderick put a flask in Jack's free hand.

Mags shifted away from him, and Jack wanted to close the distance, but the room details wove into focus.

Maeve huddled between Sinead and Alannah, their arms intertwined.

Niamh sat on the floor beside the wolf, a frightened Taylor clinging to both of them.

Warren hovered over Roderick's shoulder.

Beside him, Bronwyn sat on the bed with Alexander standing at her side.

"Hey, Magsie." Bronwyn inched closer. "Can you give me your hand?"

Mags held a shaking hand out to Bronwyn.

"There you go." Bronwyn took Mags's hand. The smell of honey and then the more earthy bite of sage surrounded them.

A soft blue glow emanated from where Bronwyn held Mags's hand.

"She's using her blessing," Alexander said. "She'll let her healing magic flow into Mags and see if it can find the problem."

Jack kept his attention on Bronwyn's face.

She closed her eyes and the blue glow brightened.

Nobody moved or spoke; they all watched Bronwyn.

In his arms, Mags's skin warmed, and her rigid muscles relaxed. Her breathing slowed.

"There." Bronwyn opened her eyes. "That should do it."

"What happened?" Jack raised the flask and took a gulp. Fiery malt burned down his throat and hit his gut like an anvil. He wheezed out a breath that must have been one-hundred proof. "Where did she go?"

Bronwyn frowned and swayed as she got to her feet. "I'm not exactly sure how to describe it."

"Steady now, little witch." Alexander snagged her around the waist and balanced her weight. "You need to transmute whatever the hell that was."

"I will." She patted his hands. "But let me talk to Mags and Jack first."

"You've got two minutes," Alexander near-enough snarled. "Speak quickly."

"The best way I can describe what I found was like the wires got tangled in her brain. The messages from her temporal lobe were getting tangled with her basic life functions in her hindbrain. I routed things back to where they should be going."

Jack didn't understand much beyond shit had got tangled in her head. "Will it happen again?"

"I can't say." Bronwyn's face fell. "I'm not really sure how it happened in the first place, but I can do some research and have another look at Mags."

"In the morning." Alexander moved her toward the door. "Right now, you need to transmute that crap and get some rest."

"But—"

"I'm okay now," Mags whispered. "I feel better than I have in days." She rubbed her temple. "Things seem clearer in here."

Bronwyn dug her heels in. "Are you sure, because I can stay—"

"I'll stay with Mags," Jack said. Like they could get him out of here without an excavator. He tucked her head beneath his chin, drawing comfort from the soft tickle of her breath against his neck. "I'll come and get you if I'm worried."

Mags looked toward the door. "Is Taylor okay?"

"She's sleeping," Niamh whispered. "She dropped off when Bronwyn was treating you."

Warren looked down at his daughter and frowned. "What the hell was she doing here?"

"She felt me," Mags said. "She felt what was happening to me and was on her way to get Jack."

"Which explains exactly nothing." Warren scrubbed his jaw with his palm. "Christ, shit gets fucked up fast around here."

The wolf bared her fangs at him.

"Yeah, I know." Warren dropped his hand and sighed. "I'm just worried about her is all. I don't mean anything by it."

The wolf nudged his hand.

"I better get her to bed." Carefully, Warren scooped Taylor into his arms.

Niamh rose and put her hand on his arm. "We'll talk to her when she's awake. We'll get the answers."

Under Niamh's steady regard, Warren relaxed a bit and nodded. "Yeah."

"Good night, Magsie." Sinead leaned across the bed and squeezed Mags's shoulder. "You scared the shit out of all of us."

"I scared the pooh out of myself." Mags gave a shaky laugh.

Jack nearly lost it and started laughing. Who the hell said pooh? His Magdalene, that's who.

Sinead left with Alannah.

Roderick stood and motioned the flask. "Hang on to that. You might need it."

"There's no might about it." Jack took another swig. The whisky went down easier and curled like a cat at a fire in his belly.

"Call us if you need anything," Maeve said. "I'll check with the sisters past and see if they can shed any light."

Suddenly wrung out, Jack could only nod.

Maeve curled her arm around Roderick's waist, and they left together.

And Jack and Mags were alone.

She wriggled around in his lap and stared up at him. Those green eyes of hers were clear as a marble. "Thank you for hearing me. And thank you for coming to get me."

"Any time and every time, sweetheart." Needing the visceral comfort of touch, he smoothed a sticky hair strand away from her lovely face. "And I'm staying right here."

"In my bed?" Mags squeaked.

In her bed, under her bed, on top of her bed, so along as he was within arm's reach. He nodded. "I can stay on top of the covers."

She stared at her bed and wrinkled her nose. "That seems a bit silly."

He wasn't going to argue her away from that point. "Do you think you might be able to sleep."

"I don't know." She sighed. "But I do feel more peaceful than I have in days."

"Maybe we could just lie down?" He sure as fuck wasn't going to sleep. He'd stay up and watch her, wake her the hell up if she even twitched.

"Okay."

A lot of Mags untangling her long limbs from covers and nighties followed. A few elbows to his ribs and almost one of her knees to his danglers before she finally got herself settled against the pillow.

Jack settled the thick quilt over her. Then he slid into bed beside her.

She still felt way too far away, and Jack eased his arm behind her shoulders and settled her head against his chest. "Comfy?"

She nodded. Her hand rested on his ribs.

Jack closed his eyes and breathed her in. The jasmine and almond of her magic, underpinned by the tart lemony fragrance of her hair. He let his muscles relax and accept her nearness, opened himself to the warmth of her tucked in close. Only the worst kind of horndog would be getting ideas after the night they'd had.

Aaand he was officially the worst kind of horndog. Blood rushed into his groin as Jack junior green-lighted his thoughts. Jack junior would have to get the fuck over it.

"Jack?"

He couldn't quite manage syllables, so he settled for an affirmative grunt.

"Would you kiss me?"

Had Jack junior developed vocal cords, or was his inner horndog learning ventriloquism? "Huh?"

She shifted against his chest and looked up at him. "I asked if you would kiss me." Her cheek warmed against his chest, and she glanced away. "I mean, you don't have to, if you don't want to, but I need…"

Oh, he had exactly what she needed. Not that he was going to do anything but kiss her. But suddenly he needed a tactile reminder she was alive and still with him.

Shifting over her, he cupped her cheek with his palm and lowered his mouth to hers.

The first touch of her mouth zapped through him on a lightning bolt of sweet and hot. But he had enough higher brain function left to keep it light and gentle.

"More," she whispered as their mouths separated. Her lids fluttered closed.

Jack wrestled his baser self back under control. "Not tonight, Magdalene." He pressed a swift kiss to her full lips. "There'll be other nights. For more kissing and more…more."

Mags sighed and opened her eyes. "You really are a decent man, Jack."

She said it like she was not entirely sure that was a good thing.

# CHAPTER TWENTY-ONE

"Heya." Niamh appeared in Warren's bedroom doorway. Just the person he hadn't been aware of wanting to see, but now that she was here, his world brightened, and a weight lifted off his shoulders. He couldn't get Taylor's terror-stricken face from last night out of his mind. As her dad, he was supposed to protect her from bad things, not dump her right in harm's way.

He took the momentary distraction of Niamh's sensual sway of a walk. Niamh's lush curves and midnight-dark cat eyes could brighten a dead man's day. "Heya, yourself."

"I could sense you brooding from all the way on the other side of Baile." She took a seat on the bed next to him. This morning, her T-shirt read, Eat Pie, Kill Demons, and it drew a reluctant smile from him. A weasel clambered up her leg and burrowed under his pillow.

He'd been sitting on the edge of his bed since waking and getting dressed, trying to find a way to broach what had happened with Taylor last night with his daughter. Everything he'd come up with so far began with what the fuck and went downhill from there. Taylor was twelve years old, for fuck's sake. He could barely wrap his thinker around what went down around Baile, so how could a girl that age have any chance of understanding?

Niamh's hand pressed warm and all kinds of amazing on the center of his back. "I guess your big, bad, growly papa bear is in charge this morning."

Dammit, she was his kind of nutter, and he laughed. "Growly papa bear?"

"Uh-huh." She stroked his back. "Talk to me."

He made a face. "Talking's really not my thing."

"Really?" She widened her eyes, her almost too-full mouth breaking into a broad smile. "I would never have guessed."

"Smartass." Being around her made him feel like he could cope. "Her face is stuck in my bloody head."

"Taylor's?" She already knew the answer to that, could feel and see it through their bond, but she was prodding him to get on with the yakkity-yak.

Then he named his greatest fear. "She's a little girl, for fuck's sake. Bollocks like last night is going to drive her mental."

"I know she's young, but she has her dad's resilience and an entire coven to help her with what's happening."

Her stroking hand worked magic—*arf, arf*—on his jangling thoughts. "She shouldn't have to."

"No, she shouldn't." She lay her head against his shoulder.

He opened their bond wide to get the full wallop of her compassion and care for him. "I've been stuck here trying to think about what to say to her."

"You could go with the truth."

Like he had a sodding clue what that might be, but he'd lay money she was about to tell him. "Which is?"

"That you're concerned about her and frightened for her, that you want to protect her and make sure things like last night don't happen to her."

Right on the button. Him and her. "But I can't stop them from happening."

"No, you can't." She wrapped both arms around his waist and squeezed. "But let's keep the blame where it belongs." She whispered, "Rhiannon. None of this would be happening if she wasn't so set on destroying us and owning the world."

"Yeah, but as much as I'd like to—and I'd really, really like to—I can't pound on her until it makes me feel better."

"You'll get your chance." She nuzzled into his neck. "Unfortunately, you're going to have to get in line on the pounding."

Warren tried to tamp down the doubt worm chewing on his intestines. "That didn't go exactly as planned last time."

"She froze you." Niamh squeezed and didn't let up until he looked at her. "She froze all of us in that cavern. You, me, Lerato, Nofoto, and Ulwazi."

The old sangoma, Ulwazi had paid the greatest price that night when Rhiannon had killed her. And he'd been able to do fuck all about it. All Roderick's nattering about coimhdeacht being the mighty protectors, and special powers courtesy of Goddess, and he'd been bloody useless to his witch. A leopard had given her the minute gap to save herself.

Head cocked like one of her dogs', Niamh sat back and studied him. "You blame yourself for not being able to do anything."

Right here was one of the reasons he didn't favor gut spilling. It made you haul out all the dusty, dirty bollocks in the back of your brain box and give it the once-over. Living through it had been enough for him.

"Oh, Warren." She cradled his face with her palms. "You're not to blame for that night, Ulwazi's death, any of it. Every time we come up against that bitch, she whips out a new trick."

He'd love to go with that, really he would, but he wasn't built that way. Niamh had been his to protect, and Nofoto, Lerato, and Ulwazi by extension. Even worse, Rhiannon had found them because of him. He hadn't kept his dick in his pants and had had sex with Edana. She'd managed to plant a nifty tracking spell on him while his pants were, quite literally, down.

Niamh's expression softened as she read his thoughts.

Fucking hell! Warren slammed up his mind barriers, but it was already too late. Roderick was so much better at keeping his witch only to those thoughts, feelings, and activities he wanted her to access.

"You were wonderful." Niamh pulled his face closer and kissed him. "You did everything you could and more. You're the reason I'm still breathing."

And she was being kind. He should have done better, more. But the kissing thing, now that idea he was all onboard with.

"Are you two, like, having a moment or something?" Taylor asked.

Laughing, Niamh released him and faced his door. "Or something."

"You two should get a room." Taylor made a gagging noise.

"We have one," Warren said. "But you're in it."

Taylor shuddered and rolled her eyes. "You're so gross."

Warren searched his little girl's face, trying to clue in on how she was. She looked the same as she always did, and he wished he could see below the surface. "I was just thinking about you."

"Snap!" Taylor clicked her fingers. "Because I was just thinking about you."

"Get over here." Niamh patted the bed between them. "We want to talk to you."

Warren liked that she used we and not him.

Taylor made a production of dragging herself over and tossing herself on the bed. "Is this about last night?"

"Yup." He only wished it was the kind of last night conversation normal Dads had with their twelve-year-olds about normal crap. At this rate, he'd take boys and periods. Strike the boys. Any little sod that came near his girl was as good as dead.

Niamh raised her brows at him over Taylor's head.

Yeah, he'd thought it, and he'd meant it too. "What happened to you?"

"Dad!" Taylor rolled her eyes so hard Warren worried they might get stuck that way. "I'm totally okay with what happened."

"Give your dad a break." Niamh nudged Taylor. "His growly papa bear is threatening a takeover."

"Okay." Taylor heaved the sigh of misunderstood and underestimated tweens the world over. "I got this bad feeling, like really bad." She scrunched her T-shirt over her chest. "And deep inside I knew something was wrong with Mags, that she was in danger."

Channeling Gary from his former anger management support group, he said, "How did that make you feel?"

"D'uh." A quarter eyeroll this time. "Scared." She batted her lashes at him and simpered. "And so I went to find a responsible adult to help me with it."

"And you chose Jack?" His mate was many things, but responsible adult, not so much.

"Jack was the only one who could help her." Taylor dropped the attitude. "I knew that too."

Niamh tilted her head. "How did you know that?"

"I don't know." Taylor shrugged. "I just knew."

By Niamh's expression, he guessed she was putting two and two together and would talk to him about it later.

"Anyway." Taylor gave the word a few extra syllables. "Can we get to my news now?"

"If you promise me that—"

"Da-a-ad!" The attitude came back. "If I start feeling freaked out, I'll tell you."

Niamh laughed. "What's your big news?"

"Internet!" Taylor did a little sitting happy dance. "Baile has internet."

Baile had started allowing the limited use of phones since they'd gotten back from South Africa.

"Full internet," Taylor said with emphasis. "Like high-speed internet."

Warren grappled with that. He didn't trust the internet. He also didn't trust those so-called smart phones. Smart phones, dumb sap using them and giving the world a way to keep tabs on them.

"Which means—" Taylor leaned into him "—I can FaceTime Mum."

His cup ranneth over. Debra being able to contact him and Taylor whenever she wanted. How lucky could one bastard get? He managed to say, "Great."

"You don't mean that." Taylor fixed him with a no-bullshit look. "But that's between you and Mum, and it doesn't involve me."

"Have you called her yet?" Niamh took the heat off him, and he wanted to kiss her for it.

He wanted to kiss her anyway.

"Yup." Taylor wriggled around to face Niamh. "I spoke to her earlier. Woke her and Adam up in the middle of the night." She made Adam sound like a venereal disease.

Part of the reason Taylor was with Warren now was because she and Adam didn't get on. Warren had met the man. He didn't seem like a bad sort, but Warren was more than happy to have Taylor with him. Of course, if things with Debra and Adam progressed the way they were heading, Taylor and Adam were going to have to find a way to coexist. Or Taylor could stay here with him. Like hell Debra was going to let that happen without a fight.

"How was she?" Warren didn't want Taylor getting the idea he and Debra couldn't play nice. Except that horse also seemed to have bolted. You couldn't hide much from kids.

Taylor thought before she answered. "She was…okay. I

dunno." She shrugged. "Once she woke up a bit, she was all super friendly and chatty." She glanced at him. "You know how she gets when she's trying to pretend everything's okay?"

Apparently, you could hide nothing from this kid, so he nodded.

"I don't think she's happy." Taylor's face fell. "So, I tried to cheer her up."

"How?" An uneasy feeling tightened his nape. He'd been on the receiving end of Taylor's nothing barred, cheerful chatter.

"I told her about the puppies and how cute they were. I even held one up for her to see."

His head throbbed. "Did you say they were dogs?"

"No." Taylor frowned. "Why would I say they were dogs?"

On cue, his phone buzzed on the nightstand.

Niamh stood and handed him the phone. She motioned to Taylor. "Let your dad get that."

Warren accepted the call. "Hello?"

"Warren." Debra might be halfway round the world, but her voice rang loud and true.

"Come on." Niamh took Taylor's hand. "I want to ask you a couple of things about how you knew about Mags."

Taylor frowned at him. "Is that Mum?"

He nodded.

"Warren." Debra's tone was strident. "We need to talk."

"Just a minute." He held the phone to his chest. "I'll catch up with you two later."

"She sounds angry." Taylor looked at Niamh. "Is it because of something I said?"

"No." Niamh even convinced him she sounded so sure of herself. "But if she wants to talk to your father, then we should give them some privacy."

Taylor looked at Niamh and sighed. "It's because of the wolves isn't it?"

"I don't know." Niamh edged her toward the door.

"Or maybe it's because I told her about meeting Goddess."

Niamh shut the door behind them with Taylor still talking.

Taking a deep breath, Warren returned the phone to his ear. "What's up?"

"Wolves, Warren, wolves?" Debra's voice went shrill. "You have my child near wolves. Have you lost your fu—"

"Okay, Debra." He breathed deep. He got where she was coming from. A few months ago, he'd have reacted exactly the same. "First off, our child. She's our child, and I would never put her in any danger. She means the world to me."

"But..." Debra sucked in a breath. "Explain."

Warren nearly checked the number. Debra had never given him room to explain before. Then again, if he could grow and change, so could she. And if she was giving him the benefit of the doubt, he could extend the same. "And they're not wolves." He prayed Goddess didn't have a lightning bolt handy for liars. "They're just big dogs."

"She called them wolves."

"Well." He steered as close to the truth as he could. "That's what we call them around here, because of the way they look. It's kind of a pet name thing."

"Oh." Silence reigned for a while. "That puppy she showed me looked a lot like a wolf."

"Yeah, doesn't it." He forced a relaxed chuckle. It wheezed out of him more like a whimper. "And that's why we call them wolves. But they're well trained and wouldn't hurt a fly."

"She likes dogs."

Warren's voice strengthened as he got back to being real. "She's really good with them. They follow her around."

"And the mother isn't protective?" Debra's tone sharpened again.

Not if you were a coven member, she wasn't. Warren didn't like an outsider's chance with the she-wolf. "Absolutely not.

They're almost weaned now, and she spends most of her day outside."

"Okay." Debra cleared her throat. "She's living in that castle with you?"

"Yup." He went with the story he, Roderick, and Alexander had concocted. "I'm a sort of handyman, and I help out with security."

Suspicion roared back as Debra asked, "Why do they need security? Is it dangerous?"

"No. It's just really old and tourists tend to wander in." And inside Baile wasn't dangerous at all. Outside the wards, though, different story. His head throbbed. As the newest and youngest cré-witch, Taylor had moved on to Rhiannon's hit list. He really didn't know how he was going to let Taylor leave Baile's wards. "It's a great place, Debra, you saw it, full of history—which she also loves—and with plenty of space for her to roam."

"That's good." Debra took a breath. "Taylor says you're seeing someone?"

"Yeah, it's new." Warren hated the half-truths and evasions, but those were the downsides to his new gig as coimhdeacht. He didn't know how Alexander had tap danced his way around the truth for hundreds of years. Although Alexander in a top hat and natty duds didn't take the imagination on too far a leap.

"Taylor likes her." A wistful note crept into Debra's voice. "If it's new, should you be introducing her to Taylor so soon? We agreed we wouldn't have a revolving door of people in our daughter's life."

Debra had more neck than a giraffe to comment on people coming in and out of Taylor's life, but he didn't want their conversation devolving into an argument. "It's new, but I'm serious about her. She's going to be around for a long time." The rest of his life, in fact.

"Wow." Debra's giggle was high and thin. "That happened fast."

"When you know, you know." Had that banality really come out of his mouth?

"True." Debra sighed. "I wish you well, Warren. I hope you're very happy."

That must have cost her an arm and a leg to get out. "I wish the same for you."

They sat in silence for a couple of breaths.

"Taylor is also chattering about magic," Debra said.

Warren's gut tightened. He didn't know how he was going to climb the magic mountain.

"I never mentioned this before because it was a phase," Debra said. "When she was younger, Taylor used to talk a lot about having magic." Debra laughed. "She used to tell all her friends she was a witch and had magical abilities."

"Really?" He hoped like hell the light at the tunnel end wasn't an oncoming train.

"She grew out of it." Debra chuckled. "But I had some uncomfortable conversations with teachers and other mothers, I can tell you."

"Right." Words jammed in his throat, and he cleared them. "How do you want to handle the magic thing?"

"I let her talk," Debra said. "It's a harmless fantasy, and as long as she doesn't decide to fly off roofs on a broomstick, I don't see any harm in it."

He forced himself to laugh with her. "I'll hide all the broomsticks."

"Good." Her voice grew serious, "Listen, while I've got you, there's something else I wanted to talk to you about. Ask you, really."

"I'm listening." This was probably the most amicable conversation he'd had with Debra in years. It was nice.

"It seems like I'm going to need to stay here for a bit longer." She cleared her throat.

Warren jumped right in, his heart giving a happy leap. "You need me to hang on to her?"

"Could you?"

"Fuck, yes." He didn't have to fake his enthusiasm. "I love having her with me."

"But listen, Warren." Debra got the tone that signaled she was going to bring the hammer down. "She's due to start school in a week. I've spoken to her teachers, and they say she can do her schooling online, but you need to make sure she does it."

He could handle that. "Got it. Do I need to speak to any of her teachers?"

"No, I've done that already. They'll send her stuff via email to her. I'll check in with them and make sure she's keeping up, but you need to make sure she does the work."

"I'm on it, Debra." Taylor staying longer meant he could defer his worry for a time. "How long do you think you'll be?"

"Why?" She snapped. "Is she crimping your new girlfriend's style?"

"No." He kept it calm and easy. "I just wanted some idea of how long I've got her for. It's a reasonable question, Deb, and has nothing to do with Niamh."

"Is that her name?"

"Yup."

Debra sighed. "You're right. It is a reasonable question. I should be home in three weeks."

"Right." Three weeks to find a solution to all of this. "I'm sure she'll be happy to see you."

"Yeah." Debra's voice got shaky. "I miss her. It's strange being here without her. I've never been away from her for this long."

Warren knew all about missing your kid when they weren't with you. "It must be." He wasn't sure what made him ask, but he went with it. "How are things going over there?"

"Fine," she snapped. She smoothed the edges off her tone as she continued, "Things are...fine."

"Really?"

"Do you care?"

"I do, actually." And surprisingly, it was the truth. Debra might be pricklier than a hedgehog and want to take a piece out of his hide every time they encountered each other, but she had been his wife, the woman he loved. And she always would be Taylor's mother.

"Things are...different," Debra said eventually. "I mean, they're fine, but not exactly as I expected them to be."

He risked his neck. "With Adam?"

"Adam's good," she said, but way too quickly. "Adam and I are good, but things didn't work out here as he expected. It's part of why I'll be delayed in coming back."

Warren waited to see if she'd give him more.

And she did. "The whole reason we came to Australia was because he had an opportunity here. A great opportunity. Much better than anything he could get in England."

"Uh-huh." Sinead had been coaching Roderick in active listening, and Warren had picked up a nugget or two.

"But when we got here, the job had gone to someone else."

"That must have been disappointing for both of you." Sinead would be proud.

"It was." Debra relaxed further. "Of course, Adam will find something else. He's very skilled at what he does. But in the meantime, we have a bit of a cash shortage."

He knew better than to offer to help. "I wish him the best with that."

"You do, don't you?" Debra sounded surprised, and he couldn't blame her.

"Of course I do," he said and meant it. "I want you to have the life you always wanted, Deb."

Debra went silent, and when she spoke, there was a wobble in her voice. "Thank you, Warren. So...I'll speak to you soon."

"Soon," he said. "And I'll keep Taylor at her schoolwork and let you know if there are any problems."

"Thank you." She took a breath. "It wasn't all bad between us, was it Warren?"

"No, Deb, some of it was really good."

# CHAPTER TWENTY-TWO

Maeve sat at the kitchen table and watched Roderick poke at something on his dinner plate with his fork. She leaned closer to him. "They're really tasty."

He frowned and speared one. Bringing it up to eye level, he glared at it. "But what is it?"

"A chickpea," Sinead said, winking at Maeve. "Eat it, big guy, they're good for you."

Alannah had made something she called a meatloaf pot roast. From what Maeve could see, the meatloaf part was the loaf-shaped piece of meat in the center of a tomato-based sauce. Strips of bacon lay across the top, and now she had a name for the nut-flavored little balls.

Jack was spooning fluffy mashed potatoes on his plate while Warren added green beans to Taylor's plate.

She didn't know why anyone would want to make a loaf of meat, but the burst of flavors that came from the dish persuaded her it was a good idea.

Roderick transferred the chickpea to his mouth as if he was waiting for it to explode. He chewed, swallowed, and pulled a face. "It tastes like chalk."

"Not ready for hummus then, I'm guessing," Sinead said.

The modern dinner table occupants all laughed at that one.

Maeve decided she probably wasn't ready for hummus either. "Put the sauce on them." She nudged Roderick. "It's lovely."

"Thank you, Maeve." Alannah smiled at her, but the smile was a lightbulb to the bright sun of Alannah's normal smile. She'd been quiet the last couple of days, as if something had extinguished her joy.

Thomas had been scarce for the same amount of time, and Maeve suppressed a sigh. She ached for the two of them. The Thomas she'd known from the time before this had been a different man, free with his favors and a great coven favorite with the witches. Thomas in this time, Alannah's Thomas, was a man—or the specter of a man—deeply in love.

Beneath the table, Roderick pressed his thigh to hers in a gesture of comfort. Their deeper level of connection meant he knew what was bothering her sometimes before she even did. She leaned closer to him. "Eat your chickpeas."

And he did, because he knew she was worried about Alannah, and that if eating chickpeas made Alannah happy, he'd eat a crate of the things.

"Ah, good." The slender man who followed Roderick around strode into the kitchen.

Andy! That was his name.

He pulled out the chair beside Sinead and wedged himself between her and Alexander. "I'm glad you're all here."

Roderick stopped with his fork halfway to his mouth.

Warren stared.

Everybody stared, come to that, and silence fell over the kitchen.

Andy helped himself to dinner before resuming his seat. Oblivious to all the attention, he forked up a mouthful of potatoes and meatloaf, chewed, closed his eyes, and sighed.

"Superlative, as always." He tipped his head at Alannah. "My compliments to the chef."

With a ghost of a smile, Alannah inclined her head back at him. "Thank you."

Chuckling, Alexander shook his head and resumed his dinner.

"Is there a reason you're here?" Warren glowered at Andy.

Andy glanced at his plate. "It is dinnertime, right?"

"Right." Alexander pushed a bowl closer. "Green beans?"

"Lovely." Andy beamed and spooned beans on his plate. "I always try to eat something green with every meal."

Roderick scowled.

Pale, but calm, Mags looked at Roderick. "It's all right. He needs to be here."

Jack watched Andy as he ate, his gaze not entirely friendly. Jack might not be Mags's coimhdeacht, but he protected her like he was. And Goddess knew, Mags needed protecting. Maeve pushed the image from the other night out of her mind. The witches past had been no help as to why Mags had been caught in her nightmare, but they were clear on the warning: Mags was in danger.

Roderick snapped his mouth shut and went back to eating. He never argued with the coven seer, but Maeve could sense his annoyance through the bond, and the speed his fork was making the return journey from mouth to plate told the same story. He wanted to know why Andy needed to be here.

Maeve would rather like to know herself. "Have you been here all day?"

"Indeed." Andy nodded and chewed. He dabbed his mouth with his napkin. "I have been here for a few days now." He shook his head. "The amount of work is staggering."

Dark eyes alive with mischief, Alexander leaned back in his chair. "What's been keeping you so busy?"

"I'm glad you asked." Andy pushed his plate away.

Maeve blinked at it. Not even Roderick could put away food that fast.

Leaning to the side, Andy snagged a leather binder from beside his chair. "Now would be an excellent time to convene a meeting."

She sensed the protest rising in Roderick and pressed her thigh into his.

Andy took a sheet of paper out of the binder. "Now, I've done an exhaustive study of the assets of the castle and the coven."

"You did what now?" Sinead leaned forward. "You can't have. We have bank accounts you know nothing about."

Flushing, Andy tapped the sheet. "I believe you will find I have been most thorough." He shook his head. "Banks are horribly lax with cyber security. It took me exactly forty-seven seconds to gain access to your accounts."

Alannah dropped her fork and gasped.

"You hacked our accounts?" Sinead yelled.

Maeve wasn't precisely sure what hacking entailed in this instance, but she got from the modern witch's expressions that it was a bad thing.

"Now, your problem is a thorny one." Andy continued as if impervious to the outrage simmering around him.

Maeve wanted to laugh but kept her lips jammed together.

"In a nutshell, you are asset-rich and cash poor. The bulk of your assets rest within the land surrounding Baile, and the castle itself. The contents of the castle are also quite extraordinarily valuable." He looked wistful. "The art alone, assuming it's all genuine, is astonishing."

Roderick growled. "It's all genuine."

"I thought as much." Andy recovered from his reverie. "It stands to reason that these treasures would have been collected over the duration of many lifetimes." He shrugged. "Of course, at the time of purchase they would have had nowhere near their current value."

"Un-fucking-believable." Sinead stood and cleared plates.

"Not at all," Andy said as he handed her his empty plate. "Many of the masters in your collection would not have been considered that in the time in which they worked."

Sinead looked at Roderick. "Can't you make him disappear."

"Apparently not." Roderick threw Mags a disgruntled look.

"You don't want to do that," Andy said to Sinead.

Warren took the bait. "Why not?"

"You need me." Andy spread his hands palms up, as if his statement was self-evident. "You cannot continue to operate successfully without somebody keeping the engine running." He nodded at Roderick. "So to speak."

"You mentioned a thorny problem." Looking thoroughly delighted by the conversation, Alexander draped his arm over Bronwyn's chair back. "Pray, continue."

"Thank you." Andy consulted his papers. "Now, I have totaled your present assets at current market value." He tapped the sheet. "I have also tallied your operating expenses, to the best of my ability. I am happy to go into detail if you'd care for it."

"Er…no." Warren looked sick. "We'll take your word for it."

Andy pursed his lips. "You really should check my figures. For all you know, I could be a complete charlatan."

"Yeah," Jack rumbled. "You could be. But that wouldn't end well for you."

"Quite right." Andy nodded.

Alannah brought a golden-brown pie to the table.

"Is that apple?" Andy pointed.

"Triple berry," Alannah said and added a second pie. "The fresh berries are lovely at the moment."

"Oh perfect." Andy rubbed his hands together and then said to the table at large, "I'm not a great one for apple pie. But berries are my favorite. I believe it's the tartness contrasting with the sweetness of the pastry."

"Good to know," Alexander murmured.

Sinead thunked a tub of ice cream on the table. "You were saying?"

"Ah, yes." Andy watched Alannah like a hawk as she cut and doled out pie servings. "Of course, you're all aware of the issue of the property taxes in addition to operating expenses."

Roderick grumbled. He wasn't taking well to the idea of Baile being taxed.

"So, the issue is this." Andy perked up as Alannah offered him a plate of pie. "Although your assets more than cover the debt, they're not liquid, and given the...ahem...more clandestine nature of your enterprise, liquidating those assets could present more problems than it solves."

He helped himself to ice cream before continuing. "So, our first priority must be to generate income. In large quantities." After taking a huge bite of his dessert, he stopped. Then sighed. "Sublime."

"When you say generating income—" Sinead jabbed at him with her fork "—you mean make money?"

Andy beamed at her. "Precisely. I thought a good jump-off point for our discussion on how to generate income would be to look at everyone's marketable skills."

"What the fuck is he talking about?" Roderick turned to Warren.

Warren tried to hide a grin. "What each of us can do to make money."

"I'm assuming that your...er...skills do not extend to poofing some cash into existence." Andy scraped his plate and looked at it mournfully.

Sinead grabbed his plate and plopped a second slice on it. "He'll never get to the point if he keeps pining after pie."

"I really shouldn't." Andy tittered and dived into his dessert.

"We had the wands," Sinead said.

Andy looked at her questioningly.

"They're Harry Potter wands," Alannah said. "We can imbue them with a little magic, and they make pretty sparks."

Maeve had read all the Harry Potter books, and she'd loved them. Not that she would tell Sinead as much.

"Uh-huh." Andy looked encouraged. "Cost to make?"

"Zero." Sinead crossed her arms, the Harry Potter wands still a sore subject with her. "The wood comes from Baile, and the magic is ours."

Andy's eyes sparkled. "Price?"

"We sell them for a fiver at the local market."

Stopping eating for long enough to dig out his smart phone, Andy tapped at the screen and then frowned. "Harry Potter wands retail on Etsy for twenty pounds. We should be charging at least ten to fifteen pounds."

"Oh no." Alannah's eyes widened. "That's too expensive, and the children won't be able to afford them. They do so love to come to our stall and swish them around."

Andy gaped at her.

"When they're a fiver, they don't have to ask their parents," Alannah said.

"How many can you make?" Andy turned to Sinead.

"Ten, twelve."

"Thousand?" Andy straightened in his chair.

"A day." Sinead glowered at him. "Ten to twelve a day."

"Ah." He deflated and looked mournful. "Well, that is lovely." He glanced at Alannah. "And I'm sure the children love them. I was...er...thinking larger scale."

"I make lotions and creams and things," Bronwyn said. "But nowhere near the quantity you want."

"Also lovely." Andy surged forward, his smile looking a bit pasted on. "But cosmetics...tricky market. Hard to break into."

"I can read tarot," Mags said.

Andy looked at her.

She giggled. "Kind of."

"Your gift is not for sale." Roderick pounded the table. "This entire fucking conversation is obscene."

"Hey!" Sinead pointed a finger at him. "Settle down. Unless you have any bright ideas for making money. Maybe we can sell off that overload of testosterone you're sporting."

"We could start a clinic." Bronwyn brightened. "One of those high-end spa-type things."

"At Baile!" Warren, Alexander, and Roderick all thundered at once.

"Well, it could work. I mean we'd have to screen—"

Andy held up a hand. "Huge outlay required." He winced. "Massive and, of course, the security concerns."

How much did Andy know about Baile and the coven? Maeve was guessing nearly everything.

"Ghost tours!" Taylor piped up. "We could run ghost tours of the caverns. Maeve could summon up the dead witches and they could, like, flit about and stuff."

Maeve strongly suspected Roderick was about to have an apoplexy. Placing a restraining hand on his arm, she said to Taylor. "They don't really work like that."

"Thomas flits." Taylor glanced around her. "Where is Thomas?"

Alannah shot a look at Sinead over the table and Maeve's gut tightened. You didn't need Mags's foresight to see that storm coming.

"No." Andy rapped the table. He made a circular wrist motion. "Let's circle round to all these ideas later. Whilst you are all remarkable, quite remarkable, I do think we need to focus on the large scale." He smiled at all of them. "I thank you all for your contribution and encourage you to continue thinking in this vein whilst I apply the old gray matter to the issue."

"Global." Taylor nodded at him. "We need to think global."

"Exactly!" He aimed his thumb and forefinger at her and fired.

Roderick rose with a chair screech. "Nobody is selling the gifts Goddess granted them. I'll break your collective necks before I allow that."

Oh dear! Maeve waited until he'd stormed out. "He doesn't mean that."

"Then he shouldn't say it," Taylor said.

Warren jerked his head toward his daughter. "What she said."

"It's this time." Maeve stood and prepared to follow her grouchy coimhdeacht. "He tries, but it's so very different."

"It's not so different." Alexander rubbed his chin. "Nothing for nothing, and death and taxes are the only sure things."

---

THE ADULTS WERE STILL CHATTING in the kitchen, and Taylor was bored. They kept arguing and arguing in circles and nobody was listening to anyone else. Really, she wanted to bang all their heads together, or stand on the table and scream at them to grow up.

She walked into the library to find something to read. The library reminded her of the one in *Beauty and the Beast*, and she liked the quiet, peaceful atmosphere.

A fox sat on the desk Niamh normally used, but it was more what the fox was sitting on that drew her attention.

As Taylor drew nearer, the fox stood and moved to the side of a large, yellowish envelope, the sort you got through snail mail. Her blessing surrounded her in a waft of coriander and apple. Prickles ran beneath her skin. She needed to do something with that envelope. The something was tied to Mags.

Taylor picked it up. There was no address on the outside,

and it was sealed. She squeezed the envelope and identified two smallish rectangular shapes.

The fox blinked at her, and for a second, she was sure it nodded.

Apple and coriander scents got stronger, and an image bloomed in her mind.

The envelope belonged in Jack's bike. She didn't know how she knew that, or why, but she left the library with it tucked under her arm. Not wanting to go through the argument still raging in the kitchen, she left through the main door.

Jack's bike stood beside her dad's, to the left of the kitchen door.

Taylor opened one of the storage compartments and slipped the envelope inside.

She knew she'd done the right thing. It didn't matter why.

# CHAPTER TWENTY-THREE

"Mags?" Jack's voice sounded in Mags's dream. "Magdalene."

The dream bifurcated, and one part of her was aware of her lying in her room in Baile. She was alone because Jack had stayed with her through the night and left early this morning to workout in the barracks. He'd spent every night since her episode sleeping beside her. As nothing had happened for three nights, he'd risked leaving her alone for a short while this morning. He'd kissed her forehead before he left. "Don't go anywhere, Magdalene."

Other than the chaste kiss on her cheek or forehead, there'd been no more of the good sort of kissing. The dream was lovely and inviting. In it, she stood by her window and her gaze was drawn to the forest.

"*Mags.*"

Jack waited for her in the dream forest. Excitement tingled through her. Even if it was only in her mind, the possibilities of her and Jack—alone—in the forest, made her heart beat faster.

Her corporeal form was still tucked up in bed, the covers snug to her chin.

Her dream self wanted to go to him.

"*Get dressed, Mags,*" Jack whispered. "*It's chilly out.*"

Dream Jack looked out for her like real Jack did.

She pulled on yesterday's caftan and a pair of shoes. To make him happy, she added a cardigan and left her room.

A strange hazy quality filled Baile's hallways as she trod through them. Cool air made her grateful for the cardigan.

"*Come, Mags.*"

"*I'm coming.*" She laughed at his impatience. Jack had a playful side very few people saw.

The kitchen was quiet as she entered. A residual heat rose from the banked coals in the cooking range. The she-wolf got to her feet and growled.

"It's okay," she whispered. "I'm going to meet Jack."

The wolf bared her teeth and tugged at Mags's cardigan with her teeth.

"*Hurry, Mags,*" Jack called. "*Before everyone else wakes up.*"

"Let go," she whispered at the wolf and pulled her cardigan out her mouth. "Go back to your pups."

The wolf wove in front of her and snarled.

"No." Mags tried to use a firm voice, but the animal was intimidating.

"*Grab the keys to the Landrover,*" Jack said.

He was only in the forest. "*Why?*"

"*I'm not really in the forest.*" Jack chuckled. "*That's why you have to hurry. Roderick won't like us being outside the wards. I want to show you something.*"

That was odd, and her mind veered back to her room.

Was the bed empty? She couldn't get a lock on her corporeal self.

"*Come on.*" Jack sounded impatient. "*We'll be back before they even know we're gone.*"

"I'll be right back," she said to the wolf, and ducked around it. After snagging the Landy keys, she closed the kitchen door on the snarling animal and climbed into the Landy.

Doubt wormed in a corner of her mind. The dream seemed almost too real.

"Everything's fine, Magdalene. I want some special time alone with you," Jack said.

Well, she did like the sound of that. Mags fired up the engine and drove out of Baile.

---

"Do it," Rhiannon screamed at Hannah. Stupid bitch didn't understand how imperative her maintained contact was at that moment.

Christ, she was so close. Rhiannon wanted to release her magic and tear the room apart, but she was inside the wards, putting her plan into action. It was almost laughably easy. All she'd had to do was use the plant Edana had created for her, along with the gap in the wards, and that crazy seer.

Hannah made a helpless motion and indicated Edana. "I can't." Her voice wobbled, and she looked like she might bawl any second. "I'll kill her."

Edana's skin looked grey, and her chest rose and fell in an unsteady rhythm.

The doctor was probably right, and Edana didn't have that much left to give, but with an even greater prize dangling, she'd ceased to be useful.

"I need that blood." Even now, Rhiannon could feel her connection waning. Crazy or not, the seer had enough moments of lucidity to be able to break free.

Hannah shook her head, her face resolute. "I can't do that."

"Can't you?" Dr. Hannah Maxwell needed a reminder of what was at stake here. Rhiannon left the room and banged into the room next door. She had mere seconds to make her point.

The boy shrank from her, eyes huge in his pale, terrified face.

Rhiannon didn't have time for their weakness, and she grabbed him by the arm.

Back in Edana's room, she held the athame to the child's throat.

Hannah paled and swayed on her feet. "Please, no."

"Get me what I need." Rhiannon pressed the sharp edge to the delicate, soft skin of the child's throat. "Or I'll get blood another way. But I will have blood."

He whimpered and stood deadly still.

"Don't move, Charlie." Hannah pulled her shit together, but with difficulty. The fear in her eyes was tangible. "Just keep really still, baby, okay?"

"Mummy?" His voice quavered.

Hannah looked from her child to Edana. If she'd had more time, Rhiannon would have enjoyed the woman's dilemma, dragged the situation out for her amusement. Mundanes were so laughably fragile. It took but a moment to remind them there was no substance behind all their bluster and bullshit.

"I'll do it." Fiona stepped forward and took the needle from Hannah's hand. Without hesitation she plunged it into Edana's arm and opened the little tap on the tubing that got the blood flowing again.

The child shook so badly he'd cut his own useless throat and spare her the trouble. She'd lost her son. Rhiannon saw no reason for this unworthy, pointless bitch to keep hers. Merely a small flick of her wrist and Hannah Maxwell would know the same mother's pain that cursed Rhiannon. Of course, her spawn drew breath yet, but he was as good as dead to her. Maybe she could add the boy's blood to Edana's and gain even more power.

"Mistress." Fiona cut into her reverie as scarlet spilling down the child's downy, white throat. "The scrying bowl."

First things first, Rhiannon shoved the child toward his mother.

Hannah darted forward and caught him to her. Cradling him, Hannah turned him away from what Rhiannon was doing. Coddling children was idiotic.

Alexander had been raised on blood magic, and his earliest memories were of watching her wield it. She hadn't shielded him and swaddled him. She'd raised him to be hard and resolute, to do what must be done.

The image in the scrying bowl came into sharp focus as Edana's blood gave its power to her. Rhiannon cut her hand and added her own.

"Here, Mistress." Fiona held her wrist over the bowl.

She served faithfully that one, and Rhiannon slashed into her wrist.

The combination of her, Fiona's and Edana's blood crashed into her with great spikes of agony. Rhiannon wrestled the magic under control. Christ, but it grew stronger with each cardinal point awakened. Soon now, she wouldn't have to suffer the pain for the reward. All of what she did here today served a greater purpose.

The connection strengthened like a sturdy rope, and Rhiannon smiled.

---

"Niamh!" A hand shook her shoulder and forced Niamh awake.

Taylor stood by her bed looking concerned.

Niamh blinked at the early morning light. A glimpse out the window had her guessing the time at too freaking early. "What is it?"

"I had a bad dream again." Taylor frowned.

The three dogs bracketing Niamh's leg were alert and

uneasy. Combined with the look on Taylor's face, Niamh was paying attention. "What kind of bad dream?"

"It's Mags." Taylor shook her head. "She's here but she's not here."

Not knowing what to make of that, but not prepared to take a chance, Niamh climbed out of bed. "Let's go and check on her."

Mags had not had a recurrence of the other night in three days, but nobody at Baile wanted to see that happen again.

Outside her room, the she-wolf waited for her. Niamh quested for the wolf and asked permission to enter her mind.

Mags's smell filled her nostrils as she perceived the world through the wolf. Mags had walked through the kitchen and out into the bailey.

The wolf licked her lips and peeled them back from her fangs.

Niamh sampled the sickly-sweet decay of blood magic from the wolf, and that got her moving faster.

"Mags," she called up the stairs as she climbed. "Are you in there?"

"She's not there," Taylor said.

Climbing faster, Niamh kept calm but firm as she spoke over her shoulder. "Go and get your dad, Taylor. And Roderick. And Jack."

Taylor's feet clattered away as Niamh knocked briefly and opened Mags's door.

Animals boiled around her feet, hackles up, senses prickling, instincts screaming.

Mags's bed was empty.

"Shit." Niamh left the room at a run.

The wolf had shown her Mags in the kitchen, and she went straight there.

Jack hit the kitchen behind her first. Warren, Roderick, and Alexander right on his heels.

"What the hell is going on?" Jack prowled up to her.

"Mags is not in her room." Niamh found the wolf's mind again and replayed the memory.

The animal didn't have the human name for things, but it showed her Mags reaching for something on the hook by the door.

"The keys." Warren caught echoes of what she saw through the wolf. "She took the Landy keys."

"Fuck!" Jack headed for the door. "She just walked out of the fucking castle, and nobody stopped her."

"Nobody saw her." Niamh sent reassurance to the she-wolf. The animal had tried to stop Mags, but short of hurting her hadn't been able to do anything.

Alexander followed Jack. "Let's not jump to—motherfucker!"

Niamh didn't need Jack's confirmation to know.

"She took the Landy." Jack stared at the spot the Landy had been parked. "I should never have left her alone. Fucking, sodding, shitting hell!"

"How did this happen?" Roderick glared around the bailey as if the answer might pop into existence.

Wearing a nearly identical expression, Alexander joined him. "And why did she go?"

"Where did she go is what I want to know." Jack stared at the tire tracks on the sand of the bailey. His face darkened. "I allowed this to happen."

"The important thing is finding her." Alexander clapped him on the shoulder. "And time's ticking as we stand here."

Maybe Taylor could help with that, but given Warren's protectiveness, Niamh was reluctant to suggest it.

Warren glanced at her and nodded. He looked down at Taylor standing beside her. "Do you have any ideas?"

Taylor went pale and shook. "Daddy, she's in so much danger. We need to find her. I see..." Her eyes went opaque. "She's moving. Fast. Scenery flying past the window."

"Can you see what scenery?" Alexander crouched beside her.

Warren's conflict roared down the bond at Niamh. His urgency to find Mags warred with his desire to protect Taylor from her frightening visions.

"It's going too fast." Tears streamed down Taylor's face. "She's going fast." Then she straightened. "She's not driving."

"Train!" Jack yelled and ran for his bike.

Warren was on his heels. "You head for the train station. I'll take the village. She might not be on the train yet." He stopped and looked at Taylor.

Niamh put her hand on Taylor's shoulder. "I'll take care of her. You go."

"It's all right, Dad." Taylor scrubbed the tears off her cheeks with her palms. "I can do this. We need to find Mags."

Warren reiterated his need for Taylor to be safe through the bond and Niamh nodded. She already loved Warren's child as though Taylor was a part of her, which in a weirdly cré-magic way, she was.

Bikes roared and dust flew as Warren and Jack took off.

Still watching them, Alexander said, "Well, Taylor girl, we now know what your blessing is. You're a seer."

"Great." Taylor grimaced. "More of this freaky stuff to look forward to."

---

JACK DROPPED his bike low as he took the twists and turns into Greater Littleton. He scanned constantly, looking for any sign of the Landy. Tight on his tail, Warren followed.

She couldn't have gotten far.

They were forced to slow as they entered the village, and the road grew busier.

The red sedan in front of him slammed on brakes, and Jack narrowly avoided rear-ending it.

"Shit!" Jack eased past the sedan, only to find a white minivan in front of that.

Warren drew up beside him and flipped his visor. "What's the problem?"

"Dunno." Jack tried to snake his way past the minivan and found himself locked in by a delivery truck. "Fuck!"

Warren rose on his toes and stared ahead. "There's a jam."

"We need to get around it." Jack ramped the pavement and had to stop. A construction crew had cordoned off the entire pavement.

Oncoming traffic was as gridlocked.

"I've never seen this in Greater Littleton." Warren swore long and steady. "I didn't even know there were this many fucking people in the village."

Frustration burned like acid in Jack's gut. Vehicles had moved in behind him.

They were trapped.

"Sod this!" He stopped his bike on the pavement. "I'm legging it."

Warren nodded. "I'll stay here. Station's that way."

Jack pounded pavement, dodging between the early risers going about their daily business. Narrowly avoiding plowing into a couple of women, he dodged left and ran like hell chased him. Alongside him, the traffic was locked in place. A harried policeman was trying to sort the problem. A huge truck carrying bottles had overturned and spread glass and whatever was in the bottles all over the road.

People scattered out of his path as he left a trail of outraged bellows behind him. Jack didn't give a crap.

He ran past the Hag's Head and charged straight through the knot of people clustered outside.

The station appeared up ahead.

Scanning the parking lot, he almost wept with relief as he

spotted the dark green Landy parked between a blue sedan and a silver SUV.

Jack hit the platform at a dead sprint.

A train picked up speed as it left the station.

It was empty.

Jack ran for the ticketing office, but it was shut.

He near enough tackled a station attendant. "Did you see a woman, long red hair?"

"Sir." The man stepped back and straightened his uniform. "I'm going to have to ask you to calm down."

The Jack of ten years ago took over and he loomed over the man. "Did you see a woman with long red hair this morning?"

Swallowing, the conductor glanced around for rescue.

Jack closed on him.

"I saw a lot of people," the conductor babbled. "The last train was nearly full."

"When did it leave?"

"Ten." The conductor swallowed. "Maybe fifteen minutes ago."

"Where's it going?" He hadn't gotten here fast enough.

"London." The man tried to dart around Jack. "It's the morning train to London."

"Route!" Jack snapped. "What's the route?"

"It's on the board." The man pointed to the overhead display. "All the stops are up there."

Taking out his phone, Jack snapped a picture.

Jack set off, running again, keying the train number into his phone.

As he entered the parking lot, a bike growled in.

Warren came to where he was standing. "Anything?"

"Conductor didn't see her get on the train." Jack was struggling to find words. "The same train we missed."

"Do you—"

"London, it's heading for London."

"Did—"

Jack thrust his phone at Warren. "This is the route."

"Right." Warren scanned his phone. "There's a change in Redruth."

"She might not get off the train." Jack wanted to rip the fucking station apart.

"You head for Redruth," Warren said. "I'll make sure she's not still around here and then start for London. Stay in contact." He motioned Jack to hop on. "I'll take you back to your bike."

Traffic had cleared as they rode back to where Jack had left his bike.

Warren stopped beside his bike, his face grim as he said, "There's too many sodding coincidences in this. First ever traffic jam I've seen in Greater Littleton, and suddenly it clears just like that." He snapped his fingers. "Just like fucking magic."

# CHAPTER TWENTY-FOUR

A pall hung over Baile, and nobody was interested in the breakfast Alannah put on the table. Sitting at the table, glued to Taylor's side, Niamh's mind held the hundreds of small connections with animals as far as she could reach.

Niamh connected with dozens of animals and Mags's image was passed from mind to mind. If there was a living thing near her, they would let Niamh know.

Alexander had located a scrying bowl, and Bronwyn sat on Taylor's other side.

"Breathe, sweetie." Her voice was quiet and steady. "Breathe and reach for water."

The scent of apples came first, and then the earthier tone of coriander: Taylor's unique magic scent. It should have been a time for celebration, a new witch coming into her power.

"That's it." Niamh squeezed Taylor's hand. "You're doing so well."

Taylor's eyes popped open. "I can't feel it."

"Yes, you do." Bronwyn cupped her chin. "Now, I'm not a seer, so I don't know how Mags does this, but when I call my element, my blessing responds."

"I can't feel—oh!" Taylor's eyes widened.

"That's great." Bronwyn smiled. "Now think of Mags and look into the bowl."

Taylor stared for a long moment, and then slumped. "I can't do it!"

"Yes, you can." Niamh put a wolf pup in her lap. "Relax and let it come to you. The magic is like a rushing river. You can't fight it or stop it. You have to let it carry you away."

The pup snuggled into Taylor.

Taylor stroked it and took a deep breath. "Okay."

"Now picture Mags," Bronwyn said.

Maeve had taken a quick trip to the caverns to find out how to scry, and they were working off what she'd discovered. The person who should be teaching Taylor to do this was missing, and the very reason Taylor needed to learn.

"Get a clear picture of her in your mind. Try to picture her face, remember what she smells like, how her voice sounds."

Taylor leaned over the bowl. Her back stiffened, and she gasped. "I see her."

Thank you, Goddess. Niamh sent a quick prayer up. The she-wolf pressed against her leg. The castle cats had even braved the kitchen, aware of the turbulent emotions and seeking to soothe.

Taylor's voice took on a hollow, unearthly tone. "Mags?"

They all leaned forward.

"Where is the train going?"

Breath quickening, Taylor grimaced. "You need to be calm, Mags or you'll lose…bugger it!"

Nobody thought to admonish her.

Sitting up, Taylor said, "I lost her." She tapped her temple. "Her mind is muddled. It's like talking to her on a mobile with bad coverage. She drifts in and out."

"Does she know how she got there?" Alexander leaned his elbows on the table. "Did you see what happened?"

"No." Taylor shook her head. "She doesn't know what she's doing on the train, and she's kinda freaking out."

Andy ran into the kitchen holding out his mobile. "It's Warren. I called him for an update."

Niamh took the phone. "Hi."

"Is Taylor okay?"

"She's trying to scry Mags," Niamh said. "And she's fine. We made a connection with Mags, and she's on a train."

"Yeah," Warren said. "She must be on the early train to London. We guessed as much from the station. I'm heading to London now. Jack is heading for Redruth, where she'll need to change trains."

"Okay." Niamh wanted to tell him to be careful, wanted to be with him. Instead, she said, "Take care and keep us posted. If we get anything else, we'll let you know."

She hung up.

Andy put his phone on the table. "I have Jack programmed in as well."

"How did you?" Niamh didn't know the words, so she waved a hand.

Andy looked apologetic as he said, "Mobile phone records are really not secure. Twenty-eight seconds."

Taylor looked at her. "Shall I try again?"

"Eat something first." Alannah put a plate of scrambled eggs and toast in front of Taylor. "We know she's on that train until the first stop, but in the meantime, you need to eat." She sent a hard stare around the kitchen. "You all need to eat."

Sinead glanced at her sister and nodded. "The weirdness in the wards." She took a deep breath. "It's growing, getting stronger. We don't even have to delve far to find it anymore."

Alexander piled eggs on Bronwyn's plate. "Wanna bet Rhiannon is behind all this?"

Nobody took that bet.

Taylor was getting tired, but she wouldn't stop. Bronwyn kept trying to get her to release the magic and rest, but Bronwyn hadn't felt what Mags was feeling. None of them had.

Water responded to her demand for strength. She tapped into the water in the pipes, the great underground springs feeding Baile, even the ocean crashing against the rocks as it answered her call.

There! She narrowed in on Mags again.

Mags's mind was clearer.

"She's getting off the train at Redruth." Taylor spoke aloud for her audience's benefit.

Niamh picked up Andy's phone and dialed Dad. "Warren? Yup, she's doing a great job, but we're going to make her stop now. Mags is getting off the train at Redruth." She paused. "You too. See you when you get home.

"Taylor." Bronwyn moved the scrying bowl away from her. "You need to stop now."

Taylor didn't want to stop. She loved the way the magic felt inside her, loved the way water leaped to respond to her. "I can do more."

"You've done an amazing job." Alexander crouched beside her. "You got her to leave the train, and Jack will find her in Redruth and bring her home."

The bad feeling in Taylor's tummy grew stronger. If they would only—

"No." Niamh must have read her mind. "I promised your dad I would take care of you. You need to rest."

Taylor wished she could see why she felt scared still. "Mags won't come back here."

"What?" Alexander frowned at her. "Did you see something?"

"It's a feeling." Taylor rubbed the spot on her chest that told her as much. "She's not coming back."

Niamh nudged Alexander aside. "Come on, lovely. Alannah has made you some of her special hot chocolate. Drink it, and then we'll take the pups out for a walk."

---

JACK STOPPED his bike in the parking lot of the Redruth station and returned Warren's call.

The London train had been and gone two minutes ago.

"Jack," Warren answered. "She got off the train at Redruth. Where are you?"

"At Redruth Station." He disconnected, and leaving his bike, ran inside the station.

People crowded toward the exit, and he had to use his size to cut through them. Looking over their heads, he read the platform allocations on the electronic board, and then hotfooted it to platform three. Across the raised walkway, over the tracks, and down the stairs he went.

A lone, shadowy figure stood on platform three, and his heart hammered. Relief almost made him giddy. He drew closer and the figure turned.

Not Mags. "Fuck."

The young woman blinked at him and looked around nervously.

The rest of the platform was empty.

Sweat rolled down his cheeks as he ran back to the station. The last of the people from the London train were making their way out the exit.

Jack studied them one by one as he followed. Woman and her child, middle-aged man, younger suit-type with a briefcase, three women chatting with each other.

She couldn't have gone far. Where the hell was she?

THE EDGES of her reality blurred again, and Mags fought the oncoming brain fog. She didn't know how she'd ended up on the train or why. She only knew she was in danger, and it was closing on her heels.

She quickened her steps as she moved away from the station. No! She had to stay at the station.

She almost turned back, but fear prodded her forward. She needed to get away from the station, go the way she was.

Her stomach roiled as the confusion in her brain worsened.

Someone had told her to stay at the station. Who was that?

Taylor had said it. Taylor had reached through the mist and spoken to her. She didn't know how Taylor had done that. Maybe she hadn't, and Mags had imagined the entire thing.

She could be dreaming again. All of this, the train, the fear, the running could all be a dream.

"*Mags.*" Jack's voice. "*Where are you, Mags?*"

"I'm here," she said.

A man walking his dog looked at her oddly and gave her a wide berth.

She must have spoken aloud.

"*Look around, Mags,*" Jack sounded urgent. "*Show me where you are.*"

"Are you coming, Jack?" She looked around her. Behind her was a newsagent, and two teen boys jostled each other out the door.

The taller one stopped and looked at her. "Did you say something?"

"I'm looking for Jack." Mags didn't think she knew these boys, but she couldn't be sure. The fog in her mind thickened and boiled.

The other teen laughed and nudged his friend. "She's fucking mad."

"Yes," Mags said. This must be what insanity felt like.

Across the street there was a coffee shop with tables and chairs set out on the pavement under bright red parasols.

"*Keep looking around, Magdalene,*" Jack said.

Next to the coffee shop was a women's clothing store with bright SALE signs decorating the mannequins.

A silver car pulled up and stopped in front of her.

"Get in." A man leaned over from the driver's side and opened the door. "Jack sent me."

That didn't sound like something Jack would do. Mags took a step away from the car and shook her head. "I'll wait here for Jack."

Hard hands fastened on her arms from behind and propelled her forward. "Jack is waiting for you," said another voice.

Mags started to struggle. Something was really off about all of this.

The man behind her picked her up and shoved her into the backseat. The car moved before he'd even gotten the door shut again, and Mags screamed.

---

TIME TICKED like a relentless metronome in Jack's head as he searched Redruth. He stopped every now and again and asked if anyone had seen a woman matching Mags's description.

He got lucky on his fourth person. A man walking his black Labrador recognized the description and pointed. "I saw her heading in that direction. She looked confused."

"Yeah." Jack improvised. "She's my sister and she has these…episodes."

"Poor thing." The man shook his head. "She can't be far. I saw her not five minutes ago."

Jack took off again.

At a newsagent, he converged on a tight gathering of two teen boys, the shop owner, and a couple of spectators.

"I think you should call the coppers," one of the boys said. "She didn't want to get into that car."

The other teen looked nervous. "But she was off her fucking head."

"I'm telling you; she didn't get into that car of her own will. The big bloke picked her up and tossed her in."

Heart in his throat, Jack grabbed the boy's arm. "Who? Who did they shove into the car?"

"Some woman." The boy shrugged his hold off. "She was standing here talking to herself, and this car pulled up and a bloke jumped out and grabbed her."

"Are you sure you're not imagining this?" The shop owner looked skeptical.

The bystanders broke into murmurs of discussion.

"What did she look like?" Jack focused on the first boy.

"Red hair," his friend said. "Tall, kind of pretty, but not all there."

"Mags." Jack knew it. His blood heated. Someone had his Mags, and that same someone would pay. If so much as a hair on her head was disturbed, he'd rain fucking mayhem down on them. "Did you see which way the car went?"

"That way." The first boy pointed down the street and then eyed him suspiciously. "Who are you anyway?"

"I'm her husband." The lie didn't even phase him. "Do you know what kind of car?"

The boy crossed his arms. "What's your name?"

"Jack." He didn't see the relevance, but he needed to keep the lad talking.

The friend nudged him. "Jack!" He flushed. "She said she was looking for Jack."

"I know that." The first boy glared at his friend and then turned to Jack. "Silver Audi A4. I didn't catch the reg, but it was this year's model."

## CHAPTER TWENTY-FIVE

Edana was dead, and Fiona had killed her. Beautiful, stupid, misguided Edana with her honey-blond mane and her toffee-colored eyes was gone from the earth hundreds of years after her birth.

"You should go, Mistress." Fiona dug her nails into her palms to stop her foolish, useless tears from falling. "They have Mags, and they will need you." She motioned Edana's body. "I will take care of this."

"See that you do." Rhiannon's eyes glittered in her victory-flushed face. She glanced at Hannah still crouched over her son as far from Edana as they could get. "And as to the other?"

"That will also be taken care of." Now that Edana was dead, Rhiannon had no further use for Hannah or Charlie.

Rhiannon nodded. "Good. I need to find suitable accommodation for our new guest."

Close to Baile would not be an option. It would be too easy for the coven to find Mags.

Fiona bowed her head. "A great outcome for us, Mistress."

"Yes." Rhiannon giggled. "Our very own seer."

Fiona kept her head bowed. Somehow Rhiannon had penetrated Mags's mind, using Edana's lifeblood to do so, and had controlled her.

"Of course, she will be an even more valuable asset once we have activated air." Rhiannon paced to the bed and back again. "But once I have her under my control, I can exert a much stronger influence." She sighed. "In the end, Edana did not fail me."

Edana had served her loyally for hundreds of years. Fiona wanted to yell the words at Rhiannon, but that would serve no purpose. Then they would both be dead, and Rhiannon would have Mags. With Mags, Rhiannon might not even need Fiona anymore.

The door slammed shut in Rhiannon's wake. In the silent aftermath, Charlie's hitched breathing filled the room.

Over at the bed, Fiona drew the sheet over Edana's face. In the short time she'd been here, Hannah had managed to start Edana's wound healing. If she'd lived, she would have been scarred, and Edana would have hated that. Perhaps it was a mixed blessing that she would never live to see the loss of her beauty.

Edana was—had been—conceited, stupid, arrogant. Fiona's friend.

A car started up outside, and a short while later passed by the window with Rhiannon in the passenger seat.

Rhiannon expected her to kill Hannah and Charlie and clean up the bodies.

For the first time, Fiona felt every one of her many, many years. Her future looked bleak.

Rhiannon had a new toy, and she would discard her like she had Edana.

Sitting on the bed beside Edana, Fiona was suddenly exhausted by all the death and the killing. So weary of walking the knife's edge of Rhiannon's temper and caprice. She hadn't been born at Baile, as Edana had. No, her frightened parents had taken her there when she was about seven. Not sure what to do with a child manifesting her strange gifts, they had taken her where she would be safe. Fiona tried to remember the year. Fifteen-something.

A couple of times a year, her parents had made the long trip to Baile to see her. They hadn't had much money, and leaving their farm had been difficult, but they'd done it to see her. Traveling on rough roads in their rickety wagon, they had come to see a daughter they were so proud of. How Fiona had hated living on that farm, doing the mundane and endless chores it required. Living at Baile had suited her much better.

She hadn't thought about her mother in years. Fiona had been the one to end those visits. At nineteen, full of herself and her own self-importance, she had told them not to come anymore. Looked her own mother in the face and told her that she had no further use for them.

Her mother had cried. Fiona remembered clearly her father putting his arm about her mother and leading her away from Baile for the last time. Her mother had been wearing her best blue dress, and the skirt had trailed and gotten fouled in the bailey's mud. Fiona had felt nothing. She had watched them go and been relieved.

Hannah rose with Charlie in her arms. "What now?"

"You know what she wants." Saying the words made Fiona ache with the fatigue of her years spent at Rhiannon's side. She didn't want to frighten the boy and say the words out loud.

"Don't do it." Hannah stood like a warrior queen with her boy in her arms, fire in her eyes. "You don't have to do it."

"No." Fiona took Edana's slim, elegant hand in hers. The bright red polish was chipped, and her nails ragged.

Edana would have hated the sight of her unkempt hands. She had taken such pride in her appearance.

"I'll fight you," Hannah said. "With every damn thing in me."

Like a lioness with her cub.

Edana's hand was cold and her skin dry.

For Edana then. One act of rebellion for the life and loyalty Rhiannon had cast aside so casually.

"Do you see that castle?" Fiona jerked her head toward Baile through the window.

Hannah frowned, her face wary. "Yes."

"Go there, and make them let you in." Baile had always smelled so wonderful. As if the combined aromas of all the magic worked within her had permeated the stones. Fiona closed her eyes and pictured her chamber, and later, when she had been made coven leader, her suite of rooms. Edana had lived there with her, in an adjacent chamber.

"W…what?" Hannah blinked at her.

"Go to Baile, and bang on their door until they let you in." She and Edana had sat beside the fire in her cozy sitting room and spun their plans. "They are the only ones who can keep you and Charlie safe." They had been so idiotically naive, believing Rhiannon's promises of greater things to come. "Go now."

She didn't open her eyes until she heard the door close behind Hannah. If Rhiannon found out what she'd done, she'd be dead too. With Edana gone, the threat didn't seem to hold the same weight as it used to.

Pulling the sheet off Edana's face, she watched the way the light played on those delicate features. She didn't see the gray pallor of death, or the jagged scars. Fiona saw the woman who had been. The deadly beauty who brought men to their knees.

Then she said the thing that she could scarcely believe was true. "I will miss you. I love you."

# CHAPTER TWENTY-SIX

Reality dissipated the fog, and Mags knew she was in deep trouble. The two men who grabbed her drove her to a quiet detached house on the outskirts of Redruth. She used the drive to piece together what had happened. The voice in her dreams couldn't have been Jack, and somehow must have been Rhiannon or one of her followers. The unmistakable taste of blood magic coated her tongue and made her want to retch.

They'd gotten her out of Baile, on a train and into a village she had never been to before. It didn't take a genius to realize there must be a good reason behind all of that. The house they stopped in front of was a seventies box with small windows that provided an uninspired view of a messy garden. They marched her quickly through an avocado-colored kitchen and shoved her into a small bedroom at the back of the house, then left her.

She tried the windows, but they were jammed shut. The door was locked. There was a single bed with a violently mauve floral duvet, which clashed with a brown and orange carpet. Nothing else. No other furniture and nothing she could use to get free.

Taylor had somehow managed to communicate with her on

the train. The coven had some idea where she was, or had been. Closing her eyes, Mags pushed her fear back and tried to concentrate. The part of her mind Taylor had entered remained dormant. She breathed deep and reached for air. Her magic rose as a jasmine and almond aroma around her. She pulled deeper on air.

Still nothing.

From the other room, the men murmured. A kettle whistled and went silent.

Mags would love a cup of tea. Her throat felt sandpaper dry.

Were they waiting for Rhiannon to get here?

A wave of fear crested and threatened to drown her. Perching on the end of the bed, Mags tried again. *"Taylor?"*

Warren's girl was a seer, like her, and she hadn't known it. Her blessing might have made itself useful and told her.

A knock sounded, and Mags stood. She might only get one chance, and she needed to be ready. Her knees shook and she was glad her long skirts hid her legs.

The lock turned and the door opened.

The one who had been driving stood in the doorway with a mug in his hand. He motioned the window. "Stand over there."

Mags moved to the window.

Not taking his eyes off her, he put the mug on the floor and retreated.

The lock turned again.

She approached the tea and stopped. As thirsty as she was, Mags left the tea where it was. She had no idea what was in it, and she'd already made her abduction too bloody easy for them.

Back to the bed, she perched on the edge.

She counted slowly back from ten. Would Rhiannon kill her? Surely, she wouldn't have gone to the trouble of kidnapping her if all she intended was to kill her?

It got hard to breathe with her heart hammering in her chest.

What was that thing Jack had done when she'd been panicking before?

Five things she could see.

She named them out loud. "Bed, ugly carpet, window, saggy curtains, grass."

She didn't know how she could have been so stupid as to follow that voice and believe it had been Jack.

Was it four things she could taste? No, feel.

"Duvet. Blinding, ghastly panic."

This wasn't working.

She stood up and paced to the window. Trying again to open it, she gave it a hefty shake.

Going back to the bed, she tried again. *"Taylor?"*

*"Mags?"* Taylor's mental voice came faintly, and then strengthened. *"Is that you?"*

As if it would be anyone else? She didn't know how much time she had. *"I'm in a house."* She tried to send Taylor the little she'd noticed on being hustled inside.

Goddess, why hadn't she thought to look around and take note?

A door slammed.

Dropping the connection to Taylor, she sprung to her feet.

She ran and fetched the tea mug. Not much of a weapon but more than she'd had before.

Her hands shook, and hot tea splashed over her hand.

A man shouted; furniture scraped. A loud crash was followed by the thump of something big.

Mags got her mug ready. The hot tea should go first, and then she could bash them with her mug.

More muffled yells, some grunting, and the door opened.

Mags threw the tea.

"Fucking hell!" Jack stepped back just in time, and the tea splashed the wall.

Mags could hardly believe her eyes. "Jack?"

"What are you going to do with that?" He pointed to the mug.

That was rather obvious. "Clobber someone. Not you, of course."

"Never mind." Jack shook his head. In two strides, he reached her. Grabbing her hand, he hauled her out the room.

The first man lay on the floor outside the bedroom.

Jack booted him out the way.

The other man was spread over the kitchen table, out cold.

"When I get you out of here and somewhere safe, I'm going to shake you. Then I'm going to hug you. Then I'm going to kiss the fuck out of you." Jack tugged her through the door and outside the house.

Mags liked the sound of the hugging and kissing part but could give the shaking a miss. "You came?"

"Of course, I bloody came." Jack growled and nudged her toward his bike. "I don't have two helmets." He shoved the one helmet at her.

"No, Jack—"

"Magdalene." He went nose to nose with her. "We have no time. None. Put the helmet on and get on the bike."

She really hoped she wasn't imagining this part. "Okay."

Jack hopped on in front of her and hauled her arms around his waist. "Hold on tight."

Then they were off. Jack gunning the bike onto the street and away.

He wove through the town, barely stopping at stop signs and sticking to quieter roads.

Mags tightened her arms around his waist and rested her head against his solid back. He was real, and he had come for her.

ALEXANDER DIDN'T RECOGNIZE the woman standing at Baile's door, but she looked like she'd been through hell. It was more than the mussed hair, the red-lined blue eyes, and the rumpled, stained clothing. Even more than the toddler clasping her neck and staring at him in terror. The woman's eyes held the kind of desperation that yanked on unwelcome memories. The night Baile had been attacked, the surviving witches had worn those eyes.

"Can I help you?" Not wanting to spook the child further, he kept his tone even and his body still.

She shoved her glasses up with her spare hand. "I'm Hannah Maxwell. I was told to come here."

Being told to come to Baile could mean so many things, but that Baile had let her in got him opening the door and stepping back. "Then, perhaps you should come in."

The coven had left the kitchen in dribs and drabs since the news had reached them that Jack had Mags, and they were safe. Warren was on his way back, and Niamh had taken Taylor to bed and left the she-wolf with the girl.

"I was told you could keep me safe." Hannah tightened her grip on her child. "That only you could keep me safe."

"Who told you that?"

"A woman called Fiona."

Every muscle in him tensed. "Did you say Fiona?"

She nodded and must have sensed the change in him because she took a step back and then two more. "I'll go."

"Wait." Alexander's head reeled. In the hundreds of years he'd known her, he'd never known Fiona to act out of anything but her own or Rhiannon's interests. Sending this woman here now could mean so many things, and he needed more information. "You surprised me." He left his hands in clear view. "Fiona's not a friend of mine."

He'd strangle Fiona on sight.

"She didn't say you were friends." Hannah backed up again

and scrabbled behind her for her car door handle. "She said I'd be safe here."

Alexander took a guess. "From Rhiannon?"

"Yes." Hannah froze. "I think I've made a terrible—"

"I can tell you if you're in danger from Rhiannon, you are in the right place." Nobody could fake looking that traumatized. "We've had some trouble with Rhiannon ourselves, and we're wary."

Roderick spoke softly at his shoulder. "Let her in."

Mastering the what the fuck ringing through his head, he kept his voice tight and low. "She said Fiona sent her."

"I heard." Roderick stepped into Hannah's view, arms loose at his side. "My name is Roderick, and I think you should come inside."

Hannah stared hard at Roderick. "I'm going."

"Nobody will stop you," Roderick said and pushed his hands in his pockets. "But you look like you've been to hell and back, and if Rhiannon is the reason, this is the only place she can't get to you."

Hannah opened her car door and slunk behind it. She seemed to feel better with the car door between them. "I don't know what she is."

"We do." Roderick radiated the sort of reassurance Alexander had rarely seen him exhibit except with animals and small children. "We are fully aware of how lethal she is."

Slumping, Hannah took a shaky breath. "I've seen things… done things."

Alexander knew what he saw reflected in Hannah only too well. "She doesn't give anyone a choice."

"We can help you." Roderick stepped into the bailey. "And we will help you, but nobody is going to force anything on you."

"What is she?" Hannah leaned against her car for support.

"A witch," Roderick said.

Now Alexander had to snap his mouth shut. It wasn't like

Roderick to go with the open and honest routine, especially not with a virtual stranger.

"She's a blood witch." Roderick kept right on laying it out. "Which means she uses blood, and people's life force to work her magic. She's also evil. If you got away from her, you're a lucky woman."

Giving a strangled laugh that held no humor, Hannah said, "I wouldn't put it like that."

"Come inside." Roderick stepped to the side, giving Hannah a clear path to the door. "I'll make us a cup of tea, and we can talk."

If Roderick could even make tea, Alexander would eat his Levi's. "I know it doesn't feel like that right now, but if you're here, it means the worst is over."

"I don't know how any of this happened." Hannah shook her head. "I only came to Greater Littleton to check on a patient of mine."

Roderick nodded.

"Gemma." Hannah glared at them, as if throwing down a challenge.

"Hermione's daughter?" Alexander connected dots. "So, you are her doctor?"

"Oncologist." Hannah nodded. "At least I was, until she..." She cleared her throat and shook her head. "That doesn't matter now."

"Until her cancer mysteriously disappeared?" Roderick said.

Hannah narrowed her eyes at him. "How did you know that?"

"Because we healed her." He shrugged.

Swallowing, Hannah looked from one to the other of them. "I don't believe in magic healing."

"I imagine not." Alexander took his cue from Roderick, not that he'd tell the big bastard that. "You're a scientist, and you believe in science." He took his next verbal steps mincingly. "But

I also imagine you have seen things in the last few days that have made you question almost everything you know to be true."

For a long moment, Hannah didn't move, and then she nodded.

"We will answer all your questions." Roderick took a slow step toward her. "But you look like you're about to collapse."

"I don't know who to trust." Hannah spoke to herself more than them.

They waited. Hannah looked poised to run at any minute, and Alexander couldn't blame her. If Rhiannon had gotten her claws on the poor woman, he could only guess what she'd been subjected to.

She looked at Roderick. "I'll come in. For a moment."

"Okay." He nodded. "May I carry your son for you?"

"No." Hannah's arms tightened around her child. "He stays with me."

---

MAGS FOLLOWED Jack into a room at the nothing-special hotel he'd driven them to. Two beds with nondescript counterpanes, a cabinet with a television, and an overlarge chair dominating one corner beside the window.

"What are we doing here?" She'd thought they'd go straight for Baile.

"I need a minute." Jack winced and shrugged out of his leather jacket. "To get cleaned up."

Blood stained the entire right side of his T-shirt.

With a gasp, Mags started for him. "You're hurt."

"Yeah." He looked down at himself and grimaced. "Fucker went for the kitchen knife."

"We need to get you back—"

"Mags." He dropped his jacket on one of the beds. "We both

need to get cleaned up, and then I need to figure out a way to get us back to Baile. If we ride without helmets, we could get stopped."

She didn't care about any of that. "How bad is it?"

"I'll live."

Jack's mobile rang, and he reached for it, and grimaced

Mags sprang into action and yanked it from his jacket pocket. She handed it to him.

"Yup," he barked at whoever was on the phone. "She's with me." Jack frowned. "No, I was about to call him."

Mags edged closer, her belly tight with concern. She wasn't much good with blood, but she'd never fainted or anything. Yet.

"What?" Jack thundered and scowled. "That can't be—"

Mags moved closer, but she could only tell it was Alexander on the line. He spoke fast, and she only caught one word in four.

And then she heard Alexander say Rhiannon.

"What is it?" She got close enough to hear. Anything about Rhiannon could not be good.

"...used the tracking spell she put on Warren," Alexander said. "It was her way behind the wards, and she used Edana's blood to scry inside."

Edana had put a tracking spell on Warren when he'd gone with Niamh to South Africa. Bronwyn had checked Warren and found nothing.

"She has some kind of way through the wards," Alexander said. "We don't know exactly how yet, but Alannah and Sinead have been talking about an anomaly for a while. It's gotten worse over the last few days."

Jack sat heavily on the bed beside his jacket. "So, what now?"

Mags perched beside him. Somehow Rhiannon must have used Warren or the chink in the wards to get to her and get her out of Baile. None of any of that should have been possible.

"You can't tell Warren where she is," Alexander said.

Jack stiffened. Hearing that wouldn't sit well with Jack. He was loyal to a fault.

Careful of the wound, Mags touched his back.

"Does he know?" Jack glanced at her.

"No," Alexander said. "Niamh called him and told him to come back immediately. We'll have to break the news when he gets here."

"Fuck." Jack squeezed his eyes shut. "That's going to mess with his head."

Alexander went silent and then said, "Yep. But until we can figure out how she's doing it, and what exactly she's doing, he's more of a danger to you than anything else."

"So, she used Warren the entire time." Jack growled.

"As near as we can extrapolate," Alexander said.

"Right." Jack straightened. "I need to think and talk to Mags. To be safe, I'm going to ditch this mobile."

"Good idea," Alexander said. "Be careful."

"Christ!" Jack ended the call and dropped his head.

Rhiannon had been one step ahead of them the entire time. They'd been hiding in Baile, believing themselves insulated from her and all her machinations. Instead, they'd played right into her hands.

Mags took the phone from Jack's hand and dropped it to the floor. "Step on it."

With a brief hesitation, Jack raised his heavy boot and slammed it on the phone.

Bits of plastic and electronic innards leaped over the carpet.

"We don't know how much she hears from within Baile," she said, as she stared at the shattered phone. "And because of that, we can't rely on the coven." The enormity of what she was about to say pressed against her like an elephant squatting on her breastbone. "We can't trust the coven. We're on our own."

Frowning, Jack stared at her. "Why do I feel like you've got an idea going?"

"Because you're that clever." Her attempt at jaunty misfired into limp. "Our passports are in those saddle bag thingies on your bike. Taylor put them there." She'd not understood what she'd seen in Taylor's mind at first, but the confusion had cleared now, and so had their trajectory.

"What are you saying, Magdalene?" Jack cocked his head. "And keep it simple, because I'm not tracking much right now."

"We're going to Moscow," she said, trying to sound like she dropped bombs like this all the time, which she kind of did. "And we're not going to tell anyone that we are."

Jack gaped at her.

She took advantage of having rendered him mute. "But first, we're going to clean your wound."

# CHAPTER TWENTY-SEVEN

Warren heard the words Alexander spoke, but it took a while for his brain to catch the meaning. When it did, it was a mind fuck for the ages. Rhiannon had used his connection to Edana to spy on all of them. She'd know each and every thing they did as they did it. Even worse, she'd piggybacked off their connection to get to Mags.

Sitting at the table, he took a long moment to dissect the statement into individual events, proof of the truth of what he was hearing. All of this because he'd been a stupid sod who let a beautiful woman lead him by the dick.

"Hey." Niamh nudged him. "Don't do that."

He couldn't oblige. He'd come to Baile to join an elite chosen called to protect the witches. Between almost getting Niamh killed, actually getting Ulwazi killed, and now this, he'd pretty much failed his probationary period. "The obvious answer is for me to leave Baile."

"You can't." Niamh stared him down. "It would never have been safe, but it's doubly dangerous now that she knows where you are. And Taylor is here. The coven needs you. Your fellow coimhdeacht need you. And me."

It was so like Niamh to put herself at the end of the list of what was important.

"Until we know more—" Alexander gave him an apologetic wince "—I think it best, if we don't discuss anything sensitive or confidential with you. I agree with Niamh, though. You can't leave, and nobody wants that."

Like a wall being erected between them, but he had no choice. "Right."

"As far as we know, she can't physically get in here," Roderick said. "But I agree with Alexander."

Fucking hell. Were these two learning to work together?

"Sinead and I will try to heal the breach in the wards." Alannah put a hand on his shoulder. "You can't blame yourself. You couldn't have known this would be the outcome."

Rhiannon definitely knew about Taylor now. All his chest beating around protecting his little girl, and he was the reason she was in even greater danger than ever.

Taylor snuggled up beside him. "It's okay, Dad. She's the bad guy, not you."

A person's kids could kill them with kindness. He kissed the top of her head. "I'm good."

She gave him those wise, grownup eyes that called his bullshit.

"Until we know how much she can still hear, I think it's best to make sure we keep future discussions away from Warren." Roderick shrugged. "I'm sorrier than I can say, my brother."

They were all being so nice about his screwup, and that made it even worse.

"There are lesser inhabited areas of the castle," he said. "It's too easy for someone to slip up and say something they shouldn't if I'm around all the time." He'd always considered himself a loner, but living at Baile with the coven and the coimhdeacht had opened a chink in his armor, and he didn't want to sequester himself.

"We'll get this sorted." Alexander squeezed his shoulder. "According to Hannah, Edana is dead, and she was the most powerful magic source Rhiannon had. It may be that she's limited now that Edana's dead."

Did it make him an awful person that he really didn't care about Edana's fate?

"I'll get my stuff moved." Warren felt twenty stone heavier as he got to his feet. "The southern tower is free. I'll be there."

Niamh rose with him and slipped her hand into his. "Let's go for a walk."

What she meant by that was a pack run, and he didn't know if he could manage that.

"You're pack," Niamh whispered. "Always."

Together they walked across the bailey and under the gatehouse.

Alpha waited with the rest of the pack beyond the moat, as if they'd sensed his turmoil.

Younger wolves rose and twined around his legs, pushing their snouts into his hand, offering their silent support.

"This is easier with fire activated," Niamh said. She closed her eyes, and strawberry and basil aromas filled the air.

His eyesight skewed into monochrome, his hearing sharpened, and his nose picked up the million scent markers surrounding them. Blood surged into his muscles, and his heart pumped. Instinct drove him with a sharp edge as the pack ran. In the rush of wind through fur, and the steady beat of paws on earth, and the sheer joy of powerful bodies doing what they were created for, Warren forgot everything. For the moment.

---

SINEAD CROUCHED BESIDE HER SISTER, as they buried their hands in the earth beneath giant fruit trees in the orchard. They were far enough from the castle for nobody to see them. They didn't know how much Rhiannon knew or could see, but they needed to try to repair the wards.

Rose and cloves swirled around them as they drew earth.

Earth responded, gathering in a gentle green nimbus around their hands buried in the soil before snaking out in thin fissures.

The wards were buried deep into the ground, a shimmering barrier both fragile and enduring. Sinead and Alannah's magic folded within the wards and traveled on the pulses of magical energy. The fissure had grown exponentially and now formed a dark, muddy sludge in the silvery essence of the ward magic. It throbbed with sickly energy, and they stopped their magic well short of the malevolence.

"It's getting stronger," Alannah whispered.

Sinead nodded. It reeked of blood magic. Her instincts recoiled from the threat. "We need to try."

Nodding, Alannah led their merge closer.

Pulses of misshapen magic rolled over them and grew stronger as they approached. It felt like diving headfirst into a hurricane. Blood magic sparked and pricked against their senses. Spikes of pain left Sinead gasping.

The recoil made her ears ring and knocked Sinead flat on her arse. Their connection to earth severed, and her head tilted and whirled. She breathed deep against the rolling nausea. Bloody hell, that hadn't been much fun at all.

Beside her, Alannah shook her head like a punch-drunk boxer, a thin trickle of blood seeping out of one nostril. She wiped at Sinead's lip. "You're bleeding."

The coppery taste of blood coated Sinead's tongue. "So are you." Then she stated the obvious. "Whatever the hell that thing is made of is stronger than us."

"Right." Alannah dusted her hands on her skirt. "I will if you want to, but I don't fancy going near it again."

Sinead considered it. For about ten seconds, before shaking her head. "We don't have the oomph to tackle it."

Their failure sat heavy with both of them. It was the closest they'd come to their former closeness since Thomas had stopped hanging about Alannah. When it came to wielding magic, however, they both had to pull on their big-girl panties and work together. Their gift worked only when they merged.

Maeve had told them other sets of twins had experienced the same thing back in her day. If either she or Alannah wanted to work magic, they needed the other.

Goddess, but Sinead would never have imagined a man—or what was left of one—could have caused the schism between them. It had always been the two of them since birth, together against all comers.

Alannah cleared her throat. "The only hope we have of healing the wards is to activate earth."

"Right." As per usual, Sinead had been thinking along much the same lines. "Then I think we know what we need to do."

Standing, Alannah held her hand out and helped Sinead up. "Will we tell them?"

"Best not." As much as Sinead hated sneaking out like a thief in the night, they couldn't risk providing Rhiannon with another road map to their plans. "Tonight then?"

Alannah nodded. "Tonight."

---

THOMAS REMAINED incorporeal as he followed Alannah through the great hall. She and Sinead had packed a backpack each and waited until Baile had fallen silent before they left.

He'd spent his time amongst the living flitting from one warm pair of arms to another. He'd genuinely liked each of those women during their affairs and regretted hurting them when he had inevitably ended things. His regret had lasted only until his next affair had begun.

Then he'd died in a battle that had wiped out every

coimhdeacht except Roderick. Thomas's end had come courtesy of a sodding pitchfork, of all things. A brawny farmer had taken advantage of him being distracted by a halfway decent swordsman and stuck him from behind.

Thomas could still feel the tines enter his body and strike vital organs. He'd known at the moment of the strike that it was fatal. Still, he'd fought for as long as he could to keep the secret passageway to the village protected.

His biggest regret about dying had been the pain it caused Lavina. His death had ricocheted through her, and he'd experienced her soul-deep pain at his passing.

Oddly enough, for a man who thrived on sexual conquest, the most important woman in his life until that point had never been his lover.

Moonlight caught in Alannah's hair as she trailed Sinead across the bailey. They moved as silently as wraiths in the quiet night, seen only by him and the she-wolf in the kitchen.

Alannah moved like moonlight, serenely and heart-stoppingly graceful. He had stood beside her in the kitchen on more occasions than he could name and watched the innate elegance of her every movement. So many times, and still not enough.

He had loved Lavina, still loved her. In his center, ached the truncated edges of their severed bond. Her spirit was trapped on the village green still, and her pain throbbed like a missing limb. Lavina had made the ultimate sacrifice the night he had died. Along with twelve other witches and an acolyte, she had taken part in a suicide blood-magic ritual that had frozen Maeve and Roderick to preserve cré-magic across time.

He had existed in an odd between time and space envelope until Roderick had reawakened. Even then he'd been distantly aware of Alannah, like she was his lodestone.

Drifting through the damp night, he followed the twins as they passed under the gatehouse and hurried across the drawbridge.

The only time he got any respite from the pain of Lavina's entrapment was when he was with Alannah.

But Sinead was right. A spirit had no business holding the heart of a mortal witch. Without him hovering about her, teasing her with impossible dreams, she would find a flesh and blood man to love and join her life with. Maybe they'd have children, Alannah and this unknown man. Thomas hated him already.

Alannah and Sinead crossed the wards, and Thomas stopped. He could go no further than the wards.

The twins walked side by side on the road to the village, Alannah's dress fluttering around her legs, and Sinead's combats crunching small stones beneath her feet. So different and yet so much the same. Not his, though. Never his to protect. Their ultimate destination was Canada to wake the earth point, but he had no idea how they would get there. He would not be there to share the dangers and triumphs of their journey.

"Fare thee well, my love," he whispered to the night wind. "Be safe and find all that you need."

Stopping on the road, Alannah turned and stared right at him. He was still incorporeal, so she could not have seen him, but she raised her hand anyway in a silent goodbye.

# CHAPTER TWENTY-EIGHT

As much as Warren would have liked to confine himself to a grim, comfortless cell and wallow in his own guilt, Baile was having none of it.

Between him finding an appropriate room and going to fetch his stuff, Baile turned his isolation ward into a cozy haven. Red and cream oriental rugs decorated the austere stone floor. A large, boxy post bed became a haven of welcoming bedding and plump cushions. In an adjoining sitting room, she surrounded him with books, a game table, a globe bar, and oversize, comfy sofas. Far from constructing the punishment he deserved, Baile had created a lush retreat for him.

He packed his clothes away in an enormous oak wardrobe. As much as he'd liked to, there was no arguing with a stroppy sentient castle.

His suite, because no other name would do, even had a spectacular view of the forest.

In a deep window seat, complete with artfully arranged cushions and a throw rug, he took a load off and let the view soak in. A green haze hung over the treetops. It did sweet fuck all to soothe his twisting emotions.

The door banged open, and Niamh stumbled in, tripping over a massive suitcase. She beamed at him. "Hi."

Warren could almost hear the strain on the suitcase's capacity as he stared at it stupidly. "What are you doing?"

"Moving in." Niamh dragged the suitcase across the floor. Jamming her hands on her hips, she scowled at the suitcase. "For a woman who prides herself on being a jeans and T-shirt sort, I have a lot of clothes."

Warren couldn't be interpreting this right. "You're doing what?"

"Moving in." Niamh beamed at him.

He stared at her.

She stared right back. Then she frowned. "You didn't think you were going to leave me alone, did you?"

"Actually, that's exactly what I thought." What part of him being a danger to all of them didn't she get?

Niamh shook her head.

A scratching at the door had her opening it again.

A badger, a three-legged fox, and four dogs trotted in. The dogs immediately made themselves at home on his bed. The badger disappeared underneath it, and the fox went to investigate his sitting room.

Before Niamh could shut the door, a large ginger cat sauntered around the jamb and beelined for him.

After leaping onto the window seat, the cat circled and then curled into a ball.

Warren addressed the real culprit. "You can't move in."

"Looks like I can." Niamh shrugged and dragged her suitcase over to the wardrobe. She opened the doors and peered in. "I'm not sure there's enough space for the two of us."

A dresser appeared against the wall beside the door.

Chuckling, Niamh shook her head. "That will do nicely."

Kneeling by her suitcase, she unzipped the thing. Clothes spewed on the floor.

"Niamh." Warren gave her his best no-nonsense tone. "You can't be around me, and you know it."

She flapped a hand at him. "Pfft! Where else would I be? You're my coimhdeacht."

"As far away from me as possible." He had to get her to see reason.

Lifting its head, the cat blinked at him reproachfully.

Warren lowered his voice as he said, "It's not safe for you to be around me."

"There's no safer place I could be than with you." Her dark eyes met his.

The thing with Niamh, Warren was learning, was that she was generally easy going and relaxed, but she got a certain gleam in her eye that meant the combined forces of all four magic elements would not budge her an inch. She stood there and slapped him with that intractable gleam. Also, he was genuinely glad to see her, and to keep on fighting would be stupid. He nodded. "Okay, then."

She nodded as if the conclusion was foregone and started shoving clothes in dresser drawers.

"Hey, Dad." Taylor poked her head around the door. She surveyed his new digs and made an impressed face. "Very nice."

"Baile takes care of her own." Niamh looked over from shoving interesting bits of lace into the top dresser drawer. The sort of interesting bits of lace he'd like to investigate in detail.

Taylor sauntered over to Niamh and stared at her suitcase. "Are you moving in?"

"Yup." Niamh grabbed a handful of T-shirts and put them away.

"Cool." Taylor's eyes twinkled as she grinned at him. "Just like a real family."

Warren liked that notion and grinned back. "You've got a lot of mouth on you."

"Yeah." Taylor wrinkled her nose. "But I work it so well."

"Here." Niamh shoved a toiletry bag at her. "Make yourself useful and put that in the bathroom for me."

Snorting, Taylor took the bag. "I won't be gone long, so don't start any of your together stuff."

"We save that for when you're not here," Niamh called after her.

Taylor made retching noises.

Warren sent a fervent prayer to Goddess to make it so.

---

Alexander watched Bronwyn bind bunches of dried lavender together. His little witch wore an unhappy expression, and he wished like hell he could take it off her face.

"I don't like this." She sighed.

He didn't either. "It's a definite turn for the worse."

Baile's residents had woken that morning to no Alannah in the kitchen. A quick search of the twins' apartments had filled in the blanks. By tacit agreement nobody discussed the conclusion they'd all reached.

Although his cooking skills nowhere near matched Alannah's, Alexander had stepped up and fed the coven breakfast. It had been a sadly depleted coven that sat down to scrambled eggs and bacon. Alannah and Sinead gone, Mags and Jack Goddess alone knew where, Warren and Niamh relegated to their tower.

Even he and Roderick had lacked the will to bitch at each other.

Bronwyn made to stand on the refectory table.

Not while he was watching, so Alexander stood, and taking her by the hips, put her firmly on the ground. "Let me do it."

"I can manage." Being his little witch, she never went down without a fight, but her objection lacked her watch-out obstinacy.

Hopping up onto the table, he said, "Now what?"

"We need to hang these from the rack." Bronwyn handed him bunches of lavender.

Obediently, he hung the dried herbs as directed.

"It's the not knowing that's getting to me," she said, handing him the last of the clumps. "I wish we could be sure of what she can and cannot hear."

"Maeve's working on that now." He finished hanging and jumped off the table. "She's seeing what the witches past know."

Bronwyn made a face. "They haven't been a whole helluva lot of use thus far."

"But they will be." Unable to be close without touching her, he pulled her against him. "Especially when we get all the points activated."

"You hear that, bitch!" Bronwyn threw her head back and yelled at the air. "We're going to activate all those points, and then we're coming for you."

Alexander had to chuckle. "I think she already knows that."

"It doesn't hurt to keep telling her." Bronwyn pressed her head to his shoulder. "I really hate your mother."

"I think the term mother is giving her more credit than she deserves." It made him want to beat his chest and strut the barnyard when his woman leaned on him like she was now. "Evil incubator is closer to the truth."

"I'm sorry." Bronwyn slid her arms around his waist. "Sorry you had to grow up with that fucker."

As he spoke, Alexander solidified a truth he'd only been peripherally aware of realizing. "I am, and I'm not."

She glanced up at him in question.

"Everything I've done, and everything that's happened has led me to this point." He kissed her. "Right here with you and our babies, and I can't regret that."

Scuffing made them look toward the door to the healer's hall.

"I'm sorry." Hannah backed out. "I didn't mean to interrupt."

"You're not." Bronwyn moved out of his hold. "Come in."

Hannah hesitated and then stepped in. "Roderick told me this was the healer's hall." She looked around her, her gaze taking in the rows upon rows of jars on the shelf behind the refectory table, lingered on the fresh herbs growing in window boxes and tracked back to Bronwyn.

"Is Charlie okay?" Alexander asked. Hannah had kept her son right beside her since her arrival. He couldn't blame her.

Hannah nodded. "He fell asleep in the administration office."

"The what now?" First Alexander had heard of such a place.

"The admin office." Hannah wandered over to the jars of shelves and scanned the labels. "Andy's office."

Andy was making himself right at home, apparently. "Right."

"Andy said he'd call me if Charlie woke up." Hannah reached for a jar, stopped, and glanced at Bronwyn over her shoulder. "May I?"

Bronwyn waved her forward. "Go right ahead."

Hannah read the label and then opened the jar and took a sniff. "Hawthorn berry?"

"For cardiovascular uses and hypertension," Bronwyn said.

"Huh." Hannah nodded and peered at another jar. "Neem."

"I use the leaves, the twigs, and the nut oil." Bronwyn joined her at the shelf. "It's a useful one. Antibacterial, anti-fungal, anti-parasite, emollient, insect repellant, purgative and skin tonic." She smiled.

Gesturing the shelves, Hannah said, "And these are what you use to…heal?"

"Partly." Bronwyn cocked her head. "These didn't help with Gemma."

Hannah nodded and faced Bronwyn. "What did then? I've been over and over her scans and labs, and I have no idea. That's why I came to Greater Littleton. I wanted to know how one appointment I'm explaining to a young girl and her mother how it's only a matter of time, and the next appointment I'm looking at a full recovery."

Bronwyn assessed Hannah for a long minute before she nodded. "You deserve an explanation, but it would be easier to show you."

"I'd appreciate that." Hannah's ghost of a smile was the first break in her perpetually haunted expression since she'd arrived at Baile.

Moving around the table, Bronwyn patted a stool before taking the one beside it. "You've already seen magic for yourself."

"What I've seen is a sick bitch bleeding someone dry." Hannah's expression soured. "I'm not sure I'm ready to come right out and call that magic."

Alexander went back to the leather sofa and let his little witch handle the situation.

"Well," Bronwyn said as Hannah sat, "assume for a moment that magic does exist."

"But—"

"Assume for now." Bronwyn kept it gentle. "Set your disbelief aside long enough to hear me out."

It took Hannah a moment before she nodded. "Okay."

"Every witch here is born into a different element." Bronwyn ticked them off on her fingers. "Air, earth, fire, and in my case, water. The element provides the power, the thrust if you will."

Still looking skeptical, Hannah nodded.

"Each witch then also has a blessing, and it changes from witch to witch. Maeve is a spirit walker, which means she can commune with witches past."

Hannah jerked upright. "You mean she talks to the dead?"

"Sort of." Bronwyn waggled her hand. "It's more a case of she can cross the veil between life and death."

Alexander might not have started there.

The skepticism on Hannah's expression bloomed into outright disbelief.

"Niamh draws fire." Bronwyn forged on as if the other woman weren't looking at her as if she'd lost her mind. "And she's a guardian, which means she can communicate with animals."

Standing, Hannah said, "That's all a bit Dr. Dolittle for me. I came here looking for answers, not fairy tales."

"Then open your mind and listen," Bronwyn said. Then she quoted Sherlock Holmes. *"When you have eliminated the impossible, whatever remains, however improbable, must be the truth."*

Hannah sat again but wasn't looking happy about it.

"My blessing is healer," Bronwyn said. "I use water as my power source, and I can go within the body and draw the illness or the injury into myself. From there, I transmute it into the earth."

Huffing, Hannah gaped at her. "That's impossible."

"May I?" Bronwyn motioned for Hannah's hand.

Reluctantly, Hannah extended her hand.

Honey and sage perfumed the air as Bronwyn drew water. Growing in her power daily, Bronwyn no longer needed a bowl of water beside her. She could draw the water from the air itself if she needed to. Taking Hannah's hand, Bronwyn said, "You'll feel a sort of tingle. It's not an unpleasant sensation."

Hannah scowled at their connected hands. "It's warm."

"That's my gift," Bronwyn said. "It's searching through you for what it needs to heal."

"But I'm perfectly healthy." Hannah's voice didn't sound as certain anymore.

Alexander mentally took his cap off to Bronwyn. Her forthrightness had worked so much better than prevarication. She'd not couched the truth in platitude but laid it bare for Hannah to poke at.

Closing her eyes, Bronwyn drew deeper on water.

"Why can I smell honey?" Hannah sniffed the air. "And something herby."

"Sage." Alexander took over the explanation. At least that part. "Each witch's magic also has a unique scent marker. Bronwyn's is honey and sage."

"That's it." Hannah glanced at him. "I smell sage."

"You broke your arm once," Bronwyn murmured. "It's an old injury."

Wide-eyed, Hannah stared at her. "You can't have—"

"Older injuries are harder to heal." Bronwyn drew more water. Then she smiled. "But not impossible. That won't bother you again." The honey-sage scent weakened as she hunted again. "You also have a scar on your uterus."

On a shocked gasp, Hannah said, "Charlie. I had Charlie by c-section."

"Let's just…" Bronwyn increased her power for the healing.

Hannah put her free hand on her lower belly. "It's like a low vibration."

"And that's enough for now." Opening her eyes, Bronwyn released Hannah's hand. "With Gemma, I found the tumor and destroyed it down to the cellular level." She shrugged. "I attempted to destroy any other cancerous cells I found, but there could be others."

"There aren't." Hannah shook her head. "I ran her DNA sequence to be sure."

Bronwyn smiled. "That's really good to know."

Raising her hand, Hannah stared at it as if it could answer all her questions. "I'm a medical doctor. A scientist."

"And I'm a witch, a healer."

"Oh my God." Hannah clapped a hand to her mouth. "Do you know what this means?"

Bronwyn smiled wryly. "I have a fair idea of what it could mean, if I could practice what I do more freely."

"Why can't you?" Hannah's laser focus returned.

"A number of reasons." Alexander stood and joined the conversation. The topic of circumspection always gave Bronwyn the screaming shits. "Your own skepticism is one of them. Imagine that on a global scale. There's an ethical component that we need to consider as well."

"Which is?" Hannah spoke, but both women focused on him.

"Say you had cured Hitler or Ted Bundy as a child?"

"We don't discriminate," Hannah said. "We treat the patient."

"And we trust Goddess to guide our path." Bronwyn added her tuppence worth.

Alexander let that one lie for now. "And then you've met the biggest reason for our caution."

Hannah shuddered. "Her."

"Yes, her." He cut the explanation short. Hannah had encountered enough to deal with for one day. "She'd love to get her hands on Bronwyn. Any of the cré-witches for that matter, but Bronwyn specifically. We can't risk that happening."

"Right." Hannah nodded, and then her expression turned misty. "But what Bronwyn can do…" She shook her head. "With that blessing, she could heal the world. Eradicate disease."

"An excellent point, Dr. Maxwell." Andy stood in the door holding Charlie's hand. "And I see definite income potential in that."

# CHAPTER TWENTY-NINE

Domodedova airport passed in a blur of thronging people, custom's officials, entrance visas, and Russian. Mags clung to Jack's hand, the only safe point in her careening universe. Alexander must have made sure all the applicable paperwork was in order, and then some, because they were cleared through passport control with a suspicious deference.

The flight had been interminable, the voice whispering in her head constantly. She concealed her problem from Jack. He was concerned enough, and the nasty gash across his ribs needed rest to heal. He'd refused to have it looked at before they left, and Mags was no expert, but she suspected he could do with a couple of stitches. Instead, she'd cleaned it up with antibacterial ointment and as many plasters as she could get him to tolerate.

"*Mags?*" At least the voice was softer than it had been when it had lured her out of Baile, but time had skewed. She'd lost the ability to discern where she was and when she was. It made her want to bang her head against stone until she could force the world to make sense again. "*Mags?*"

She shook her head.

Jack squeezed her hand. "Magdalene? Look at me."

Relief made her sag. That voice had been real and not in her swirling thoughts. She turned to Jack. "Yes."

"What's wrong?" His big handsome face wore a fearsome frown that would have made her smile in different circumstances. "You need to talk to me. I don't have the bond. I can't read your mind."

"Let's get somewhere quiet." The rushing people, the loud conversations, the ebb and flow of activity didn't help. "And I will tell you."

Nodding, he tightened his grip on her hand and led her outside.

Hot, sticky air rushed at them and coated her skin. The air smelled like tar and exhaust fumes.

Jack hailed a taxi. "Metropol hotel," he said.

With a grunt, the taxi driver set the vehicle in motion.

Mags closed her eyes and rested her cheek against Jack's shoulder. Thank Goddess for him. She would like to have looked around her. She was in Russia, for goodness' sake, Russia. The place of ancient folk tales, mystery, and intrigue. Here was where James Bond had tackled some of his biggest baddies. They were in the land of Tolstoy, Dostoyevsky, and Chekov. They were traveling in the land the infamous Stalin had come to power and ruled with his iron fist. Vladimir Lenin had led an uprising, and the last of the Tzars had been executed. And all she could do was pray the nightmare would end soon.

"I've got you, Magdalene." Jack pressed a kiss to her head. "I'm here."

And that's all that kept her breathing.

"*Mags,*" Taylor sobbed. "*I need you Mags. Where are you?*"

Tears stung beneath Mags's shut lids, but she kept her face down so Jack couldn't see.

"*I'm frightened, Mags,*" Taylor whispered. "*Tell me where you are.*"

Mags was frightened too. Terrified even. What if Taylor's voice was real, and she ignored it, and Taylor needed her? What if she wasn't even in Russia?

"Jack?" She breathed deep of the salty, woody scent that was all him.

He grunted.

"Tell me." Her voice stuck in her throat, and she had to force words past the tightness. "Tell me something real."

Shifting, he put his arm around her and drew her even closer. In a low, husky murmur, he said, "You are Magdalene Cray, and you're with me. I'm Jack Langham, and I'm here to take care of you."

"Where are we?"

"We're in a taxi on our way from the airport to the Metropol hotel in Moscow."

"Is Taylor here?"

He paused before he responded. "No, Taylor is back in Baile. Safe and sound with Warren watching over her, and Niamh and Alexander. Roderick and Maeve are there, and Alannah and Sinead. Nothing is going to happen to Taylor."

That was good. She let relief wash over her. "She's in my head."

"I thought as much." Jack hugged her close. "You stay with me, Magdalene. You keep talking to me and I'll tell you what's real and what's not."

---

JACK HADN'T PANICKED when the police had told him he'd killed Martin all those years ago. Even standing outside the nightclub where the fight had taken place, with police lights splashing blue across the faces and the buildings. He'd been shit scared, true, but calm and kind of resolved. He hadn't panicked all through his trial. He hadn't even panicked when he'd looked around prison for the first time and realized what and who he was trapped behind bars with for the foreseeable future.

Jack was panicking now.

He couldn't fight the living nightmare happening to Mags. He couldn't even fucking see it.

Her tension vibrated through him as she tried to keep hold of her sanity. And he could do fuck all but keep telling her shit and try to keep her grounded.

Weird thing about help and needing people, you never knew how much you needed a lifeline until you were cut off. He'd have given anything to call Warren and tell him what was happening. They were on their own, fighting invisible demons that, unless he missed his guess, had upped the ante.

Mags's face was tight with tension. White lines bracketed the grim line of her mouth, and her nails dug into him.

The trip from the airport to Moscow took two thousand years, and he kept talking the entire way. At least, when he spoke, some of the tension left Mags.

"I didn't mean to kill him." He'd gotten to his conversational dregs. He hadn't even told Warren the kind of detail about the night he'd killed someone that he was now divulging. "My sister was there, and she was a bit clueless about men. Somehow, she managed to get herself cornered outside a nightclub with this fucking animal from our neighborhood, Martin Sherman."

"Did he hurt her?"

Mags's quiet question surprised him. He hadn't been sure how much she'd heard. "Nah. But all three of them were surrounding her, and Martin had her pinned against a wall. Her top was ripped open."

As if sensing his turmoil, Mags wrapped her arm around his waist. "But you got there in time."

"Yeah." Helen's scream had told him exactly where to go. He hadn't hesitated. "It was three against one, but they were all smaller than me. Even then, I was a big lad."

"It wouldn't have mattered," Mags said. "You would still have tried to save her."

True that. He'd waded right in and taken them all on. When the dust had settled, two of them had run off, and Martin had been lying on the ground, not moving. Involuntary manslaughter had been the charge.

"I only hit him once." A bad punch that would follow Jack for the rest of his life. "He went over backwards and hit his head."

Mags nodded. "I know. And you were right; he was going to hurt her."

"You saw it?" He didn't know when he'd suspended his disbelief to the extent that he now believed Mags, but there it was.

She shrugged. "I dreamed about it. A while ago. Before you came to Baile. I didn't know you or why I was dreaming about you at the time."

"Huh." Because, for the life of him, he couldn't think of a single syllable more. "So, what other juicy details do you know about me?"

"I couldn't possibly say." Mags giggled, and the almost carefree sound made his heart swell.

Jack was glad he'd told her all he had. If only because of the tiny moment of respite that had followed.

Outside the taxi window, huge square apartment blocks crowded together like stacked dominos. The roads widened, and the traffic grew heavier. Jack had never seen so many cars, coming from all directions and crowding the five-lane road they were on. Billboards and signage were all written in Cyrillic, and he had no idea how to decode their meaning. Their taxi driver weaved through the mayhem like a rally veteran, crisscrossing lanes, squeezing into impossible gaps, and flooring it through amber lights.

The Kremlin came up suddenly, large red walls with arc lights atop them. Lush parkland with towering trees surrounded the oxblood walls then gave way to meticulous paving. Rows of flowers bobbed and swayed in their regimented beds like good little soldiers.

The Metropol, when the taxi finally stopped in front of it, was a throwback to a far more opulent era. A grand old Art Nouveau dame, showing off her gold filagree, and shining green marble.

He sent a silent thank you to Alexander for the small packet of information, along with a credit card, tucked into his passport. No way his bank account could have stretched to anything close. The poker-faced check-in clerk didn't twitch a muscle at their lack of baggage or that they looked like they'd slept in the clothes they were wearing.

Up in their room, the magnificence continued, and Jack didn't dare sit on any of the delicate gold and brocade chairs. A huge silk draped bed resembled the closest thing to heaven he'd seen.

Mags was drooping again. She leaned against him, a deep frown etching parallel lines between her eyebrows.

His ribs ached liked a motherfucker, and he'd need to clean the wound again, but first he'd see to her. Taking her with him into the en suite marble splendor, he ran water into the bath for her.

Standing by the vanity, Mags shivered like a whipped dog.

"Magdalene?" He cupped her face and turned her gaze to his. "Level with me, sweetheart, how bad is it?'

She grimaced and wrapped her arms around herself. "It comes and goes." A shudder wracked her body. "It's bad now."

*Fuck, fuck. FUCK!*

"Okay." He checked the water temperature and turned the taps off. "This is what we're going to do."

The childlike trust in her incredible green eyes wrenched his balls into a knot. She needed a better man taking care of her. But all she had was him, so he'd better sac up and deal.

"You're going to have a bath."

"But—"

"And I'm going to be right here with you." He pointed to the floor. "I'll turn my back, but I won't leave the room."

She nodded.

"Then I'm going to put you into bed."

"But—"

"I'm not leaving then either." It would take an act of God. That fucking bitch doing all this shit to his Magdalene could bring it; he was ready. "I'll be right there beside you. It doesn't matter what voices you hear or what you see in your dreams, I'm going to make sure you're safe."

"But—"

"No." He slashed the air with his hand. "That's how it's going to be."

She clapped a hand over his mouth. "Jack, you need to rest too."

"Then I'll tie a fucking rope around your wrist and attach it to me." He nudged her arms up. "But until we get that stupid air point active and working with you to get rid of what's buggering with your head, we're going to do it my way."

She opened her mouth, then shut it again.

Smart girl. Beautiful, brave, clever, kind, and so many different kinds of wonderful.

He tugged her dress over her head.

Underneath, her bra was white cotton and virginal. Her vulnerability killed him.

Mags put her hands up. "I can do the next part."

White cotton knickers rode the soft rise of her hipbones.

"Then get on with it." He winked at her. "Or I will."

Jack turned his back and ignored the sounds of her removing her bra and knickers. Forced his head not to dwell on images of her long, elegant, pale limbs climbing into warm water. Refused to focus on what her breasts looked like under the bra. Absolutely did not, in any way, linger on the thought of the naked vee between her long, slim legs.

Nope. He did none of that.

Sick fuck! He did all of that.

Her bath lasted another two centuries, and then she said, "I'm done."

Heart hammering, he turned.

She'd twisted her long hair into a messy knot atop her head. A white, fluffy bath towel swathed her from chest to midthigh. A gentle pink flush crowned her high cheekbones.

Shrugging, she said, "I've nothing to wear."

Jack whipped off his T-shirt. "It's not the cleanest, but it'll do for now."

Her eyes widened as she took her time examining each inch of his bare torso.

Her eyes lit up like she appreciated the view. "Oh, Jack," she whispered. "We really need to do this again sometime. Under different circumstances."

His groan came from way, way, way deep inside him. "Not helping, Magdalene. Not helping one fucking, tiny bit."

Her giggle almost made up for his pent-up sexual frustration. Almost.

# CHAPTER THIRTY

Jack paced the suite, his steps following Mags's soft breathing from the bed. She was sleeping, and as far as he could tell, it was peaceful. They were on the second floor, but he'd locked the windows anyway. He'd bolted the door and put a chair in front of it, and when he did allow himself to catch a few minutes, he napped in that chair.

Mags wouldn't get out of the room without alerting him.

Rubbing at his gritty eyes, he moved to the window. Moscow at night was lit in soft, yellow light. Across from the hotel, the Bolshoi Theatre had long since fallen still and silent, the patrons already home and safe in their beds.

Traffic had slowed considerably, but a city of almost twelve million people never really slept. A figure moved, more shadow than form, in the lee of the building. Jack moved to the side and out of sight from the street.

The figure strolled into the light. A man in a light summer windbreaker over jeans. He tugged his baseball cap lower and moved away down the street.

Jack stayed where he was.

Two men approached, crossed the street, and disappeared

from view beneath the window. After long minutes, they didn't reappear again.

He was jumpy as fuck. It could be nothing, but he was taking no chances.

His knife wound throbbed in a way he prayed didn't mean infection. When he'd cleaned it earlier, the sides had been red and swollen. He'd taken a quick shower, door open and his eyes on Mags the entire time, and done his best with some soap, water, and a ton of washing to get it clean.

Tomorrow, he'd need to find them something else to wear.

Mags had washed their underwear and left it hanging over the bath to dry. She'd climbed into bed wearing one of the hotel's white, fluffy robes.

Jesus, he was tired. He hadn't caught more than a catnap since Mags had disappeared from Baile.

Night quiet wasn't his friend. It gave him far too much time and silence to think. He didn't get about eighty percent of the turn his life had taken.

He'd ridden to Baile to find Warren when he hadn't heard from him in a few days. His first confrontation with Roderick and Alexander outside the Hag's Head in Greater Littleton had dominoed his life to this point. How long ago had that been?

The view outside the window stayed quiet, and he paced to the minibar and opened another bottle of water. Taking a swig, he tried to tally the time.

Then gave up. It didn't matter anyway. He was here now, and he was staying.

Mags murmured in her sleep and drew his attention. She burrowed deeper under the covers and went quiet again.

She'd twisted beneath his guard and grafted herself to his soul. He wasn't a romantic, had never given much credence to maudlin pathos about soulmates and "the one," but there she lay sleeping, his one, his soulmate.

Jesus, he wanted more than anything to be her coimhdeacht. To get even closer to Mags was a possibility he ached for.

Back to the window.

One of the two men from earlier now stood in the shadows of the Bolshoi across the street, and he wasn't a big believer in coincidence. During his night watch, he'd registered three of those handy coincidences, and they reminded him to stay sharp.

He had tomorrow's destination picked out. An internet search on a loaner laptop from the hotel had delivered a program at the Russian State University for the Humanities, and a Dr. Emma Fletcher. Dr Emma Fletcher, late of Cambridge, was here and studying the myths and folklore of Russia. A long list of google hits assured him Dr. Fletcher was the person to talk to about Russia and her tales and legends. Magic, Alexander had told him, always left a trail, most of it whispers and campfire stories, and dismissed by the modern world as make believe. It was a longshot, but they needed to start somewhere. Hiding in this mega stretch of land was the cardinal point for air, and his Mags needed him to find it for her. Failure, not even a remote option.

---

WARREN EASED Taylor's arm away from his throat and tried to find a comfortable position. His big ideas about him, Niamh, a large bed, and no interruptions had ended abruptly when Taylor had taken up residence in his suite. She'd offered to sleep on one of the couches in the other room, but no man let his daughter take the couch. So, Taylor and Niamh shared his big, beautiful bed, and he got neck cramp on the couch.

Taylor was having nightmares about Mags. The sort of nightmares that woke her screaming and crying, and he wasn't leaving his daughter to battle those demons alone. Tonight had been bad enough that he'd had to lie down beside her on the bed before she would go back to sleep.

The dog lying across his ankles raised its head, grumbled, and resettled.

Warren had to laugh. Why had he ever thought he'd share a bed with Niamh alone?

Current occupants: him, Niamh, Taylor, two dogs, eight—yes, eight—cats, and an injured squirrel. Baile couldn't make a bed big enough.

Niamh rolled to her side and looked at him. "Can't sleep?"

He shook his head because she already knew that much.

Grunting, Taylor tossed out her arm and whacked him in the chest.

Niamh giggled softly. "Does she get this restless sleeping thing from you?"

"Couldn't tell you." He turned his head and met Niamh's gaze. Her dark eyes sucked him into the void, and happily he went. "Other than Debra, I've never slept with anyone before."

Blinking, Niamh said, "You mean actual sleeping versus euphemism sleeping?"

"Yup." And he wouldn't be euphemism sleeping with anyone else either. Not in his near future, at least.

Niamh's smile bloomed slow and sultry and made him almost forget his daughter was sleeping between them. "That is so unfair," she whispered.

"You have no idea what's going on in my mind right now."

She sucked the corner of her bottom lip into her mouth. "I know exactly what's in your mind right now."

Yeah, she did, and through the bond, she broadcast her wholehearted approval. He and Niamh had a date. Of the naked and alone variety.

Then she frowned, clearly catching his concern for Taylor. "She's getting visions of Mags."

He nodded, Taylor had told them both as much before falling asleep and hogging the bed.

"I hate that for her," he whispered. "She shouldn't be worrying about this shit."

Niamh's understanding and support came through the bond like a warm internal hug. "It doesn't seem fair, does it?"

"No." He'd come to Baile, compelled by a driving need he hadn't understood. At the time, he'd thought it would only affect him.

Niamh lifted the squirrel and moved him behind her head. "Would it have made a difference if you'd known?"

"I don't know." Lying to a woman who could roam your thoughts and feelings was pointless. "I only know that I wish my daughter wasn't being plagued by fucking nightmares."

"She's a cré-witch, Warren." Niamh reached over Taylor and touched his shoulder. "I don't think there was ever any avoiding that."

Fate was a fucker. Endless questions within questions that had no answer. "Maybe."

"I was born to cré-magic." Niamh spread her fingers over his shoulder. "It was always there, and always going to be part of my life. I know this is hard for you."

He could sense the truth in what she said. "Did you ever resent it?"

"All the time." Her soft chuckle stroked his senses. "Why did I have to be one of those strange Cray women who lived in the castle on the hill? Why couldn't I play with the other children? Why did people get so freakily obsessed with me?"

"That last one is easy." He took her hand off his shoulder and kissed it. "You're incredible."

"Don't make this weird," Taylor murmured. "Child, literally, right here."

# CHAPTER THIRTY-ONE

Bronwyn loved Hannah's brain. The more she worked with her, the more she learned. After breakfast—and even her loyal self had to admit Alexander's pancakes paled in comparison to Alannah's—Hannah had trailed her into the healer's hall.

Playing in a patch of sunshine by the window, Charlie was more relaxed than he'd been since his arrival.

Poor little guy. Nobody should have to deal with Rhiannon, and certainly not a child that young.

It made her doubly frightened for her two, and she touched the rounding curve of her belly.

"You're pregnant." Hannah turned her eagle focus on Bronwyn.

They'd gone beyond half-truths and platitudes at this point in their relationship, so Bronwyn nodded. "Twins."

"Oh." Hannah's eyes widened. "Not the same twins she wanted to know about?"

Bronwyn couldn't suppress a grimace. "The very same."

Hannah looked over at Charlie as if having the same thoughts as Bronwyn about his vulnerability. "Why does she want them so badly?"

Oh boy! How to answer that question. "It's complicated."

"Really?" Hannah gave her a look that called her bullshit. "You're going to pull that one with me?"

Well, the woman had taken all the other hits to her belief system quite well. "Alexander is their father."

"Right." Hannah nodded, not surprised.

"And he is…" Bronwyn hunted for the right words. "Her son."

Hannah gaped. "Her son?"

"Yup."

Sitting down, Hannah took a breath. "Someone actually impregnated that and survived?"

The praying mantis had nothing on Bronwyn's mother-in-law. "Actually, we're not sure who his father is. We have our suspicions though."

"Hmm." Hannah frowned in Charlie's direction, but Bronwyn doubted the frown was aimed at her son. She turned back to Bronwyn, her eyes keen and direct. "Could you do something for me?"

"Within reason."

"Can you stop dancing around the truth and give it to me straight?"

All right, then. You didn't get much clearer than that, and after all Hannah had been through, she deserved the right to choose what she believed and what she didn't. "I can." Bronwyn got it all lined up in her head. "Rhiannon managed to get herself pregnant and had Alexander. He's hundreds of years old, and she had him to fulfill a prophecy. The exact wording isn't important, but it states that he will have a child with me, although we didn't know it was me at the time, and that child will be the ultimate of all magic." She amended for the sake of clarity. "Or children, in this case. Like I said, I'm having twins."

"Wow." Hannah stood and walked over to the window. "That's…um…"

"A lot. I know." Bronwyn didn't know if she'd be a good enough mother to one normal child. Let alone raising these two, upon whom so much depended.

"F'ed up," Hannah said. "I was going to say f'ed up."

That about covered it. "She wants my children, so she can control the end game."

"Which is?"

"World domination." Bronwyn managed a light shrug. It sounded stupid to her too. "Your basic evil nemesis plotline."

Hannah made a face. "Huh."

"Ah, here you are." Andy strode through the door dressed in a pair of breeches and a flowing white shirt. He looked like an 80s music video escapee. "I'm glad I've found you together."

"What does he do here?" Hannah glanced at her.

"We're not quite sure," Bronwyn whispered back. "But he seems to have made himself at home and is sorting out our finances."

Hannah stared at Andy as if he might grow wings. "An accountant?"

"I can hear you." Andy gave them a tight smile. "And accounting is only a small portion of what I do."

The sooner they got to the reason for his visit, the sooner he would leave. "What did you need, Andy?"

"I'm glad you asked." Andy beamed and produced a folder from under his arm. He gestured them to take a seat at the table. He sat and opened his folder.

Bronwyn took one stool and Hannah the one beside her.

"Now, I've run some numbers." Andy handed out sheets of paper to her and Hannah.

Hannah squinted at the paper. "Are these clinics?"

"Yes." Andy grinned. "I'm so glad you picked that up. These are clinics with global reputations for exemplary service and unprecedented results." He leaned forward and tapped a column on Hannah's paper. "As you can see, the best percentages in terms of medical results are disappointing."

"I don't know about that." Hannah scowled at the numbers. "These are some top-notch institutions providing the cutting edge of what medical science can offer."

Andy chuckled. "Exactly."

Clearly, Bronwyn was missing the punchline. "What does all this mean?"

"Now, Blessed—" his use of her title made Bronwyn blink "—what you can do is so far superior to anything on the sheet in front of you."

Hannah glanced at her and Andy.

"As Dr. Maxwell said the other day, you can potentially eradicate disease and injury from the world."

Bronwyn got an inkling of where he was heading. "But—"

"You need to be circumspect." Andy nodded. "And I fully understand, and in fact, actively encourage that. But now we have Dr. Maxwell."

Leaning closer to her, Hannah murmured, "What is he getting at?"

"He wants to sell what I can do." Bronwyn would love to be a fly on the wall when Andy ran his idea past Roderick. "And, I'm guessing, using you to give the entire thing legitimacy."

# CHAPTER THIRTY-TWO

By the dark circles under his eyes and the harsh lines of his face, Mags knew Jack hadn't slept. He paced their hotel suite like a hunting bear, peering out the window, back to the minibar, two seconds on the sofa, up again and at the window.

She hadn't the heart to tell him how bad her head spun this morning. Having slept well, she'd woken to the voice whispering urgently and repeatedly in her head. It wanted to know where she was, demanded she let it inside. Brick by careful brick, she spent her lucid moments building a wall. However, the voice tried to force its way inside as though the wall was like a membrane.

Jack had ordered a room service breakfast, and she managed to choke down enough food to get the grim expression off his face. To be honest, she wasn't confident he wouldn't get her in a headlock and pry her jaw open if she refused to eat enough to satisfy him.

*Mags?*
*Magdalene?*
*Listen to me.*
"No."

Jack's head snapped her way.

"No more coffee." She pushed her cup away and managed a smile.

It couldn't have been entirely successful, because his gaze narrowed on her. "How bad?"

"Not bad." She spread butter on a sweet roll she had no intention of eating.

Jack folded his arms. "That bad, hmm?"

*Bugger*! And she'd thought it was only coimhdeacht who could ride around in a witch's head. "It's under control." Kind of.

He finished his enormous plate of bacon, eggs, sausage, potatoes, and grilled tomato. "I did some research last night when you were sleeping."

"You should have—"

He glowered at her.

Mags changed tack. "What did you find?"

"Well—" he wiped his mouth on a starched white napkin "— we don't have any leads, or any idea where this cardinal point is, and contacting the coven is not an option."

Mags spread jam on her sweet roll. She missed Alannah and her homemade jam, and homemade rolls. She missed Baile and her other coven sisters. "And?"

"Based on everything I've heard around the coven, these cardinal points don't exist in a vacuum. Magic has resonances, folk stories around places that have magic, strange happenings, superstitions."

She nodded and broke a tiny piece off her roll.

Jack stared pointedly at the bread morsel.

Obediently, Mags chewed and swallowed.

He pushed the fruit platter her way. "I made an appointment this morning with a professor at a local university." He gave the fruit a nudge.

Mags took a strawberry and ate it.

"She specializes in folklore, urban legends, Russian mythology."

*Yes, there.*

It sounded like her premonition, but the last time Mags had trusted a voice she'd ended up alone on a train to London and headed straight into the hands of Rhiannon's minions.

*Emma.*

"A Dr. Emma Fletcher. She's English, but she's been working out here for a few years now." Jack prodded the fruit platter at her again.

Feeling more like herself than she had in weeks, Mags stood. "Let's go."

"Magda—"

"If you shove that fruit plate at me one more time, Jack Langham, you're going to end up wearing it."

---

MAGS WAS LYING TO HIM. The rigid set of her shoulders and the way she clung to his hand told him as much. He couldn't risk leaving her alone at the hotel, so he had no option but to take her with him. The parking valet hailed them a taxi.

Navigating their way around the towering architecture of the university took time. Blocks of seventies-style bureaucracy cozied up beside neoclassic monoliths as they found their way to Dr. Fletcher's department.

Students thronged the spaces between the buildings, looking much like students the world over with their backpacks, jeans, and to-go coffee cups. They were friendly enough, and few spoke sufficient English to help him and Mags on their way.

A young couple, hands perma-glued to each other, pointed out the correct building.

Mags tensed, and then dropped his arm. Her longs legs ate

up the ground as she strode up the steps and between the columns bracketing the glass doors.

"Mags." He almost had to break into a run to catch her. "Where are you—"

"There." Mags turned left down a corridor and increased her pace.

She was a tall woman, and those long legs of hers could make rapid progress.

"She's here." Mags glanced at him with opaque green eyes. He remembered something one of her coven sisters had said about when Mags was having one of her things. They all described her eyes glazing over like they were right now.

Mags came to a junction and swung right and up a flight of stairs. She tripped over her skirt and Jack caught her arm and righted her. "She's here. It's her."

"Take it easy, Magdalene." He'd prefer if they could get there in one piece.

"You don't understand." Mags shook her head. "I know it's her. I can feel it."

Oh-kay. And what else could he do but follow her?

At nearly a run, their footsteps slapped against the polished floor. Mags took another right and stopped in front of a wooden door with Dr. E. Fletcher embossed on the frosted glass panel.

Stopping her before she could throw it open, Jack knocked.

"Come," a woman called from the other side.

Mags threw open the door and smiled. "I'm Mags."

Jack hadn't met a lot of university lecturers in his time, but Dr. Emma Fletcher wasn't even a little bit like what he would have expected. Around five nine, toned and fit, with a long blond braid over one shoulder, she stood from behind her desk as they entered. Glacial grey eyes locked on him, assessing the greatest risk, and then Mags. Dr. Emma Fletcher was a fighter, and by the way she stood, poised and alert, a highly effective one. "Who are you?"

Mags strode forward, both hands out.

Moving quickly, Jack got in front of her. "We're your ten o'clock."

Dr. Fletcher frowned and looked at her arm. Starting where her cream T-shirt ended, faint markings rippled beneath the skin of her left arm. It took Jack a moment to connect them with the same markings on both Warren and Roderick.

"You're my coimhdeacht." Mags slid around him. "And you're a woman."

Emma blinked at Mags and shook her head. "I'm sorry?"

"Oh my." Mags giggled. "Roderick is going to be so surprised."

As he watched her, Emma's mask slid back into place. Cool, calm, and unruffled, she took Mags's outstretched hand. "I beg your pardon?"

"Dr. Fletcher—" Jack got between Mags and Emma and held out his hand "—thanks for seeing us on such short notice." He didn't get what the hell was going on here, but he did get how responsible for Mags's safety he was, and nothing about Emma Fletcher was giving him the trusty-happys.

"Mr. Langham?" Emma shook his hand in a strong, sure grip. Callouses on her palm proved she spent her time doing more with her hands than tapping away at a keyboard. She motioned the two chairs in front of her desk.

A neat stack of papers perched to her left, a keyboard and computer monitor to her right. Framed degrees on the wall to their right proved her credentials. A large bookshelf underneath her framed degrees housed rows of books in ascending order. A couple of awards nestled in amongst the books.

Mags took her seat but perched on the edge like an excited child. "You've seen me before."

If Jack hadn't been watching her so carefully, he would have missed the flicker in Emma's eyes. She did recognize Mags but wasn't about to give up that information.

"I'm sorry." A polite smile spread over her face. "But this is the first time—"

"In your dreams." Mags flapped one hand. "You've seen my face in your dreams. And you've heard a voice." She wrinkled her nose. "But the voice wasn't me."

Emma's face hardened, and she looked at Jack. "Is this a joke?"

"No." That much he knew for sure.

Coimhdeacht? Had Mags called this woman coimhdeacht? Fucking hell! Her coimhdeacht. Fucking, fucking hell.

"We need information from you," Jack said into the tense silence.

Emma dragged her gaze back to him. "About?"

"We need to find the air cardinal point," Mags said. "And you're going to help us."

"The air cardinal point?" Emma frowned and gave a small laugh. "I'm afraid you have me at a disadvantage. I have no idea what you're talking about."

"Yes, you do." Mags sounded stronger than she had in days, her eyes clear and lucid. "You know exactly what I am. You also know exactly what we're up against."

Emma stood, her body tense and ready to fight. "I think you should leave."

## CHAPTER THIRTY-THREE

Jack held it together until they shut their room door at the Metropol, and then he lost it. Mags was so fragile, he kept it to a dull roar. He was tired, his knife wound hurt, worry chewed at his good humor, and she'd gone and thrown herself in front of what could be an eighteen-wheeler of trouble and mayhem. "Want to tell me what the hell that was all about?"

The white lines were back around Mags's mouth, and she moved stiffly to an overstuffed chair and perched on the edge. "You'll have to remind me."

"Magdalene?" Concern flushed his fear and anger as he crouched at her feet.

"I don't know where we've just been." She pressed her fingers to her temples. "We went out?"

She'd been so different in Emma's office, more like the Mags he had first met. The shell of a woman, clenching her hands in her lap, tightened his heart into a fist.

Jack got her a glass of water and wrapped her hands around it. He went for one of the small bottles of whisky in the minibar for himself. Was it a good idea in light of the amount of sleep he'd been getting and his wound? Nope. Did he give a shit? Also, nope.

He'd wanted to shake the crap out of Mags for opening her mouth and spewing to Emma, but in that moment, she'd seemed normal. Well, as normal as his Magdalene got. Taking the other seat beside her, he said, "Mags, we're in Moscow."

"Moscow?" She glanced around the room. "The voice wants to know where I am."

"Did you tell it?" His gut clenched.

Her eyes flit his way. "Tell who?"

He'd do anything to get Mags back, and to not have to keep doing this again and again. "Mags, I'm Jack."

"I know that." She nodded. "Jack Langham, and we're going to have four children."

If he got her out of this alive, he'd give her twenty fucking children. "Yes. I've brought you to Moscow to wake the air cardinal point." He took one of her hands. It was corpse cold, and he chaffed it between his larger ones. "We're here in secret. You can't trust the voice."

She stared down at their joined hands. "I do know that."

"Okay." He took his first proper breath. "Try not to tell it anything until we know who it is." Jack would bet his nuts he already knew the answer, but her mind was like a spiderweb, delicate and tangled. "We went to see someone this morning."

"Emma." Mags straightened. "Emma Fletcher, and she's my coimhdeacht."

That detail she managed to keep straight. "Are you sure?"

She laughed and it nearly killed him with how much she looked like his Mags when she did. "I can't make a mistake about that, Jack." She touched her breastbone. "I can feel her, in here." She pointed at the door. "You should get that."

"Get what?"

A knock came from the door.

A young guy dressed in hotel livery handed him a note. "This came for you, Mr. Langham."

Before he could reach into his pocket for a tip, the guy darted off.

Jack turned the note over in his hands. He couldn't remember the last time someone had sent him a note on real paper, and this was the thick and expensive kind.

"We should go." Mags stood beside him.

"Go?"

"The note." She reached for the door. "It's from Emma, and she wants us to meet her in the restaurant downstairs." Looking over her shoulder she said, "Come along."

Swearing, Jack got to the door before she opened it and put his palm against it. "Just a bloody minute."

Mags rolled her eyes. "Read the note then."

Jesus, she was giving him whiplash. One minute lost and fragile, and the very next clear-eyed and straight in the head.

Not taking his palm off the door, Jack opened the note. Exactly as Mags had said. It was from Emma with a request to meet her in the restaurant. He didn't know what to do. The Mags tapping her foot at him seemed to have her shit together, but not two minutes ago she hadn't had a bloody clue where they were.

"It's okay, Jack." Rising on her toes, she kissed his cheek. "It's me and only me in my head right now. The note really is from Emma, and we need to see her."

"Why?" He played for time while he waited for the solution to drop out the sodding sky.

"Because she has information we need. She knows where the air point is situated, and she can help us activate it."

"Mags." He stepped into the conversational tornado. "I don't know if I can trust what you say."

"I understand." She patted his cheek. "But it's the hotel restaurant. Even if I'm completely nutty, we have to eat lunch."

As if complicit, his stomach growled.

"See." Mags laughed and rattled the door handle. "Let's go."

Jack's misgivings escalated as they entered the restaurant. Above them, the elaborate stained-glass ceiling filtered gentle light over the starched white tablecloths.

From a table near the back of the rectangular room, Emma stood. She had a man with her, and he stood as well.

"Emma." Mags weaved through the tables with a wide smile. "It's so lovely to see you."

Emma rubbed her left arm, her gaze stuck on Mags. "Hello."

"And Jack." He inserted himself in the conversation.

"Yes, Jack." Emma shook Jack's hand and then motioned the man beside her. "This is Sasha, my…colleague."

"Oh, Emma." Mags giggled and shook her head. "That's a bit of a euphemism."

"Right." Emma took her seat again.

Picking up the menu, Mags said, "What's good here? I'm starving."

The waiter appeared, and Jack ordered himself a stiff scotch. Being clear headed hardly presented as an advantage at this point.

Mags ordered herself a glass of white wine and chewed on her bottom lip as she perused the menu.

Jack wasn't the sort of bloke to beat around the bush. "What's this all about?"

"Jack." Mags touched his arm. "We'll get to that, but I'd really like to order first."

Getting food into Mags had been hard enough, and who was he to argue with her if she was going to eat willingly. "Fine."

They waded through the tense atmosphere and ordered lunch. Jack hadn't a bloody clue what he was getting.

Once the waiter had disappeared, Mags leaned forward and sipped her wine. "Tell him now."

"Right." Emma blinked at Mags.

Jack almost felt sorry for her. Unadulterated Mags took some getting used to.

"Sasha?" Emma nudged her companion. "Maybe you'd like to take this part."

Dark, with fine features, Sasha pushed his gold-rimmed glasses up his nose. "It's a somewhat complicated story." His lightly accented voice was pleasant and smooth.

Jack resisted the urge to tell the man to get on with it and sipped his scotch.

"Start with Baba Yaga," Mags said.

"How do you know that?" Emma blinked at Mags.

Jack had this part. "She knows things. It's what she does."

"Quite extraordinary." Sasha smiled and dropped his eyes. "Forgive me, but when you have always believed a thing to be true, and then that thing sits before you…" He shrugged. "You are Blessed, of course."

"I am."

Jack's hackles rose. "You best get talking, mate."

"They're on our side, Jack." Mags touched his wrist.

Sasha glanced at Emma, got a nod, and spoke, "Baba Yaga is one of the most enduring figures in Slavic folklore. At times she is represented as a forest mother, at others, she eats children, often lives in a hut on chicken legs. She may help or hinder those who seek her out, but there are accounts of her taking a maternal role. She's most often depicted as a hideous old woman, and sometimes as three sisters, but the first clear reference to her can be traced to 1755 in Mikhail—"

"Stick to the basics, Sasha." Emma patted his shoulder.

"Sorry." Sasha flushed. "I've made an extensive study of Baba Yaga."

Sitting back in his chair, Jack wanted to wrap the conversation up and get Mags somewhere safe. There were too many people in the dining room. "I'm not hearing anything worth listening to yet."

"Jack." Mags looked at him reproachfully. "You're being rude."

"I'm being cautious." And also, maybe, rude. "I need to keep you safe."

Emma gave him an approving nod.

His jury was out on Emma. If she was Mags's coimhdeacht, she'd have to prove to him she could keep his girl safe.

"However, the etymology of Baba Yaga is much, much older, and references to variants of her can be traced to medieval times. The first instance of these being *Ježibaba* in Western Slavic tales." Sasha paused as the waiter put their meals in front of them.

Looks like Jack had ordered steak. He got to work keeping his mouth busy chewing. As he did, he scanned their fellow diners for any sign of trouble. Anything off, and he was getting Mags out of there.

"A lot of folktales have some basis in fact," Emma said as she picked up her cutlery.

Mags grinned at the table's occupants. "Well, in our case, that certainly proved to be true."

"Right." Emma scrutinized their fellow diners. "About a hundred years after the legend of Baba Yaga came up, so did a group of people who believed where there was smoke there was fire."

"She's real?" Jack would have had a much harder time even giving this brain space if the last few weeks of his life hadn't gone the way they had.

"In a way." Sasha grimaced. "What is true, is there is a malevolent female figure who has played a significant role in Slavic history. She's hidden behind children's stories and folktales, but we believe she's real."

"The we includes me," Emma said and her grey eyes locked on Jack.

Jack's mind scrambled and refused to find traction. "Break it down for me in simple terms."

"Plain speaking it is then." Emma put her knife and fork precisely together in the center of her plate and leaned closer. "We believe Baba Yaga has existed all these years. We believe she's still around and still causing shit. We believe she's the same blood witch you call Rhiannon, and we believe she's getting ready to launch something big." She started eating again. "Clear enough for you?"

Mags clapped. "Quite succinct, Emma. You gave it to him straight all right."

"Everything except who the *we* you keep talking about is." There was so much about what he was hearing he would need to cogitate slowly.

"We are a watchdog organization," Sasha said. "We are almost as old as the legend herself, and we have gathered a large body of evidence and data to support our theories."

"Legends like Baba Yaga exist all over the world, and we're damn sure they're connected," Emma said.

"What matters in all of this is that they're here to help," Mags said.

"Why?" Jack hoped they kept the explanation simple again.

Emma rubbed the markings on her arm as if they itched. "As much as we know Rhiannon to be true, we also know the cré-witches are real and the physical manifestation of Goddess on this earth. Members of our organization have given their lives to prevent Rhiannon from ascending to Goddess. If you've encountered her, you'll know exactly why her power needs to be limited and eventually eradicated." She dabbed her lips with her napkin. "The only being who can accomplish her end is Goddess."

Sasha put his elbows on the table and lowered his voice. "All our studies indicate matters are rapidly approaching their conclusion."

Jack was never one to not take a long gander at the gift horse's mouth. "What gives you that idea?"

"Goddess wakes," Sasha said. "Water is active and so is fire, and now we have a cré-witch in Moscow and she's here to wake air. Once all the points are active, magic will quicken, and the battle will begin in earnest."

"Rhiannon is growing in power too." Emma leaned her elbows on the table and took over the good news recitation. "As you wake the points, she has access to greater power. Although she uses blood magic, the more magic there is to be had, the more she can use. Not waking the points, however, is not an option, because without activating them, Goddess can't incarnate. And if Goddess doesn't incarnate, nothing and nobody can stop Rhiannon."

Jack filed that under things he wished he hadn't known. "So, you're saying we're damned if we do and damned if we don't?"

"Pretty much." Emma fisted her hands. "But the battle's not over yet, and you're not on your own."

# CHAPTER THIRTY-FOUR

Sasha disappeared after lunch to set matters in order for that night. Mags wasn't sure what matters were, but Emma stayed with her and Jack in their room. She did a thorough check of the room and made a couple of phone calls before she relaxed enough to sit down and talk.

Lifting her sleeve, she stared at the faint markings on her arm. "I've heard about coimdeacht," she said. "But I never thought I'd be one."

"Surprise." Mags held her hands up and tried to keep it light.

Emma chuckled and stretched her legs out in front of her. "So, if I'm your coimhdeacht, then who is Jack to you?"

Jack loomed behind Mags's chair. "I'm her man."

Mags really liked the sound of that. "Yes, he is."

"Tell me about yourself." Emma sat on the edge of her chair.

"I'm an air witch," Mags said, "And my blessing is seer, which means—"

"I know." Emma grinned. "And you live at Baile?"

"I was born there. There were only four of us. Niamh is a guardian and fire. Alannah and Sinead share the warden blessing, and they're earth. A couple of months ago, Bronwyn joined us, and she's the healer. She's also the one who woke water."

Emma folded her arms over her chest. "Is she the one? *The son of death shall bear the torch that lights the path. And the daughter of life shall bring forth water nascent and call it onto the path of light. Then they will bear fruit. And this fruit will be the magick. The greatest of magick and the final magick.*"

"You know about that?" Mags hadn't considered there might be other people in the world like them.

"Like Sasha said, we have done extensive studies. We have watchers all over the world. Since water woke, we've been on high alert. Part of our organization's purpose was to guard the air point until the right witch came to wake it." She tilted her chin at Mags. "And now you're here."

Until very recently, she'd been living at Baile with the twins and Niamh, and assuming they were the only people in the world with strange gifts. "If your organization knew about us, why didn't you make contact before?"

"A good question." Emma grimaced. "Like any organization, we're made up of different opinions. Some of the older members had concerns that by making contact we risked exposing you further. As long as Rhiannon was keeping a low profile, those of us who disagreed were prepared to keep a distant eye on you."

"And then Bronwyn came." Mags could see the logic in what Emma said. Until Bronwyn, they'd all been woefully ignorant of their legacy.

Jack perched on her chair arm and slung his arm across the back. "You said something about Rhiannon gathering power and a final battle."

Emma crossed her ankles and stared at the ceiling. "How much do you know about Rhiannon's organization?"

"It's an organization?" Fury pulsed in Jack's voice.

"Very much so." Emma looked at him, her face grim. "She's

had hundreds of years to spread her tentacles everywhere. She has influence at the highest level." She sat up and rested her elbows on her knees. "The very highest levels."

"To what end?" Mags's blood visions were starting to make a horrible sort of sense.

"Primarily destabilization," Emma said. "And she's been moving her chess pieces into place so she's ready when she makes her move."

"Do you know when?" Jack's hand tightened on her shoulder.

"We don't." Emma looked back at Mags. "That's more your department."

Other than Jack, Emma was probably the person she could trust most in the world. "I've been having some trouble with my gift."

"Waking the air point should help," Emma said. "We have studies of seers and what were called prophets over history. We have a theory that your blessing has become unstable with Goddess having been latent for so long, and the cardinal points being dormant."

Jack tucked her closer to him. "We were hoping that would be the case."

Something else occurred to Mags. "Are there others like your organization?"

"We don't know." Emma held her palms up. "Our priority has been keeping ourselves on the DL. Rhiannon has managed to kill a fair number of our members over the years. We've learned to keep what we do secret. The hard way."

"I'm sorry." Mags took Emma's hands.

A warm tingle spread up her arm from the contact.

Emma shuddered and smiled. "That is the strangest thing I've ever felt, and I've spent my life dealing with impossible shit."

Jack shifted.

Feeling like she was being disloyal to Jack in some way, Mags dropped Emma's hand. "We need to talk about what your being my coimhdeacht means."

"Yeah." Emma got to her feet and fiddled with her braid. "We will need to talk, but let's get that air point active first."

Mags didn't need her gift to read a disturbance in Emma's energy. "Agreed."

"I thought coimhdeacht became life partners," Jack said, an edge in his voice.

"Not necessarily," Mags said. "Sometimes those relationships become romantic, because the bond is so close. It's hard for another person to work around the bond."

Emma smirked at Jack. "Worried?"

"Nope." Jack shrugged. "I'm not walking away from Mags without a fight. Don't care who or what you are."

"No, you wouldn't." Mags wanted to kiss him but resisted the urge. "I told you. Four children."

"Right." And the way he said it made it sound like a vow.

Emma laughed and shook her head at Jack. "Settle down, big man. You've nothing to worry about."

"I'm not worried." He folded his arms and glowered back.

Nobody felt much like eating as dinner time came and went. Outside, night settled, and the lights of Moscow flared to life.

Under Emma and Mags's combined urgings, Jack agreed to sleep for a while, but not without a long lecture to Emma about not leaving Mags alone and not taking her eyes off Mags.

Funny, but the voice had been absolutely silent.

Night wore on, and Mags peeped in on Jack. Flat on his back, he was fast asleep. As anxious as she was to get going, it was good that he rested.

Emma joined her at the door. "He's a good man."

"The very best." Mags's heart warmed. "He's been injured, but he's trying to hide it from me."

"I'll have a look before we go." Emma grinned. "He won't like it, but I reckon I can take him."

Mags got the feeling that was not an idle boast. "So, you're a hard arse?"

"Yep." Emma laughed. "My dad was special forces and saw to it I could take care of myself. Turns out I liked it so much I kept finding new ways to do it."

"Was your dad involved in your organization?" Not wanting to wake Jack, Mags moved back to the chairs.

"No." Emma strode to the window and stared out. "But my mother's parents were. My grandmother had…gifts."

Mags wanted to know all about Emma and her family. "What kind?"

"She could predict the weather." Emma looked wistful. "Nothing like you can do, but she had a sense for the weather, and a really good way of reading people."

It was such a relief to be able to talk openly with someone. "Alexander has this theory that our blessings are spread throughout the world in a distilled form. Since Goddess has been dormant, the magic has dissipated. That there are people who are our descendants and have partial blessings."

"The Alexander?" Emma turned and raised her brows.

"The same." Mags kept forgetting how much Emma knew. "All it took was falling in love with Bronwyn."

"Actually, we've been watching him for years now, and he's been working against Rhiannon for a long time."

Mags loved hearing that. She'd never gotten an evil read off him, even before Alexander had defected. "Really?"

"Oh, yes. We even debated contacting him, and then Bronwyn came along. There are also rumors that he took a more active part in making sure some witches survived the night of the coven massacre. They're unsubstantiated, but there are several historical accounts of a mysterious man who got the few witches that did escape to safety." She leaned against the wall beside the window and stared out. "We were hoping his father's genetics would show."

Mags had been keeping that secret to herself for some time now. "They're very alike. You should see them together."

Emma made a noncommittal sound. "Sasha shouldn't be much longer."

"What are we waiting for?"

"The metro system to get quiet."

Mags didn't think she'd heard her right. "What does the metro system have to do with any of this."

Emma grinned. "You'll see."

---

"Wow." Mags turned in a full circle to take in Komsomolskaya metro station. Even Jack was struck dumb as they stood beneath the impressive yellow dome. Baroque scrollwork and huge chandeliers crowned stylized Corinthian columns. In the wee hours of the morning, only a few people still lingered in the echoing space.

"Beautiful, isn't it?" Emma led them to a down escalator. Dressed in leather pants and combat boots, she looked every inch the badass. "It was designed to express the Russian fight for freedom."

On the platform, she strode forward as if she knew exactly where they were going.

Mags trailed behind, still awed by the baroque ceilings and marble pillars. More chandeliers lit their way. She'd always imagined Moscow to be a dreary, cold place but her assumptions were being flipped.

Toward the end of the platform, Emma slipped behind a pillar. She counted the wall-mounted torchères and turned to them with a grin. "This one. Stand back."

"Why?" Jack scowled.

"You'll see," Emma said, and tugged on the torchère.

Stone grated against stone as a square opened in the floor beneath them.

Jack's hand shot out to keep Mags back. "What the bloody hell?"

"Like I said." Emma shrugged. "Our organization has been around for a long time. This was built when the metro station was, back in the thirties."

Mags peered into the darkness. Her magic rippled beneath her skin, a warm caress blooming deep inside her. "I can feel it."

"You're shining." Jack gaped at her.

"What?" Mags raised her hands. A faint golden glow surrounded her hands and arms.

Emma stared at her in wonder. "It really is you."

"You just decided that now?" Jack glared at her.

Emma shook her head at him. "I knew it was her, but seeing it…"

"Right." Jack nodded. "Well, come along sparkle fairy; let's get your magic fixed."

With a torch from her pocket, Emma led the way down the shadowy staircase inside the hole in the floor.

Jack went first, keeping a secure grip on Mags's wrist. "Go slowly. These steps are steep."

The air point was here. It resonated through Mags, and if Jack hadn't been holding her, she would have run toward it. The power was so thick and potent around her, she felt like she could float on it like a cloud. "I never felt it until you opened the floor."

"It was designed that way." Emma trained the torchlight on each stair as they descended. Shadows played over the delicate, clean lines of her face. "Back when this was built, they had access to enough magic knowledge to ward the air point."

"Clever," Jack said.

Emma stopped suddenly. "Wait!"

Mags and Jack froze.

"Did you just say something nice?" Emma batted her lashes at Jack.

Jack growled, but a small grin twitched around his mouth. "Let's get this done."

"As far as we know, our enemy has no idea this is here. They know it's somewhere in Moscow, but that's as close as they can get." Emma resumed walking, her boots near soundless. "Still, we take nothing for granted where that bitch and her followers are concerned." Emma held up her hand. "Just a minute." She felt around the dark wall and pressed. "We don't want anyone following us."

The opening above them grumbled closed.

Jack tensed.

"Just a precautionary measure." Emma kept her gaze on the diminishing rectangle of light. "We're willing to bet they've had eyes on Mags since she landed in Moscow."

"We're also trapped in here." Jack barricaded her with his body.

"It's okay, Jack." Mags put her hands on his barnlike shoulders. "She really is my coimhdeacht, and I can trust her."

After a long pause, Jack motioned Emma to continue.

The stairs went down and down. They came to a landing and started on another downward staircase. The pull of air grew stronger as they went. It tugged at Mags's core like a heavy rope was connected to her.

Another landing. More stairs.

Mags's legs ached as they descended farther and farther into the dark.

The air smelled stale and dry, and the darkness intensified as they went.

"What's that?" Jack pointed downward.

Mags squinted into the darkness, and it took her a moment to see what he was talking about.

Somewhere down below there was light.

"Sasha scouted ahead of us."

"Are we nearly there?" Mags could barely contain her excitement. To have her magic in all its power and to have it so close was nearly killing her. Her skin prickled, her blood pulsed, and her magic swelled with each step closer.

Emma grinned at her. She was startlingly pretty when she smiled. "We're heading for Sasha and that light."

They sped their descent.

The light grew stronger until they could see without needing Emma's torch.

At the bottom of the staircase, a small arched opening forced them into a sharp right turn.

Mags blinked against the sudden light after all the dark.

"What the fuck?" Jack jumped in front of her. "Who the fuck are all these people?"

Mags peered around him and gasped.

They were in a large subterranean chamber. Roughhewn rock walls supported a stone roof that almost brushed Jack's head. The chamber was full of people.

"Blessed." Sasha stepped forward. "It is our honor to serve."

As one, the seventy or so people in the chamber lowered to one knee and bowed their heads.

"I'm sorry," Emma whispered, her face fierce and determined. "But most of these people have families who have served going back generations. To see the culmination of all that work and dedication was an opportunity I couldn't rob them of."

Mags couldn't make sense of people bowing. To her. "They don't need to bow to me. I'm just Mags."

"You are the embodiment of Goddess on earth," Sasha said. "We have dedicated our lives to keeping the air point safe for you. Now you will activate it and our purpose will be fulfilled."

Mags stepped out from behind Jack.

He dropped behind her, so close he almost trod on her heels.

"Please." All the bowing made Mags want to fidget. "Please stand."

Sasha stood and spoke in Russian.

As one, the people surged to their feet. All eyes locked on her, and she fought the urge to fidget.

"Magdalene." Jack's deep voice rumbled close to her ear. "You've got this. This is what you do."

Taking a deep breath, Mags managed a smile for her audience. "Right then. I'll get on with it."

People parted, and as if she hadn't already felt its unmistakable draw, they formed a human passageway leading straight to the air point.

Two rough pillars stood at the end of her body corridor. About four feet separated the stone columns, and a faint golden glow surrounded them. Sigils like the ones marking Baile's caverns ran over the two pillars.

As Mags walked toward the pillars, the air in the chamber stirred. A soft breeze ruffled her long skirts and lifted tendrils of hair around her neck and face.

A low murmur stirred the crowd.

And Mags knew exactly what to do.

She motioned for Jack to stop and wait.

Stepping between the two pillars, she put a hand on each. Reaching deep inside, Mags pulled air. The breeze stiffened around her. Mags reached deeper. Jasmine and almonds perfumed the air. Power started at her feet and traveled up her legs. It strengthened as it climbed higher until her entire body vibrated. Her teeth chattered together, and her hair streamed out behind her.

Wind howled through the chamber.

Power surged through her blood like a narcotic. She wanted more and more of it. She needed all of it.

"I call Air," Mags yelled.

Wind battered against her and everyone else in the chamber.

Her clothes and hair whipped around her, stinging her skin. The columns blazed with golden light. It burned her palms, and stung her eyes, but Mags held the connection.

Magic exploded inside her, lighting her like a torch. The wind howled and screamed. Her blood felt like lava. Her muscles screamed. Her bones strained like they were being pulled apart. Her joints shrieked under the strain.

People shouted and fell to the floor, sheltering their heads with their arms.

*BOOM!* The walls and floor shuddered, dust and pebbles rained down on everyone's head.

And then it was over.

The columns flared and subsided into a gentle amber glow.

Mags took her hands from the columns. Inside her, the power whispered beneath her skin. She turned to face the chamber again. "It is done."

Jack caught her as she fell, and everything went dark.

# CHAPTER THIRTY-FIVE

The hair on Maeve's nape rose, and her skin prickled. Near the entrance to the central Baile cavern, Roderick shot to his feet. "What is it?"

Crystals chimed, and more light filled the caverns.

"Look." Tears sprang to Maeve's eyes as she pointed to the walls. "The air crystals are active."

Amongst myriad crystals studding the cavern walls, a new color had joined the red of fire and the blue of water. Yellow for air.

"She did it." Roderick stared about them in wonder. "Mags has woken Air."

He yanked Maeve toward him and kissed her hard.

"She did it!" Maeve wanted to laugh and cry and cheer all at once. "She did it."

Roderick smiled down at her, his arms locked around her hips, keeping her close. "She most certainly did."

She so rarely saw Roderick with his expression open and unguarded, his pale blue eyes full of emotion. What she read in those lovely eyes now made her heart miss a beat. "Roderick?"

"I'm relieved Mags activated air. I'll be more relieved when she's home safe." He dipped his head closer. "But most of all, I love you."

"Roderick." Her voice squeezed past the constriction in her throat. She barely managed to whisper back, "I love you too."

He looked smug. "I know."

"Even when you're being a dickhead."

"Dickhead?" He raised his eyebrows. "Did Sinead teach you that one?"

"Who else?"

"We should tell the coven that air is active." Roderick pressed his hot mouth to her neck. "But they're all asleep." His deep voice vibrated through her. "We should wait until they wake up."

Tingles spread over her skin, and she shivered. The way Roderick could light her up inside left her breathless. "Any ideas how we should pass the time?"

"A few ideas have popped up." He pressed her hips to his.

Maeve's knees melted. "Yes, they have."

His mouth traveled to the crook of her shoulder and stopped. "Maeve?"

"Mmm." The man had the most talented lips and tongue. He could do things to her with his mouth that made her think she'd reached paradise.

His tone had changed completely as he said again, "Maeve."

"What?" She didn't want to chat now.

"Goddess Pool." Straightening, he turned her around. "Look."

The water had split into three bands of color: red, blue, and yellow.

Water swirled, slowly at first, and then faster, blending the three colors into one small whirlpool in the center. Mist rose over the water.

Roderick dropped to his knees. "My lady."

"Lady?" A shadowy figure rose from the water.

Maeve's knees gave way and she joined Roderick on the

cavern floor. Like her head was weighted, it dropped forward on her neck.

"Beloved." Goddess's voice was loud and a whisper all at once. It filled the cavern to overflowing and vibrated through Maeve's center.

"My lady," she whispered.

"You have done well," Goddess said.

Maeve's heart pounded in her chest. Tears sprang to her eyes.

"We thank you, my lady," Roderick whispered.

"Roderick." Goddess's tone warmed. "Always so worthy."

"My humble thanks."

"I cannot stay long," Goddess said. "My strength grows, but I cannot maintain this form for long." Her voice deepened. "The seer is in much danger. I cannot say more, but she is caught in a web."

Maeve shivered and grabbed Roderick's hand.

His strong fingers clasped hers and helped against the dread filling her gut.

"What must we do?" Roderick spoke.

Maeve didn't have the presence of mind to manage any words.

"What can be done has been done," Goddess said. "The web will untangle when it must. But there are other webs you must break, my spirit walker."

"My lady." Maeve didn't dare look up.

"In the sacred grove, you will find the answers you seek. Those who came before can help you break the bonds that should not be."

"My lady?"

Silence.

Maeve waited as long as she could and then looked up. Goddess Pool had returned to a soft amber and the mist had disappeared.

Confusion swirled inside Maeve. "What did that mean?"

"Walk the sacred grove." Roderick stood and held his hand out for her. "It seems you have a job to do, and it must be an important one for Goddess to deliver the message in person."

---

DRAWING fire was so much easier now that the fire point was active. Orange and lily perfumed the air as Maeve pressed her palms against the sigils for the ancient ones. The cavern walls shimmered and melted, and she entered the grove.

Small clumps of grass peeped out in sparse patches on the earth beneath her feet. Her toes pressed into the soil that had been hard-packed and barren on her last visit. More buds swelled from the bare branches of the trees all around her.

Mist swirled and stirred around the tree trunks, dense blue and gray, and coalesced into a woman. Maeve recognized a face in the ephemeral figure, and she bowed her head. "Deidre, Blessed be."

The original healer clasped her hands prayerlike before her chest and bowed back. "Blessed be, Maeve."

"The grove reawakens." Maeve gestured around her.

Breathing deep and closing her eyes, Deidre smiled. "It does. Goddess is almost ready to walk amongst us. Once the fourth point awakens, she will take form again."

"That is good news."

Deidre had never been conventionally beautiful. Her features combined in an unassuming plainness that was often overlooked. Deidre's beauty lay in her eyes, the deepest brown and infinitely kind. Her walnut-colored braid hung over one shoulder. "Remember that to all things there must be a balance, sister."

Maeve's nape prickled a warning that she was not going to like what she heard next.

"As Goddess grows stronger, so does the enemy." Deidre nodded. "As the points awaken and more magic floods your plane of existence, so more magic becomes available to her." Deidre winced, even after hundreds of years not able to speak Rhiannon's name. The betrayal had been most keenly felt by the original three witches. It was they who had cut their fourth sister off from Goddess.

*Shit*! To borrow Sinead's favorite curse. "But we have no choice but to wake the points."

"Always balance must be maintained." Deidre inclined her head. "The path is set and must be followed. When earth awakens, she will reach her zenith."

"But so will we." Maeve tried to draw comfort from the message of balance as much as being terrified by it.

Deidre smiled, her eyes warming. "Aye, sister. I have come to impart a task for the healer."

"Bronwyn?"

"A fitting name." Deidre's smile widened. "She has much to offer the world, and she will shine like a beacon of hope."

"You know about the prophecy?"

"Aye." Deidre sighed. "She bears a heavy burden, but she is a strong one, and Goddess makes no mistakes."

Deidre's serenity irked Maeve. It was easy to be serene when you were not in the front lines fighting this battle but tucked away in the sacred grove. Then she felt wicked for her reaction. The first three had suffered through their own trials and tribulations. If Goddess disappeared from the world, they would cease to be as if they never had existed. "What is the task for the healer?"

"The evil one has buried a tendril of her malignancy within my coimhdeacht, Warren. The healer must search, and she can break it."

Maeve didn't like to contradict an ancient being. "But she searched before and never found it."

"She must widen her search," Deidre said. "A healer deals not only with the physical body, but with the heart and spirit as well. The evil one has buried her work deep within his psyche, where it is not immediately obvious."

"I'll tell her." Maeve bowed and winced internally. Bronwyn wasn't a big fan of cryptic messages.

More mist swirled, and a stunningly beautiful brunette with deep indigo eyes stepped out of it.

"Tahra?" The original guardian, and Roderick's first bonded witch and first love.

Tahra held her hands to her chest and bowed. "Blessed be, my sister."

"Blessed be." Maeve returned the greeting. It was hard not to feel pale and insignificant beside the dark, willowy loveliness of Tahra.

Then Tahra smiled, and didn't she get even lovelier. "Maeve, I feel Roderick's bond within you."

Cheeks heating, she nodded. They'd both shared Roderick's bond and his bed, and she felt like the interloper.

Tahra laughed and shook her head. "Our bond was a thing of ages past. Your bond is bright and alive and shines a light in our shadowy landscape."

Okay then. Maeve didn't know how to respond to that.

"He is happy, Maeve." Tahra gestured to her. "And you are the reason for that happiness. Thus, I am able to rest peacefully."

As nice as the words were, Maeve would rather they move away from the topic of Roderick. If Tahra asked her to send Roderick her love, she'd do it, but it wouldn't be her favorite task.

"We have a task for you too," Tahra said.

More mist arose, and Brenna coalesced. She had the same opaque green eyes as Mags, and her hair was a rich, sable brown. "Our sister's lost souls cry out to us."

"Lost souls." It took Maeve a minute to stumble on to their

meaning. "You mean the ones who did the unthinkable?" For her. Thirteen witches and one, barely grown novice had taken their own lives in a blood-magic rite to send her and Roderick into stasis. The punishment for that action had been the permanent removal from the cycle of death and rebirth. Their souls were trapped on the village green forever in the moments of their death. "Are they not separated from Goddess now?"

"Goddess suffered much that awful day." Deidre looked forlorn. "So many witches broken and murdered, so much loss and blood. It drove her deep into the center from which all is born to heal her wounds."

Is that where Goddess had been all this time?

"Indeed." Tahra nodded. "And there was not enough magic remaining on your plane to sustain her. She is now able to recover and return."

"And she would welcome the lost souls home," Brenna said. "The magic was wrought for you, and it is you who must unravel it. The spell has come to full fruition and now must be released. It was cast in four, and when the time comes, it must be undone in four."

## CHAPTER THIRTY-SIX

S asha looked like a whipped puppy as he gazed at Mags. "Are you sure you cannot stay longer?"

"Nope," Jack cut in before she could say a word. "I need to get her safely back to Baile."

Jack had told her that after she'd woken the air point, she'd passed out cold. He'd carried her from that subterranean cavern and back into the metro station. From there, Emma had taken them to a waiting car and whisked them back to the Metropol. She'd apparently stayed unconscious for a good few hours.

Jack and Emma had stayed with her.

"But there are many who would meet you, Blessed." Sasha blinked at her and looked like he might cry at any moment. "They may never get this chance again."

"Those who can must go to her in England." Emma put an arm around his shoulders and manhandled him to the door. "We will make plans for our people to visit Baile. They have earned it after all their sacrifice."

"Indeed." Sasha nodded and cast a longing glance at Mags over his shoulder. "There will be many who will wish to make the trip."

"Good." Jack handed Mags a cup of tea. He was back to force feeding and watering her. "Greater Littleton's a nice village. Very picturesque. Good seafood."

At the door, Sasha wriggled away from Emma and turned to Mags. One hand on his chest, he dropped to his knee. "It has been an honor without equal, Blessed."

All this bowing and stuff didn't sit well with Mags. She had no idea how to respond, so she managed a stiff smile and said, "Thank you. It was lovely to meet you too."

"So gracious." Sasha sniffed. "And so humble."

"Yup." Emma hustled him out the door and shut it. Leaning her back against it, she rolled her eyes. "Really nice guy. Excellent researcher and not bad in a fight either, but way too intense."

Jack laughed. Actually laughed for the first time in—

Mags couldn't remember when she'd last heard him laugh.

"Right, then." Emma strode toward them. "Let's get to the airport. Time to get you safe."

"Too right." Jack grabbed the few things Emma's organization had managed to gather in their short visit and shoved them into a duffle Emma had brought. "Finish your tea and bring your sandwich."

"I'm not hun—"

"Got it." Emma snagged her sandwich and wrapped it in a hotel napkin. "You can finish it in the car."

She had two of them now.

Emma had a luxury black sedan waiting outside the hotel. She opened the door and shut it behind Mags and Jack then hopped in beside the driver.

Mags reached for her gift, the access instantaneous, and now hers to control. No more sudden flashes of intuition or visions forcing themselves into her dreams. She now controlled when, where, and what she saw. Her shoulders felt lighter than they had at any point in her life. Until she'd woken air, she hadn't been aware of the burden she'd lived with. Taking a long, relaxed breath, because she could, she sat back in her seat and stared out the window.

Too busy hanging on to the tangled remnants of her sanity, she'd seen none of the sights on their drive from the airport.

Emma pointed out the bigger tourist attractions as they drove: Red Square, the Kremlin, the Seven Sisters. They passed out of the central ring of Moscow and drove through the land of the impersonal tower blocks thrown up by Khrushchev. Row upon row of them stacked beside each other, each housing thousands of people.

It took a long while to clear the city, and then they were in the countryside. Willow, larch, birch, and spruce rose up in large forests interspersed with thick summer-green waist-high grass. Occasional towns and villages battled back the greenery with more gray blocks and a few traditional log houses.

Emma told them about her work in Russia, how her position at the university had given her access to so much information and made it easier to track the origins of Baba Yaga and draw the inevitable parallels with Rhiannon.

"There are stories and folk figures like Baba Yaga all over the world," she said, as she scanned the cars around them. "I wouldn't be surprised if there were more organizations like ours."

Jack grunted. "It would be a good idea to find them."

"Right." Emma nodded. "The organization is going to need a new purpose now that the old one has come full circle." She turned and grinned at Mags. "That was one helluva show you put on there at the end."

"You're most welcome." Mags returned her grin. She did like Emma. Their bond wasn't active, but the connection was there already.

Her intuition prickled, but she would wait until she got to Baile before she opened to her gift again. Poor Jack had dealt with more than enough as it was. He deserved a drama free trip home.

The car dropped the three of them off at departures. Domodedovo airport reminded Mags of a fat, glass sausage, and she nearly giggled.

Sensing her amusement, Emma winked at her. "I'd keep that opinion to myself."

"This is going to be fun." Jack glowered at them and rolled his eyes. "Not."

They stopped at the check-in and Jack handed over his and Mags's passports to the smiling attendant.

She took them and glanced at Emma.

Emma shook her head.

"She's not coming," Mags said and turned to Jack. "She's not ready."

Jack gaped at Emma, and his expression turned thunderous. "But she has to."

"No, she doesn't." Mags forced a smile over her sadness. "Free will is always a thing, and Goddess respects it. We need to do the same."

"I'm sorry." Emma's gray eyes gleamed her regret. "My work is here. My studies, my students. The organization." She cleared her throat. "They need me. Now more than ever."

Jack's voice dropped into a growl. "Mags needs you. You're her coimhdeacht."

"No, she doesn't." Emma raised her chin and met his glare. "She has you, and you're more than capable of doing what needs to be done. Besides." She shrugged. "If you're honest, you'll admit that you really don't want me around cramping your style."

"But—"

"It's all right, Jack." Mags took his hand. "And I do have you."

"But this is not how it works." Jack's jaw set in a hard line. "Warren got the calling, and he answered it."

"Warren didn't have the sort of life Emma does." Mags took Emma's hand with her free one. "He didn't have the same responsibilities that Emma does."

"He had a daughter." Jack scowled. "And he had friends. He had me."

"It's okay, Jack." Mags didn't have all the answers for him, but she had known Emma wasn't coming. Not her gift telling her that, but her common sense. Emma had never once said she would come to England. She'd even avoided answering when the issue had arisen. "Each must respond to the calling as they see fit."

"Take care of her." Emma's voice wobbled, and she dropped her head. When she raised it again, she was cool and collected. "Take care of her, Jack Langham. She's more precious than either of us deserve."

Turning, she strode away.

"Come." Mags tugged at Jack's hand to get him moving. "We've got a plane to catch."

After one last glare, he dropped into step with her. "I can't believe she's walking away from her responsibility."

"Is she?" Mags took their boarding passes and passports and handed them to the airport official at security. "Or is she honoring her current responsibilities?"

"There's nothing more important than making sure you're safe," Jack grumbled.

Mags had to stop and slide her arms around his waist. "I love that you think that."

"Well…" He cleared his throat and glanced at the watching security official. "You know how I feel."

Her Jack. Mags had to laugh. Such a mixture of marshmallow and metal. She patted his barrel chest. "And because I believe in free will, I won't even make you say the words."

JACK FOLLOWED Mags to a gift shop beside their departure lounge. He couldn't believe Mags was okay with Emma staying behind. Sure, he'd had a few stray thoughts about how this would work with him and Mags and Emma, but it had never occurred to him Emma wouldn't come with them.

He'd seen the bond with Warren and Niamh in action. Seen how close Roderick was to Maeve, and although they told him the relationship was different, Alexander and Bronwyn. Which reminded him. "What was that about Alexander's father?"

Mags glanced up from studying a collection of bears dressed as Cossacks. "Hmm?"

"You and Emma were talking about Alexander and how like his father he was."

"Ah. I thought you were sleeping."

"I was." As much as he could sleep with Mags out in the world and not safely tucked away at Baile. "Mostly."

Mags smirked. "I'm surprised you haven't worked it out yet."

"Worked what out?"

She raised an eyebrow at him. "Who Alexander's father is."

He hadn't really given it much thought. He'd kind of assumed the man was dead ages ago. "He's alive?"

"Oh, yes." Mags handed him a bear. "I think Taylor will like this one?"

"Huh?"

She drifted over to a stand of Matryoshka dolls. "Do you think Niamh would like one of these or prefer a bear?"

"Bear," he said. Alexander's father was alive and kicking?

Mags nodded. "I think you're right." She held up two Matryoshka's. "The red one for Sinead, and the green one for Alannah?"

"Blue for Alannah." He picked up a doll and handed it to her. "Bronwyn would like one of those scarves."

Mags gasped and closed in on a display of brightly patterned silk. "Yes, she would."

She picked a yellow one and handed it to him.

"Do you think Roderick, Alexander, and Warren will be offended if I get them all a bottle of vodka?"

The truth resounded in his mind like a brass fucking gong. "Fucking hell."

"They will?"

"What?" He focused on her again. She stood beside a display of vodka with a concerned frown. "No, get the bloody vodka."

Mags glanced around. "I need a basket."

"Madam." A dapper little man appeared at her elbow. He took the bears, dolls, and scarf away from Jack and placed them in a basket. He then rescued the three large bottles of vodka. "Allow me."

"Do they know?" Jack spoke to empty air and hurried to join Mags.

She was examining the contents of a bookshelf. "A book for Andy, I think. I know he's just arrived, but it seems wrong not to get him anything."

Jack took her by the shoulders and turned her. "Do Alexander and Roderick know they're father and son?"

"Oh, no." Mags giggled. "Baile would not be standing if they did. Now." She held up two books. "The History of the Tzars for Andy, or Moscow Architecture."

---

MAGS ATE everything on her tray and enjoyed each bite. She didn't get why people complained about airplane food. Then again, not everybody got to travel first class. She remembered nothing of their first flight together, but this one she was going to thoroughly enjoy.

Already into her second mini bottle of crisp chilled white wine, she was starting to feel pleasantly drowsy.

Jack had his earbuds in and was flipping through the movie selection on his screen in front of him.

His big, strong form beside her made her feel safe and cherished. She even thought he might be coming around to the idea of four children. Not that it was going to make a button's worth of difference if he did or didn't. She'd seen it clearly. Two girls and two boys. Not a redhead amongst them.

She must ask Maeve why the modern witches were all redheads. Maeve was blond, and if the stained-glass depiction of the original three in the great hall of Baile was accurate, all of them were brunettes, and Rhiannon had hair as black as her soul.

Snuggling into her duvet, she rested her head on Jack's solid arm. His skin warmed her cheek, and she watched his movie without really taking it in. Being with him was enough. For now. He was hers.

Her eyes grew weighted, and she blinked to keep them open. She lost the battle on the third blink and kept them shut.

*"Mags. Have you missed me? I've missed you."*

# CHAPTER THIRTY-SEVEN

Warren eyed Bronwyn with suspicion as she approached him. On the surface, nothing to be worried about. Diminutive redhead, cute and sexy. Although he'd never say the latter when Alexander was in the room. The man got seriously territorial. Bronwyn's pregnancy was beginning to show beneath the snug fit of her T-shirt.

"Stop it." Niamh clipped his ear. "Or I'll tell on you."

He hadn't only been looking at her…never mind. "It was purely academic."

"Right." Niamh smirked.

Bronwyn stopped and stared at them. "What?"

"Nothing." Warren jumped in before Niamh could out him. He really hadn't been lusting after Bronwyn, but her T-shirt had never stretched over her—

He blamed sexual frustration. Sharing a room with Niamh and Taylor had been pure fucking torture. And that sounded all kinds of wrong, even in his own head. His continued confinement wore on him.

"What are you going to do?" He focused on Bronwyn's toffee-brown eyes.

She pulled a face. "Not exactly sure, but apparently, I can get rid of your uninvited guest."

How reassuring. Not. But he'd do anything to rid himself of his lingering tie to Rhiannon. He held out his hand to Bronwyn. "Let's do it."

"Right." Frowning, she took his hand. "This may take a while."

Hannah peered over Bronwyn's shoulder. "They said it wasn't physical, which implies you need to tackle this on the metaphysical plane."

"Any idea how to do that?" Bronwyn glanced at Hannah.

"Nope." Hannah shrugged. "I deal with the physiological organism."

Warren felt the stringent need to object. "I'm not an organism."

"Well, technically..." Bronwyn shrugged.

He glared to shut her up.

Hannah chuckled. "Why don't we approach this from a psychological point of view."

"Meaning?" Bronwyn cocked her head.

"Well, if you were looking from a psychological standpoint, you'd look for an emotional causality. A person has a certain response to something, and you'd search their memories, their past experiences to find the root cause." Hannah perched beside Bronwyn on Warren's bed. "Can you do that?"

"I don't know." Bronwyn grimaced. "Any other healing I've done has had a definite physical origin."

Hannah thought that over. "Well, to an extent most diseases are psychosomatic. We could use that as a starting point."

"You're suggesting I try to dig around in his mind?"

*Hang about!* Warren withdrew his hand. "Dig around in my mind?"

"Hmm." Bronwyn frowned. "I mean, I could try. You know, root out the memory of Edana and see what happens."

Warren did not want anyone mining that particular memory. He tried his best never to go there. "That sounds like a horrible idea."

"Don't be a big baby." Niamh poked his arm. "It can't have been that bad."

Would a little empathy be too much to ask for? "It was not my proudest moment."

"But hardly your worst." Niamh shrugged. "And it's not like none of us know about it."

He shot exactly what he thought of her statement down the bond. Guardians were so pragmatic; it could be maddening. Especially when it came to sex.

And he was back to sex and Niamh in the same head space.

"You'd have to trust me enough to let me in," Bronwyn said. "I don't think I could barge into your memories without an invitation."

Then again, if this worked, he would be free to join the rest of the coven.

"We're bound by patient confidentiality," Hannah said.

When had they become a we? Although it made sense. Bronwyn and Hannah may approach healing from very different perspectives, but their goals aligned.

"Okay."

"There you go." Niamh patted his shoulder.

Alexander poked his head around the door. "How's it going?"

Marvelous! Now he had witnesses. "It's not."

"Bronwyn wants to access Warren's memory of him having sex with Edana," Niamh said. "And Warren's gone all bashful."

"I am not bashful." Why didn't she lop his balls off with a rusty spoon? Oh, right! She'd done it already. "I'm not sure how I feel about granting access to private parts of my mind."

Alexander winced. "Couldn't perform, eh?"

"What!" His eyes must be bugging out his head. "It's got

nothing to do with that. I performed fine. Thank you very much."

"Well, of course you did." Niamh patted his shoulder again. "I'm sure you were an absolute stud."

"Nothing to worry about, mate." Alexander winked. "Gave her a good seeing to."

"For fuck's sake." Warren ran out of words. And then he started to laugh. They were such unmentionable shits. And they'd also given him the only kind of reassurance he could stomach. He thrust his hand at Bronwyn. "Get on with it."

Niamh moved closer and put her palm on his nape. Whatever Bronwyn unearthed, she would be there beside him. Whatever demons came up, she would fight alongside him.

He took a deep breath as Bronwyn closed her eyes.

His hand tingled where she held it. The honey and sage smell of Bronwyn's magic tickled his nose.

The ascent of her gift through his system and into his brain was like a warm light flowing beneath his skin.

Pressure pushed at his inner mind. On an inhalation, Warren lowered his barriers.

His room in Baile disappeared, and he was back in the Hag's Head. Only in an odd way, he wasn't alone. Bronwyn stood right beside him. A man and a woman embraced by the bed. Only the man was him, another version of him, an earlier version of him.

His gut clenched, and he wanted to hurl.

Reassuring pressure at his nape centered him again.

The Bronwyn standing beside him took his hand, and they walked toward the him wrapped around the blonde. Then went right into him.

Loathing, self-hatred, distaste, an odd sense of detachment all broadsided him. Aroused, but hating it, he'd let his base emotions run his higher mind. It was all about fucking, and the way he despised himself and the act tasted bitter in the back of his throat. Edana's perfume clung to the inside of his nostrils, cloying and pervasive. Her hands petted his body, left his higher self retreating.

Edana pushed her tongue into his mouth, hand tight in his hair.

And there.

A gleaming, oily black thread extended from her mouth and into his as they kissed. It wriggled down his throat and sunk its claws into his sternum. He heaved to rid himself of it.

Bronwyn's hand shot out and fastened on the slimy tendril. With a twist of her wrist, Bronwyn snapped it. It recoiled like a striking snake and disappeared.

Warren returned to his now body, rolled to his side and retched.

Dimly, he was aware of Alexander speaking softly to Bronwyn. "Get rid of it, little witch. Transmute it now."

Forcing his eyes open, he trained his gaze on Bronwyn until he could focus.

Bronwyn looked as sick as he felt. Pale, and slightly green, she swayed, and Hannah caught her.

Face grim, Alexander scooped her into his arms and carried her from the room. Hannah followed them out.

"You're okay." Niamh climbed on the bed behind him and curled her body around his. "It's over now."

Warren shuddered. Every part of him felt unclean and violated. He wanted to scrub himself inside and out with bleach and a wire brush. It was more than what he'd done with Edana, and what Edana had done to him, it was Bronwyn bearing witness to the entire sordid mess.

Niamh's warmth seeped into him, wriggling into all the dark, cold places and bringing light.

He couldn't stop shivering, and she tightened around him. "Bronwyn says it's done. You're free."

Warren lay there, not able to do anything but shake like a cowering mongrel. "Fuck, that sucked."

"But you did it." Niamh curled her leg over his. "You did it, for you, for the coven, for all of us. You did it, and it's over now."

He didn't know if that experience would ever be over, but Niamh being here certainly helped.

Every regret, every bad deed and thought, every ugly part of him felt as if it had been ripped open.

"You're a good man, Warren." Niamh pressed her face into his neck. "You're the best man."

"The things I did." He couldn't stop the deluge of memories. His actions in the forces, bringing Rudy's body home, the ugliness of the last years of his marriage, his angry, violent youth. The slideshow through hell flicked on and on, like a harrowing edition of *This Is Your Life*.

Bonded to him, for better or worse, Niamh had to be getting all of it, but he couldn't force the floodgates shut again.

"I love you," Niamh whispered. "All of you."

It helped. A lot. His shivering subsided slowly, and the memories grew dimmer.

Niamh kissed his neck. "Now we need to teach you to love yourself."

## CHAPTER THIRTY-EIGHT

"Dad?" Warren woke to Taylor standing by the bed. Her pretty face was tight with concern. "Are you okay."

He forced his mouth into a smile. "I am now."

"Niamh went to get you something to eat." Taylor touched his cheek. "She said you would be fine."

Rolling into a sit, he suppressed a grimace. He felt like he'd gone twelve rounds with Mike Tyson. "She's right. I'm already better."

"Right." Taylor gave him the tween eye of doubt. Then she scrambled onto the bed next to him. "Maeve has been teaching me how to use my blessing."

That still sent a chill through his middle. "Yeah?"

"Roderick said it was safe to talk to you about stuff again."

Chill followed by a gut punch. "It is. So, what's Maeve been teaching you?"

"How to be a seer." Taylor shrugged like the idea was commonplace. "She did a spirit walk for me—and isn't that crazy?"

He managed a quick nod before she went on.

"She asked the old seers what I should do and how I should do it."

Those dead witches could be all kinds of useful. "And?"

"Well, the best part is they said I could control it. Because I'm water, and water is active, it's me in charge." Taylor sat cross-legged and wound a strand of hair around her finger. "That I turn it on and off like a tap, so it doesn't crowd my mind all the time."

"That's great." It actually was. He'd not been able to stop his own visions of his daughter with the same look of confusion and panic Mags had worn. Or worse yet, like Roz. "That's really great."

"They also suggested that part of what is happening to Mags is because Air isn't active and her gift is running away with her, and she doesn't have enough magic to keep stable." She grimaced. "Kind of like what happened to Niamh's aunt. It's never happened before, but they said that was their best guess."

He loved hearing that. Not one tiny bit. "Did they teach you how to use it when you try?"

"Yup." Taylor nodded. "I can direct it to a specific time, or a specific person." She wrinkled her nose. "It takes practice, but I'm working with it every day."

"Hey." Niamh pushed the door open with her foot and carried a tray into the room. "I brought you a sandwich and some stuff." She eyed the tray. "I'm not much in the kitchen, but I make a good sandwich."

"Hey, Niamh." Taylor leaned over and made space for the tray on the bedside table. "I was telling Dad what I've been learning."

Niamh put the tray down. "She's been working hard. Maeve keeps an eye on her. And Roderick, of course."

"And I wanted to ask you something." Taylor snagged a crisp from the pile beside his sandwich.

"For a crisp?"

She giggled and took another. "Could you call Mom?"

Niamh's surprise wriggled down the bond.

A dog nudged the door back open and sat beside him giving him hungry eyes.

A crow flapped in and cawed from the top of the dresser.

A coincidence the crow appeared at the mention of Debra? With Niamh here, the rest of whatever menagerie were hanging around Baile today wouldn't be far behind.

He wasn't hungry but he forced himself to eat. "You want me to call your mother?"

"She's not doing well." Taylor crunched another crisp. "Things are not going well."

"She told you this?"

Taylor shook her head. "I scried her."

Dear Goddess, that habit needed discouraging. "That's a bit invasive, Taylor. It's like eavesdropping."

"I have to practice on someone, and I was worried about her." Taylor grabbed the other half of his sandwich. "Last time she called, she seemed kind of depressed, so I peeked in on her." She bit into the sandwich and chewed.

Scrying adults could lead to all kinds of things being seen, in addition to being intrusive and stalkerish. "That doesn't really excuse invading your mother's privacy."

"I didn't see anything." Taylor rolled her eyes. "Just her and Adam arguing."

That was bad enough. "Taylor, you can't—"

"I won't do it again. Okay?" She glanced at Niamh for support, but Niamh was keeping her focus on a hedgehog and trying to feed it.

"I mean it." Warren fixed Taylor with a look.

"Okay." Taylor bit into the sandwich and chewed with a resentful glint in her eye.

Warren didn't know how to handle the situation. Taylor didn't have the right to spy on people, and he needed to make her understand that. Bringing down the rules, however, got him attitude, and Taylor shut him out. There had to be a useful parenting cheat sheet somewhere. He owed Debra for the years she'd done the hard-core parenting without him. "Now, why do you want me to call your mother?"

"Maybe you could help." Taylor dropped the sulk. "I mean, I know you guys aren't really friends or anything, but she doesn't really have anyone else."

Niamh raised her head and looked at him.

And Warren grabbed his phone.

Down their bond came all the stuff she didn't need to put in words. Basic message: Be kind, Warren, be the good man I know you are.

*Motherfucking shit and hellfire.*

"Warren?" Debra picked up on the third ring.

He'd been hoping for voicemail. "Hi."

"Is everything all right?" Debra's concern bled into her voice. "Is Taylor okay?"

"She's fine." He glared at Niamh.

She winked at him.

"Everything's fine." He took a deep breath and plunged. "How are things with you?"

A long pause, and then, "Why are you asking?"

Warren searched for an answer to a very fair question. He and Debra had never had the sort of relationship where they talked shit out. Not even when they'd been together.

"Taylor is worried about you." He went with the truth. His options were limited. "And I thought I'd check on you."

Pause.

"Really?"

He didn't blame Debra for her skepticism. He couldn't believe he was doing it either. "Yes."

Only the phone's subtle crackle broke the silence.

"Um…" Debra cleared her throat. "I'm okay."

And Warren knew that tone. It was the one that came before Debra's "I'm fine."

"Are you really?" He tapped into Niamh and used her innate kindness and empathy to color his tone.

Debra sniffed. Her voice hitched. "No."

"What's going on?"

When she answered, she was crying. "I don't really know. Just a feeling."

"Tell me." And what do you know? He really didn't like Debra crying. True story.

"Things with Adam. They're...not what I was expecting." Debra sighed. "Go on. Tell me you told me so."

"I didn't," he said. He'd met Adam. Didn't really think of the guy as any kind of way. "He seemed okay to me."

"Yeah." Debra took a deep breath. "Me too."

He searched for words in the ensuing silence.

Taylor and Niamh watched him. A fox hopped on the bed and sat next to him. Keen, amber eyes fixed on him and told him to get on with it. "What happened, Deb?"

The floodgates opened and between sniffs, sighs, and sobs Debra gave him the whole story. She'd quit her job and sold her house and everything she owned to go to Australia with Adam.

Warren hadn't known that part and probably would have given her shit if he had. He wouldn't have been happy about Debra's plans to leave England for good and take their daughter with her. Now, he listened.

Adam had told Debra there was a great job opportunity for him in Australia. The kind of job that would have left Debra farting through silk. She didn't add that part, it was more his extrapolation. Only when they'd arrived in Australia, it turned out, Adam needed her to tide him over financially until the opportunity became reality. Except, that reality was still not happening. Three months, Debra had been footing the bill for the fucker, and the original opportunity had turned out to be more speculative than certain. So had all the other six opportunities that couldn't fail but had.

Now, Debra was running out of money. Along with being on the bones of his ass, Adam also had expensive taste. She'd mentioned on their last chat she couldn't afford the ticket back to England to get Taylor, but he'd had no idea how broke she was. He should have offered to help her then. Jesus, he had a lot to learn in the decent human being department.

Warren didn't like Taylor listening to the conversation.

Standing, Niamh nudged Taylor and took her out of the room.

The fox curled up beside his thigh and wrapped its tail over its nose.

Warren sunk his finger into its soft, silky fur.

Debra went on about how she couldn't get a job because she didn't have a work visa. Adam spoke about marriage to help her stay, but when pressed, didn't commit to a date. Adam had an answer for everything, and a solution for nothing.

When Warren had been married to Debra, her relationship with her family had already been strained. Her mother was a piece of work who couldn't get over her jealousy of her daughter. Her dad stayed in the background, never wanting to rock his wife's steamship. There'd be no help from either of them. Most of her friends had been against her selling up everything and going. If she'd asked him, Taylor aside, he would have agreed with her friends. But people screwed up, made decisions they regretted, and he was not one to hold that against anyone. Not that he had any ground to in the first place.

"What do you want to do, Deb?" He wasn't good at emotional chats. If he had a sensitive side, he must have left it behind somewhere.

She gave a huge sniff. "I want to come home."

"Let's get you home then." Part of him couldn't believe he'd made that offer, but it felt right. Debra was Taylor's mother.

She'd also been his girl for a long time before things went tits up.

Her bitter laugh crackled down the line. "Did you miss the part about me having no bloody money?"

"I've got money, Deb." A bit saved up and his expenses at Baile were about zero. "Enough to get you back here."

She went quiet. "You'd do that for me?"

"Yeah." He didn't want to get into why. He didn't really understand it himself.

"And then what?" Debra blew her nose. "I have no job and no home there."

"You come here." Bloody Roderick had best agree. "You come and stay with Taylor and me until you sort your next step."

If the silences before had been loaded, this one carried an abnormal cargo. "What?"

"There's plenty of room where I am, and you can stay here until you get settled and make a plan for what happens next." Plus side, it would keep Taylor with him. Downside—so many potential pitfalls they made his head hurt.

Niamh's support and validation glowed warm and comfortable in his chest. She was letting him know she had his back.

"But aren't you living with your girlfriend?" Debra asked. "How does she feel about your ex-wife crashing with you."

He responded with absolute certainty. "Niamh will be okay with it. And we live in a big place. Lots of people."

"How big?"

"It's a castle, remember."

"Right. I thought maybe you didn't actually live in the castle."

"We do."

He could almost hear the gears grinding in Debra's mind. "It's not some weird commune type setup is it?"

"Would I bring Taylor into that?" He had, in a way.

"Niamh lives with her cousins." He improvised. "It's not like a cult or anything."

It was exactly like a cult. Except they were here to stop the bad thing from happening.

"That's really kind of you, Warren." She sighed. "I'll think about it."

"You do that." Then he went one further. He had her account details for child support. "I'll move money into your bank account, so if you decide that's what you have to do, you get yourself on a plane."

She laughed. "Okay. But what if I decide to stay?"

"Then you keep the money, and hopefully Adam will get back on his feet, and everything will be good again." The money meant very little to him now. Living at Baile, dealing with what they had going on, had given him a new perspective. If Rhiannon got her way, money would be irrelevant.

"Wow." She went silent for a while. "I never expected any of this from you."

Neither had he, but everyone deserved redemption.

## CHAPTER THIRTY-NINE

Niamh waited in the kitchen with Taylor for Warren to finish his call. She didn't know the details but felt his conflicted emotions.

Taylor sat by the range playing with the wolf pups. Her affinity with animals would have had Niamh marking her as a guardian witch. She'd never have guessed seer.

She sensed Warren ending his call.

"Ah, Niamh." Andy trotted into the kitchen with his computer tucked under his arm. "I'm glad I found you."

"Hey, Andy." Taylor looked up from the rambunctious litter with a grin.

Andy waved at Taylor. "How was your maths homework?"

"All correct." She fist pumped. "Thanks to you."

"I enjoy maths." Andy took a seat opposite Niamh at the table. "Always happy to help." He opened his laptop. "As you know, I have been expending considerable effort on solving our current difficulties."

"Difficulties?" He pulled her attention away from Warren. Were they still talking about Taylor's homework? And how long had Taylor been going to Andy for help? At this rate, he'd be indispensable by the end of the week. He might already be.

"Cash flow." Andy winced. "And by extension, how to use the ample gifts abounding from Baile in a manner which doesn't draw undue attention."

News to her. She'd had no idea he was working on any of that. "Right."

"Social media." He grinned and spun his laptop to face her. "In your case, YouTube and TikTok seem our best course."

She'd heard of YouTube. "TikTok?"

"Videos." Taylor picked up a pup and kissed it. "People post videos and stuff to it that they make themselves."

Andy grinned and nodded at Taylor. "Exactly. Huge reach."

"Okay." Warren's emotions sat like tar in her solar plexus, and she wanted Andy to get to the point.

He tapped the mousepad of the laptop. "Watch."

A compact man with salt and pepper hair was talking to the camera about dogs. "What am I watching?"

Pup in arms, Taylor came to stand beside her. "That's Cesar Milan."

"Right." Andy nodded and turned the laptop back to him. He went tapping again and turned it back. "That's Jeff Corwin." He leaned over and clicked another link. "And that's Kevin Richardson."

Taylor leaned in. "The lion whisperer?"

"Exactly." Andy smirked.

"And you're telling me this why?" Warren was heading their way, and she wanted to find out what had happened on his call to his ex.

"No." Taylor gasped and looked at Andy. "You're not suggesting…"

"Right?" Andy's cheeks flushed, and his eyes sparkled. "It would be perfect."

"It would." Taylor breathed and stared at Niamh. "And she's a total thirst trap."

Niamh got an inkling of what that might mean. "I am not."

"You really are." Andy blushed. He turned back to Taylor. "I thought we could start small. A couple of TikToks, see if they got attention."

"They totally would." Taylor nodded. "We could build her into an international sensation, because the difference between all of these guys and Niamh is that Niamh can actually talk to animals."

"I don't talk to animals." Because animals didn't talk like humans did. Sure, they communicated and could do so with her, but nobody could talk to animals. She pulled the screen closer and clicked a video to watch it. The Kevin Richardson guy was cozying up to a male lion. "You've lost me, Andy. Give it to me straight."

"Your blessing is about being the voice for animals, right?" Andy nodded at her as if encouraging her.

"Right."

"Well, what better way than to build you a platform and then let you use that platform to make a difference?" Andy did a tiny jig on his side of the table. "There's already a precedent. We build you a viewership of you doing amazing things with animals—"

"Everyone loves animal videos," Taylor said.

"—and you leverage that to work your blessing. These people." He tapped the top of his laptop screen. "Have already paved the way. Nobody would see you as anything more or less than another person who has a great way with our four-legged friends."

She could communicate with animals. "I don't believe in using animals to perform."

"It won't be a performance," Andy said. "We get a few

TikToks of you with birds and beasties, post them, and see what happens."

None of that sounded onerous or disrespectful to her charges.

"All these people who are already famous have established foundations and trusts to preserve wildlife or protect and help animals," Taylor said. "It would be using your blessing right out in the open, and nobody would have to know exactly how you did it."

"Right." Andy rubbed his hands together. "Nobody's sure exactly why Cesar is as good as he is. I mean, he explains it to people, but he has a way with animals that's magic."

Taylor held up her hand. "Good one."

Tittering, Andy high-fived her.

Niamh couldn't believe she might be considering their idea. However, if she could do something with her blessing that didn't endanger the coven... She'd be hiding in plain sight, and people only saw what they wanted.

"The best part is that you don't have to even leave Baile," Andy said. "We can do a few videos. If they aren't popular, we drop it."

Taylor's eyes sparkled and she breathed, "But if they are…"

"You're doing what you do, right under people's noses, and they won't even know it," Andy said. "Being a money person, I'm thinking merchandizing opportunities, but we can get to that later." He tucked his laptop away. "Now, Roderick requires my assistance."

---

ALEXANDER STOOD with Roderick in the practice yard in the barracks. Bronwyn had made an excellent suggestion that he involve Roderick in exploring his new abilities. Such that they were.

Thomas stood by, uncharacteristically silent. He'd been much the same since Alannah had left, but any attempt to engage him on the matter got shut down. The poor sod was suffering, but determined to do it in a stoic, manly way. Well, you could take the man out of the sixteenth century...

Roderick, the bastard, watched Alexander like a hawk, but that also had the advantage of the dagger-eyed dickhead taking careful note of what Alexander could and couldn't do. He had Andy by his side taking notes on his laptop. Which was another thing messing with Alexander's allover sense of worldly rightness. Roderick using phrases like, "google that, would you" or "is there anything like it on YouTube."

"It seems to be linked to emotion." Roderick stared over Andy's shoulder at the laptop screen. "Specifically, when he feels threatened."

Andy hummed his agreement and pointed. "Yes, when you threw the brick at his head, he created a kind of barrier."

"Right." Roderick nodded. "Also, when we tied him down and tried to set fire to him, he changed into a large sort of puddle and doused the flame."

Thomas shook his head at them and threw Alexander a look of profound sympathy.

For his part, Alexander considered his reaction to Roderick's various torments way beyond good natured.

"But when we ask him to change into something. You know, concentrate and think about it." Andy shook his head. "Nothing."

"I don't feel any particular element," Alexander said, before they forgot he was in the yard.

"No." Roderick pursed his lips and kept right on analyzing the data—another verbal gem Roderick was getting warm and snuggly with. "But there is a definite light when he conjures."

Goddess forbid Roderick called what Alexander did magic. He rumbaed around the issue, calling Alexander's gift conjuring, spells, tricks, and even sleight of hand. But the stubborn shit would be dragged into a consent discussion with Sinead before he called it cré-magic or even a blessing.

"The light is white," Thomas sat on a bench with his back to the wall and stretched his legs out. He'd also stopped wearing modern clothes and was back to breeches and a flowy white linen shirt. The look had worked well for him in his day, if gossip was to be believed. And according to what Niamh had discovered in the journals of the dead witches, it was very much to be believed. Thomas had been pretty much the coven amenity.

Roderick glanced at him. "Meaning?"

"White is not a color." Thomas studied his boots and folded his arms. "But is made up of other colors."

"Right." Alexander's gut tightened as he absorbed Thomas's meaning.

"And?" Roderick might have stumbled on to his inner computer geek, but science he still poked at like a suspicious peasant with a stick.

"Meaning my magic—" And most definitely Alexander stressed that word "—is made up of all four elements."

"Spirit." Andy breathed. "The fifth element is spirit."

Roderick scoffed. "There is no fifth element."

Alexander resisted the urge to make a snide remark about Bruce Willis movies and said, "Common magic lore states otherwise."

"Modern lore." Roderick went back to studying Andy's data. "Not everything modern people believe is the truth," quoth the man staring at a MacBook as if it would show him the light.

"But in this case—" Andy pushed his glasses up the bridge of his nose "—I think it applies. The facts strongly suggest Alexander would be using a combination of all elements." He raised one finger. "There is no pull on any of the known four elements. There is no corresponding light that correlates to one of those elements. Also." He raised a third finger to join the other two. "There is none of the fragrance associated with the witches using their blessing."

Roderick straightened, folded his arms, and glared at Alexander. "That doesn't mean he's drawing all four."

"But it does mean we should consider the possibility." Andy looked apologetic to be contradicting his hero Roderick.

"I'll consider it." Roderick huffed. "Why don't we try hanging him and see what he does?"

"Or we could have a go at decapitation." Thomas sneered and stood. "This is bullshit, and stop torturing the man. You know his magic has defensive possibilities. The next step is to find out if he can conjure it offensively at will." With that he vanished.

Roderick stared at the spot Thomas had occupied. "We need to do something about him."

"Leave the poor sod alone." Alexander flexed his fingers and got ready to test his offensive abilities. "He's trying to do the right thing, and it's killing him."

"Right." Roderick nodded and looked pensive. "It would never have worked between them. She's mortal and—"

"And he knows it." Alexander didn't like to think how he'd be feeling if he couldn't be with Bronwyn.

"I'll talk to Maeve and see if she's any closer to releasing the witches on the green," Roderick said and shrugged. "It won't help him where Alannah is concerned, but it might grant him a measure of relief."

Just when Alexander was convinced the stubborn prick was a block of emotionless wood, he went and said something insightful. "Yeah, that can't be easy. Carrying around Lavina being trapped and in torment."

"Let's test his suggestion." Alexander didn't want to entertain the possibility of liking Roderick. He concentrated on his hand and turning it into a sword.

His hand stared back at him.

He tried again, something less ambitious, a dagger.

More speak to the hand.

A fucking stick, for the love of Goddess.

Hand.

"Umm…" Andy held up his forefinger. "I've been giving the matter considerable thought."

*Uh-oh.*

Roderick's expression mirroring his thought almost got Alexander laughing.

"I read a lot of fantasy." Andy placed his laptop on the bench beside him like a mother putting her baby down for a nap. "Actually, I read a lot of science fiction and fantasy." Andy tilted his head and thought it through. "And a lot of political commentary, and I'm also really partial to historical biographies. Also, I do enjoy a well-researched, strongly written historical nonfiction. Peter Ackroyd's *London: the Biography* is particularly—"

"Your point!" Roderick got there before Alexander could.

"Right." Andy chuckled and jabbed a thumb at his chest. "Geek and book nerd. So, fantasy novels."

Roderick shifted. "What kind of fantasy?"

"Not that kind." Alexander didn't even want to go where Roderick's brain had beelined. "They're stories based in mythology in which realms of magic and magical creatures are created."

"Eh?" Roderick shook his head.

"Now the idea of magic being triggered by strong emotion is hardly new. Fictionally speaking." Andy waggled his hand. "There is—"

"And?" Alexander didn't want to hear the recitation of several trilogies.

"Right." Andy blushed. "So, as I was saying. The concept of magic needing strong emotion to work is not new. In said novels, the hero—" he pointed at Alexander "—in this case, you, must learn to focus their emotion and draw their magic."

Was Andy going anywhere? "Okay?"

"He's not a hero," Roderick grumbled.

Andy patted his arm. "But they also have to visualize what they would like the magic to accomplish."

He'd been visualizing the sword, fuck you very much.

"Which got me extrapolating." Andy stood and paced the sand. "Your skills strongly suggest a martial nature." Up went that forefinger again. "When we tested you on becoming an inanimate object such as a bench or table. Nothing." Finger number two. "When we asked you to become a creature. Nothing."

At this point, Alexander might break finger number three.

"But when called to defend yourself." Andy snapped his fingers. "Every time." He grinned at Alexander and Roderick. "You're a battle mage."

"What?" It was hard to tell whether Alexander or Roderick bellowed louder.

"A battle mage." Andy ta-daed his hands. "It's a spell caster whose abilities are linked to war and fighting. And if we follow the established mythology, you must enter the mindset of the warrior to work your magic."

All Alexander got was *blah, blah blah.*

"He's right." Roderick thwacked Andy's shoulder.

Andy stumbled forward and righted himself. "Well, I don't know about that." He smoothed his shirt front. "But it might provide a useful starting point."

"Eh?" Now Alexander felt like the dumb one, which given that Roderick was in the room, was hardly a pleasant possibility.

"It's dirt simple." Roderick shrugged. "Think like a warrior."

Damn it all to hell and back, but he was going to do it again. "Eh?"

"Channel your inner warrior." Andy raised his arms in an arc over his head and wiggled his fingers in what Alexander could only assume were channeling motions.

"You definitely have one of those." Roderick snorted. "It's the part that's tried to kill me on countless occasions."

Well, that was easy enough. When he reached for his inner Roderick-slayer, Alexander's skin tingled, and power surged to his muscles. His acuity increased. "Sword," he whispered.

Sparks stung his forearm. His arm shimmered and then morphed into six feet of steel.

Roderick went on alert.

Andy clapped his hands. "Battle mage." He threw his hands out to the gods. "Alexander is a battle mage!"

Folding his arms, Roderick dropped his chin to his chest. "He's a pain in the fucking arse is what he is."

# CHAPTER FORTY

A neat man dressed in a suit and tie and carrying a placard with their names printed on it stood beneath a sign about diplomats as Jack and Mags stepped off the jet bridge and into the terminal.

Not about to be caught napping, Jack eyed the man.

Mags—bugger it to shit and back—marched straight up to the man. "Hello." She pointed at the sign. "That's me. I'm Magdalene Cray."

The man inclined his head and cleared his throat. "I have a message for Jack." He glanced at Jack and then down at his feet. "Emma says to tell you to stop being a suspicious bastard and get in the…er…fucking car."

"Emma who?" Not his first trip around the block, nor was he taking any chances with his Magdalene.

She touched his arm. "It's okay, Jack."

Jack kept his peepers trained on Suit-boy. "Emma who?"

"Fletcher. Dr. Emma Fletcher." The man dragged a card out of his back pocket and handed it to Jack. "She suspected you might not believe me, and said I was to say…um…that air was called."

"See." Mags bounced on her toes. "Emma sent you?"

"Dr. Fletcher, yes." The man nodded and seemed relieved to shift his attention to Mags. "She's one of our regulars."

Not going along that easily, Jack said, "And what is it that you do?"

"We're a car service." The man handed Jack the card. "We do…um…pickups and VIP customs clearance for a select clientele. I'm to make sure you get out of the airport as quietly as possible and take you where you want to go." The man's pocket buzzed, and he held out a finger. "Excuse me, I need to take this." He fumbled with the mobile while muttering something about his line of work and always being in touch. "This is Delta Foxtrot five niner."

He listened for a moment and then held the phone to Jack. "She wants to speak to you."

Jack took the phone and pressed it to his ear.

Emma's voice came down the line. "Jack? How's our girl?"

"Fine." He hadn't gotten over Emma's defection yet. Maybe never would. "Is this guy on the up and up?"

"He is," Emma said. "He'll get you out of the airport with fewer people being any the wiser and get you straight to Baile." She lowered her voice. "He's not one of us, but the firm has been thoroughly vetted." She sighed. "I wouldn't trust Mags with anyone else."

"Right." But she'd let Mags get on a plane without her.

"Don't be such a hard arse, Jack," Emma said as if she'd read his mind. "I'm doing what needs to be done. Get in the car and take Mags to Baile. Drop me a line when you get there so I know she's safe."

"Maybe I'm not going to Baile."

Emma laughed. "Fair enough, you suspicious bastard. And I'm a big fan of that, by the way. Tell him where you want to go, and he'll take you there. Without letting me know. He has a package in the car with a new mobile phone. We made sure it's clean, and I have the number."

"Do you have a lovely car?" Mags smiled at Suit-boy. "I bet you do."

"Umm..." He blinked at Mags. "It's a Mercedes."

"How thrilling." Mags twinkled up at Jack. "I've never been in a Mercedes."

"Newest model. Top of the line," Suit-boy added. "With a couple of special modifications. If you know what I mean?"

Jack didn't have a clue, but he reckoned Suit-boy was legit. He hung up on Emma and handed the phone back to him. "Let's go."

Suit-boy, who gave up his name as Lester to Mags, took them to a special customs area and stood by while they were checked back into England. Then he led them through an endless maze of passages and eventually into an underground parking garage.

His Mercedes, as promised to Mags, looked brand spanking new. The engine was already running and the car interior a comfortable temperature.

"There is bottled water in the center console." Lester pointed out the amenities as he held the door for Mags. "And a couple of nibbles if you didn't fancy the plane food. Also, a package I was told to give to you."

Opening the package, Jack found a mobile and turned it on.

Mags bounced into the backseat and went for the console. "Look, Jack, they have all sorts of tasty things."

"If there's anything further you'd like—" Lester smoothed his sleeves into place "—I am happy to stop and obtain it for you."

Mags beamed at the man. "Thank you, Lester. This is more than we expected."

Jesus, her insane childlike enthusiasm for shit got him in the ticker. As much as it worried the crap out of him, he never wanted her to lose it. When Jack was with Mags, he could imagine himself as a better, purer, and more open version of the grumpy shit he was. He accepted a bottle of water and insisted Mags eat something.

Lester got behind the wheel.

The car slid out of the parking garage like it ran on a pocket of air. Lester merged with the day's traffic in a flawless, intricate waltz. Jack swore he never even felt the fucker touch the brakes, but they slowed and sped up, and did all the driving things mortals who were not Lester did every day.

He watched Mags constantly. She'd tried to hide it from him, but the weirdness was back. Jack wanted to pound the elegantly appointed leather interior of the car. Midflight, she'd gotten that vacant spacey look. The one he'd thought would disappear once she'd activated air.

Right now, she was doing all right, and a bang-up job of hiding it from him.

She took a deep breath and turned to him. Dark shadows lurked in her eyes. "Jack?"

"I know." He took her hand and kissed it. "It started on the plane."

She gave a short laugh. "How did you know?"

"I know you." He shrugged. He might not be her coimhdeacht, but he understood his woman. "How bad is it?"

She made a half-half motion with one hand. "It's not as strong as it was in Moscow, but it's there. The voice is back."

"Motherfucker."

Mags laughed. "My thought exactly. Get me to Baile, and we'll sort this out."

He didn't ask how. He suspected she didn't know. He chose distraction versus dwelling on the fucking impossible. "So, about these four children."

She smiled and nudged him. "Accept it; it's going to happen."

"Two boys and two girls?"

"Yup." She opened a water bottle and sipped. "You're going to make a wonderful father."

If she said so, he'd try, and if that's what she wanted, that's what he'd give her.

---

It felt good to be back in the barracks. Warren flexed his shoulder and straightened his sword.

Roderick was determined to make up for his absence by trying to hack him into pieces.

"Your guard is sloppy." Roderick slapped Warren's sword with his. "This is supposed to protect you as well as carve a trench through me."

The burn in Warren's muscles felt good, and he grinned. "Can't I just get to the carving."

"If you can get past me." Roderick smirked.

That might take a while, so Warren tightened his focus. He still didn't see a time when he'd need to whip out a sword, but the training was good for strength and acuity.

"Any news from Mags and Jack?" He circled Roderick searching for an opening.

Roderick pivoted with him, light as a dancer on his feet. Alert, relaxed and ready, the perfect fighting machine. "No. They don't know it's safe to contact us yet."

"And Alannah and Sinead."

Roderick lunged, and Warren's hand stung as his sword wrenched out of his hold and sailed across the practice yard. "Same." Roderick pointed to the lost sword with his. "You're no use to yourself without that. Let's go again."

Any time Goddess wanted to give him some more of that superhuman strength and agility, Warren would take it. "This is hardly a fair fight."

"Why's that?" Roderick snorted.

"You've had about twenty thousand years more practice."

Roderick laughed and raised his sword. "Now you're whining."

"True story." Warren picked up his sword, his tired muscles bellowing their objection.

"Dad?" Taylor walked across the practice yard toward him. Niamh and the wolves followed her.

Her pinched expression grabbed his attention, and he dropped his sword and went over to her. "What?"

"She was practicing scrying." Niamh made a face. "I suggested Mags because she's reached her before."

Roderick was by his side instantly. "And?"

"Daddy." Taylor's voice wobbled. "Something bad is coming. Something really bad."

Fuck! Could they not get a fucking break? He kept his tone level as he asked, "Can you see what?"

"No." Taylor shook her head. Tears spilled down her cheek. "But there's this dark cloud surrounding Mags, and she's in terrible danger. Jack too."

Roderick crouched and pulled Taylor into a hug. "You did well, sweet girl. You did well to tell us."

"She's back in England," Taylor said. "She's in a car with Jack, and she's trying to get to us."

"Thank you." Warren cupped her cheek. "I know this is horrible for you."

"Help her," Taylor whispered against Roderick's shoulder. "Please. She needs you."

Niamh put her hands on Taylor's shoulders and looked at him. "Go. We'll make sure Taylor is okay."

"Get Alexander." Roderick stood and strode from the room. "And prepare yourselves."

Taylor took a deep breath and wiped her face. "I can show you where you need to go."

# CHAPTER FORTY-ONE

They'd turned off the highway. Jack stared out the window looking for Baile to appear on the horizon. The castle had become his embodiment of safety, and he itched to get there.

A flash drew his attention, and he turned his head.

A car's grill loomed in his window, heading directly their way. "Watch out!"

Jack had barely enough time to grab Mags and cover her before impact.

Lester swore but kept his cool. He jerked the steering wheel to the right and back again. Tires squealed, metal screeched, and burning rubber turned the air acrid.

The blow pushed them into the oncoming lane.

Correcting, Lester jammed the accelerator and they lurched forward.

Another car closed from the other side and t-boned them, trapping them.

"Stay down," Jack yelled. He and Mags were thrown across the backseat. His shoulder hit the door with a crunch, and the coppery taste of blood filled his mouth.

Whipping his head around, Lester threw the car into reverse. "Shit."

A third car closed off that retreat.

Another car fishtailed into position in front of them, finishing the fourth side of the box.

More cars arrived behind the first four, and doors opened.

People bailed out, all of them heading their way.

Eyes wide, Lester stared at him. "The car has a bullet—"

*Boom!*

Blinding light hit the car, and Jack blinked against the retina-burning glare. He tightened his hold on Mags.

She whimpered but clung to him.

"What the fuck?" Lester's door was wrenched open, and hands reached in and yanked him out.

Cool air hit Jack's back, and then more arms were grabbing and tugging. He wrapped as much of him as he could around Mags.

His arse, then his back hit the asphalt, and he tried to roll over and shield Mags.

Hot, arcing pain shot through him from his lower back, but he refused to loosen his hold.

A blow to the side of the head made his vision wavy and his ears ring.

He kicked out blindly, making contact with something.

People bellowed and yelled, but he couldn't make sense of the words. Hands everywhere ripping at his hold on Mags. More pain, this time from his shoulder.

"Get her," a man shouted. "Get the fucking witch. Kill him if you have to."

Jack grit his teeth and clung to Mags. Another sharp pain registered in his side. He'd felt that kind of pain before. They were using knives on him. Blood dripped down his arms and covered Mags as she cowered against him.

Mags sobbed. "Let me go, Jack. Please let me go."

"No." He grit his teeth as he felt another knife sink into his thigh. Not while he had an ounce of life in him.

"What the—"

A man bellowed.

"Fucking get her!" Hands ripped at his hold.

Jack's strength waned, but he clung on.

The shouting intensified and grew more desperate, an edge of panic to it now.

Gunshots cracked through the air.

The multiple grips on him loosened, and Jack managed to roll on top of Mags.

Beneath him, she shivered but held it together.

More gunshots. More yelling.

The hands loosened, and suddenly a voice he knew. "Jack!" She shook his shoulder. "Jack, it's Emma." She gasped. "Jesus! You're bleeding from everywhere."

"I got Mags." His jaw felt fused together. "I got her."

"You did well, Jack." Emma gripped his wrist. "Can you let me see her?"

They'd left her in Moscow, but he was struggling to breathe, let alone speak. "How?"

"Explanations later. We've got company." Emma dropped his wrist and stood. She braced her legs. "Back off." Her voice came out grimmer than death and twice as cold. "Back the hell away or I'll shoot you."

"Mags!" Warren called. "Mags, I don't know who this woman is, but tell her it's us."

Jack almost lost it and bawled as Warren's voice registered. "Warren?"

"You know them?" Emma glanced down. She looked like an avenging angel above him, handguns leveled at Warren.

"Yes." Jack managed to nod, but he couldn't let Mags go. That had been close. Too fucking close.

"He's hurt. We need to see to him. Lower your weapons." There was no mistaking Alexander's posh tones.

"Get out of the way, wench!" Good old Roderick.

And Jack nearly laughed. The fucker never changed.

"Did he just call me wench?" Emma blinked in the direction of Roderick's voice.

"Please." Warren sounded nearer now, and his black combats entered Jack's field of vision. "We're from Baile. We're not the enemy."

"He's bleeding," Alexander said. "Make up your fucking mind, but do it fast."

Jack's vision wavered. His head swum.

Lowering her weapons, Emma stepped back. "One wrong move, and I'll make a fucking swiss cheese of you."

"Who are you?" Roderick's size fourteens appeared next to Warren's combats.

"All you need to know is I'm with Mags," Emma said. "And that means I'm with Jack as well."

Roderick stared at Emma's arms. "Those are—"

"Not now." Alexander crouched beside them. "Jack? Can you move? We need to get you sorted, and we need to check Mags."

Mags wriggled beneath him. "Jack." Tears streaked her beautiful face. "You're hurt. Please let go so they can help you."

Only for her, Jack rolled to his back and loosened his hold. His head thwacked into the road, but it was one more pain in the lancing agony all over his body. He was leaking blood all over the road.

"Fuck!" The look on Warren's face as he studied Jack wasn't encouraging.

Jack coughed and more blood filled his mouth. "That bad, hmm?" At least, that's what he tried to say but his words got tangled in the bloody mess in his mouth.

"We need to get him to Baile." Alexander's lips flattened into a tight line. "She can—"

"Incoming." Emma lifted her weapons again.

Alexander cursed and whirled to his feet.

"This is going to hurt." Warren jostled him as he slid his arms under his body.

"You'll never—"

Jack screamed and nearly blacked out as Warren lifted him.

A battle cry jerked him back to consciousness.

Roderick!

Over Warren's shoulder, the big bastard swung into action.

There were people everywhere.

Where was—

"I'm right here." Mags took his hand. "I'm right with you."

Emma joined Roderick, her guns blazing hot, orange trails of flame.

So many. So fucking many. "I can fight."

Warren glanced at Mags. "Open the door."

Jack screamed as Warren maneuvered him into the back of the Landy.

Mags clambered into the back beside him. Blood streaked the side of her face, but otherwise she looked okay.

And Jack let the darkness take him.

---

"Jesus!" Warren took a moment to survey the situation and wished he hadn't. There were people everywhere. Alexander, Roderick, and the blond woman gave it their all, and it was an impressive all, but the waves of people kept coming.

Bodies dropped around them, only to be replaced by more. They couldn't win.

"Retreat!" He bellowed.

The three fighters gave no indication they'd heard him, but they inched back toward him.

More people moved between the Landy and them.

Warren threw himself at the newest wave of attackers. Relentlessly, he cut a hole in the mass of writhing, fighting forms.

Alexander was the first to reach his side. His clothes were splashed with blood; sweat poured down his face. "Can you drive?"

Warren nodded and punched a man out the way. He clambered over the Landy's hood to the driver's side. Christ, Jack was a fucking mess, but he couldn't think of that now. Bronwyn. He had to get Jack to Bronwyn.

The fight ended. Suddenly. As if an invisible signal had been given. The mass of attackers peeled off like a flock of wheeling birds and flung themselves into vehicles.

Tires screeched and engines roared, and they were gone.

The quiet rang around them.

"Get in." Warren gunned the engine. "Let's go."

Roderick turned and sprinted. The blond woman kept pace with him. Tall and lithe, she looked like the fighter she'd proven herself to be. She stopped at the driver's side. "I have my own vehicle. Go. Get her safe."

Later they would do the Q&A.

The Landy rocked as Alexander climbed in beside him.

Roderick hauled the back door open. "Where's Mags?"

---

ALEXANDER JERKED AROUND in his seat. His mind screamed a denial as his eyes confirmed the truth.

Jack lay unconscious in the back, his blood pooling around him, but Mags was gone.

"Fuck." That's why the fight had stopped. They'd gotten what they came for.

"Where is she?" The blond woman peered past his shoulder. "Where is my witch?"

"Your witch?" Roderick blinked at her.

Alexander made a snap decision and looked at Warren. "Get him back to Baile. Now." He turned to the blonde. "You have a car?"

She was already running toward it.

Roderick raced after her.

"Get him there. Fast." Alexander hopped out. "We're going after Mags."

Warren gunned the Landy before Alexander was half out.

He and Roderick barely had enough time to throw themselves into the blonde's car before she was punching the metal and following the disappearing line of cars.

"Who are you?" Roderick clung to the door handle as she swung them around the bend.

"Emma." She focused on the road, eyes narrowed, jaw clenched. "Emma Fletcher."

"Coimhdeacht." Alexander had a hard time believing the umber markings on Emma's arm were real, but there they were. "For Mags."

Roderick shook his head. "No—"

"Not now." Alexander gripped his shoulder. "Let's get to Mags first."

## CHAPTER FORTY-TWO

Warren prayed like he never had before as he pushed the Landy to its limit. Fortunately, they'd found Jack fighting for his and Mags's life a few kilometer the other side of Greater Littleton. The village flashed past the windows, as he flat-footed it through. Horns blared, people dived out of the way, but he didn't have time to be careful. Jack didn't have time.

Goddess let the others find Mags. Goddess let him be on time for Jack.

The witches stood in the bailey as he screeched through the gatehouse and slid to a stop.

Bronwyn clambered into the back beside Jack.

She put her hands on his chest. Blood soaked over her fingers. So much fucking blood.

Closing her eyes, she drew water. Blue light filled the inside of the Landy as Bronwyn got to work. The scent of honey and sage almost made him throw up.

And then Niamh was there. Standing beside him, sliding her hand into his.

He hadn't been aware of climbing out the driver's side and coming to the back.

"Bronwyn's got him." She tightened her grip on his hand. "She'll fix him."

Warren didn't have the words to voice his question.

"He's breathing," Niamh said. "You got here in time."

Blue light intensified around Bronwyn.

"Dad." Taylor took his other hand. "It's okay, Dad."

He wished he could believe it. He'd seen too many men die to believe it. Seen men die from half the wounds Jack had sustained. They'd made a fucking pincushion out of Jack.

Hannah shoved past him and climbed in beside Bronwyn. She put her stethoscope to Jack's chest. "Heartbeat steady," she said. "Respiration labored."

Bronwyn nodded and pulled more water.

With quick, thorough hands, Hannah examined Jack. "Kidneys," she said.

Bronwyn nodded. Blue light followed Hannah's hands.

And on they went. Hannah identifying areas for Bronwyn's healing. Their voices hushed and intent. Their expressions grim.

Nothing stirred in the bailey as waves thundered against the rocks beneath the castle.

"Look." Niamh released his hand. "He's breathing easier."

Jack's big chest lifted and fell.

"It's okay now, Dad." Taylor hugged his arm. "Bronwyn saved him."

Hannah glanced up and nodded at him before returning her attention to Jack.

Was Warren imagining it, or did Jack's color seem better? No more blood was joining the pool under Jack.

"Stop." Hannah touched Bronwyn's arm. "You've got him stabilized." She gestured at Jack. "The rest are superficial. I'll stitch them while you recover."

"I'm fine." Bronwyn opened her eyes and tried to move.

Warren caught her before she crumpled into Jack's blood on the Landy floor.

---

Hours stretched longer than years as they waited. After he'd carried Bronwyn to the cavern and seen her restored enough to walk back under her own steam, Warren took a shower and got out of his blood-stained clothes.

In the kitchen, Niamh and Maeve had put together soup and sandwiches, which nobody touched.

Silent and alert, wolves stood sentinel around the kitchen.

Alpha looked over at him. *Pack.*

Hannah came into the kitchen looking tired and drawn. "He's resting comfortably."

"We put Charlie to bed." Maeve nudged Hannah into a chair. "I left the dogs and Taylor with him."

With a nod, Hannah accepted a mug of tea and cradled it between her palms. "Thank you."

A cat jumped into her lap and settled.

Hannah shook her head and gave a wan smile. "This is the craziest place on earth." She stroked the cat. "How's Bronwyn?"

"Asleep." Niamh handed Hannah a sandwich. "She's exhausted."

"I'm not bloody surprised." Hannah sipped her tea. "I've never seen..."

She didn't need to finish her sentence. The knowledge of how close they'd come to losing Jack hung like a funeral dirge in the air.

"Any news?" Andy entered the kitchen, for once without his laptop.

Warren shook his head. No news was good news. Right? Goddess, he wished he could believe that.

"They'll find her." Maeve took a seat beside him. "They have to."

"Everyone needs to eat." Hannah bit into her sandwich and chewed mechanically.

Niamh grimaced. "I don't know how you can eat."

"Habit." Hannah grimly took another bite. "When you're an intern and resident, you learn to eat and sleep when you can."

Warren forced a couple of bites down. Soldiers learned the same lesson. If you didn't fuel up, you were no good for whatever came next. He pushed Niamh's sandwich closer to her. "Eat."

Maeve sipped her soup. "Can you tell us what happened?"

"We found Jack fighting for his life." He recounted the details like a robot, viciously severing any tendrils of emotion from his recitation. "We thought we'd got the situation under control, and then the next wave struck." He couldn't believe he'd been so sodding stupid as not to recognize a classic distraction for what it was. He should have—

Alpha nudged him and put his muzzle on Warren's thigh. Those keen yellow eyes focused on him, steadying him.

Warren dragged breath into his tight lungs. "While we were fighting them off, they took her."

"They'll find her," Maeve said.

Andy nodded. "They will." He took a smartphone from his pocket. "Are there any details you can remember? Car registrations? Faces? I can see what I can find."

Warren nearly shook his head, but he had remembered a few things. His soldier's mind had taken over and absorbed small details here and there.

Andy tapped it all into his phone and then excused himself.

Night limped toward morning.

THEY HADN'T FOUND HER. Bitterness turned Alexander's stomach to bile. After three days of searching, barely stopping to eat and sleeping in shifts, finally he, Roderick and Emma returned to Baile.

Shocked faces greeted their return without Mags.

Bronwyn walked into his arms and slid hers around his waist. "We'll regroup and try again."

"I'm going now." Emma turned for her car.

Roderick cut her off. "Get inside."

"Get out of my way." That Emma had to look up to return his glower in no way diminished her power.

"Inside."

"Don't make me go through you."

They'd barely spoken above sharing information and planning their next steps. But it was time.

"Emma?" Maeve stepped between Roderick and Emma and held out her hand. "My name is Maeve. I'm Mags's coven sister, and Roderick is my coimhdeacht."

Emma dragged her glare from Roderick and blinked at Maeve. "Then get him out of my way."

"Have you met Roderick? Nobody makes him do anything." Maeve touched her arm. "Come inside. Please. We're all here for Mags. We all love her and want to get her back."

Sweet, lovely Maeve disarmed Emma in a way none of them could have, and tension drained out of Emma. "I should have been with her. This would never have happened—"

"Don't." Alexander was on best friend terms with regret. "There's no point."

"A coimhdeacht never leaves his witch." Roderick scowled. "Never."

For fuck's sake. Alexander wanted to pound the prick.

Emma stiffened. "I know." She took a breath. "This is on me, and I will find her."

"We'll find her." Jack limped out of the kitchen.

Considering the last time Alexander had seen the bastard, that he was even breathing was a wonder, let alone walking and talking. Alexander suspected his little witch had pulled a miracle. He looked down at her. "Are you all right?"

"I am." She winced. "It was a difficult healing."

As much as he wanted to yell at her for pushing herself, he was glad to see Jack.

Alexander held out his hand and Jack clasped it. "I'm glad to see you."

"She saved me." Jack gestured Bronwyn. "Or I'd be a goner for sure."

"Everyone inside." Maeve took Roderick's arm and tugged him to the kitchen. "We need to share information and plan our next steps."

"She is not coimhdeacht." Roderick allowed Maeve to pull him into the kitchen. "There are no female coimhdeacht."

"There never have been before." Maeve pushed him into a chair. "But that seems to have changed as well."

After three days of working with Emma, Alexander had no doubt the woman was up to the task. He took the seat opposite her. "Care to fill in the blanks now that we have a moment?"

Emma glanced at the door. "I should be out there."

"Not without me." Jack sat beside her. "I thought you weren't coming to Baile."

"I lasted until I left the parking lot at Domodedovo," Emma said. "Sasha was way ahead of me and had a plane ready to go before you'd even left Moscow. I was right on your heels. I had just landed at Heathrow when I called Lester." She grimaced. "I had this fucking stupid idea I'd surprise Mags."

Roderick sat forward. "What does he mean, you weren't going to come?"

"Just that." Emma met his stare. "I had responsibilities keeping me in Moscow."

Roderick gaped. "You answer when Goddess calls."

"And where does that leave free will?" Emma didn't back down.

As much as Alexander enjoyed seeing someone give Roderick a hard time, they really didn't have capacity for bickering. "We need to focus on Mags and finding her."

"Mags was okay with it." Jack nodded at Emma. "I agree with Roderick. You should have come with us."

So much for everybody listening to him. "We have time to sort that out later, but for now—"

"That is why women have never been chosen before," Roderick said. "They lack the mettle for the challenge."

All eyes snapped Roderick's way.

Alexander almost choked on his own tongue. Roderick could be a sexist prick, but he'd never...

The gleam in Roderick's eye stopped Alexander.

The big fucker was goading Emma.

Emma shot out of her seat and slapped her palms on the table. "What did you say?"

"You heard me." Roderick sneered. "You think you can walk in here, after losing your witch, and become part of this brotherhood?"

"I never signed on for any brotherhood. Even the name is a sexist joke." Emma's eyes blazed.

Sitting back, Roderick folded his arms. "No, you did nothing instead. Did you think we'd grant you special favors because you're a girl?"

Wow! Alexander's brows hit his hairline. Roderick was ladling it on with a forklift, backing up, and dumping another load.

Tension vibrated through Emma's every pore. "I don't need any favors from you or any man."

"Right." Roderick chuckled. "And next you'll tell us you deserve to be here and can hold your own?"

"Fuck you." Emma snarled.

Roderick grinned. "No thank you. I prefer my women to be proper women."

Warren choked. Beer spurted out his nose and mouth, but he was onto Roderick as well.

Maeve shook her head and stared at the table.

"You mother-fucking piece of shit." Emma sucked in a deep breath. "You need to learn some manners."

"And who's going to teach me those manners." Roderick sneered. "You?"

Jack put his hand up. "Now, let's all—"

Alexander kicked him under the table. He wasn't entirely sure where Roderick was going, but Roderick had trained and managed thousands of coimhdeacht in his time, and he was going to give him the benefit of the doubt. He shook his head at himself. If anybody had heard that thought he'd have denied it.

Jack glanced at him.

Alexander shook his head and hoped the man took the hint.

Frowning, Jack studied Roderick and then Emma and subsided into silence.

"Outside." Emma stalked to the door. "Right now."

Smirking, Roderick followed Emma out.

The rest of them stayed hot on his heels.

Emma barely waited for Roderick to adopt a fighting crouch before she was on him. She moved with the deadly, focused precision of a fashionista at a seventy-five percent off designer sale.

At hand-to-hand combat she was the best Alexander had ever seen, and he'd been around for a long, long time.

Roderick was a born warrior, and he held his own through the first volley of blows. And the second. He managed to land a few telling hits, but Emma shook those off and came in for more.

She was relentless. She was determined, and she was drowning in self-loathing.

Roderick let her work it out physically.

Eventually, Roderick's lack of experience in martial arts landed his arse in the sand.

Emma raised her right hand for the killing blow.

"Enough." Warren stepped in and caught her hand. "Are you done?"

Ripping her hand away, Emma did an impressive flip through the air and landed in a crouch. "You want to be next?"

"Decline the lady's invitation." Roderick rolled to his stomach and heaved himself into a sitting position. Wiping blood from his mouth with the back of his hand, he looked at Emma. "Are you done?"

Emma's gaze flit from Roderick to Warren. "Done what?"

"Wallowing in guilt." Roderick brought his knees up and propped his elbows on them. "Or do you want to beat the crap out of Alexander first?"

How the hell had his name come up?

Roderick stood. "Personally, I never miss an opportunity to fuck Alexander up. But your choice." He held out a hand to Emma. "You are one of us. Your witch needs you. There is no time or place for guilt and regret."

"What?" Emma blinked at him.

Alexander stepped in with the Roderick translation. "You needed an outlet for your rage. Roderick provided that outlet. I would keep going, if I were you, but your choice." He leaned closer and whispered. "He can take more. So, by all means, keep going."

Roderick looked at Emma and said, "You are called, Emma Fletcher, and now there is somebody you need to meet."

# CHAPTER FORTY-THREE

"Is he always like that?" Emma followed Warren across the bailey and through an arched wooden door in the seaward wall. On the far side of the wall, wind buffeted them as they descended a narrow stone staircase carved from the cliff face.

Warren grinned over his shoulder. "Mostly."

Good thing heights didn't bother her, because there was nothing between them and the sea foaming and churning around jagged rocks below.

She had to force her hand not to trail the rockface for reassurance. A lifetime spent proving her worth to men wouldn't allow her to show any weakness. "We couldn't just talk?"

"Could you, though?" Warren stopped three steps below her and turned. "Would talking have done it for you?"

Not wanting to give that much ground, she shrugged. "Maybe not, but now we'll never know."

Warren raised a brow like she wasn't fooling him for a second and got moving again.

The stairs ended in a dark hole in the rock.

She should have been on the plane with Jack and Mags. Fuck it all, she should have used the organization plane for all three of them. But she hadn't been thinking straight. She hadn't been thinking at all. A lifetime spent tracking witches, and when she'd been swept into the heart of the storm, she'd frozen. Not for a second had she imagined she would be coimhdeacht. If she'd been with them in the car—

"Don't." Warren barely turned his head. "There's no point."

"Right." Emma nodded, but she'd failed Mags. She'd had one job; to get Mags safely to Baile and she'd totally screwed that up.

"These are the caverns." Warren motioned the Stygian black beyond.

Excitement chased her lingering annoyance with Roderick away. "The sacred caverns?"

"Do people really call them that?" Warren grimaced.

"They do if they aren't lucky enough to live right on top of them." Emma stepped through the entrance.

Tinkling chimes filled the air. The crystals in the walls glowed red, blue, and yellow and lit the embedded fossils and shells that combined with them to make the legendary patterns.

Emma wanted to touch, and her hand was halfway out before she reconsidered. "May I?"

"Of course." Warren put his palm against the wall. "You wouldn't be here if Baile didn't welcome you. And whoever Baile welcomes, the caverns permit as well." He shook his head. "I wish I'd known that before I brought Taylor here."

She ran a reverent finger over the nearest swirls and whorls of shell, crystal, and fossil. A tingle shot up her arm and she laughed.

Warren laughed with her. "Total mind fuck, isn't it?"

"Not really." She'd grown up steeped in magic and lore. "I've known about this place since I first understood about the organization and Rhiannon. I never thought I'd actually see it." Never thought her link to Baile would be so direct. It was a sorry excuse. She'd been unprepared for the new responsibility.

Her dad would be ashamed of her. He'd trained her better than that.

"You need to tell us more about your organization and what intel you've gathered on Rhiannon."

"I will." She touched another sigil and got another pleasant shockwave. "But my priority has to be Mags."

Warren nodded. "Understood."

He turned and led the way deeper into the caverns. Arched openings linked the caverns to each other as she trailed him deeper and deeper into the mountain Baile was built atop.

"Taylor is your daughter, right?" she whispered, more in awe of being there than anything else.

"Yup. Turns out she's a water witch and a seer." He dug his hands in his pockets. "I still have to share that little ditty with her mother."

Emma didn't envy him that. Growing up as she had, she'd had plenty of experience with how badly people reacted to the idea of there being more to their world than they perceived.

"The chamber holding the air point is similar to this." She motioned the caverns. "But without as many sigils, and of course, the Goddess portal."

Warren grunted. "Jack said you hid it under the metro system."

She nodded. As they moved deeper, prickles of awareness ran over her skin. The marks on Warren's arm glowed in the dim light from the crystals. Her own markings were more shadowy, but still there.

They entered the final cavern, and Emma's feet gave up on walking and planted her.

Sigils ran riot over the walls and ceiling, but the water pool in the cavern's center held her gaze. It glowed with an unearthly golden light.

"I'll leave you here." Warren clapped her shoulder. "She's waiting for you."

That nearly made Emma panic and run. Goddess waiting for her? *Shit!*

"It won't swallow you." Warren gave her a nudge. "And, like I said, you're expected."

His footsteps chuffed softly on the cavern's sandy floor as Warren walked away.

Emma took three steps toward the pool and couldn't go any further. When you'd learned about a thing since childhood, spent your adult life in service to that very thing, facing it for the first time with failure pressing down on your shoulders, it felt way too daunting.

*Emma.*

She cleared her throat and croaked, "Yes."

*Beloved.*

Stupid tears prickled beneath her lids and tickled her nose. Her knees sagged and smacked into the sand. She bowed her head. "I have failed you."

*Ah, Beloved.* The sadness in Goddess's voice brought a fresh onslaught of tears. *Roderick is wise beyond even his considerable years sometimes.*

Emma wasn't prepared to go that far. Her thigh and bicep ached from the couple of solid blows he'd landed, and a dull headache throbbed behind her eyes. Fresh waves of grief closed over Emma, and breathing got difficult. "I let them take her."

*We are all players in this game, and the game will follow its course.*

Air stirred above her, and a pair of bare, ethereal feet appeared in her line of vision. "What are you saying?"

She didn't know if she was allowed to question a deity.

*Ask your questions, Emma Fletcher. You are my Beloved, and your service has long been known.*

Only one question and it burned through her. "Why?"

*There must always be balance. Even in this war, balance must be maintained.*

"What does that mean?"

*Find Mags, Beloved. Your duty is clear. Find Mags and bond her to you.*

Emma risked a glance up. More light and shadows than corporeal, Goddess stood two inches from her. Her face was unremarkable, a pleasing collection of features that wouldn't stand out in a crowd.

*The war enters its final stages. Soon now I must take form again and enter the field of battle.*

Goddess's face didn't change, but now Emma found her pretty.

*I can say no more. Nor can I influence the outcome. I am bound in my power and abilities.*

That didn't make any sense. "Rhiannon doesn't seem to have any such restrictions."

*Rhiannon is who she is. She is the cold to my warmth, the dark to my light. She acts only in the manner in which she was created.*

As she studied Goddess, Emma found it hard to believe she'd thought her unremarkable at first. Goddess had an intrinsic beauty that drew the gaze and held it. Emma wrestled with Goddess's statements about Rhiannon. It if were up to her, she'd be cranking up a thunderbolt or something.

Goddess laughed and was now almost too exquisite to look at. *But that is not your role in this.*

"My role is to find Mags?"

Goddess nodded. The most ravishing being Emma had ever clapped eyes on, yet her features hadn't changed. *Use the tools I have given you.*

"What tools?"

*Emma Fletcher.* Goddess's voice rang around the cavern and made the crystals peal. *You are called. Do you answer my call?*

"Yes. My answer is yes." Emma's head couldn't remain upright, and she lowered it. "I obey and serve."

When Emma woke, her face was pressed into the sandy floor, and her body ached from her fight with Roderick.

The pool glowed amber and then pink, and then aqua.

She unkinked her knotted muscles and stood. She'd met Goddess and spoken with her. Damn, but she didn't have words to sum that up.

Outside the caverns, full night had fallen and she took the stairs to the bailey.

A square of yellow light spilled into the darkness from the open kitchen door, and she trudged toward it. She'd been given her mission, and she absolutely accepted it.

Inside the kitchen, Taylor looked up first from where she sat between Warren and Niamh. The smile she gave looked oddly ancient and out of place on such a young face. "I can help," she said. "Sometimes when I scry Mags, I can find her." She winced. "But only sometimes."

"The animals will be our eyes and ears." Niamh put her arm around Taylor's shoulders. "If they see, hear, or scent anything, they'll let me know."

The nerdy looking guy, Andy she thought his name was, cleared his throat. "If you'll give me as many details as you can, I'll get on the internet. Very little happens in the world today without someone seeing something somewhere and posting about it."

"Sit!" Roderick pushed a chair out from the table with his booted foot. "We need to hear what you and your organization know."

Maeve bustled over from the cooking range with a big pot of something that smelled good. "Let her eat first." She put the pot on the table. "It's not as good as Alannah's, but it'll keep us from going hungry."

Taking her seat beside Roderick, Maeve touched his wrist.

The big bastard seemed to deflate a tad.

Bronwyn looked well rested and bright eyed. Beside her, Alexander looked at Emma, but she had the feeling most of his attention remained on Bronwyn.

Emma eased into the seat and suppressed a wince as her bruised thigh protested. "How much do you know?"

"I've told them what you told Mags and me." Jack handed her a plate. He looked almost recovered. "That you're part of an organization that has been tracking Rhiannon and her lot from way, way back when."

"She's getting stronger." Emma started with the bad news. Actually, it was pretty much all bad news. "Don't underestimate the size of her following, or the extent of her reach."

Alexander frowned and handed her a bowl of salad. "You know who I am?"

"I do." Emma took some salad and passed it to Roderick.

He grimaced and put one leaf on his plate.

Maeve nudged him and he took another and a slice of cucumber.

"As far as we can tell, no one person in her setup knows the extent of it."

Alexander nodded. "That would make sense. Information with her is strictly need to know. She likes to hold all the cards close."

"I've been thinking about that." Andy tapped a forefinger on the table. "My instructions to audit Baile came out of the blue and from very high up. I still haven't found the source." He narrowed his eyes. "But I will."

"Chances are, she's behind it." Emma would tell him not to bother but by the look of determination on his face, it would be a waste of breath. "She has influence at the highest levels of government, society, and economics. If there's a pie, you can bet your arse she's got her whole hand in it."

As he straightened in his seat, Andy's eyes gleamed. "I'll take all the details you know."

"I'll connect you with Sasha." She didn't have time to brief Andy fully. It would take a while to impart hundreds of years of intel. "He's our recordkeeper and knows all there is to know."

Andy rubbed his palms together. "Great."

"I need an encrypted secure line to Sasha." Emma had resources in her search for Mags. Tools for her use, as Goddess had said.

Andy chewed and swallowed. "No problem."

"Can your people help?" Jack more pushed food around his plate than ate.

"Yes." Emma sure as hell hoped they could deliver what she was so confidently promising. "We're good at watching her and not getting caught. As soon as I have that secure line, I'll contact Sasha and let him know what's happened. I didn't dare risk it from the road."

Roderick went for a second helping.

Emma had not even seen him finish the first.

"Good." He piled beef stew on his plate. "Alexander and I will put together a list of places we know she's used as bases in the past."

"And I can give you descriptions of the few people I saw when she had me imprisoned," the doctor, Hannah, said. "I didn't see many, but…"

"It all helps." Emma hadn't heard Hannah's story, but for her to be alive was a major miracle. Very few encountered Rhiannon and lived. "We can cross reference Alexander and Roderick's list with the places we know about."

"I'll run some scenarios," Andy said. "How far they could get using various modes of transport."

Roderick clapped him on the shoulder. "Good thinking. We can start there and widen our search."

On her next point, Emma wasn't taking any argument. "I'll leave in the morning. You can update me as you travel."

Jack met her stare with a hard one of his own. "We'll leave in the morning."

# CHAPTER FORTY-FOUR

Warren stood beside Roderick and Alexander as Emma and Jack left Baile.

"They need to find her." Roderick's face was gray in the predawn light. Losing Mags had to be hard on the guy—sodding hell, it was hard on all of them—but they hadn't watched an entire coven slaughtered in front of them and been unable to prevent it.

If they'd been women, Warren would have hugged the guy. He slugged him on the shoulder instead. "They're both determined, and we'll do everything we can to help."

"Aye." Roderick swallowed, his lapse into medieval speak more telling than a two-thousand-word essay. "The cré-witches belong within Baile."

Alexander rubbed his nape. "What does she want with Mags?"

None of them needed more than a pronoun to identify who Alexander was talking about.

"She's a seer." Warren had been thinking about Alexander's question most of the night. "She can give Rhiannon insights into the future." And then, he said the thing they were probably all thinking. "And if what Jack says is true, Mags is not that aware of who she's talking to."

"Fucking hell." Alexander's jaw clenched. "Mags. She's so…"

Warren couldn't even begin to imagine how Alexander felt about Mags's abduction. Rhiannon was his mother, and he'd been part of her schemes for longer than he cared to admit. Yup, harder on him too.

"Vulnerable." Warren completed Alexander's sentence and winced. Way to go with kicking a man when he was down.

Roderick and Alexander nodded.

"She won't hurt her," Alexander said, but his tone lacked conviction. "She's too valuable."

"God's bones." Roderick rubbed his nape. "I have never lost a witch. And since I entered this time, I lost Bronwyn, had to put Niamh in a vulnerable position and now, Mags."

Alexander folded his arms. "That's not your burden to bear alone."

No, it wasn't, and Warren nodded. "We are all brothers in this war, and we all lost Mags."

"They're not brothers," Taylor spoke from right beside him, and Warren jumped.

Alexander and Roderick spun to look at her.

With an evil grin, Taylor looked from Roderick to Alexander and then to him. "Those two." She jabbed a thumb and forefinger at Roderick and Alexander. "Are father and son. I got it out of Mags's memories."

Alexander and Roderick glanced at each other and stared pointedly ahead.

"Not possible." Roderick shook his head.

Alexander cleared his throat. "Not even a minute possibility."

"Well…" Warren totally saw the similarities.

"No." Both men yelled at once.

Alexander's mobile ringing broke the tense silence.

"Oh hi, Hermione." He gave Warren a WTF look. "You what?"

He nodded and ah-haed for the remainder of the conversation, then hung up.

Alexander ended the call and turned to Warren and Roderick. "Apparently, Hermione has a visitor. In her house. A woman trying to get to Baile."

Three hours later, the three of them wound down a street of whitewashed homes and stopped in front of Hermione's bright red door. They climbed out, and as they approached the house, the door opened, and Hermione leaned out. She glanced left and right, and then motioned them inside.

"Alexander." She nodded. "Warren. Roderick." She shut the door behind them. "Thanks for coming."

Alexander raised a brow. "You have us intrigued."

Hermione lowered her voice. "One cannot be too careful in these turbulent times."

"Indeed." Roderick nodded and touched her shoulder. "We appreciate your discretion. You said you have a visitor desirous of reaching Baile?"

"She's upstairs. Sleeping." Hermione glanced toward the staircase. "Come into the kitchen."

She led them down a narrow corridor, the wood floorboards creaking beneath their weight. The kitchen was large and airy, cabinets painted a soothing sage and cream. Hermione motioned the four-seater oak table in the kitchen's center. She grabbed a kettle and held it under the faucet. "Tea? Coffee?"

Warren suppressed the desire to ask for something stronger. He had the nasty feeling he might need it.

Hermione finished filling the kettle and flipped on a gas burner. "She arrived a few hours ago. Dead tired, the poor thing. She'd tried to get into Baile and village gossip brought her to me."

Roderick's chair creaked under his weight as he took a load off. "Does that happen often?"

"All the time." Hermione grimaced. "I'm afraid word of Gemma's healing has not died down."

"That could be a problem." Alexander sat as far from Roderick as the table allowed. "So, she came here? Who is she?"

"Apparently—" Hermione rolled her eyes "—she's looking for Warren."

That got Warren's attention. "Her name?"

"Debra." Hermione took a matching teapot from the cupboard. "It would be very useful if I was informed better." Hermione glared at him. "I can't know what I can and cannot say, if I don't have the necessary information."

Before Warren could respond, Alexander said, "If this happens again, email Andy. He's in charge of this sort of thing."

Now they had an organization? Next, they'd be making flowcharts and handing out year-end bonuses.

Roderick's rabbit-in-headlights expression echoed Warren's thoughts.

"Andy?" Hermione's eyes narrowed. "Can we trust him?"

Roderick cleared his throat. "We?"

"Well, I'm part of this." Hermione flushed. "I know the rumors are true." Her face grew solemn. "You healed my daughter. The legends are true, there's magic in that castle, and it's the good kind that can change people's lives for the better." She held up one finger. "If properly managed." Then she shrugged. "Besides I've made my income as a tour guide for Baile for most of my adult life. I'm part of this."

She had a point, and with the increased activity in Greater Littleton, Hermione had had plenty of opportunity to make their story viral.

Warren's belly tightened. He had invited Debra here after all, but with all that had happened in the last few days, he hadn't had a chance to bring Debra up. Apparently, she'd accepted his offer.

"She says she's your ex." Hermione looked at him. "And she's not best pleased she can't get into Baile. She says she was there before."

Now all gazes locked on him.

Alexander spoke first. "Your ex is here?"

"Yup. I...um...sort of invited her."

"Lovely." Alexander's tone could cut diamonds. He always got more proper when he was going to hand you your arse. "Now, we can add bitter exes to the coven mix. That should work a treat."

"Ex?" Roderick frowned. "This is the woman you repudiated?"

How to tackle that one? Warren gave up. "If you like."

"Bloody hell." Alexander rolled his eyes. "We need to get Sinead back here as soon as possible. Your education is lapsing."

"And she is Taylor's mother?" Roderick had a nifty way of tuning out what he didn't choose to hear.

"Yup." Warren braced for a fight. Sure, he was one of the newer residents of Baile, but Roderick didn't get to make all the decisions.

Roderick raised his palms. "Then, of course, she must enter Baile."

When Warren and Alexander gaped at him, Roderick shrugged. "Is the mother of a blessed not as treasured as the Blessed herself? She requires our protection."

"Huh." It was the best Warren could manage.

"Quite right." Hermione took the boiling kettle off the hob and filled the teapot. "You might even find she has some latent magic in her." She smiled at them. "One can never underestimate the influence of genetics."

Tension rolled between Alexander and Roderick, and they stared at Hermione pointedly.

"What?" She glanced at Warren.

"Long story." Warren wanted to bang their heads together but settled for an eye roll. "But Alexander and Roderick have both received a recent shock."

---

NOT THAT WARREN had any previous experience to draw on, but he was twitchy about the upcoming meeting of the women in his life.

Hermione was driving Debra to Baile.

As the car approached the bailey, Warren waited with Niamh and Taylor beside him. Roderick and Maeve were holding hands on the far side of Taylor. Alexander stood on Warren's right, one shoulder in front of Bronwyn and visibly unhappy that his attempt to get her to wait inside had failed.

"Ah." Andy bustled out of the kitchen. "Our guest. We have her chambers prepared."

Roderick raised a brow at him. "We?"

"I took the liberty of requesting our lady make ready for our visitor." Andy straightened the cuffs on his crisp blue button-down. "That was after I spoke with her about increasing security measures." He sniffed. "We cannot allow all and sundry entry to Baile. Really, the manner in which I entered the castle was most remiss on our lady's part."

From the look on his face, Roderick couldn't agree more.

Maeve giggled and leaned into Roderick.

After Hermione parked, Debra climbed from the passenger side.

Dressed in painted-on white jeans and an off-the-shoulder leopard skin top, she prickled and bristled like a pissed-off hedgehog. Large, white-rimmed sunglasses hid her eyes. She pushed them up and into her platinum hair as she stalked toward him. "Warren."

"Debra." He resisted the urge to put his arm around Niamh. That might send Debra over the top.

Taylor ran for her mother. "Mum!"

Debra thawed enough to fold Taylor into a tight hug. The relief and joy on her face were all too real. Warren understood the feeling. Being separated from Taylor was not a fate he'd wish on anyone.

With Taylor tucked by her side, she closed in on him and Niamh. "Hello." She held out one hot-pink-clawed hand to Niamh. "I'm Debra. Warren's ex-wife."

"Welcome." Niamh pulled her into an enthusiastic hug.

Debra stiffened, and then the Niamh-magic took effect. She relaxed against Niamh and tears brimmed in her eyes.

Pulling back a bit, Niamh said, "I'm Niamh, and I'm so relieved you're here. Taylor has really missed you."

"Warren said it was okay that I come." Debra looked uncertain and vulnerable.

"Of course it is." Niamh put an arm around her shoulders. "Let's go in and see if we can scare up something to eat and drink."

And that was that. Warren stood there and stared as his current woman ushered his ex-wife into the kitchen. He should have trusted Niamh more, and he should have known better than to make assumptions.

# CHAPTER FORTY-FIVE

Alexander really couldn't put the conversation off much longer, so he tracked Roderick down to the practice yards. To be clear, he could have lived the rest of his life without jawing this out, but Bronwyn had insisted. She kept banging on about closure and healthy relationships. Whatever the hell all of that meant.

He stood a moment beside a rapt Andy watching the old man—his old man, apparently—go through a kata with Warren. Roderick might be new to martial arts, but he was picking them up with his typical warrior aptitude. Alexander suspected Emma showing Roderick his arse so easily had a fair amount to do with Roderick's new enthusiasm for different fighting forms.

"Magnificent, isn't he?" Andy breathed. "The quintessential fighter. How I wish the Marauders could see him."

"They're welcome to him," Alexander said.

Andy chuckled. "You're such a joker."

If only.

Roderick bowed and faced him, like he'd known Alexander was there all along.

A poke in the back, and then Bronwyn said from right behind him, "Go on. Talk to him."

"Must I?" It came out a bit whiny, but really. He and Roderick had hated each other for centuries. Even tried to kill each other on more than one occasion. They weren't going to suddenly start kicking around a football and picking out matching Christmas sweaters.

A nasty sentimental niggle tweaked in his chest. As a boy, he'd often wondered who his father was, where his father was. When Rhiannon had made being her son a living hell, he'd even fantasized about a mythical father, like a cross between Father Christmas and Thor, arriving and rescuing him.

*He doesn't want you as his son.*

Sodding hell! He'd be breaking out the bloody tissues in another minute. "Do you have a moment?" he said to Roderick.

Roderick looked like he dearly wanted to refuse but then gave Alexander an uncharacteristically jerky bow. "Of course."

Another poke from Bronwyn got Alexander moving. "It will be all right," she whispered.

"Of course it will." He knew she knew he was bullshitting but his man card demanded stoicism.

In silence they walked out of the practice yard and into the central barracks area.

"Will this do?" Roderick motioned the chamber.

"Yup."

Now what?

Roderick cleared his throat.

Alexander cleared his.

"I believe a sincere apology is owing," Roderick said.

Alexander had to snap his sagging jaw shut. "Eh?"

"You are my get." Roderick took a deep breath. "And I have failed you."

"Eh?" He needed to manage at least one more syllable. "I don't know about that."

"I should have seen it." Roderick sat heavily on the table. He gestured to Alexander. "We bear a marked similarity in both looks and temperament."

Alexander hadn't expected Roderick to admit to being his father, let alone accept it so fully. "I'm not sure I would go that far."

"Of course you wouldn't." Roderick smiled ruefully. "We share the same stubborn intractable nature."

The words burst out of Alexander before he could censor them. "You can't be happy about this."

"I'm...shocked." Roderick scrubbed his face with his palms. "And I'm not sure how Rhiannon managed to bring this about, but I have no reason to doubt the truth."

Not a glowing endorsement or acceptance of him, but what had he expected?

"It is going to take some...rethinking." Roderick shook his head and stared at the floor. "I tried to kill my own son more times than I can count."

"Well." Alexander couldn't in fairness let him carry that one alone. "Apparently I specialize in patricide."

"Attempted," Roderick said.

"Attempted." He concentrated on the other part of Roderick's earlier statement. "So, you and Rhiannon?" He couldn't finish the sentence.

"Never." Roderick shook his head.

Alexander hated to end their brief moment of accord in a biological argument. "And yet, here I stand."

"You're well aware of my...er...exploits as a younger man." Roderick flushed. "But she was not one of them."

"Then how?" And while they were on it. "And if not, why are you so sure this is true?" Hope glimmered. "Maybe Mags got it wrong?"

"No." Roderick shook his head. "It makes too much sense not to be true." He blushed. "And I checked with Goddess."

"Ah." That stung more than it should. After all the hating each other, and the lack of physical evidence, any man would have doubts.

"She wanted to create the strongest son." Roderick shrugged. "She would have chosen the strongest sire she could. Plus my link to Goddess would have made me even more suitable."

"Right." The old prophecy that shaped so much of his life, even now. The very reason he'd been brought into being. "So, what now?"

"We could try not killing each other." Roderick's eyes gleamed with tentative humor.

Alexander had to laugh. "Really?"

"We could try."

Silence stretched between them, filled with words it would take countless years to fill.

"I would have you know this." Roderick stood. "If I had known, matters would have been different betwixt us."

The lost, lonely, frightened boy inside Alexander won control of his mouth. "They would have?"

"Most definitely." Roderick nodded. "Had I known she held my son, I would have moved the world to retrieve you and raise you by my side."

The room wavered, and Alexander blinked hard. He was not fucking tearing up. He was not.

# EPILOGUE

Exhaustion dogged Fiona as she followed Rhiannon into the farmhouse. Wooden shutters covered the windows and kept the stone interior cool in the midday heat.

Rhiannon hadn't questioned her story about Hannah and Charlie being dead. At some point, they might reappear, and then Fiona would have questions to answer, but she regretted nothing. Letting them escape to Baile had been for Edana. One brief moment of defiance as retaliation for the death of her best friend.

Fiona had been alive a long time. Death no longer held her in its grip of fear.

As they walked, their feet clopped loudly against the stone floors. Cooking smells permeated from the kitchen: garlic, butter, and frying onions. She and Edana had once spent months in this farmhouse in the south of France, enjoying the bright, hot summer.

Rhiannon's excitement thrummed in the air about her and sparkled in her dark eyes.

After Warren's connection had severed, Fiona had expected

rage and volcanic tantrums. Rhiannon, however, had been ridiculously chipper. Fiona suspected she was about to discover why.

As she climbed the stairs behind Rhiannon, she wondered what Edana would have made of the new development. She probably wouldn't have noticed. Edana had been many things, but sharp and perceptive had not counted amongst that number. A more likely scenario would have been Edana picking out bikinis and planning her tanning schedule for days spent in southern France. The same bikinis would have made Fiona want to throttle her.

Stopping at a large, rough wooden door, Rhiannon turned to her. "This will be your priority. You will take care of our new guest."

With that, Rhiannon opened the door.

On the bed, a figure lay, concealed by the room's gloom.

Fiona approached the bed.

The woman on the bed stared at them, her green eyes unfocussed, a frown creasing her brow. "Jack?

"Right here, Magdalene," Rhiannon said.

The woman took a deep breath and her face relaxed. "Jack?"

"Yes, it's me," Rhiannon said. "You're safe now. You're in Baile. I've got you."

Mags relaxed, and a faint smile curved her mouth. "Good."

The repercussions ricocheted around Fiona's brain. Mags was here, and Rhiannon was controlling her. A seer with her cardinal point active could do many things, see many things, predict even more. "That's—

"Indeed. Pure genius on my part to take advantage of such good fortune." Rhiannon smoothed her hair and looked smug. "We are no longer working blind. We have our own Seer."

*What happens next?*
Will Jack and Emma find Mags in time? Will Sinead and Alannah locate the earth point and activate it? More to come in
**Cradled In Earth**

---

**The Gathering Storm**

With tension mounting between them, twin earth witches Sinead and Alannah are forced to work together to hunt for the missing earth point. That search puts them directly in the path of enigmatic, mysterious Noah Rivers, and Sinead's attraction to Noah is immediate and incendiary.

Noah is torn between his sworn duty to protect the earth point and the heady call of his new bonded mate. It's a decision that will affect the future of magic and life as they all know it.

Sisters Sinead and Alannah also face an unprecedented choice around activating the life point, and theirs is life or death. As blood-witch Rhiannon's trap closes around the cré-witches, the coven back at Baile Castle wades against the onslaught of the shifting magical tide.

Forces are gathering, the rules are changing, and the final battle looms.

## Chapter 1

NOAH COULDN'T BELIEVE what he was seeing. Of all possible scenarios this one hadn't crossed his mind. *Go to Montreal,* Zach had said. *Find the earth witch, watch her, and report back.*

Earth witch, singular!

"There are two of them," Abe whispered.

Zach had insisted Noah bring Abe with him. As the strongest fighter, Abe was a good man to have at your back. All that muscle, however, had squeezed the guy's brainpower into a poppyseed.

Two witches. Both of them reeking of earth magic. Long reddish hair, tall and toned, faces that made him want to worship. From this distance he couldn't see the color of their eyes, but their pale, creamy skin made his fingers twitch to touch.

Noah had to laugh. Goddess had a sense of humor sometimes. One of the knock-out redheads standing beside the construction site would have been enough for anyone to handle. Two was doubling down the hotness factor to off the charts.

"What's so funny." Abe frowned and then whistled through his teeth. "Do you think they're twins?"

"Seriously?" There were days when Noah didn't understand how Zach managed to lead this bunch without throwing throat and nut punches. Guess that's why Zach was their leader and not him. He couldn't wait to tell the big cheese about this little wrinkle.

Abe grunted. "They could be...those things...I watched a TikTok about them. You know, double bangers."

It took Noah a hot minute to work that one out. "Doppelgängers?"

"Yeah." Abe nodded and scrunched his face as he brain chewed that one. "You know like people who don't know each other and look the same." He leaned in closer, the waft of garlic steak making Noah's eyes water. "Did you know everyone has a secret twin?"

Abe stared at him, waiting for an answer.

Noah didn't have the fucking strength. A tantalizing scent rode the light breeze coming down Sherbrooke street. Earth magic, for certain, but mixed with cloves and roses, and something else. It was that something else that made Noah almost forget about the dumb ass at his side. It made his mouth water, his skin prickle, and his cock harden in his jeans.

---

**For first dibs on news, deals, and giveaways, and so much more, join the @Home Collective**

Or if Facebook is more your thing, join the Sarah Hegger Collective

Anything and everything you need to know on my website http://sarahhegger.com

# ABOUT THE AUTHOR

Born British and raised in South Africa, Sarah Hegger suffers from an incurable case of wanderlust. Her match? A hot Canadian engineer, whose marriage proposal she accepted six short weeks after they first met. Together they've made homes in seven different cities across three different continents (and back again once or twice). If only it made her multilingual, but the best she can manage is idiosyncratic English, fluent Afrikaans, conversant Russian, pigeon Portuguese, even worse Zulu and enough French to get herself into trouble. Mimicking her globe trotting adventures, Sarah's career path began as a gainfully employed actress, drifted into public relations, settled a moment in advertising, and eventually took root in the fertile soil of her first love, writing. She also moonlights as a wife and mother. She currently lives in Ottawa, Canada, filling her empty nest with fur babies. Part footloose buccaneer, part quixotic observer of life, Sarah's restless heart is most content when reading or writing books.

# PRAISE FOR SARAH HEGGER

**Drove All Night**
"The classic romance plot is elevated to a modern-day, wholly accessible real-life fairy tale with an excellent mix of romantic elements and spicy sensuality."
Booklife Prize, Critic's Report

**Positively Pippa**
"This is the type of romance that makes readers fall in love not just with characters, but with authors as well."
Kirkus Review (Starred Review)

"What begins as a simple second-chance romance quickly transforms into a beautiful, frank examination of love, family dynamics, and following one's dreams. Hegger's unflinching, candid portrayal of interpersonal and generational communication elevates the story to the sublime. Shunning clichés and contrived circumstances, she uses realistic, relatable situations to create a world that readers will want to visit time and again."
Publisher's Weekly, Starred Review

Hegger's utterly delightful first Ghost Falls contemporary is what other romance novels want to grow up to be." – Publisher's Weekly, Best Books of 2017

"The very talented Hegger kicks off an enjoyable new series set in the small Utah town of Ghost Falls. This charming and fun-filled book has everything from passion and humor to betrayal and revenge." –
Jill M Smith, RT Books Reviews 2017 – Contemporary Love and Laughter Nominee

### Becoming Bella
"Hegger excels at depicting familial relationships and friendships of all kinds, including purely platonic friendships between women and men. Tears, laughter, and a dollop of suspense make a memorable story that readers will want to revisit time and again."
Publisher's Weekly, Starred Review

"…you have a terrific new romance that Hegger fans are going to love. Don't miss out!"
Jill M. Smith – RT Book Reviews

### Blatantly Blythe
"Ms. Hegger has delivered another captivating read for this series in this book that was packed with emotion…" Bec, Bookmagic Review, Harlequin Junkie, HJ Recommends.

### Nobody's Fool
"Hegger offers a breath of fresh air in the romance genre." – Terri Dukes, RT Book Reviews

### Nobody's Princess
"Hegger continues to live up to her rapidly growing reputation

for breathing fresh air into the romance genre." – Terri Dukes, RT Book Reviews

"I have read the entire Willow Park Series. I have loved each of the books ... Nobody's Princess is my favorite of all time." Harlequin Junkie, Top Pick

## ALSO BY SARAH HEGGER

Sports Romance

*Ottawa Titans Series*

Roughing

Contemporary Romance

*Passing Through Series*

Drove All Night

Ticket To Ride

Walk On By

*Ghost Falls Series*

Positively Pippa

Becoming Bella

Blatantly Blythe

Loving Laura

*Willow Park Romances*

Nobody's Angel

Nobody's Fool

Nobody's Princess

Medieval Romance

*Sir Arthur's Legacy Series*

Sweet Bea

My Lady Faye

Conquering William

Roger's Bride

Releasing Henry

*Love & War Series*

The Marriage Parley

The Betrothal Melee

Western Historical Romance

*The Soiled Dove Series*

Sugar Ellie

*Standalone*

The Bride Gift

Bad Wolfe On The Rise

Wild Honey

CPSIA information can be obtained
at www.ICGtesting.com
Printed in the USA
LVHW081143180922
728655LV00025B/597